SEEDS OF EDEN

A.P. WATSON

SEEDS OF EDEN

THE *CONCILIUM* SERIES

A.P. WATSON

SEEDS

OF

EDEN

THE *CONCILIUM* SERIES

A.P. WATSON

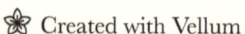 Created with Vellum

For Marie & Guy,
Whom I've always called Mom and Dad.

I

AWAKENING

"No! Please don't," I sobbed. Collapsing to my knees, I stole a glance at the man kneeling to my left. The sight of him, bound in chains, was agonizing, and my need to save him intensified with each passing moment. "I'm begging you to spare his life." My heart felt as if it were being torn asunder. An enormous axe blocked the prisoner's face from my view, its harsh blade stained with red.

"Who are you to beg anything from me?" A voice sneered at me from the shadows, mocking my very presence. The sound came from the direction of a grand throne looming in front of me, but his face was drenched in darkness.

"There was a time when you would do anything I asked of you," I answered, my voice shaking.

A shrill laugh echoed off every surface of the great hall. I could see his hands clench the arms of the throne as his nails gouged the gleaming wood. "Unfortunately for you, that time has come to an end." He lifted his hand and beckoned the masked executioner to proceed.

"No!" I buckled forward, bracing myself with trembling hands.

The stone was frigid, shocking. Breath caught in my throat—I was suffocating. The tips of my fingers clawed against the floor as I began scrambling toward the prisoner. If my pleas couldn't free him, my hands would.

"Hold her still!" the man from the shadows bellowed. Someone grabbed my arms from behind. I thrashed wildly, desperately trying to free myself, but the grip was too firm. "And pry her eyes open if you have to. I want her to see this." His words oozed with triumph and satisfaction. Dread settled in the pit of my stomach, gnawing at my insides. The man kneeling next to me was about to die, his life snuffed out as easily as a candle, and there was nothing I could do to stop it. There was nothing I could do to save him.

"Please, no!" Panic coursed through every inch of me, causing my muscles to convulse violently with the need to act. I couldn't help but focus on the axe. It lifted, and the man's face became visible. Brown locks of hair offset the brightest blue eyes I'd ever seen. I wanted nothing more than to stare into those eyes until the end of time, but even as I had the thought, the axe sliced through the air with a *whoosh*, severing the man's head from his neck. "*No!*" I screamed with all the power I could muster, but my plea rang hollow with the finality of the scene in front of me.

I woke up clutching my hand to my chest, fingernails dug into my skin, dotting the area over my heart with tiny crescent moons. Sweat trickled down my arms and neck. "A dream," I said to myself. "It was just a dream." I glanced at the clock next to my bed. The bright red numbers glared at me. *6:07 a.m.* It was almost time to get ready for school. I collapsed on my pillow in defeat. My dreams had gotten steadily worse over the summer. Every night, they became more detailed. Colors sharpened, smells grew more potent, and the nightmares began to feel more like reality than fantasy. An unrelenting sense of terror riddled my body. I couldn't shake it, couldn't explain it. What was happening to me? I was a normal girl. I should be picking out prom dresses and visiting colleges, not holding myself accountable for the imaginary execution of a mystery man.

Electric blue monarch butterflies fluttered in circles above my head. I exhaled deeply, causing the mobile to pick up speed. As it spun, it morphed into a blurry halo. The jarring sound of my phone's ringtone cut through the silence of my room. I jumped, answering it quickly and pressed the phone to my ear.

"Hey Caroline," I whispered.

"Morning! Did I wake you up? You sound out of breath."

"No," I answered with a yawn. "I woke up like a minute or two before you called." I wanted to talk to Caroline about my dream, but I couldn't let these nightmares dictate my entire existence. At the end of last school year, I let them get the better of me. I started hanging out with my other friends less and less. Caroline stuck with me; she was the only one who knew about the things I saw when I closed my eyes at night. While I knew she was cool with just the two of us hanging out after work every night, I couldn't make her forgo every social event. Senior year would be different, and I was going to make sure of it. Caroline was going to have enough exciting and amazing pictures to fill up her Instagram account for five years by the time we graduated. "The ridiculous tune you programmed into my phone as your contact ringtone disrupted the serenity of my room. It nearly gave me a heart attack."

"Disrupted the serenity of your room?" she asked with a laugh. "I love how you always sound like an SAT prep book when you talk. Seriously, Dr. Sawyer cried when she announced your perfect score on the state writing exam last year."

"I almost forgot about that!"

"She was so proud," she replied. "And she practically hugged me when I confessed to her that I'd added a thesaurus app on my phone just so I could look up some of the words you use. It's like she knew you were a good influence on me."

"I guess I'm just weird."

"I like it! Remember the note you wrote me in third grade asking if I wanted to be your friend? In that note, you told me you appreciated my sassy disposition. We were nine then! You have a better vocabulary than most of the English teachers we've had. It's just who you are."

"That was a killer note," I agreed. Caroline and I had been best friends since my fateful note in the third grade. From then on, we'd been pretty much joined at the hip. Being an only child could get lonely at times, and she was the closest thing I had to a sister."So, I'm guessing you called because you want to know what I'm going to wear to school today, huh?"

"It's the first day of our senior year of high school. Honestly, would you expect anything less from me?"

"Not really, especially since you've called me every morning for the last four years to discuss clothes."

"Wardrobe can make you or break you in high school, Evey!"

"But we don't care what people think," I countered. I heaved myself out of bed and headed to the opposite side of my room. I needed to stare at my dream board for a minute. Looking at it always made me feel better, especially after having a nightmare. It was covered with pictures of Caroline and me among print-outs of famous monuments. Caroline and I dreamed of traveling the world. One day, we'd see the Eiffel Tower, Big Ben, and the Colosseum. I added a picture of the famous Las Vegas sign to the collage. This small town wouldn't be able to hold us for much longer.

"Of course we don't."

"So the point is to look fabulous while not caring?"

"My thoughts exactly," she replied. "And what can I say? I'm a creature of habit."

I shook my head and laughed. Walking away from my desk, I moved to stand in front of my closet. Any day now, it was sure to bust and spit out a mountain of clothes. Why was it that I could never bring myself to throw anything away? "I'd be a liar if I said I hadn't noticed. I think I'm going to wear some jeans and that new loose-fitting tank top I got at the mall last week with a pink cardigan."

"Oh, that sounds cute! I'm going to wear jeans, too, but I think my green button-up shirt will look good with some sandals . . . I'm so excited! I've been waiting for senior year for so long," she said.

"Me too!"

"Just think, one more year and we'll be in college! Co-ed dorms, here we come!"

"Somehow I don't see my dad moving me into a co-ed dorm. The thought of us living ten feet away from college boys will probably make him have an aneurysm," I said with a laugh. "When will you be here to pick me up?"

"Seven thirty. I want to get to school a little early since it's the first day, and we'll have the dreaded opening assembly."

"Ugh," I groaned. "Don't remind me!"

"I know. Every time Principal Louden goes into his 'Aim for the Stars' speech, I have to fight the urge to hurl."

"Tell me about it," I replied. "Last year, I thought about performing a makeshift lobotomy on myself with a pen."

"Let's not rule that out this year. If the speech goes from awful to agonizing, it might be our only option," Caroline added, her tone the epitome of seriousness.

"I'll have my pens at the ready."

"Okay, I'll see you soon!"

I trudged from my closet to the bathroom, dragging my hand along the lavender-colored walls. Once I was by the shower, I turned the knob to hot and waited to step in until steam started to rise over the curtain. Warm drops pelted my neck, easing the tension away. As I soaked my hair, I replayed the execution again in my mind. The overwhelming sense of despair permeated my soul and tainted my every thought. I wanted to know the prisoner, wanted to know why he was being killed. His blood was on my hands. The king wanted me to suffer, and the man's death was my punishment. No matter how many times I had this dream, there was always one thing that stood out in my mind: how utterly real it felt.

But it wasn't real, I reminded myself. Maybe I had an overactive imagination, or maybe I was mentally insane. Regardless, there had to be a logical explanation for my nightmares. I wanted answers, wanted to know why I saw such things. But at the same time, the unknown held a certain advantage. How could I ever recover if I found out I was crazy? I pushed the thought to the back of my mind. Making it through my last year of high school was more important. I needed to focus on that before I could even start thinking about anything else. Except, I did need to put some energy into dating. Caroline was always nagging me to give some of the guys at school a chance. I was definitely overdue for some kind of distraction.

Once my hair was dry and curled to perfection, I started on my makeup. As I finished getting ready, I began to feel more relaxed. Today was the first day of my senior year, and I couldn't let one nightmare ruin it. I was determined to stay optimistic. Throwing on my clothes, I ran my fingers through my tousled curls and headed down the hall for a quick bite to eat.

My feet made their regular route past the living room, curving around the corner into the kitchen. I walked over to mom and gave her a quick kiss on the cheek. "Morning."

"Good morning! How does it feel to officially be a senior?" She turned from the kitchen counter to pull me into a quick hug.

"Same as last year." I shrugged. I stuck my head into the dining room and saw my dad sitting at the antique mahogany table reading the newspaper with a cup of coffee in his hand. "Morning, Daddy," I said, sitting in the chair beside him. His dark brown eyes looked at me over the square rims of his reading glasses. His black hair and beard were peppered with gray, while soft lines fanned out from the corners of his eyes. Just as I finished pouring myself a bowl of cereal, my mom handed me a piping cup of coffee.

"Good morning," he said and smiled.

"What's going on in the news today?" Dad read our town's newspaper religiously, though Estill Springs didn't register as more than a speck on a map of Tennessee. Even the dictionary made for a more fascinating read than the *Springs Sentinel*.

"A couple of kids spray-painted some stuff at the city park, but that's about it," he stated with a shrug.

"Why do you even bother reading that? It's not like anything ever happens here." Grabbing the creamer, I poured a teaspoon into my coffee mug.

"And I like it that way," he replied, smiling over his drink.

"Oh, Guy, can you believe it? After this year, she'll be graduating and then she'll be leaving us to go to college." My mother had her light brown hair pinned on the top of her head, and I could see her gold locket hanging around her neck. It had been a gift from my father when they first started dating. I knew it was her favorite piece of jewelry because she never took it off. Her light green eyes sparkled, and I could just make out the faint lingering of tears in them.

"It seems like just yesterday I was carrying you around on my shoulders."

"Both of you act as if I just grew up overnight," I said, shaking my head at them.

"Well, for us, it feels that way," she answered.

"The schools I'm looking at are still within driving distance. It's not like I'll be moving across the country after I graduate."

"Wouldn't you rather go to Murfreesboro?" she asked.

"Yeah," my dad added. "You can stay here and go to school."

"If I didn't know any better, I'd think the two of you were plotting against me." I laughed. I loved my parents. They'd always been there for me and always would be. I knew a lot of people at school who either hated or barely talked to their parents, but that wasn't the way it was in my family. That thought made me ponder Caroline's suggestion from a few weeks ago. Lately, she'd been encouraging me to talk to my parents about my dreams. At first, I didn't want to involve them in my drama-filled nightmares. But Caroline and I were at a loss for what was happening to me, and they may have more insight as to why I thought of such horrible things. Besides, didn't they deserve to know if something was wrong with me?

I could feel my confession forming with each breath I took, but as soon as the courage to tell them surfaced, I stopped myself. What if they blamed themselves for my condition? I could handle nightmares of executions and people being tortured, but I couldn't bear the thought of causing my parents pain. "We wouldn't dream of it," he replied with a wink. "Are you working after school today?"

"Yeah, Caroline and I have our regular school shift at Pat's. I should be back by ten though."

"Is Caroline going to join us for breakfast this morning?"

"Not today," I replied, answering mom's question. "We have an assembly this morning so she wants to get there early."

"Well, you wouldn't want to miss that."

I smiled at her, unable to rid myself of the thought that missing the assembly would be a blessing. "Not at all." Breakfasts like this were what I needed. A few minutes ago, I'd been so close to confessing everything to my parents, I'd almost forgotten the promise I'd made to myself. I was determined to have a carefree senior year, and if ignoring my dreams would help me attain my goal, then that's exactly what I'd do.

Before we could continue our conversation, two honks sounded from the driveway. That was my signal that Caroline was ready to go. I headed for the kitchen to gather my things.

"Here you go, Evey." Mom's arm was extended, holding my leather messenger bag. The brown exterior was faded from years of use. It had been my mom's, and like most of my other possessions, it was an antique. "Do you need money for lunch?"

"No, I have some. Love you!" I called to both of them over my shoulder and rushed out the door.

I waved to Caroline as I approached her car. A Chanel compact was perfectly poised in her hand as she applied a layer of lip gloss. Flashing me a grin, she flung the car door open. She drove a beat-up Nissan Sentra, but you couldn't tell her that. She was one of those people who felt an emotional connection to her car, even if the majority of the white paint was peeling from the hood. Her motto was *the car chooses the driver*, though she'd inherited this pile of junk when her cousin got a new one for college. I plopped down in the seat, wedging my messenger bag in between my feet.

"Hey, you look so cute!" I told her.

"Thanks, you do too!"

"Can you believe this is our last year at Tulson? I've been freaking out all morning."

"I couldn't be more excited! We're going to have so much fun in college."

"I know! I can't wait!"

"This is such a good song. Let's turn it up!" Reaching forward, I turned the volume dial on her radio as she backed her car out of my driveway.

"Senior year, here we come!" she shouted. We continued singing along to the radio throughout the drive and, ten minutes later, found ourselves pulling into an empty space in the parking lot. When we got out, there was already a multitude of cars around us. It seemed that, like us, everyone else was ready to start the new school year.

Walking through the side entrance, we filed in line with a mass of other students. Posters decorated the brick walls, advertising afternoon meetings for the French and Spanish clubs. Weaving through the sea of bodies, we headed to the assembly.

A crowd of nervous freshmen hovered at the entrance to the gymnasium, and we squeezed through to find two open seats. The room was buzzing with conversation. Everyone was running around, saying hellos and giving out hugs to all the people they hadn't seen during the summer. Kristen stood as we approached the bleachers, waving her arms at us. Caroline and I returned her wave, scanning for two empty seats, but every empty slot around her was filled.

"Find us after the assembly!" I shouted to her.

"Okay! I will!" she called out.

We made our way up to the only empty space, which was at the top of the bleachers, and sat with our backs against the gym wall.

As Principal Louden walked to the center of the gym, Caroline and I pulled out our schedules to see which classes we had together. English IV, Economics, World History, and then Physics.

"We have every class together." I nudged her shoulder.

"I can't believe it! Which guidance aide did you sweet talk into doing that?" she asked me, looking both pleased and incredulous.

"Who me?" I asked as innocently as possible.

"Yes, now spill."

I smiled at her. "If I told you, I'd have to kill you."

"I love it when you're diabolical!"

"Good morning, students!" Principal Louden bellowed from behind a small podium in the center of the basketball court. "How are all of you this morning?" He cupped his hand around his ear, gesturing his eagerness to hear our replies. His shining cheeks mirrored the majority of his head, which was almost entirely bald. "I'm so excited for the start of another school year here at Tulson High! I know we have the best students in the world, and all of you have the potential to do something great with your lives," Principal Louden continued. "But you have to learn in order to earn that potential. You have to search for success within yourselves!"

"It's like watching a wreck; it's so terrible and yet I can't look away," Caroline said.

"I guess we can count out getting nominated for 'most school spirited' in the senior superlatives," I replied. When Principal Louden entered the fifth minute of his speech, I couldn't take any more. "Can I talk to you about something?"

"What's up?" Caroline asked, leaning in so we could whisper.

"I just wanted to say thanks for sticking with me after all the craziness last year. I know all my drama caused you to kinda stop hanging with our old group and I feel bad about it."

"You don't have to apologize for that! We're besties, it's what we do for each other."

"Regardless, I wanted to say thanks and make you a promise that this year will be different. We're gonna have an awesome senior year!"

"Really?" she asked. I nodded in answer to her question. "A year filled with hot boys and maybe an appearance or two at one of my cousin's college parties?"

"Whatever you want, I'm down!"

She squealed with delight, wrapping her arms around my neck. "This is gonna be the best year ever, Evey!"

"Only if we can get the hell out of this assembly."

When Principal Louden finally dismissed the student body to go to their first period classes, everyone jumped out of their seats, rushing toward the gym doors in a mass exodus. "I guess this means we're free to go to English. Thank God!" Caroline shouted.

"Come on, let's go before Louden starts preaching again," I added, laughing.

"Hey, Evey! Hey, Caroline!"

I turned in the direction of the voice. Kristen stood on the gymnasium floor, waving wildly. "Hey!" I called to her. "Wait for us!" We jumped down the remaining bleachers, catching up with her quickly.

"Did y'all have a good summer?" she asked.

"It was pretty good. We had a few interesting customers in the diner," I answered. "We missed you!"

"I missed y'all too!"

"What about you?" Caroline asked.

"I know summer was only a couple months, but I felt like I spent an eternity in Maine. My grandmother insisted I spend my entire vacation with her," Kristen groaned.

"That sucks," I said.

"Tell me about it! Do either of you have Advanced French first period?"

"Nope, we've both got English," Caroline replied.

"Boo." Kristen pouted.

"We'll walk with you to class though!" Caroline added.

"Okay!"

As Kristen moved to loop her arm through mine, she hit the strap of my messenger bag, jerking it from my shoulder. The bag crashed against the floor, spitting out my belongings in every direction. Lip gloss, paper clips, hairpins, and a pack of mints scattered around me. "Y'all go on without me. I'll catch up in a minute," I said, dropping to my knees.

"You sure? I can stay and help," Caroline replied.

"Nah, you go on. I'll see you in a minute. Besides, aren't you always telling me I carry around too much crap?"

"True." She grabbed Kristen's arm. "See you in a bit."

I scrambled, frantically trying to gather my stuff as quickly as possible. Scooping up a final bobby pin, I was suddenly struck with the strange feeling that I was being watched. By now, I had to be the only soul left in the gym, but when I looked up, there was a stranger leaning against the far wall. His arms were crossed over his chest nonchalantly. My gaze slid upward, halting as his stare met mine. He had the most beautiful blue eyes I'd ever seen. Blood coursed through my veins, causing my heart to pound. The prisoner from my nightmares stood before me, mere feet separating us. He seemed too real to be a wild hallucination. My hands grabbed my bag, swinging it over my shoulder so forcefully that I lost my balance. Turning around, I quickly regained a stable footing, but when I glanced back to where he'd been standing, he had disappeared. Sprinting into the hallway, I searched in both directions, but the man from my dreams wasn't there. He was gone.

2

A STRANGER
FROM THE PAST

I shook my head, desperately trying to dispel my state of shock. The only logical explanation was that I had imagined it. Human beings couldn't vanish without a trace. As much as I might wish my affliction were something slightly supernatural, like being a psychic or a telepath, I knew it couldn't be possible. When it came to my dreams, there had to be a reasonable cause, even a scary one like an underlying medical condition. As I stood there, praying for divine intervention to ease my suffering, the bell rang. My footsteps echoed down the hall as I sprinted in the direction of the English wing.

Silently, I slid into the seat Caroline had saved for me and opened my book to the page Mrs. Burleson had written on the board. I was determined to shrug off any negative thoughts and focus on school. While most teachers simply cover the attendance roster and assign books on the first day, Mrs. Burleson, it seemed, had spent the summer preparing a detailed syllabus outlining the course objectives for the entire semester. She even made partner assignments for our first presentation. The rest of the class flew by as we read *Macbeth*, and before I knew it, the bell signaled for us to report to second period.

I was beyond ecstatic when Caroline and I were assigned to be partners for a project in Economics. By the time Mrs. Harper dispensed the textbooks and curriculum overview, it was time for another class to start. Even though I liked my previous two teachers, I was relieved for history because it was my favorite subject. Stories of battles, treaties, and revolutions fascinated me. I could pore over my textbooks for hours, absorbing all the facts.

Caroline and I filed into Mr. Rieder's class and found two empty desks in the back left corner. Caroline took her seat and I slid into the one directly behind her. Pulling out my purple notebook and a pencil, I placed them by the textbook in front of me just before the bell rang.

"Everyone quiet down," Mr. Rieder ordered. "Your book for the semester is already in front of you. Write your name in the front page and make sure you bring it to every class." Mr. Rieder was a short plump man who was as round as he was tall. His black hair was littered with streaks of white, and his gold circular spectacles always rested on the tip of his nose. The way his mouth was shaped always reminded me of a turtle, as if at any moment his head might recede beneath his dark green sweater. "Now I want all of you to turn to page 256. We will be talking about the Spanish Inquisition today." I flipped my book open and immediately began studying the first paragraph. "Read over that section while I go through the class roster. When you hear your name, please raise your hand so I can see who all is here." I perused the page as he called out various names, barely hearing mine. My hand shot into the air for a second before resuming my reading.

"We're going to start off talking about the two rulers of Spain who initiated the Inquisition." He turned back around and started scribbling various dates and names across the white board. "Essentially, the purpose of the Spanish Inquisition was to punish converted Jews and Muslims who were thought to be insincere in their conversions. Authorities of the church instituted it, but it was under the control of the Spanish monarchy. It was established in 1480 by Ferdinand the Second of Aragon and his wife Isabella I of

Castile. If you turn the page you can see a painting of Isabella in the top left corner."

Flipping the page over, I glanced at the picture. The first thing I noticed was the pendant hanging around her neck. Its beauty perfectly complemented the delicate gold and pearl crown she wore. An ornate gown clung to her fair skin, making her appear every bit the queen she was. I heard the door open and shut with a slam, but my eyes remained on the woman in the picture. Something about her seemed familiar to me, as if I were looking at a picture of an old friend whom I hadn't seen in years. I was unable to tear my eyes away from her, even when Mr. Rieder announced that a new student was joining our class.

"Class, this is Conrad Bourdet. He is a new student here at Tulson, so I want all of you to make him feel welcome! Where are you from, Mr. Bourdet?"

"Los Angeles."

"Well, you certainly did come a long way from Los Angeles, but we're glad to have you in our class! Why don't you take the open seat in the back by Claire?"

Suddenly, Caroline elbowed me in the shoulder.

"Ouch! What was that for?" I asked, shooting her a glare.

"Because the most gorgeous guy that's ever been to this school just walked into class and you're staring at that stupid book!"

"You assaulted me over a guy?"

"Heck yes, I did!" she whispered. "Just look at him!"

I glanced up from my book, only to see Conrad's back as he turned away from me. Claire sat in front of him, chatting flirtatiously. He had a deep, golden tan and short chestnut-colored hair. He ran a hand through it, causing the brown locks to become slightly disheveled. As I looked at him, I noticed he had to be at least six feet tall, and despite his height, you could see the well-developed muscles in his arms stretching underneath the tight black shirt he was wearing. Confidence seemed to roll off him in waves, which was fitting because every girl in class was ogling him. I turned to see the notes Mr. Rieder had added to the board. When I put my pencil to my notebook, the point broke off, smearing a line of graphite across my white paper.

"Oh crap!" I said, muttering silent curses at my pencil. "Hey Caroline, my pencil just broke. Can I borrow one of yours?"

"I only have the one. I forgot to grab an extra out of the locker," she whispered back. "Sorry, Evey."

"It's okay. I might have something in my bag." Before my hands could slide off the table, a voice stopped me.

"Here, use mine. I don't really need it." Following the voice, I caught sight of the new student leaning across the aisle, a pencil in his outstretched hand. My mouth fell open in surprise. The stranger from the gym now sat across from me. I appraised his features before settling my gaze on his bright blue eyes. They reminded me of a pair of brilliant sapphire earrings my mother kept in her jewelry box. "See something you like?" he asked with a wicked smile.

A rush of heat warmed the apples of my cheeks. "Don't you need it to take notes?" He knew I was blatantly gawking at him, but at this point, I didn't care. The prisoner from my dream wasn't just a figment of my imagination. He was real, tangible, and there was nothing to stop me from reaching out to touch him.

"Nope, I never take notes." He reached even further. "Seriously, just take it."

"Thanks," I replied, stretching toward him. As I took the pencil, something within me snapped and my fingers wrapped instinctively around his wrist. Conrad tugged on my arm gently, pulling us closer to one another. My free hand grazed the side of his cheek. He wasn't a dream, he wasn't a symptom of a mental illness—he was reality.

"Evey." I could hear Caroline whispering my name, but I continued watching the stranger across from me. "Evey!" This time her voice jerked me back to the present. Every set of eyes in the classroom focused on me.

"I'm so sorry," I muttered, releasing Conrad's arm. The moment my fingertips fell from his face, a jolt of electricity shot up my arm. After another second, unease began to churn in the pit of my stomach. Swiveling around to hide my humiliation, I tried to refocus on the lesson.

"Now that we're all focused on class again, who can tell me what the controversial part of the Inquisition was?" Mr. Rieder asked. He scanned the room, searching for someone to answer his question. "Anyone?"

When I finally mustered the courage to glance at Conrad again, he was leaning back in his chair with his hands behind his head and his feet on the desk. He was acting as if nothing strange had transpired between us at all, and he wasn't even trying to pretend like he was paying attention to Mr. Rieder's lesson. What a dick. Although when you're that attractive, I guess you could do whatever you wanted.

"Well, they tortured people in an attempt to coerce confessions or information out of them," Conrad answered.

"Yes. Yes, they did. Although it has been exaggerated as to how many cases actually involved torture, it's true that this form of punishment was used in some of the trials."

Suddenly, a flash from one of my dreams leapt into my mind. A mangled body lay on its back, its arms twisted in an unnatural pose. My stomach bubbled with disgust. Then, a sharp metal spear was being heated over a fire. The end glowed orange. I watched as the spear was thrust into the stomach of the writhing soul. It sliced through the flesh like a hot knife through butter. Acid burned my throat, and I could feel my breakfast begging to come back up. I placed my fingers on each temple, massaging lightly. Had touching Conrad sparked this glimpse of my nightmares to play before my eyes? Or was there some other power commanding my mind at will? Glancing around, I hoped no one noticed my uneasiness, but unfortunately, Conrad had. He surveyed me with curiosity. I shifted in my seat, not wanting to be seen by him or anyone else. Instead, I concentrated on Mr. Rieder, who was busy scrawling more notes across the board. It seemed to take all my willpower to focus on his lesson, but I had to distract myself from the imagery of my dreams and Conrad sitting beside me. No matter what horrible things plagued my consciousness, I needed to be normal. I *had* to be a normal girl.

Thirty minutes into the lesson, Mr. Rieder dismissed us from class to go to lunch. School would be dismissed at 1:00 p.m. as it was the first day of the school year.

"Hey, aren't you eating today?"

"Huh?" I was so disoriented I hadn't heard Caroline's question until the third time she asked it.

"It's time for lunch. Didn't you hear Mr. Rieder?"

"Oh yeah," I replied. "I don't feel up to it; my stomach's not really cooperating right now."

Sensing there was an underlying problem to my sudden lack of appetite, she stared at me. "You're pale. What's up?" she asked as we filed out of the classroom behind everyone else, putting as much distance between us and our classmates as possible. As much as I wanted to, I knew I couldn't ignore Conrad's presence in my dreams. Caroline deserved to know what my odd behavior in class was all about, and I had to be certain we wouldn't be overheard.

Grabbing her hand, I pulled her into a small brick alcove off the main hallway. "I had that dream again last night."

Her mouth curved into a frown. "The same one you've been having since last year?"

"I can't get it out of my head."

"Well, you are watching someone die in it! I'd say that would be pretty hard to forget."

"I know."

"But it's just a dream."

"Is it?" I asked, wringing my hands nervously as I scanned the area around us to make sure we were still alone.

"Yes! It's just teenage hormones and stress. We have ACT and SAT exams to take this year, colleges to visit. You're just stressed, that's all."

"Seeing a man murdered every night is stress?"

"That and a combination of Harry Potter and Charlaine Harris. I know you stay up late reading Sookie books."

"I wish it were that simple," I replied. "You know the new guy,

Conrad? He looks exactly like the guy getting executed in my dream."

"What! How?"

"I don't know. I understand if you don't believe me, but that man and Conrad are identical."

"You're sure?"

"Positive."

"Okay, I believe you," she replied with a hug.

"You do?"

"Actually, yes. The way you were looking at him in class can't be faked. You stared at him like he was someone you hadn't seen in a hundred years. It gave me goose bumps."

Leaving the alcove behind, I followed her to the cafeteria. She stood in line, a plastic tray held firmly in her hands. "Whatever is happening to me, I think it's getting worse," I whispered, hoping no one could hear our conversation.

"We'll figure it out. Try to block it from your mind. I know it's almost impossible, but try to focus on something else." Just as she was talking, I turned to see Claire catch up with Conrad at the front of the lunch line. She wrapped her arm around his and leaned in close to whisper in his ear. "Or maybe you could focus on someone else," Caroline added, following my gaze.

"I don't think focusing on him is a good idea."

"I didn't mean him specifically. Maybe you could just think about what his abs look like."

"Caroline!"

"Hey, a distraction is a distraction."

"Either way, I believe he might be taken."

"Oh please, you could have him eating out of the palm of your hand if you wanted. The Chemistry Club practically worships the ground you walk on, and even if Claire is the most popular girl in school, you can't deny the fact that you possess a certain sway with guys."

"Well, what am I supposed to do? Flirt with him in the middle of class?"

"It seemed to work pretty well for you before Mr. Rieder

dismissed us for lunch. You only live once. What's it going to hurt to put yourself out there?" she asked. "At the very least, cozy up to him and see what you can figure out about him. Maybe you met him as a kid and you just can't remember it."

"That could be a valid reason as to why I dream about him, and it's definitely a better alternative than believing I belong in an insane asylum."

"Go for it!"

Caroline was right, I needed a distraction. And hadn't I promised myself all morning that this year would be different? "Okay! I will."

Filtering through the lines of students, I passed the registers to the main seating area. The popular seniors always sat at the benches in the center of the lunchroom, but since Caroline and I belonged to a smaller social circle, I found us some seats in the far corner of the cafeteria. Our usual place was by the wall of windows, directly across from the other seniors. Claire, of course, took her typical seat at the center benches with Conrad right beside her.

"She is certainly trying to mark her territory, isn't she?" Caroline placed her tray on the table as she glanced over at Claire.

"I don't think he seems to mind," I added.

"Maybe not." Conrad and Claire were the center of a large group of laughing seniors. I watched as she touched his arm and threw her hair over her shoulder. She was a shoo-in to be nominated for football homecoming court, and she was the queen of Tulson. No doubt she felt the need to introduce Conrad into her exclusive social circle. I couldn't blame her though; if any girl in school had a chance with him, it would be her. While I was watching the two of them, Conrad looked up from his tray and caught my gaze. He smiled at me, and I returned the gesture. Maybe it was idiotic to think I could have a shot with him, but at the very least he'd make for a good distraction.

When we returned from lunch, it was time to report to our last period of the day. For the first time in my life, I was ecstatic to leave history class. Discovering the prisoner from my dreams was real was exhausting. And how could I ever forget the distorted figure I saw being mutilated? You would think after all the dreams I've had, I would be used to it, but that wasn't the case and it never would be. As hard as I tried to be a normal girl, a small voice in my head was screaming that I was the exact opposite.

I followed Conrad to the door, stopping him just before he could disappear into the hall. "Thanks for letting me use your pencil," I said, holding it out to him.

"You keep it. Like I said, I don't take notes."

"How—how can you come to all your classes and not take a single note?"

"Because people like me don't need to take notes."

"What do you mean, people like you?"

"Ridiculously attractive people. Obviously."

"Right, because everyone on the face of this earth thinks you're ridiculously attractive."

"You mean that thought didn't cross your mind when you were staring at me earlier?" he asked with a smirk. His nonchalant attitude toward school grated at my nerves. I was in no mood to be taunted by someone so cocky, especially not today.

"Are you hitting on me?"

"Am I that obvious?"

"Arrogant and apathetic aren't really my type," I replied, shrugging.

"So, if I showed more attention to my studies, I'd be your type?"

"You'd have better luck with me."

"Interesting," he said with a grin, before slipping into the hallway.

"What was that about?"

I turned to Caroline, confused. "What do you mean?"

"He is *so* good looking and lets you borrow his pencil, but you thank him by accosting him for not wanting to take notes in class? I mean, *I* barely take notes in this class!"

"It's not just about the notes! He's arrogant and kind of a dick," I replied in a defensive tone.

"I thought you were going for it."

"I am! At least I was, until he started acting like he is God's gift to the female sex."

"You're hopeless, Evey," she chuckled. "Come on, let's go to Physics."

I reluctantly grabbed my messenger bag and trailed her to the door. Maybe I had been rude, but it wouldn't matter. After hanging out with Claire, Conrad would never be interested in me, and a small part of me preferred it that way. By the time we got to Physics, I was already feeling better. I listened to Mr. Liner's lecture intently, answering questions whenever he posed them. I was once again fixated on my studies, and it was a welcome relief to be able to do so. This is who I really was. I was an intelligent girl with a penchant for exams and writing papers, not a clairvoyant basket case. My welcome reprieve was short-lived since our last class only lasted forty-five minutes. While unfortunate for my mental health, it was advantageous for my appetite because I was famished from skipping lunch. Caroline and I changed into our pink waitress uniforms before heading out to the parking lot. A few spaces down, I could see Conrad sitting on the hood of his car. He had a red Mustang convertible, and Claire was leaning over it, talking to him.

"At least he knows his value to the world," I said, throwing my bag on the back seat.

"Apparently, so does Claire."

"She isn't capable of engaging in an intelligent conversation."

Caroline and I slid into our seats, making the quick drive to work. Though most of our friends thought the 50s themed diner was a little dated, Caroline and I had always loved the authentic retro feel at Pat's Place. It had a long bar that spread across the back of the room with a row of barstools in front of it. The counter was a sparkling white, matching the tops of the tables. Booths with red seats covered the remaining wall space inside, breaking up the black and white checkered floor. Kit was at the register ringing up a customer when Caroline and I met her behind the counter.

"Hey girls," she said as she smiled at us.

"Hey," we answered in unison. Kit's mother's name had been

Pat. When her mother died, the diner became hers. Kit and her father, Mickey, have been running it since.

"How was the first day of school?" Kit brushed a stray brown curl from her cheek. Though she was in her mid-thirties, Kit could pass for twenty-five any day.

"It was pretty good. School is school." I shrugged.

"There was a new student in our history class today, and he is gorgeous!" Caroline added.

"Well, in that case, I hope you girls are focusing on the assignments and not the scenery in the classroom," Kit replied with a wink.

"You know I will, but I make no promises for Caroline."

"Hey!" Caroline yelled, smacking my arm lightly. "I think it'll be harder for you than you think. Besides, Conrad didn't seem to mind when you practically massaged his face in class."

"Oh, that is so not what happened!" Instantly, warmth flooded my cheeks. "I borrowed a pencil from him, that's all."

"If that's the case, then why were you staring holes through Claire in the parking lot?" Caroline questioned.

Glaring at Caroline, I walked over to the serving window between the kitchen and eating area. Kit came up to snag a hot plate of fries off the window, before walking it over to a customer seated at one of the bar stools.

"Hey, Mickey!" I called out. Mickey had graying hair and a set of creases that cut across his forehead. I'd never met any of my grandparents, so Mickey was the closest thing I had to a grandfather. He always referred to Kit, Caroline, and I as "his girls." Caroline and I had been working at the diner for the past two years, but we'd practically grown up in it. My parents knew Mickey and Kit before I was born. They'd been my family for as long as I could remember.

"Hey!" He looked up from the grill and beamed at me. "You have a good first day?"

"It was pretty good. I felt sick at lunch though, so I didn't really eat anything."

"If you give me a minute, I'll cook you up a burger and fries. Does Caroline want anything?"

I pulled myself over the bottom of the window and pecked him on the cheek. "Thanks! Hold on, I'll ask her." I turned to face the opposite end of the bar. "Caroline, you want a burger?"

"No thanks, Mickey," she yelled. "I'm not hungry right now."

I braided my hair into a single plait to get it out of my face and tied a white apron over my dress. Then I slid an order pad and pen into the pocket of my apron. Caroline started cleaning the windows on the opposite side of the restaurant while I ate my late lunch. When I finished my meal, I began refilling the ketchup bottles and salt shakers. I was about halfway finished with all the tables when the bell on the front door rang out, indicating the entrance of a customer. My eyes followed the sound, only to see Conrad stepping inside the diner. Immediately, my heart began to pick up its pace. He stalked past me and took up a seat in the back corner of the room. I waved at Caroline in an attempt to get her attention, but her head was already bent toward Kit, deep in conversation. They both motioned for me to go over to him, but I shook my head no. After I blatantly insulted him, I figured there was no chance he wanted me as his waitress. Ignoring my apprehension, Caroline scowled and mouthed the word, "Go." Nervously, I wandered over to his booth and pulled out my pad and pen.

"Hi, what can I get you to eat today?" I asked, a hint of anxiety creeping into my voice.

Conrad studied the menu for a moment before meeting my gray eyes with his shocking blue ones. "Can I tell you my order or do you need to insult me first?"

"Sorry about that. I can be pretty opinionated sometimes."

"Don't worry about it." He laughed. "I'm really not that conceited, it was just amusing to get a rise out of you. I'm Conrad, by the way. You're Evey, right?"

"Yeah."

"It's nice to meet you."

"Yeah, you too."

"You still don't seem to like me much."

"I don't really know you," I answered.

"I see. Well, if there is something you would like to know about me, all you have to do is ask."

"Thanks, I guess. So what can I get you?"

"I'll have a burger, fries, and a Coke."

"Okay," I said, writing down his order. "I'll have that out to you in just a few minutes." I could sense him watching me as I walked back to the counter and handed the slip to Mickey. After filling a cup with soda, I slowly made my way back to Conrad's booth. "So what made you move from Los Angeles to Estill Springs?" I set his Coke in front of him, waiting for a reply. He held the cup to his lips, draining the dark liquid.

"It seems like a nice enough place." He shrugged. "Why don't you sit down and join me for a minute or two?"

"That might be doable if I wasn't currently at work."

He glanced around and smiled. "Because the diner is so preposterously busy at the moment?" Other than him, we only had two other customers.

Preposterously busy? Any time I met his gaze, my heart fluttered inside my chest. But his word choice definitely piqued my interest. Maybe there was more to him than what met the eye. When I glanced back at Kit, she was already motioning for me to sit down with him. As I took my seat, I noticed Kit and Caroline staring in our direction, watching Conrad and me like a couple of hawks. "Fine, but just for a minute though."

"The truth is I moved because I have some family business to attend to. My uncle recently passed away, and he left me his house here. Because he was the last living family member I had, I decided to come and live in his house."

"Oh, I'm sorry to hear about your uncle."

"It's okay. I didn't really know him all that well," he replied. "I only met him a couple of times."

"What about your parents?"

"They died a long time ago," he answered, looking away.

"I'm sorry. I didn't mean to upset you." I dropped my gaze,

biting my lip slightly. He was trying to be friendly, and all I could do was bring up a past he probably didn't want to talk about.

"Don't be sorry. It's not your fault."

"I know, but it was rude of me to pry. It must be hard to be alone."

"I'm not alone. You're sitting with me, after all."

"Have we met before?" The words rolled off my tongue before I could stop them.

"Why would you ask me that?"

Before I could reply, the order bell dinged. Conrad's food was ready.

"Excuse me, I'll be right back." As I picked up the plate, Mickey winked at me. What in the world was going on? It seemed like everyone wanted me to get to know this boy better. Setting the food in front of Conrad, I resumed my seat.

"Do I look familiar to you?" he asked.

"Why would you ask me that?" I repeated his question from earlier. We stared at one another, locked in a theoretical stalemate. Conrad and I had both asked questions the other was evading. "So how come you don't take notes in class or anything?"

"That really bothers you, doesn't it?" he asked with a surprised look on his face.

"I just don't see how you can act like school isn't a big deal. I don't know. I guess I just take my studies seriously and want to do well."

"When I lived in Los Angeles, I was homeschooled. I had a private tutor, and I've already studied pretty much everything the teachers were going over in class today. Believe me when I say my education was a top priority before I moved here."

"Oh, okay." It was official, I was a jerk. I'd made an assumption about him and it turned out to be completely wrong. Luckily, Conrad didn't seem to mind. We sat in silence for a few minutes while he ate his food. I knew I should've returned to work, but some inexplicable force almost seemed to be pulling the two of us together all day. What was the point in trying to fight it now?

"If you're worried about what you said to me at school, don't be.

You didn't insult me," he replied with a smile. "I've always admired women who weren't afraid to speak their minds."

"Are you saying you admire me?"

"Maybe," he answered. "I like your hair like this." He wiped his hands on a clean napkin before reaching forward to touch my braid.

"Thanks. I wear it this way for work." As I fidgeted underneath his scrutiny, a flush of heat warmed my face and neck.

"I'm sorry. I didn't mean to make you uncomfortable."

"You didn't." He briefly rubbed the end of my braid before letting it fall back to my chest.

"Why did you grab me in class today?"

Once again, my heart began to race. I'd held onto his arm while caressing his face intimately. "I didn't feel like myself." In that moment, my need to learn whether or not Conrad was real super-seded everything else. How could I care about manners or embar-rassing myself when proof that I may not be as crazy as I thought sat mere inches from me?

"Is that so?"

"Of course." I plastered a soft smile on my face. "What would make you think otherwise?"

"I just thought it was strange you held on to me like you were afraid I'd disappear before your very eyes."

"Maybe I was," I whispered.

A new intensity crossed his face and he took my hand, holding my gaze with his bottomless blue eyes. "Do you know who I am?" He pressed my hand to his chest. "Do you know me?"

Surprised by his reaction, I froze, searching for some memory of him. Was I cursed with amnesia? Had I met Conrad before only to have the memory erased from my mind as soon as it was made? The tone of his voice broke my heart. All I could respond with was a weak, "Should I?" I wanted to. It almost sounded like he was begging me to remember. I wanted to know why I dreamed of his face for months before ever laying eyes on him. Frustrated at not having the answers, and seeing his face change with my question, I took the easy way out. "I better get back to work. Let me get you another Coke."

"That's okay, I need to go anyway. I pay up at the register, right?"

"Yeah."

"I'll see you later," he said, brushing past me. For a moment, I considered grabbing his arm and pleading with him to stay, but the chime of the order bell distracted me. I took the steaming plates from the window and carried them out to two customers. Then, I refilled their cups with sweet tea before going back to Conrad's table to clear it off. As I collected his dishes, I found a black velvet box tucked between the salt and pepper shakers. Picking it up, I saw the napkin underneath had a short note written on it: *I thought you would like to have this back −C.* Slowly, I lifted the lid. Inside laid a pendant on a gold chain. I had the strange sensation I'd seen this necklace before. It had a bright red stone cut into the shape of a diamond, which was encased inside a larger diamond comprised of gold. A gleaming pearl hung from the bottom tip of the gold pendant. My fingers delicately brushed against the large pearl. I looked around, but no one was watching me, so I slid the box and the note into the pocket of my apron. I'd been right. Conrad wasn't a complete stranger. My stomach did a couple somersaults at the revelation of this new information. Each interaction I'd had with him from the gym to our conversation just a few minutes ago flashed before my eyes. It was all too much. This entire day had been hard, but the combination of his note and the necklace sent me over the edge. I slumped to the checkered floor, my chest heaving with frantic breaths as I contemplated two questions that were sure to haunt me the rest of the day. Why on earth would he give me such a gift? And what did his note mean?

3

THE NECKLACE

When I got home from work, I dumped my bag by the front door and headed straight to the den to find my parents. I grasped the black box in my hands, my fingers rubbing the soft velvet exterior. My parents owned and operated their own auction house in town. They appraised and sold a variety of antique furniture, jewelry, and paintings. I wanted to find out more about this necklace, and they were just the people to ask.

"Hey, Mom," I said, walking up to the couch where she and dad were reading.

"Hey! How was your first day?"

"It was good, kind of busy though. The teachers jumped straight into the lessons today."

"Did you and Caroline get any classes together?"

"Somehow, we got every class together," I replied, suppressing a grin.

"I wonder how that happened," she stated with a knowing smile on her face.

"Let's just say I called in a favor to one of my friends in the guidance office."

"You'd think they'd exercise more discretion with student sched-uling," dad answered.

"The computer software at Tulson isn't the most up-to-date," I countered. "What can I say, Dad? It's a faulty system."

"Of course it is, angel," he replied with a wink. I watched as his attention shifted from my face to the box in my hands. "What do you have there?"

"I have a necklace for you guys to look at, and I was wondering if you could tell me anything about it."

"Where did it come from?" my mother asked, reaching for the box.

"Actually, one of my customers gave it to me as my tip. At first, I thought he might have gotten it from the theater department since they have tons of costume jewelry, but I wasn't sure."

She opened the lid and stared at the necklace. "Oh wow," she gasped, glancing at my father.

"Do you think it's real?"

"It's definitely real, and I'd say it's a ruby, not a garnet."

"How old do you think it is?"

"I'm not sure. Here, Guy," she said, handing the box to my dad. "You're always better at dating things like this than I am."

He removed the necklace and turned it over in his hands a few times. I watched as he readjusted his reading glasses, moving the pendant as close to his face as possible. "Hmm. It looks pretty old. I'd say late fourteenth century, possibly even older. It's quite a stun-ning piece, and it's still in great condition. It could be in a museum even. I haven't seen anything of this quality in quite some time."

"That's incredible." After he handed me back the box, I closed the lid over the necklace, handling it as if it were made of crystal.

"And you said a customer gave it to you?"

"Yeah, he left a note on his table saying he wanted me to have it and to consider it my tip." I cringed. It wasn't a complete lie, but it wasn't as if I could tell them it was a gift from a strange guy I'd just met.

"So a boy gave it to you?" mom asked, smiling slightly.

I nodded, already knowing where this was headed.

"Is it the boy you dated last year?" dad questioned.

I groaned inwardly, recalling the brief month Rob and I dated last year. When you've only ever had one boyfriend, if Rob could really even be called that, I suppose it was imperative for your parents to bring it up periodically. Even though we had fun and I enjoyed hanging out with Rob, there was always something that didn't feel quite right to me. It was part of why I broke up with him; the other part was my dreams. "No, someone else gave it to me."

"Someone else?" she asked.

"Yes, someone else," I answered in exasperation. "Look, I'm exhausted. Are the two of you going to keep interrogating me about my love life, or can I go to bed?"

"You know we're just teasing you, angel," dad replied, holding out his arms for a hug.

"Yeah, yeah."

"We love you," mom added.

I hugged my mom and dashed for my bedroom before either of them could stop me.

Stretching beneath the covers of my bed, I tried to rest but I couldn't get Conrad or the necklace out of my mind. The only thing more puzzling than his note was the pendant itself. What did a six- hundred-year-old necklace have to do with me? And why did he keep asking if I remembered him? I had nightmares from the time I was a small child. I'd always shrugged them off as the result of an overactive imagination, but my dreams had recently turned darker. Torture, murder, and human suffering now plagued my mind as I slept. The sensible part of my brain told me I was clinically insane, but if that were true, how could a complete stranger claim to know me? How would Conrad be able to return one of my possessions, one I had no memory of owning, if I was simply schizophrenic? As I finally began to slip into the realm of unconsciousness, I envisioned Conrad's piercing blue eyes staring at me from a pit of darkness.

My dream was the same as the night before. I begged the merciless king to spare the man's life. I pleaded with him on my knees, but it was all to no avail. When I fell to my hands, I saw a glistening pendant swinging around my neck. However, before I could think about it any further, the axe swung through the air while laughter resonated throughout the room.

I awoke with a start. A glance at my alarm clock informed me it was 4:07 a.m. A fire burned in my throat. When I tried to speak, a hoarse croak escaped, as if I'd spent hours screaming at the top of my lungs. Grabbing the glass of water off my bedside table, I drained every last drop. The cool liquid soothed the sore muscles of my neck. The black velvet box beckoned to me from my dresser. I threw off my comforter and carefully inched over to it. Even in the dim light, the pendant shone, and I couldn't resist the temptation to wear it. The pearl reached the middle of my chest, and the deep red of the stone was almost the same color as my hair. I was captivated by the beauty of it. Looking at my reflection, I couldn't fight the feeling that I'd seen this necklace before. It seemed to belong around my neck. Reluctantly, I put it back in the box, sliding it into my messenger bag. I needed to figure out what Conrad was doing with such an extravagant piece of jewelry and why he believed I was its owner.

I tried going back to sleep, but there were too many questions nagging at my subconscious. After a couple hours, when I finally realized no more rest was to be had this morning, I decided to take a hot shower. Like clockwork, Caroline's call came just as I shut off the faucet.

"Hey!"

"Hey."

"So, what did Conrad talk to you about at the diner? You were really quiet last night, so I thought it better not to ask you about it."

"Oh, you could've asked; I was just a little surprised by every-thing, especially since I insulted him after class. He was nice. Really nice, actually, but there's something different about him."

"You mean other than the fact that he's starring in your latest recurring nightmare?"

"It feels like I've met him before. He seems so familiar."

"Like déjà vu?"

"Exactly! A very odd and twisted case of déjà vu."

"In this day and age, I think it's safe to say stranger things have happened," she replied. "But on the bright side, I don't think he's interested in Claire anymore."

"How can you say that? We only talked for a few minutes."

"Yeah, but you obviously didn't see the way he was looking at you."

"And how did he look at me?"

"Like you were something he wanted."

My heart raced uncontrollably at her words. When I caressed Conrad's cheek in class, his skin felt soft and familiar, and suddenly, I realized I wanted him to want me. Just as I was about to express my excitement at her statement, I couldn't help but wonder why he would want me. Surprise, elation, and trepidation hummed through my body all at once. "Oh," I finally mumbled, cursing myself for ruining such a wonderful train of thought.

"It's not a bad thing! There was a lot of desire and passion behind those eyes."

"Shut up!"

"I'm being serious, Evey. He likes you," she added.

After we said goodbye, I finished getting ready for school. I styled my hair back into soft curls and applied a thin layer of red lipstick. After all, it couldn't hurt to look nice just in case Caroline happened to be right. Retrieving a dark green sweater and a cream-colored skirt from my closet, I dressed quickly. My skirt flowed behind me as I ran down the hall to meet my parents for breakfast.

"Hi, Mom. Hi, Dad," I called out cheerfully.

"Oh, you look beautiful today, sweetie," my mom said.

"Thanks," I answered, sitting at the table beside my dad. He was already working on a stack of blueberry pancakes, and my mom set an identical stack in front of me. The room smelled like hot syrup and bacon grease. Digging into my breakfast, I ate as if I hadn't seen food in days.

"How late will you be tonight?" my dad asked me.

"I should be home around nine. It's Caroline's night to work late."

"Oh okay, do you need us to pick you up from the diner?"

"Yeah, I'll call you first though, in case the time changes."

"Sounds like a plan." He smiled. Just then, I heard Caroline's honk from the driveway.

"That's my cue. Have a good day at work!" I gave my dad a swift kiss on the cheek and my mom pulled me into a tight hug before sending me out the door.

"Love you," my parents called out in unison.

"Love you too!"

I raced to Caroline's car and jumped in the front seat.

"Hey, you look good today," she intoned with a grin.

"Shut up." I could feel the heat rising in my cheeks.

She started laughing. "I'm being serious. Does it have anything to do with a certain someone in our history class?"

"Maybe. He probably won't even notice me."

"Oh please." Rolling her eyes dramatically, she released a loud sigh. "Half the student body will be gossiping about you and Conrad's relationship status by the end of the day."

Time passed at the pace of a snail during my first two classes. The monotony of the lectures was completely vexing. A million different questions churned inside my brain, and I was eager to see the only person who could provide me with answers. Because school wasn't going to dismiss early like it did yesterday, we were supposed to head to the cafeteria and eat lunch before reporting to third period. I nearly sighed with relief when the bell rang, because I would finally have a chance to talk to Conrad. When we got to the cafeteria, I searched for him, but Claire whisked him away before I could even wave in his direction. Her persistence in pursuing him was really starting to irritate me. So while he sat at the coveted table in the center of the cafeteria, I hovered on the outskirts. We smiled at each other a couple times, but smiles weren't what I wanted. I needed to talk to him.

After lunch, Caroline and I took our seats in the back corner of Mr. Rieder's room. Conrad strolled in just before the late bell, taking his seat between Claire and me. Leaning toward her, he whispered something in her ear. As though he could feel my eyes on him, he glanced in my direction. I averted my gaze as Mr. Rieder began scribbling information across the board.

"He's staring at you," Caroline whispered, leaning back in her seat to cup her hand

around my ear.

I fought against my better judgment and stole a look at him. In an instant, our eyes met, and he mouthed a silent "Hi" at me. I replied with a "Hi" of my own and felt a smile spread across my face. Reluctantly, I grabbed my pencil and began taking notes on the lecture, but as I was writing down the composition of the tribunals during the Spanish Inquisition, a small paper airplane landed on top of my notebook. Unfolding it quietly, I read the message that was scrawled along the inside. *You aren't wearing the necklace.* When I glanced at Conrad, I noticed he was frowning slightly. I scribbled a note back to him. *It's a really beautiful necklace, but I can't accept it. It's very valuable and rare. Why would you give it to me?* He responded quickly, sliding the paper to me. *Meet me in the hall after class.* I looked back at him and nodded.

The moment the bell rang, my pulse increased to the speed of a jackhammer. "You go on to physics. I'll meet you there," I said to Caroline. Moving to my feet, I followed Conrad to the door. Once we made it to the hall, he grabbed my hand and pulled me into the janitor's closet. Space was limited, and his body hovered mere inches from mine.

"Didn't you like the necklace?"

"I do. I just don't understand why you would give it to me."

"I thought you would like it."

"But you don't even know me," I replied.

"Is that really what you believe?" He bent forward, closing the distance between us. His lips brushed the skin on my cheek, causing my body to tingle all over. "Did you bring it with you?"

"It's in my bag." He removed the necklace from the box and unclasped it. Then leaning toward me, he circled his arms around my head, sliding his hands beneath my hair. My hands found his waist as he fastened the chain at the base of my neck. His palms rested on either side of my face, the warmth from his touch transferring to my skin. Tilting my head back, I gazed up at him. His lips parted ever so slightly, and I found myself wondering what they felt like.

"Evey," he whispered. Suddenly, the late bell rang, pulling me away from his eyes. "I guess we better go." He opened the door for me, and we immediately set off in opposite directions. Pausing for a moment, I watched him turn the corner toward the English wing as I took off in a run toward my physics class. Sneaking in the room a little late, I sat beside Caroline. Her eyebrows arched dramatically as she noticed the necklace.

"Don't ask," I laughed, rolling my eyes.

"Oh my God! Is that real?" I scowled at her and held my finger over my lips, urging her to be quiet. Mr. Liner surveyed us suspiciously from the front of the classroom.

"Ms. Brewer, is there something you would like to say to Ms. Rhodes?" he questioned, staring at her through his thick Coke-bottle glasses. He always reminded me of the old cartoons of Mr. Magoo, especially with the way he squinted through the lenses.

"Well, yes actually." Shaking my head, I couldn't suppress the groan escaping my lips. Great. There was no doubt she was going to land both of us in detention. However, instead of being furious, her answer seemed to surprise him.

"Just continue your conversation after class," he answered, turning back to the board.

Glancing over at Caroline, I noticed that she was grinning triumphantly. "I'm going to kill you," I mouthed at her. When I bent over my notes, the necklace bumped against my chest, and my hand instantly closed around it to keep it steady. As soon as I touched the necklace, flashes from my dream replayed in my mind. I was in the same grand hall, kneeling in front of the king on his throne. Again, I felt consumed with despair, and as I hunched over on the floor, I saw the necklace.

"I'm begging you to spare his life," I heard myself call out. I turned toward Conrad. The executioner jerked his head to the side, causing him to wince. "Please release Conrad. Your fault is with me, not him."

"As a queen, I expected you to conduct yourself with more dignity than this," the king sneered.

"Punish me any way you see fit, but spare Conrad. That is my only request."

"No!" Conrad shouted. "Torture me if you'd like, but you'll not touch her!"

"No!" I screamed. My heart stalled in my chest. Conrad's eyes locked onto mine, the expression in them full of regret. To my horror, the axe came down, extinguishing the light in his eyes.

Shaking my head from the glimpses of my daydream, I slammed my hands down on the table, causing Caroline to jump. My chest heaved with frantic breaths. I was mistaken. Had everything in my dream really happened? Did Conrad sacrifice himself in order to save me? Sensing something was wrong, Caroline pretended to drop her pencil on the floor and bent down close to me to retrieve it.

"Are you okay?" Her voice was so soft I could barely hear it.

"Yeah, I just have a bad headache." Just as I rested my forehead in the palm of my hand, I was hit with an epiphany. I knew where I'd seen the necklace before. I saw it the same day I met Conrad. Not caring to be quiet, I reached down for my bag and pulled out my history book. I flipped through the pages, not worrying when I ripped a few, and landed on page 256. When I turned it over, I saw Isabella I of Castile smiling at me. My eyes widened with shock and recognition as I focused on her necklace. It was identical to the one hanging from my neck.

4

PIECES OF
THE PUZZLE

"So, he just gave you that necklace?" Caroline asked incredulously as we changed into our work uniforms after school. "But why?"

"Because he seems to think it belongs to me," I answered. "That's all I know."

"You're going to ask him about it, right?" Caroline looked into the bathroom mirror as she applied a fresh layer of lip gloss.

"Of course. Honestly, I can't figure out the bizarre connection we have or deny it exists. How is this even possible?" I asked, deciding to withhold the history of the necklace until I had more answers from Conrad.

"Well, whatever you find out, I think you should keep it. It's beautiful, and it looks great on you."

"You would say that," I stated with a smile.

"All I'm saying is if a man gives you jewelry, you don't give it back."

"I feel like someone should needlepoint that on a cushion."

"You see? This is why we're best friends!" She laughed, hooking her arm with mine as we emerged from the restroom.

Walking out to the parking lot, we headed toward Caroline's car. Across the way, I could see Conrad sitting on top of his. Claire was stuck to him like glue because she leaned against his front tire, her elbows resting on the hood beside him. The two seemed to be having a simple conversation when she stroked the length of his arm in an obvious attempt to garner his attention. Throwing my bag on the back seat, I closed the door.

"Hey, wait for me a minute. I'll be right back," I called to Caroline as I ran toward

Conrad.

He slid off the hood as I approached him. "I need to talk to you."

"Conrad and I were in the middle of making dinner plans," Claire said, inching closer to him.

"That's absolutely fascinating, Claire," I countered with an eye roll. "However, I need to talk to Conrad right now. So, why don't you go over there for a second and practice one of your little cheers."

Her face flushed at my words. "You need to watch what you say, Evey." In a huff, she sauntered over to the football field behind the parking lot. The rest of the cheerleading squad was there, running through drills and tumbling passes.

"Don't you think you were being a bit hostile toward Claire?"

"Not really. She's been pissing me off lately."

A slight smile spread across his face. "I wonder why."

"Can we please cut the formalities?"

"What would you like to talk about?" He was trying to be coy, but instead of being cute,

it was irritating.

"I think you know what."

"Personally, I think the necklace looks like it was made for you."

"I've had dreams about you."

"I must say, it does seem a little early for you to be having dreams about me, but I do tend to have this effect on women," he replied with a suggestive wink.

"You're infuriating. Has anyone ever told you that before?"

"Maybe once or twice."

"Could you please try to focus? We were talking about my dreams," I spat in exasperation.

"Right," he answered, pausing for a moment. "If you would like to compare your dreams with reality, I'd be happy to assist you." When he took a step toward me, a knot lodged itself in my throat.

"I didn't mean dreams like that!" I didn't need a mirror to know that the color of my face now matched my hair. "The dream I had felt real. You were executed in it, and I had on this necklace," I said, holding up the pendant.

He frowned slightly. "I see."

"You know more than you're telling me, that much is obvious. Right now, I have to go to work, but can you come to the diner around nine? I want to finish this conversation."

"I'll see you later tonight."

Turning on my heel, I headed back to Caroline's car. Frustration pumped through my veins like a raging river. I slid onto my seat and slammed the door with more force than I intended. "Is he still staring at me?"

"Oh yeah," Caroline answered, sounding breathless. "Then again, I don't think he's stopped since history class today."

We rode in silence all the way to the diner. Because it was Thursday, the Springs Gardening Committee would be having its weekly meeting, so by the time we got there, the diner was already packed. Immediately, we made ourselves busy by taking orders and serving hot plates of food. I knew I would eventually have to tell Caroline about everything with the necklace, but I just couldn't until I had more answers myself. When things finally started to slow down around eight, Kit eyed the pendant as I cleaned out the milkshake blender.

"Pretty necklace," she noted, sliding the clasp on the chain back behind my neck.

Pulling on my braid, I couldn't stop myself from groaning at her comment. "Can we please talk about something besides my love life?"

"Of course."

"I'm sorry, Kit. It's just been a really long day."

"Don't worry about it! Why don't you, Caroline, and I go shopping together next week? Isn't Homecoming right around the corner?"

"We do need some killer dresses for the dance," I stated.

"Good." She returned my smile and shooed me in the direction of the kitchen. "Go help out Dad with the grill and I'll finish up here."

"Got a lot on your mind?" Mickey asked, looking at me as he scraped off excess grease with a wire brush.

"I was just thinking about the lesson we were going over in history today."

"And what might that be?"

"The Spanish Inquisition." I grabbed an onion and began slicing it so Mickey could fry up some onion rings. The vapors from it stung my eyes, making them water.

"Ah. The persecution of Muslims and Jews by the Spanish monarchy."

I turned to him, unable to mask the surprised expression covering my face. "How did
you know?"

He let out a deep belly laugh. "I went to school too, and it wasn't all that long ago."

"Sorry," I replied innocently. "It's just hard to picture you as a high school student."

"It's fine," he laughed. "Actually, it was such a long time ago I hardly remember it. I prefer it that way though. I cringe at the thought of being eighteen again. Speaking of which, have you given any thought to what you want to do for your birthday next month?"

"I really want to have a small party here again like last year. That is, if it's okay with you
and Kit."

"You're one of my girls; of course it's okay with us." He beamed at me. "Just name the date, and Kit and I will decorate the whole diner."

"Thank you!" I flung my arms around him in excitement and he gave me a tight squeeze back. A soft jingle sounded from the front of the diner. When I looked through the window, I expected to see Conrad, but instead it was Claire. "Oh great," I muttered to myself. She strolled over to the bar like she was a contestant on *America's Next Top Model* and took a seat. Not a minute later, Caroline stuck her head into the kitchen.

"She's requesting to have you as her waitress."

"Of course she is. I'm on my way." Sighing heavily, I pulled out my order pad and pen as I approached her. "What can I get you today?"

"Oh, there you are, Evey. It's so hard to see through all the smoke in here. I guess that's what happens when you cook everything in grease," she noted in a superior tone.

My fingers gripped my order pad, and I sucked in a deep breath to calm myself. "I don't see any smoke, but whatever you say. What do you want?"

She perused the menu for a few minutes, clearly enjoying the fact she had the power to make me wait. "I'll have a sweet tea and some fries, I guess." She set her menu down, watching as I retrieved her drink. "I hate to eat carbs right after cheer practice, but that's all you have here."

If I hadn't been at work or cared about keeping Mickey and Kit's good name, I would've let her have a piece of my mind right then and there. "I'm sure," I replied with a fake smile. "I'll have your food out to you in just a minute." Heading into the kitchen, I watched as Caroline prepared Claire's fries. "I swear to you if she doesn't eat her food and go, I'm going to drown her in the milkshake machine."

"What is she saying?"

"Basically just insulting the diner and saying it's a terrible grease trap."

"Well, if she doesn't like it, tell her not to let the door hit her in the ass on the way out!"

"I think she's pissed because I embarrassed her in front of Conrad today."

"She better be lucky I'm a classy waitress, because otherwise, I'd be spitting in her fries."

"I'm just sick of her thinking she's the center of the universe." I took the plate of fries Caroline handed me and carried them out to my least favorite human being on the planet. "Enjoy," I spat, dropping the plate in front of her.

"There are a couple more things I wanted to discuss with you."

"I absolutely refuse to tutor you again. Last time went terribly. You didn't want to learn and you just expected me to do the work for you."

She crossed her arms in exasperation. "I don't need a tutor anymore, and that wasn't what I wanted to talk about."

"Well, what did you want to talk about?" I planted myself across the bar from her, watching as she nibbled on her fries.

"Homecoming and Conrad."

"I don't see how either of those things have anything to do with me."

"On the last day of school before summer, Mrs. Burleson had the next group of seniors nominate several girls to run for Homecoming Queen."

"I know, I was there."

"At the student council meeting today, she named the nominees."

"Are you campaigning for my vote?" I questioned. "Because blatantly insulting the place where I work isn't the most solid campaign strategy."

"I'm trying to tell you that you're one of the nominees for Homecoming Queen."

"What? Why?"

"We both received the most nominations, so it's between you and me."

"That's ridiculous."

"Those were my exact words as well."

"Look, Claire, I know you're pissed at me, but I never asked to be Homecoming Queen. I don't know of anyone who would even nominate me."

"I was just as surprised as you are."

"Well, I didn't knowingly throw my name in the hat, so don't blame me for ruining your dreams of being crowned queen of Tulson."

"Sure you didn't. We all know that crown belongs on my head."

Anoyance simmered in the pit of my stomach. Was she for real? "Maybe you should actually try being nice to people for a change. You might win more votes that way!" I shouted slamming my order pad on the counter.

"You girls doing okay over here?" Kit came to stand behind me, setting her hand on my back.

"We're okay," I replied. "Just talking about school stuff."

"All right, if y'all need anything, I'll be right over there."

"Thanks," I added with a stiff smile. "And what about Conrad? What could we possibly need to discuss about him?"

"I want you to stay away from him."

"Interesting. May I ask why?"

"I like him; he's charming, sexy, and he likes me too. We would make the perfect couple and with Homecoming just around the corner . . ."

"You think dating him will secure your place as Homecoming Queen."

"Every girl has been drooling over him the past two days, and he's well on his way to becoming the most popular guy in school. I might not be as smart as you, but I can put two and two together."

"I have no claim on him, so I don't understand why you'd feel the need to tell me to stay away from him."

"You were seconds from making out with him in Mr. Rieder's class the other day."

"That was nothing," I defended. "I wasn't feeling well."

"Really?"

"You wouldn't understand. I—"

"You want him to be all yours? Join the club, sweetie."

The annoyance I felt only moments ago transformed into a swell of anger. What I was dealing with was more important than some stupid popularity contest. My own sanity hung in the balance, and the only person who could explain the mystery of my nightmares was Conrad. "Maybe he just wants to be my friend. Is that such an impossible notion?"

"Guys like Conrad aren't interested in being friends. He'll take what he wants from you and then move on to someone new. It's best to let a real woman handle his needs." Before I could utter a reply, she tossed a wad of cash on the counter and strutted out of the diner. I threw the money in the register and removed my apron.

"I'm going for a short walk. I need to cool down."

"I'll go with you if you want," Caroline said.

"I just want to be alone. Thanks though."

"Be safe and come back whenever you're ready. There's no rush, Evey," Kit replied.

I walked by a few parked cars and made my way to the far end of the lot. It was already dark outside and the street lamps glowed, lighting the path in front of me. Cars passed by, shooting down the highway. I couldn't fathom Claire's nerve. She acted as if Conrad wanted to use me up and then discard me like I was a piece of trash. Of course she considered herself the only girl at Tulson worthy of being with Conrad, but I certainly wasn't inferior to her.

"Evey!" The sound of my name broke my daze. "Evey!" Conrad shouted as he ran toward me.

"What do you want?"

"I came to meet you at the diner, but when I drove by, I saw you walking outside. I figured something was wrong."

"I'm fine."

"No, you're not." He moved closer to me but I backed away. "Tell me what happened."

"What do you want from me, Conrad?" I asked. "Because Claire seems to think I'm some kind of sexual conquest to you. She basically told me once you've had your fill, you'll toss me aside and move on to someone new."

"Claire is wrong."

"Is she?"

"Yes," he answered, taking my hands in his.

"How can I know you're telling me the truth?"

"Tell me exactly what happened in your dream."

"I don't see how that is going to make me trust you."

"Just think back to your dream. What happened in it?"

Closing my eyes, I replayed the nightmare in my mind. "We're in a grand hall, kneeling before a king. The executioner has ahold of you, ready to strike as soon as he's given the order. I beg the king to show you mercy and he laughs at me. I keep pleading with him, but it's all to no avail. I even offer to take your place, so I can be punished instead of you."

"And what did I say when you offered to take my place?"

"You didn't want him to hurt me. You said he could torture you if he wanted but he wouldn't touch me." Conrad's hand lifted my chin. Seeing the truth swimming in those crystal blue irises, I asked, "You would endure torture for me, wouldn't you?" He nodded once in reply, his gaze never leaving mine. "I should get my bag from the diner before we continue this conversation."

He followed me into the diner, waiting out front while I went to the break room to retrieve my messenger bag. By the time I gathered up my things, Conrad was already talking to Caroline and Kit at the counter.

"My name is Conrad Bourdet. I'm just going to give Evey a ride home," he said, holding out his hand to Kit.

"It's very nice to meet you. We've certainly heard good things about you," she replied, taking his hand. "I'm Kit, and that's my father, Mickey, back in the kitchen. We own the diner."

"It's nice to meet you." He nodded slightly to Mickey. Despite his air of cockiness, no one could say Conrad didn't have perfect manners and posture. Now that I was watching him, I noticed he stood up straight, like a soldier at attention, just waiting to be given the order to relax. "Are you ready?" he asked, walking over to me.

"Yeah."

"Here, let me." He reached forward to take my bag and slung it over his shoulder.

"Bye, guys," I called to everyone. "I'll call you later, Caroline."

"Oh I can't wait," she snickered. I scowled at her over my shoulder and saw they were all waving goodbye to me. I followed suit and stepped out of the diner with Conrad right behind me. He maintained his close proximity as he trailed me to the passenger side of the car, opening the door for me.

"What was that look for?" he questioned.

"I don't know. I just wasn't expecting you to be so chivalrous."

"Despite what you might think about me, I was raised to be a perfect gentleman."

"Honestly, I don't know what to think of you, and that's the problem," I countered, sitting in the passenger seat. He jogged around to his side of the car and slid behind the wheel. Then he set my bag in the back seat before pulling out of the diner parking lot.

"Where do you want to go to talk?"

"Let's go to the park." I pointed for him to turn right and continued talking. "It's just a half mile down that way, on the left."

"Sounds like a plan."

A few minutes later, we pulled up to the basketball court by the playground, and I felt an odd sense of relief, as if all my questions and uncertainty would soon be resolved. Needing some fresh air, I decided to walk over to the swings. Conrad followed my lead. The chains on the swing shook slightly as he placed his hands above mine. I shuddered. A cool wind blew through the park, chilling the air.

"Cold?"

"Just a little." I turned to see him.

"Take my jacket," he said, pulling it off. He waited for me to hold out my arms before sliding it over my shoulders.

"Won't you get cold?"

"Nah, I'll be fine." He returned his hands to the metal chains, sliding them down closer to mine. "Besides, I'd rather me be cold than you." I stood, spinning around so I could face him.

"You're so confusing sometimes."

"How so?"

"It's like you're two different people," I replied. "One second, you're this cocky jerk, and the next, you're looking at me like you've known me for hundreds of years. It's completely puzzling."

"There's an explanation for that."

"Really? Because I'd love some clarity at the moment. You know,

I must have had that dream a thousand times, and until I met you, I thought I was losing my mind. I tried to rationalize the horrific things I saw every way possible and finally concluded I was just crazy." I was tired of waiting; it was time for him to start talking. "And when you gave me this necklace, it fit into the dream too. I have it on when I watch you die."

"That's rather depressing."

"See, there you go again with your jerk routine," I spat in exasperation. "This necklace is the same one Isabella I of Castile is wearing in a painting from our history book! How did you come to have a necklace that is nearly six hundred years old?"

"The dreams you've been having aren't really dreams."

"Oh really?" The sarcasm in my voice was unmistakable. "And what are they exactly?"

"Memories."

His confession hit me like a ton of bricks. Instinctively, I tightened my grasp around the chains on the swing. "No, that's impossible. How can I be having the memories of someone that was alive almost six centuries ago?"

"Because you aren't seeing someone else's memories. You're seeing your own

memories."

I could feel the blood rushing in my ears. Somehow I knew my knees were giving out, but I was too stunned by his revelation to react. When I finally came back to reality, Conrad sat next to me, his hands caressing my face.

"My memories?" I shook my head, not wanting to believe his confession.

"Are you okay?" He scanned me from head to toe, searching for any indication of an injury.

"I'm fine, but how can they be my memories?" I asked. "And how are you in them?"

"They're your memories because you were there when everything happened, and I'm in them because I was too."

"I don't understand," I gasped, my eyes filling with unshed tears. I wanted to push away from him, to release myself from his touch, but his gaze glued me to the spot. At any moment, the rational part of my brain would kick in and I'd make a run for it. But as the seconds ticked by, I realized there was nowhere else I wanted to be. He reached forward to brush a strand of hair off my face, his fingers softly trailing along my skin.

"Do you trust me?"

"I don't even know you."

"That doesn't matter. Do you trust me?"

"I don't know," I answered reluctantly.

"Evey, look at me. Look in my eyes and tell me if you think I'm lying to you."

I stared into his eyes for what seemed like ages. "Okay," I finally whispered. "I trust you."

"Well then trust me when I say I want to tell you everything, and I will, but I can't just yet."

"What do you mean you can't?

"I mean exactly that. It's not time for me to explain everything to you, but it will be

soon."

"But—"

"Evey, trust me." He leaned forward, softly pressing his lips to my forehead. Despite conventional thinking, I knew what he was telling me had some truth to it. My dreams had always seemed so real to me. Thinking they were memories made more sense than believing I was psychotic. I had memorized every feature of Conrad's face months before I ever knew he existed. How could I dream about a real person before I'd even met him?

"Okay, I'll wait, but I have one more question."

"What's that?"

I raised my hand to his face and gently traced the outline of his lips with my fingers. "So, you're not interested in Claire?"

He held onto my wrist, tilting it slightly to kiss my palm. "Not at all." Pulling me up from the ground, we made our way back to his car. "Come on, let's get you home." His hand stayed against my back to steady me as I walked. When we were almost there, he suddenly said, "I know this is going to seem like the wrong time, but can I ask you something?"

"Sure," I replied. His presence was reassuring, and it made me realize the more he touched me, the more I didn't want him to stop.

"Claire is having a party at her house tomorrow night, and I was wondering if you would like to go with me."

I fought unsuccessfully to hide the grin unfolding across my face. "I don't think Claire invited you to her party with the intention of you bringing a date."

"Who cares what she thinks? Besides, I want you to go with me."

"You're asking me out on a date?"

"That depends," he said with a roguish tone.

"On what?"

"On whether or not your answer is yes."

"What do you think my answer is?"

"I guess I'll pick you up at eight," he answered with a devious grin. I gave him directions to my house and watched the trees meld into a murky blur outside my passenger window. From the corner of my eye, I saw that half of his attention was focused on driving, while the other half stayed on me.

"I don't know if you realize it, but you're staring at me," I said, breaking the silence in his car.

"I tend to look at things I find beautiful."

"You think I'm beautiful?"

"I've met many people, and I don't believe I've ever seen anyone as beautiful as you."

"You're very sweet . . . when you want to be."

He parked the car in my driveway and switched off the ignition before making an attempt to reply. "I'll be sure to try harder in the future." He jumped out and rounded the front end to open my door.

My feet trudged reluctantly up the walkway to my house as the sound of Conrad's footsteps echoed from beside me. Who was this mysterious stranger, and why did he move to Estill Springs of all places? A tiny voice in my head dared to state the obvious; it dared to say he moved here because of me. However, if that were the case, why would he come for me? I didn't want to say good night, at least not yet. "You know, I'm putting a lot of faith in you, trusting you aren't lying to me and that you'll eventually explain all of this," I whispered, glancing down at my white sneakers, unable to meet his eyes. "Please don't let me down."

"You say that as if you expect me to."

"I really don't know what to expect." I shrugged off his leather jacket, handing it back to him. "Thanks for letting me wear your jacket. Good night."

"Good night, my lady," he replied with a slight bow. "And for the record, I'd never let

you down."

I shook my head at him and stepped inside the house, locking the front door behind me. What a day it had been. The more answers I got out of Conrad, the more questions I seemed to have, but my train of thought was interrupted when I bumped into my mother in the kitchen.

"Sorry, Momma. I didn't see you there."

"That's all right. Your father and I thought you were going to call us to come pick you up."

"Oh," I replied. "I ended up catching a ride with a friend from school." Mom furrowed her eyebrows. She knew all too well that Caroline was pretty much my only friend.

"Who is this friend exactly?"

"His name is Conrad. He's a new student in my history class," I said, pouring myself a glass of milk.

"I see. And is this the boy who gave you the necklace?" She placed her elbows on the kitchen counter, leaning over them as she waited for me to answer her question.

"Yeah."

"It's quite an extravagant gift."

"He's just trying to make friends." The expression on her face told me she didn't believe a single word coming from my mouth. "Okay, so he asked me on a date tomorrow too." Instantly, my cheeks filled with heat.

The stern look on her face was replaced with a soft smile. "So, just how important is this

date?"

"Pretty important," I replied. "Caroline would think it was a huge deal. All the girls in the school want to get to know him." I took another gulp of milk, letting the cool beverage coat my dry throat.

"It's getting late," she added, giving me a kiss and ushering me off toward my room.

"Evey?"

I spun on my heel so I could look at her. "Yeah?"

"Just be sure to bring him by to meet your father and me before the two of you go on

your date."

"I will."

That night, when I slept, I watched the execution again. Only this time, I could see everything more clearly—the gnarled scar that spread from the executioner's upper lip all the way past his chin, the dark eyes of the king glowing in the shadows, and the desperation with which I tried to save Conrad. As I scrambled toward Conrad's kneeling figure, I saw he was trying to reach out to me too. His fingers almost touched mine, but the hands that restrained me prevented it. Our eyes locked onto one another. "I'm so sorry, Conrad, please forgive me," I said to him.

"It's not your fault," he replied. He said something else, but I couldn't make it out. Then the executioner dealt his fatal blow.

I rolled over in bed, groping for my phone. I groaned. It was barely three. When I unlocked the screen, I saw there was a missed call from Caroline. I decided to send her a quick text. *Sorry I didn't call you last night. I have a lot of stuff to tell you. See you in the morning!* Then, I burrowed myself down into the covers and was finally able to have a few hours of restful, dream-free sleep.

5

POPPIES

I slapped the buzzer on my alarm clock, silencing it, and headed to the bathroom to take a shower. It was Friday morning, and excitement bubbled in my stomach as I remembered I had a date with Conrad tonight. Hot water flowed over me, erasing any negative feelings that remained from my dreams. I dried and curled my hair and then applied a couple coats of mascara to my long eyelashes. I grabbed a white skirt printed with red and yellow roses from my closet and pulled it on. A hunter green tank top and soft yellow cardigan completed my look. Grabbing my leather bag, I took off down the hall, sliding into the kitchen.

"Woah. You seem like you're in a hurry today," my dad said as I almost collided into

him.

"Oh, sorry, Daddy."

He laughed at me, his expression softening. "That's okay. Ready for the weekend?"

"You have no idea."

My mom was waiting for us both at the stove. "What kind of eggs do y'all want this

morning?"

"Fried," I answered, pouring myself a cup of coffee. I added a fair amount of cream before sitting down at the table.

"I'll have scrambled," my dad replied, wrapping his arms around his wife, kissing her cheek.

"Evey has a date tonight," my mom said as she glanced at my father.

"Is that right?" He turned to me, his eyebrows practically disappearing into this hairline.

I choked on my sip of coffee and wiped away the brown beads running down my chin. "Yes."

"What is this boy's name?"

"His name is Conrad Bourdet. He just moved here from Los Angeles. His uncle died
recently."

"Oh, that's got to be Jim Bourdet's nephew," my mom replied, adding two eggs to my
plate.

"Oh yeah, that's right. Jim brought a couple of his antiques into the store to get appraised before drawing up his will. I always liked Jim. He was a good man and had quite an assortment of collectibles."

"Conrad is a little old-fashioned. He always opens doors, and last night, he carried my bag when he dropped me off at the house."

"That's good," he answered. "Just be sure to bring him in when he comes to pick you
up."

"I will," I promised with a smile.

"I remember the first time I saw your mother like it was yesterday."

"And what did you think?" I questioned.

I watched my dad's eyes as they followed my mom. She bent to him, setting down a plate full of eggs. Taking advantage of her closeness, he leaned forward and planted a kiss right on her lips. "I thought she was beautiful."

"And I thought you were my knight in shining armor," she replied, smiling.

I finished my breakfast with a few minutes to spare before Caroline arrived, so I washed some dishes in the sink. The sun shone brightly, casting shadows across the neighbor's yard. It was a wonderful start to a beautiful day, and it was only going to get better. Just as I dried off our breakfast plates, I heard a honk.

"Caroline's here. I'll see you tonight," I called to my parents.

"Have a good day," my dad replied.

"We love you."

"I love you too," I said to my mother, pecking her on the cheek before running out the

door.

I jogged to the passenger side of the car and jumped in the front seat, fastening my

seatbelt.

"You have a lot of explaining to do," Caroline hissed, glaring at me over her sunglasses.

"I know, and you'll never guess what happened!"

"Oooh! What?"

"I have a date with Conrad tonight."

"Seriously?"

"Yeah, he's picking me up at eight, and we're going to Claire's party!" I beamed at her, unable to keep my excitement under control.

"That's awesome!"

It might sound horrible, but I didn't take a single note during my first class of the day. My mind kept replaying the conversation I had with Conrad in the park. Thinking about his lips against my forehead made my whole body tingle, and my attention span didn't improve during economics either. I was simply too preoccupied with my evening plans to even care what was going on in class today. For the first time in my life, I had been transformed into a bad student. I felt a twinge of guilt that Caroline was assigned to be my partner for the first budget analysis report, especially since I couldn't focus for more than five minutes at a time, but she didn't seem to mind.

"So, are you excited about tonight?" She had to repeat her question four times before I even realized she was talking to me.

"Huh?"

"I said, are you excited about tonight? Wow, you're really distracted today."

"Sorry, I was thinking about last night, when Conrad and I went to the park."

"Oh? What happened?"

"Nothing much, we just talked."

"Uh-huh." She gave me a disbelieving look.

"Oh, shut up. It's true!"

"Okay, okay. I believe you." She laughed, holding her hands up in defeat.

"Really?"

"No, not even for a second."

"You realize I'm not you, right?"

"So, I kiss and tell. Is that such a bad thing?"

"Not when it comes to your dating life," I teased. "Are you going to the party tonight too?" I slid the budget report over to her so she could review all the financial data included on the balance sheet. Mickey and Kit had given us both the night off because it was the first Friday night of the school year.

"I can't. My cousin's birthday dinner is tonight. My parents and I are going to Murfreesboro to eat at some restaurant up there."

"Oh yeah, I forgot about that. That kind of sucks."

"Tell me about it! I wanted to go to the party so I could watch you on your date."

"Don't worry, I'll call you and give you every detail after it's over."

"I bet Conrad is a better kisser than Rob, so you better not leave anything out! I want full kissing and groping descriptions, with lots and lots of adjectives."

I laughed at her, shaking my head. "Your wish is my command."

"Good!"

When it was time for lunch, I felt my heart quicken its pace. I tried to seem calm as Caroline and I made our way to the cafeteria, but the task proved to be harder than I anticipated. Conrad was already in line when we got there, and he smiled as we picked up our trays.

"Hey." I could see him looking me over, taking in the features of my face. "You look nice

today."

"Thanks," I replied, nervously tucking a strand of hair behind my ear. "Do you want to eat with us?"

"Absolutely," he answered. At that moment, Claire came up behind him and put her hand on his shoulder, turning him away from me to whisper in his ear. "Oh yeah, I'll be there." I could hear his reply, even though I couldn't make out what she had asked him. "And Evey will be there too. I asked her to come with me as my date." Claire's cheeks reddened as she contorted her face into a scowl. Conrad, it seemed, didn't notice because he flashed me another smile.

"Just come find us when you're finished getting your food," I said, following Caroline to the register.

We were already digging into our food by the time Conrad emerged from the lunch line. He spotted us and waved, but before he could head in our direction, a voice stopped him.

"Conrad, come sit with us! I've got to talk to you right now!" Conrad barely had time to process what Claire was shouting when she grabbed his hand and led him over to the benches in the center of the room.

"Wait," Caroline began. "What the heck was that? He was clearly coming to sit with us!"

"I guess she's making her last stand. Maybe she wants to make it clear to everyone that she already marked her territory."

We watched Conrad as he bent over his food. He nodded his head absentmindedly as Claire talked to him. He must have known we were staring because at that moment, he glanced in our direction. In a dramatic act of defiance, he held an imaginary gun up to his head and pulled the trigger. At the sight, Caroline and I burst into giggles. "Sorry," he mouthed.

I smiled slightly and shrugged to let him know it wasn't a big deal.

"That was such a bitch move. I can't believe Claire did that," Caroline said.

"I can," I replied. "Besides, let her talk to him. I'll get him all to myself tonight."

"I have to say, catty looks good on you."

"Where do you think I learned it from?"

"If you don't say me, I might cry."

I nudged my shoulder into her arm softly. "Of course you! Honestly, who else do I know with that much attitude?"

"You do make an excellent point," she agreed. "So, I assume your mom and dad are cool with you going out with Conrad?"

"Yeah, they really are," I answered. "I don't know. It just seems like ever since Conrad moved here, fate has been trying to push the two of us together. Does that sound ridiculous?"

"I don't think it's ridiculous at all. It's in the way he looks at you. I know I've given you a lot of flak about it, but I'm just teasing. He really likes you, and it's so obvious every time the two of you are in the same room." Instantly, my mind replayed our conversation from the park. The way he made me feel was undeniable. "Just look at him right now. He can't keep his eyes off you," she added.

I turned my attention away from my lunch tray and met his eyes once again. As soon as he noticed I was looking back at him, a wide grin covered his face. She was right, he really couldn't stop staring at me. After lunch, Mr. Rieder lectured while Caroline and I commenced with our diligent note-taking. When he mentioned the Spanish Inquisition, I couldn't resist the urge to pull out my book and turn to the page with my necklace on it. There was no difference between the two pendants—they were identical. When I glanced to my right, Conrad was staring at me. He nodded his head, and I knew he wanted to answer all my questions. When it was time to go to fourth period, Mr. Rieder continued speaking through the first bell, too engrossed in his lesson to realize class was dismissed. I'd been hoping to talk to Conrad after class, but Caroline and I only had one minute to run to physics, and there simply wasn't enough time. We barely made it through the threshold before the tardy bell rang. Panting, I took my seat beside Caroline and removed a notebook from my bag. I only had one more class to go before this torturous school day was over.

Physics class passed in a blur. I only heard snippets of the lecture, something was said about joules and Newton was referenced a couple times, but nothing stuck. Mr. Liner asked several questions, but I was so busy thinking about the date I was going on tonight, I was incapable of providing answers.

"You really are out of it today. You didn't even answer a single question in physics, and you always answer them," Caroline said as we climbed into her car.

"I know. I keep thinking about tonight."

"I can't say I blame you. Although, you might want to watch out for Claire at the party tonight, because after the stunt she pulled at lunch and all the stuff she said to you at the diner yesterday, I'd say she isn't finished with Conrad."

"I was thinking the same thing."

"Just don't let her ruin your night! You deserve to have fun!"

She pulled into the parking lot of my parents' auction house. Rhodes' Auction House

was in an old, two-story white house just off North Jackson Street. My parents opened it right before I was born and had been running it together ever since. The entire inside of the house was gutted to create an open floor plan that was ideal for a showroom. Upstairs was their office space and downstairs housed all the antiques. Paintings and mirrors hanging in expensive gilded frames occupied every inch of wall space. "Call me later and let me know how your date goes!"

"I will! Have fun tonight in Murfreesboro."

"I'll try my best. Don't do anything I wouldn't do," she said with a wink.

"Don't worry, I won't leave a single adjective out," I replied.

"Can't wait. Love ya!"

"Love ya!" I waved goodbye to her as I stepped through the door of the auction house.

"Hey, Mom. Hey, Dad," I called out.

"Hey," my mom said, walking around the corner to the entryway.

"Where's Dad?"

"He's upstairs, balancing the books. How was school?"

"It was good, I was ready for it to be over though. I'm glad it's the weekend."

"Are you and Caroline working tomorrow?"

"Yeah, Kit asked us to come in and work from 11:00-9:00."

"That's good. I think I'm going to talk your dad into helping me paint the kitchen

tomorrow."

"Good luck with that."

Before she could say anything else, a customer came in, drawing her to the other side of the room. I walked around, admiring the delicate vases and tables scattered about, only to stop in front of my favorite piece in the whole house. It was a small painting hanging next to the window on the back wall. The painting depicted a young girl lying in a field of red poppies. The soft glow of the sun shone off the girl's golden hair, and the flowers looked as if they were dancing in the wind. When I was little, I always liked to pretend I was the little girl. I would imagine myself in the white dress that seemed to jump out against the reds and greens of the flowers. I couldn't think of anything better than a bed made of poppies, smelling their sweet perfume as I drifted off to sleep.

I could hear footsteps behind me on the aged wooden floors, and I turned to see my mother approaching.

"This has always been your favorite painting," she said, smiling at me.

"How come it's never been sold?"

"People have made several offers on it, but your father never agrees to sell it." She put her arm around me. "I don't think he ever will."

"Why not?"

"Because it reminds him of you," she answered. "When you were really little, he used to take you out to Penny's farm to pick blackberries, and there was a field right beside the blackberry patch. After the two of you had filled your baskets with fruit, he would take you to the field, and you'd both lie down in the wildflowers to nap."

"I'd forgotten about that."

"You were really young, only four or five years old."

"Do you think Dad would let me have it?"

"I have a good feeling he might."

I spent the rest of the afternoon reading my tattered copy of Jane Austen's *Persuasion* while my parents went through some new inventory in the showroom. My father came up to get me when five o'clock rolled around and it was time to close the store.

"You ready to go?" He leaned against the doorway with his arms folded across his chest. His gray streaks suited him, and I couldn't quite remember what his hair looked like without them or if he had ever been without them.

"Yup," I answered, turning off the computer. "Hey, you know the painting of the girl in the field?"

"Yeah, what about it?"

"I was wondering if I could have it. It's my favorite piece in the whole store, and I'd just be heartbroken if someone else got it."

"Actually, I was saving it to surprise you on your birthday."

"Really?"

"Really," he replied with a laugh. "Eighteen is a milestone birthday after all, but I guess it would be all right if you got it a little early."

"Thank you!" Running over to him, I threw my arms around his neck. I couldn't believe they were going to give me my painting, and I knew just where to put it in my room.

"I guess we shouldn't be surprised that you figured out your present before your birthday. You always did have a knack for finding where your mother and I hid them," he replied. "Do you remember Christmas when you were ten?"

"How could I forget?" I asked. "I found the stash of presents in your bathroom closet, and Mom threatened to return every one. I cried for hours. I was so distraught because I thought the two of you were mad at me."

"She wouldn't have returned a single gift. I think your mother was just upset because you were growing up and it would be that much harder to keep things from you when you were older." He held his arm around my shoulders and followed me out of his office. "Let's get you home so you can get ready for your date."

Excitement fizzled in my stomach as I got ready. I was so anxious to see Conrad it seemed impossible for me to stand still. I danced around my bathroom, humming the lyrics to any song that popped in my head, as I curled my hair and drew my eyeliner way out past the corners of my eyes. I'd been waiting for this date all day, and it was finally going to happen. Not only would I get to do something a normal girl would do, but I'd also be able to find out more about Conrad and my necklace. Setting my maroon dress on the bed, I retrieved a pair of tan heels from the closet. I changed into my dress and ran my fingers through my hair, tousling the soft curls. When I checked the clock, it was 7:55. Conrad would be here any minute. I had just enough time to brush my teeth and straighten out my necklace before I heard the doorbell ring.

"Evey, Conrad's here to pick you up," mom called from the living room.

I grabbed a black sweater and purse before heading down the hall. Conrad was perched on the love seat across from my parents, and he was deep in conversation with my father when I walked in. Sensing my presence, he turned his head to look at me, and I couldn't deny how happy it made me to see the smile spread over his face.

"Are you ready to go?"

"Absolutely," he replied. "What time should I have her home, Mr. Rhodes?"

"Try and have her back by midnight."

"Don't worry, I'll have her back on time," Conrad said, extending his hand for my dad to shake. "It was nice meeting both of you."

"Same to you," my dad answered. "Be sure to take good care of her." This was my first date in quite a while, and I could already tell dad was starting to have separation anxiety.

"She's in good hands, Mr. Rhodes," Conrad replied with confidence.

"You kids have fun tonight," my mom added.

I walked over to my parents. "Love you," I said, hugging my mom and kissing her cheek.

"I love you too, sweetie."

Then I walked over to my dad. "Bye. Daddy. I love you."

"Be safe, Evey," he said, pulling me into a hug.

"We will." I stood on the tips of my toes to kiss his cheek before following Conrad to the front door.

6

THE DATE

"You look so beautiful tonight," Conrad said, opening the car door. He took my hand in his, guiding me into the passenger seat.

"Thanks. You look pretty good yourself." He donned dark jeans and a black button-up shirt, which seemed to make his eyes look even bluer, if that was possible. I followed his every movement as he rounded the front of the car and slid behind the steering wheel.

"I thought we could go to the party for a little while and then head over to the diner and grab a bite to eat. Does that sound good to you?"

"Yeah, that's fine with me," I replied, fastening my seatbelt. "So, what do you like to do for fun?" He pulled out of the driveway and began the drive to Claire's house on the other side of town.

"I don't know. I like lots of different stuff."

"Such as?" I pried.

"I like sports, especially fencing, and I listen to music a lot."

"You fence?" I asked, surprised.

"Yeah, I've taken fencing classes for years."

Do you do any fencing competitions or stuff like that? I mean, do they have competitions?"

"Yeah, they have competitions," he laughed. "But I'm not big on doing tournaments anymore."

"Why?" I asked surprised. Given his cocky nature, I would have thought he

thrived on the rush of competition.

"Because it's just play fighting. It gets old after a while."

"Oh, okay." I nodded. "Well, what kind of music do you like?"

"Why so many questions?"

"I'm just trying to get to know you. Is that a crime?"

"Not at all," he answered. "Am I really that much of a mystery?"

"You moved from Los Angeles to a tiny town in the middle of nowhere, and you gave me a six-hundred-year-old necklace. What do you think?"

"I guess you're right. And you want to know about my music tastes?"

"I do."

"I really like Bob Dylan, Muddy Waters, the Black Keys, and lately, I've really gotten into Mumford and Sons."

"Oh, me too! I love Mumford and Sons!" I added. "So, is there an ex-girlfriend you left back in Los Angeles?"

A sly grin crossed his face. "Nope, no ex-girlfriend back there. Why would you think there is?"

"You've only been at Tulson for three days, and all the girls are clamoring over each other just to sit next to you. I want to make sure you haven't left a trail of broken hearts in your wake."

"You don't have to worry about that. I would never hurt you," he said, reaching out to take my hand in his.

I interlaced our fingers, feeling his gaze on me once more. "You stare a lot, did you know that?"

"Only when I'm around you."

Claire lived in a large Tudor-style house in one of the nicer subdivisions in town. As we pulled up to her house, we saw her driveway already filled with cars. Every window glowed with light, and we could hear the music getting louder as we approached the house. Conrad took my hand in his and led me inside. Immediately, we were thrust into a swirling mass of people. They were dancing, singing, and having a good time. We slowly made our way through the crowd and arrived at the kitchen to pour ourselves some drinks.

Just as I filled the second cup Conrad was holding with punch, Claire sauntered up, flipping her long blond hair over her shoulder. "I'm glad you guys could make it," she said.

"Thank you for inviting us," Conrad replied politely.

"Of course I would invite you." Apparently I was invisible, because she stood there making eyes at Conrad throughout the entire exchange.

"I really like your outfit, Claire," I said.

She snapped out of her daze and acknowledged my presence for the first time. "Oh, aren't you so sweet! I love your necklace. It's simply gorgeous."

"Thanks. Conrad does have exceptional taste."

At my words, her eyes narrowed. "Evey, you wouldn't mind if I borrowed Conrad for a dance or two would you?" Without waiting for an answer, she grabbed his hand and pulled him out to the dance floor.

He stopped to look back at me. "It's okay," I reassured him. After Conrad told me I was the only girl he was interested in last night, I didn't see the point in causing a scene with Claire. "Go ahead." Reluctantly, he followed Claire's lead. While they danced, I sat down in a chair in the corner of the room. The guests all seemed to be people I either didn't know or would never talk to, so I decided to keep to myself. I watched Claire put her arms around Conrad's neck as they danced. Every time she attempted to move in closer to him, he backed away. One dance quickly turned into three, and I was starting to get tired of watching Conrad's attempts to end the dance session. He was too polite to cause a scene, and Claire was using every trick she had. Tired of the scenery surrounding the dance floor, I headed back to the kitchen to refill my drink. I was about to pour more punch when another flashback took hold of my mind. I glanced all around me, praying the party wouldn't fade from sight, but to my dismay, I found myself kneeling on the floor of a familiar grand hall.

The floor was like ice against my skin. I pushed myself upward, resting on my hands. Air caught in my throat, making it difficult to breathe. My eyes fell upon a stream of blood flowing in front of me. I followed the crimson pool, tracing it back to its source. "Please no," I whispered. "Not Conrad." His head lay two feet away from the rest of his body. To my horror, I found his eyes staring into my own, wide with death. In an instant, my chest felt as if it was caving in on itself. Blood. There was so much blood. My eyes slammed shut. This wasn't real. He couldn't be dead.

"Evey, what's wrong?" The touch of a hand against my arm startled me, making me drop my cup. "What happened?"

"You . . . you were dead," I replied with a sob. "I saw your face staring at me, but your body was nowhere near it."

His arms encircled me, pulling my face into his chest. "I'm not dead. I'm right here."

"What's wrong with me?"

"Nothing. There's nothing wrong with you."

I watched with envy as everyone around us continued partying. In the living room, people laughed and swayed to the music without a care in the world. These people weren't like me. They weren't haunted by images of decaying flesh and gore. Somehow, I wasn't like them, and no amount of smiling or pretending would ever be able to change that. "I'm different from them, aren't I?"

"You're not different, you're special."

"Then why do I keep seeing such horrible things?"

"You're remembering things from the past, that's all."

"Am I the one to blame for the things I see? Is that why these visions haunt me?"

His hold on me tightened at my words. "No, you aren't to blame. You've just been witness to a great many things. Some have been good and some bad."

"I must've done something wrong to deserve this. Normal people don't see corpses everywhere they turn."

"You didn't do anything wrong," he insisted. "I think it's time I told you everything." His hands slid from around my waist, our fingers intertwining as he grasped mine. I held onto him tight, not wanting to be separated, even for a second. When we finally stepped outside, I sighed with relief.

"Please don't let go of me."

"That is something you'll never have to worry about," he said, tightening his grip. "I'm sorry, I should've picked a better first date for us. It's just been so long since I've done this."

"It's fine, don't worry about it. And you keep saying that, but you're eighteen. How long could it have been?"

"Actually, the last time I went on a date was 1926."

"So you haven't been on a date in almost a hundred years?" I asked sarcastically. "May I ask who the lucky girl was?"

His eyes flashed a knowing look as he ushered me into the car. "Who do you think it was?" he questioned, sliding behind the steering wheel.

"Me? Are you insinuating that the last woman you went on a date with was me? I—I don't even . . . Wait, so do you, like, never die or something?"

"Oh no, I can definitely die. I have many times, in fact."

His confession threw me for a loop. "No, that doesn't make any sense. How could you have died multiple times?"

"You tell me. You've already seen me die once in your dreams."

I shook my head. "No, it can't be. There is no way you could have died before and still be alive right now. It just doesn't happen."

"Evey, stop denying what you already know to be true."

My mind was racing; unease coiled in my stomach like a snake. I'd watched him die so many times, seen the axe hovering over his neck. As much as I didn't want him to be right, I knew he was. "Do you realize how horrible it is to watch you die every time I lay down to sleep?" The slight catch in my voice was unmistakable. "Can you blame me for wanting to deny something like that?" I shuddered, recalling all the times I had woken up from that nightmare and cried until there were no more tears left to shed.

"I know and I'm sorry, but this is the truth. This is what you keep saying you want to know."

"I know, but every time I have that nightmare, I'm so heartbroken, so completely overtaken with despair, and . . ." I said, my voice trailing off.

"I came back to you," he whispered, taking my hand in his. "Just remember that."

"Okay."

"Look, I know everything I've told you is hard to comprehend, but when did you start having the dreams?"

"I guess I was about six."

"They always felt real, did they not? I mean, to a certain extent, most dreams seem that way, but these were frighteningly real, weren't they? What child has dreams like that, Evey?" He waited for me to answer, but no sound poured from my lips. As the car made its way down the highway, silence lapsed between us. There were so many things I wanted to ask him, but I couldn't force my mouth to open. His hand grasped my shoulder and I jumped at the feel of his rough skin next to mine. "Stop thinking so much."

I let out a deep breath. My mind had been analyzing every possible explanation ever since I first saw him, so I cut off my own objections and decided to hear him out. "Fine, but answer one thing. How can it be that you've died and are still here, talking to me?"

"I'm alive right now because of you."

"What do you mean because of me?"

"I was brought back to life in order to protect you," he answered in a matter-of-fact tone.

"Like reincarnation?" I asked. "That's ridiculous."

"Why?"

"Because it goes against everything I believe in. People are born, they live, and then they die. That's it."

"Why do you believe in that particular cycle of events?"

"It's what my parents taught me, it's what I learned from going to church every Sunday. The Bible doesn't necessarily preach about the miracle of reincarnation."

"Doesn't it though?" he asked. "Jesus brought Lazarus back from the dead."

"That was different."

"Was it?"

"You said you were brought back to protect me. What could I possibly need

protecting from?"

He pulled into the diner parking lot and killed the ignition. "Not from what, from whom."

My fingers clenched the edge of my seat, gouging into the soft leather. I swallowed hard, forcing myself to ask the question that was probably best left unanswered. "What do you mean 'from whom'?"

"Someone from your past has been hunting you for a very long time."

"Someone?"

"I won't go into any more detail about who that person is right now."

"Why?"

"Because remembering him will only bring you pain."

"Conrad—"

"I meant what I said; I won't tell you any more about it."

I sighed, reluctantly deciding to concede the point for now. "So, you were brought back

from the dead to protect me. Why you?"

"Because there was a time when I was the person you trusted the most, and because of everything we've shared together."

"I hope you realize how bizarre all this is for me."

"I do, but I also know you can handle it." He grabbed his jacket out of the back seat of

the car. "Let's get something to eat before I continue."

"All right," I said, unfastening my seatbelt. We walked into the diner and sat down in two empty seats at the bar.

"Hey," Kit called to us in a cheerful voice.

"Are we too late to eat?" I asked. It was already thirty minutes after nine, and the diner would be closing at ten. I looked around and saw an older woman sitting at the opposite end of the counter and a couple perched in a booth near the back corner by the windows.

"Of course not," she replied, handing each of us a Coke. "What do y'all want to eat?"

"I'll take a burger and fries."

"Same for me," Conrad added.

She jotted down our orders and hooked it to the clip that hung on the kitchen side of the window. She then scurried away to ring up the couple that'd been sitting in the back of the diner. Mickey glanced up from the kitchen and grinned at me.

"I'll have it right out," he called out with a wave.

"Thanks Mickey!"

I swiveled in my seat to face Conrad, and our knees knocked together as he mirrored

me.

"Sorry." He bent forward to rest his hands on my legs. "What would you like to do after we eat?" he asked.

"I don't know. What did you have in mind?" Even though the diner was warm, a cold

chill came over my body, causing me to shiver.

"You're cold. Here, take my jacket," he said, holding it out for me.

"Thanks." He slid the jacket over my shoulders and I stuffed my arms through the holes. "Would you be up for watching a movie after we eat?"

"Sure. Where do you want to go?"

"We can go to your house. I haven't seen where you live yet."

"Yeah, that's fine," he answered with a grin.

A minute later, Kit was setting our food in front of us. I dived right into the piping hot fries, not realizing how hungry I was.

"Mmm. There's nothing like a good burger and fries," Conrad said, devouring his food.

"Did they even have them when you were born?" I asked in a sarcastic tone.

"No, they didn't. Are you trying to imply that I'm old or something?"

"Maybe," I teased.

"Well, I hate to break it to you, but you're a hell of a lot older than I am."

"What?" Coke sprayed out my mouth in surprise. "I'm older than you?" I enunciated every word just to make sure I was asking the right question.

"Oh yeah, by thousands of years actually. But don't worry, I like older women." He uttered his confession with a quick wink. "I'm going to the restroom. I'll be right back."

I wiped my face with a napkin and stared at him, unsure how to react. I watched as Kit went back in the kitchen to help Mickey start cleaning off the grill. A glance to my right told me the old woman from the end of the counter was moving toward me. Her long gray hair fell in tangles to her shoulders, and her brown coat looked like the moths had gotten the better of it. Bits of dirt clung to the visible skin under her baggy clothes and her face was covered with scars, as if her very flesh had been scorched to the bone. She sat down on the stool next to mine and smiled at me.

"Excuse me, dear, is your name Evey?" Her raspy voice shook as she spoke my name.

"Yeah. How did you know—" The words fell from my mouth before I could form them. Her bony hand clenched around my wrist, and despite her frail appearance, the grip was firm. As she tightened her grasp, my skin started to feel like it was on fire. Steam billowed from where she grabbed me. "Let go! You're hurting me!" I screamed. I tried to wrench my arm away from her, but she responded by digging her nails into my skin and squeezing like some kind of sinister vise. "Conrad!" I screamed, the smell of burning flesh smothering my senses. Hot tears flooded my eyes as I tried to break free. Her other hand rose, preparing to strike my face, when she was suddenly knocked away from me. I dropped to my knees and saw Conrad standing over the woman holding a chair. Blisters marred my skin, marking where her hand had been.

"Evey, are you all right?"

He bent over me, but I had already started screaming again. The woman scrambled over the floor, lunging toward him. Conrad reached down to his leg, pulled up his jeans, and withdrew a long knife before thrusting it into the woman's throat. She reeled backward. A wail escaped her lips and black liquid began to pour from her mouth as she crumpled to her knees. Conrad stepped forward and kicked the handle of the knife, splitting her throat. The back of her head collided with her shoulder blades while dark sludge coursed from the wound, spilling to the floor. The woman began disintegrating into a puddle. Her eyes bore into me until they burst, dissolving into the tarry substance that was quickly starting to engulf the checkered linoleum. Conrad lifted me onto my feet as Mickey and Kit materialized from the kitchen, staring at where the woman had been.

"Fulton, it's not safe here anymore. I need to take her to the house," Conrad said to

Mickey.

"Of course," he replied with wide eyes. "Go get Marie and Guy. Kit and I will clean this up and get in touch with you later."

"How did they find her?" Kit's eyes were wide with shock.

"I don't know," Conrad answered. "We'll have to figure that out later. Right now, we have to get her out of here." I glanced back and forth from Mickey to Conrad, wondering what they were talking about. "Evey, we have to go," Conrad said, grabbing my hand. Just as I was about to speak, the window behind us shattered, shards of broken glass showering us like drops of rain. Ten more deranged homeless-looking people crawled through the hole. Their clothes hung in shreds from their bodies. The edges of the rotting fabric were singed, as if they had been held over an open flame.

"Oh my God. There are even more outside!" Kit yelled, pointing to the glass door.

"Bourdet, you take Evey and head out the back of the restaurant. Kit and I will fight them off. Take her to Guy and Marie, we'll meet up with you later," Mickey instructed in an authoritative tone.

"Okay." Conrad nodded, pulling me to the break room.

"No, I'm not leaving without them!"

"Evey, there isn't any time to explain. We have to get you out of here," he pleaded.

"Not without Mickey and Kit. I won't leave them." Another window exploded to our right.

"Evey, get out of here! Go with Conrad. He'll protect you," Mickey ordered.

The strange people stumbled over to us with their arms outstretched. Mickey ran behind the counter and pulled out an axe and a sword. He tossed the axe to Kit and swung his sword, slicing off the outstretched hand of a man with long black hair. I kept expecting a river of red to flow from the stump, but to my horror, more of the tar-like substance seeped from the appendage. I could feel my knees starting to give out. I held on to Conrad even tighter, praying I'd stay on my feet.

"Go!" Kit yelled. "Now!" Conrad jerked my arm, and we sprinted to the back door in the break room. I peeked behind us and saw a tornado of black. Mickey and Kit were slicing people left and right, splattering their tarry insides on the floor. Their weapons moved at surprising speed as they plunged into the swarming mass of bodies. The once pristine interior of the diner was now a tomb, reeking with the smell of decaying flesh. Conrad gave my arm one last tug and we burst outside, almost knocking into the dumpster.

"Come on," he called, jogging ahead. I tried to keep up with him, but he was moving too

fast.

"Conrad!" He looked back at me, and I pointed to the left where a throng of people, or whatever they were, was charging at us.

"Run!" He reached out for me, racing for the front of the diner. "We have to get back to my car." I followed but couldn't maintain his pace. My feet tripped over a rock, and I was sent on a collision course with the ground.

"Damn it, Evey! Why the hell are you wearing those shoes?" Bits of gravel stuck to my palms and shins.

"Because I wanted to look good," I answered in a defensive tone. "And up until just now, you didn't seem to mind."

"Yeah, well, we weren't exactly trying to outrun a horde of tortured souls earlier!"

"Tortured what?"

"Souls. Never mind, I'll explain later," he replied, gripping my waist and throwing me over his shoulder. Then he took off in a sprint toward his car.

"Put me down!"

"Not until we get to the car."

"I'm not helpless!"

"It's not safe out here!"

"Look out!"

A melting body hurtled itself toward us, narrowly missing Conrad. A small woman coughing up black bubbles of tar reached for me. Without having to look, Conrad spun around, slashing her face with another knife. She stumbled, erupting into a shrill screech that set my teeth on edge. When we made it to the car, Conrad opened the driver's door and threw me across to the passenger seat. As he revved the engine, his headlights illuminated the ghastly scene inside the diner. Twenty bodies were clawing through the windows and headed right for Kit and Mickey. I could still see the silver of their weapons glinting in the dim light. "We have to help them!" I yelled.

"We can't. I have to get you out of here."

I yanked the handle, shoving the door open. "If you won't help them, I will." As I set my feet on the gravel, he wrenched me back inside. He slammed the car in drive and spun out of the parking lot, stirring up a cloud of dust. My eyes scanned the diner one last time, only to see more forms flooding the entrance. As we raced away, the building slowly dissolved into the distance.

"You need to put on a different pair of shoes. Look in the back."

"Turn the car around. We have to go back for them."

"That's not happening."

"You had no right to leave them there!"

"Aden would have you right now if I hadn't gotten you out of there!"

"I don't care! They're my family!"

"Mickey and Kit are warriors. They know what they're up against. In the grand scheme of things, Mickey, Kit, and I—we don't matter. You do, and we'll do whatever it takes to protect you."

"You're an ass."

"Think whatever you want about me. The only thing I care about is keeping you safe. Now, look for a bag in the back seat," he ordered. I obeyed him and found a purple duffel bag. I grabbed it, immediately searching through its contents.

"Why do you have my stuff in your car?"

"I brought it just as a precaution. I knew Aden was looking for you, and I wanted to be ready for him."

"Who is Aden?"

"All you need to know right now is that he is a very bad guy and he wants to hurt you."

"You went through my underwear drawer?" I held out a pair of undies and waved them in anger. "That's an extreme invasion of privacy."

"Do you not wear underwear or something?"

"Of course I do," I replied, my voice starting to quiver with rage.

"Stop blushing like a child. We must be prepared for anything, and clothes are a necessary provision to have." I was flung sideways as the car made a sharp turn. "And believe me when I say I've seen you in far less," he said, lunging over me to secure my seatbelt.

"What about you?" I asked, eyeing his seatbelt still flat against the side of the car.

"I'm fine." When we rounded another curve, I leaned across him, grabbing his seatbelt. "Thanks," he muttered. "We'll be at your house in a few minutes."

I sucked in frantic gasps of air. My eyes darted to the clock on the dashboard. It was 10:00. Could all that have happened in thirty minutes? As I glanced at Conrad, I noticed his jaw was clenched and the veins in his hands bulged as he gripped the steering wheel so tight I feared it would snap in half. "What are tortured souls, exactly? Why don't they bleed?"

"In basic terms, tortured souls are people who have been released from hell. They're pretty fast, but they are not as tricky to kill as demons. However, when you get a ton of them, they can be deadly." His eyes studied my arm. "How's your arm?"

Red welts now covered the flesh around my wrist. "It hurts, but I'll be fine."

"When souls are destroyed, their bodies decompose and turn into the *cibus inferni*."

"What does that mean?"

"In English, fuel of hell."

"Fuel of hell?"

"They're the fuel that keeps the fires of hell lit."

I gasped. "But that's horrible! Those poor souls."

"If it makes you feel any better, they were in hell for a reason."

"It doesn't."

"I can't believe Aden found you. Someone has to be helping him," he said, more to himself than to me. "I wasn't expecting him to send souls." He stepped on the gas even harder, causing the car to lurch forward. "We need to get to the meeting place as soon as we've got your parents. It's not safe here. I'll bandage your arm when we get out of town."

"Her hand . . . Because they become the cibus inferni, is that how she burned me?"

"Tortured souls burn with the fire of hell, that's what makes them deadly if you get a large number of them. Their touch burns like a hot flame."

"So, souls are controlled by the devil or something?"

"Yes, but I'm certain Aden is the one who sent them here. He's definitely up to something, and it's not good." Blood trickled from a small gash on his temple.

"You're hurt," I said, pointing to the cut.

"It's nothing. You're sure you have no other injuries?"

"I'm okay." I wiped the blood from his head with my hand. "Thank you for saving me from that woman."

"Like I said, it's my job."

"You almost make it sound like a burden."

"That's not—we don't have time for this conversation. We'll talk later."

I rummaged through my stuff, sliding on a pair of socks and pink Converse shoes. I finished tying my laces as he parked the car on the street. He checked the road in each direction before getting out, and after deciding there were no immediate threats, he opened the trunk.

"What is that?" I asked, pointing to a lethal-looking weapon.

"A mace." He picked up another long knife and stuck it in the back of his pants. Then he grabbed the mace while supplying me with a small knife. I'd never used a weapon before and it felt foreign in my hand. "Get behind me," he instructed, creeping toward the front of my yard. The light blue paint on the siding glowed in the darkness. The house looked perfect, untouched, and the white door loomed ahead of us. However, as soon as we reached it, I saw the front door was slightly ajar. Conrad squeezed my hand before heading inside. "No matter what happens, stay behind me, and if I tell you to run, you do it. Understand?"

I wasn't usually one to follow orders blindly, but after everything I'd seen tonight I knew I had a better chance of surviving if I listened to him. "Yes."

"Good. Follow me."

My heart hammered inside my chest. Instinctively, I grabbed onto the back of Conrad's shirt, positioning myself as close to him as possible. His muscles were tight beneath his clothes, and he raised his weapon, ready to strike. Glass crunched beneath our feet as we tiptoed cautiously around the overturned furniture.

"Where are my parents?" I choked on the last word, not really wanting to know the answer. I couldn't help but stare at the pictures from my childhood that lay in fragments on the floor.

"Let's keep going," he whispered. "There's a light on in that back room," he added, pointing ahead of us.

"That's my room."

"Have your knife ready." I gripped its handle in my right hand, pointing it out to the side. An eerie silence filled the house, making me tremble. Conrad was calm, completely ready to attack and kill anything in his path. He pushed the door to my bedroom open. The room had been ransacked. Remnants of my possessions littered the floor, and within the chaos, I saw a mangled body.

"Dad!" I screamed, running toward the center of the room. I rolled him over. His entire face was covered in red welts. Every inch of visible skin had been burned beyond recognition. I gaped in horror. The area around his eyes was swollen and his lids only opened to slits. "Daddy, I'm here," I cried. Bending low enough for him to see me, I gently took his hand in mine.

"Evey?"

"It's me."

Conrad knelt beside me. "Rhodes, there was an ambush at the diner. Twenty, maybe thirty souls attacked us there. We barely made it out."

"Fultons?" He coughed and blood spurted between his teeth. I dabbed at the crimson drops with the bottom of my dress.

"We had to leave them behind. The souls were in a swarm, and I had to get Evey out. I'm sorry, I didn't want to leave them."

"You made the right call."

"We have to get him to a hospital," I said to Conrad.

"It's too late," my father wheezed, spitting up more blood.

"No, you're going to be all right. If we can just get you to the hospital, you'll be fine."

"Evey," he said, reaching out to me with blistered hands. "Go with Conrad. He can protect you."

"I won't leave you."

"Listen to me. They came for you, but you weren't here, so they took your mother. They'll use her to find you, and if she doesn't help them, she'll be killed." His voice cracked at the effort it took for him to speak. "You have to leave. You're more important than any of us."

I shook my head. "I won't do it." He winced as I touched his cheek.

"I love you, but you have to leave." The small puddles of scarlet on his shirt grew by the second. "Right now," he demanded.

"I love you too."

He grabbed Conrad's arm. "They're looking for a *consiliarius*."

Conrad's brow furrowed. "But all of them are still in hiding."

"I know, but he has already found one, and he won't stop until he's destroyed all of them. He wants the rest of their powers."

"Do the other *secundae* know about this?"

"No time to warn them."

"How do I get in touch with the nearest consiliarius?"

Conrad waited for an answer, but my father started convulsing. Blood oozed from his mouth and nose. With the last of his strength, my father took my hand. "It's in the field."

"I don't understand, what's in the field?" I asked.

He looked back and forth from Conrad to me. "The consiliarius . . . How to find them is in the field."

"What field?"

He stared right into my eyes. "The field." I attempted to wipe the blood away from his mouth, but there was too much. "I love you. I love you so much." He smiled at me.

I shook my head. I knew he was trying to leave me, but I couldn't accept it. The mutilated form in front of me couldn't be my father. He'd always been so strong. Even as a child, I had marveled at the strength of his arms when we would climb trees together. I couldn't fathom a world where that man ceased to exist. "I love you too, Daddy." My tears rained down on his burnt skin. "Please, don't leave me," I begged.

"I'll see you again." Then he released his last breath, and his eyes went blank.

"No!" I threw myself at him, but Conrad held me back.

"We have to go." He stood from the floor, lifting me up. "Now!" Startled by the tone in his voice, I looked at him. "Is there anything you need from here?"

My room was in shambles. I walked over to the table beside my bed and picked up a photograph of my parents and me. "Just this." I stared at my father's body. "We can't leave him here."

"We have to. He wouldn't want me to risk your safety."

"I don't care. I'm not leaving him!"

"Then you leave me no choice." Conrad scooped me up in his arms and carried me down the hall.

"Put me down! I'm not a child!"

"I know you don't understand why, but I can't. I have to get you out of here."

"I never asked to be saved!" I screamed. Unable to stop it, I burst into a fit of heaving sobs. His hold on me tightened at the sound of my tears. Still holding the photograph, I wrapped my arms around him and buried my face in his neck. I was so loud, we barely heard the shattering of a window down the hall. Conrad stopped short of the front door.

"Can you run?" He eased me onto my feet. "Evey, can you run?"

"I think so." A loud wail rang through the house. Panic overtook my body. The howl sounded just like the one the old woman had made at the diner. "Is that—?"

"More souls." He seized my hand and peered out the open door. "The front yard looks clear, but they run fast. Faster than we can."

I swallowed hard, trying not to choke. "What do we do?"

"Hold on to me and run as fast as you can to the car." He interlaced our fingers, raising the mace in his other hand. "Let's go!" We tore out of the house, sprinting across the yard as we headed for the car down the street. A mass of bodies charged at us. Conrad's feet moved quickly, dragging me behind him. A tall bald man was gaining ground on us; his brown teeth were bared in a snarl. When we reached the car, I leapt inside. Conrad spun around and hurled his mace at the man. It flew through the air with speed, crashing into the man's face. The force of the blow sent him stumbling backward as his face turned black. Conrad jumped in the car, speeding away before he even closed the door. I looked in the rearview mirror and saw the souls hot on our tail. I grabbed my seatbelt, flung it over my waist, and clicked it shut, quickly turning to Conrad to do the same for him.

"What do we do now?"

"Try to get to the safe house without anyone following us."

"Where's the house?"

"About an hour away. It's an old farm in the middle of

nowhere." The car sped around another curve, and I set my hands on the dash to brace myself.

"I want to go get Caroline."

"No, it's too risky."

"If they knew how to find me, they know about her. We have to get her."

"That's not an option." His voice was firm and unyielding.

"Why not?"

"Because I won't compromise your safety so you can get your friend."

"I just want to be around someone I know."

"No."

"If you don't, I'll find a way out of this car and head straight for that mass of tortured souls."

"Then I'll chase you down and drag your ass back to the safe house," he warned. "I said, no."

"But——"

"There's no time."

I placed my hands on his shoulder, demanding his attention. "Conrad, please," I begged. "I know you didn't ask to risk your life protecting me tonight, but I need her. I can't handle all this on my own."

"I'm following your father's orders and getting you out of here. We're not making any stops."

"I've lost every single person I've ever loved within the last couple hours," I whispered. "Please, just let me have this one thing."

He was silent for a minute before he responded. "You're too damn stubborn for your own good," he whispered, sighing slightly. "Where does she live?" I pointed for him to turn left and directed him to her house. "Call her and tell her to be ready."

I searched for my leather bag and found my phone on the bottom. I punched the familiar digits and waited anxiously for it to ring.

"Evey?" Her voice sounded groggy with sleep.

"Caroline, I need you to do something for me."

"It's almost eleven."

"I know, there isn't time to explain, but I need you to trust me. Pack a bag with some clothes and leave a note for your parents. We'll be at your house in a few minutes."

"We? We who?"

"We as in Conrad and me."

"What's going on? You sound strange."

"I know. I promise I'll tell you everything later. Please, just pack a bag and meet me outside. It's important."

"I'd be lying if I said you weren't kind of freaking me out, but you know I'd do anything

for you," she replied. "I'll get my bag ready."

"I'll see you in a few minutes," I said.

She was waiting for us in her front yard wearing penguin pajamas by the time we pulled up. Her bag was strung over her shoulder, and she clutched a pillow in her hands. Conrad jumped out of the car and took her stuff. After he threw it in the back seat, she climbed in. Without waiting for us to say anything, Conrad stepped on the gas and the car took off speeding down the road.

"What the hell is going on?" She looked at my face and gasped. "What happened to you? Why are you covered in blood?"

"I'm fine."

"Your arm. It's covered in burns. How did that happen?"

I paused to take in a deep breath. "What I have to tell you is going to sound crazy, but you have to believe me."

"Okay," she said reluctantly.

"Someone bad is after me. I'm not quite sure what he wants, but he had my dad killed and he took my mom."

A look of horror crossed her face. "What?"

"Please don't make me repeat it," I pleaded. "Conrad and I were eating at the diner, and all these bad people came in and attacked me. Conrad saved me and got us out of there."

"What about Kit and Mickey?"

"They didn't make it," Conrad answered.

Her hands shot to her mouth, stifling a choking noise. "What do you mean they didn't

make it?"

"They held off the people while Conrad and I escaped. We haven't heard anything from them since."

"And your parents are gone too?"

"We don't know where my mom is exactly, but yes." I brushed a stray tear from my

face.

"Oh my God. I'm so sorry, Evey." She reached forward, pulling me into a hug. I held onto her tight, sobbing into her shoulder. As I wept, an overwhelming silence filled the car. My head was throbbing and I didn't know what else to do, so I laid it down on the console between the seats. Any minute now, my skull was sure to explode into a million tiny pieces. After the things I'd seen tonight, how would I ever be happy again? How could I continue with my life when those I held dear were left to burn? Seconds seemed to extend forever as the car tore down the deserted interstate. The only things I could be certain of were despair and exhaustion.

7

GENESIS

It took five minutes for us to drive down the narrow road before stopping in front of an old two-story house. The brick on the outside had been worn by weather and time. White paint peeled from trim encasing the front porch. A small barn was barely discernible in the distance.

"Where are we?" I asked as we crept down a dark driveway partially camouflaged by low-hanging branches.

"Just outside of New Hope, going toward Chattanooga," Conrad answered.

"What is this place?" Caroline leaned forward, shifting between our seats to get a better look.

"It's a sort of safe house for our group."

"What group?" she asked.

"The group consists of Marie, Guy, Mickey, Kit, and me. We're called secundae. We are guardians, warriors really, who were assigned to Evey in order to protect her."

"Why do I need to be protected?"

He let out a sigh and turned off the car. "Let's go inside and I'll tell you everything." He grabbed our bags and led us up to the house. There was a small potted tree that had long since dried up sitting by the front door. He picked up the cracked blue pot and pulled a key off the bottom of it. When he slid it into the lock, it clicked, allowing us to enter. Caroline and I stepped into the dark house, our hands glued to one another. Conrad followed behind us and turned on the light. Immediately, he fastened the door shut, barricading it with a large wooden beam.

"That should keep us safe."

The inside of the house was much nicer than the exterior. A kitchen, living room, and dining room seamlessly flowed into one another. All the walls were painted a light sage color and a narrow staircase with wooden steps led to the second floor. Conrad toted our bags as he climbed the stairs.

"There are three rooms upstairs, so everyone can have their own." We trailed him and saw the three bedrooms ahead of us. One bathroom separated two of the bedrooms from the other. "You can stay in here, Caroline," he said, walking into a small room with soft yellow walls. He set her bag on top of the rose-colored bedspread, ushering her inside. "There should be clean towels in the dresser and empty hangers in the closet."

"Thanks," she replied, running her hand across the bedspread.

"This room is yours, Evey," he said, motioning to the room next to Caroline's. The walls of my room were lilac. It instantly reminded me of my room at home and my heart ached at the thought. In the center of the room was a large canopy bed with a white crocheted comforter. He set my bag on the bed just as he had Caroline's. "This next room is the bathroom, and my room is just over there." Caroline and I stared at him, speechless. In the light of the house, I could see her face had the same tear streaks across it as mine. "Why don't you take a shower, Evey, and I'll make us all some food. Then I'll tell you everything you want to know while we eat."

"Okay." I agreed with a nod. I watched as he and Caroline descended the steps and turned toward the kitchen. Pulling the family photo from the pocket of Conrad's jacket, I set it on the dresser in my room. The picture was taken last year at Christmas, and it showed my parents and me in front of our tree. My chest tightened as I gazed at their smiling faces. I needed them now more than ever. With a heavy heart, I shuffled over to my bag and pulled out a nightgown and an old cardigan.

I slouched into the bathroom and started the shower. The water turned a reddish brown as I washed the dirt and blood from my body. I tried to wrap my head around everything that had happened tonight, but it proved to be impossible. Defeated, I sank down, allowing the scalding stream to engulf me. I sobbed until the water turned cold, unable to do anything else. When the drops of water stung like ice upon my skin, I finished my shower and dressed before heading downstairs. The air smelled of pancakes as I hit the bottom step. Caroline sat at the table watching Conrad cook.

"Hey," I said. Startled at the sound of my voice, Caroline jumped as she turned to face me. Conrad, however, seemed unsurprised at my sudden reappearance.

"How many pancakes do you guys want?" He set three plates on the table and poured us each a glass of water.

"Two," Caroline replied.

"I don't want any," I answered. "I can't even think about eating right now."

He slid a stack of pancakes on the table, quickly adding a pitcher of syrup. I watched Conrad devour his meal. How could he be so calm? His demeanor provided no indication that he was the least bit perturbed by leaving my loved ones behind to die. My fists clenched. He acted like they were expendable, like they didn't matter at all. As if he could read my thoughts, his attention shifted from his empty plate to me.

"I know you're pissed at me, but there's nothing we could've done. We wouldn't have been able to save them."

"Gee, your powers of perception are extraordinary."

"There was nothing we could do."

"We could've at least tried," I spat.

"Maybe once I explain everything, you'll see I made the decision —to get you out of there instead of going back—because I had to, not because I wanted to."

"I hope you're right," I replied.

"Me too. Well, I guess the only place to start is at the beginning." My stomach began twisting into knots as I waited for him to continue. Now, I'd finally have my answers. "Are either of you familiar with the Bible?"

I was surprised by his question. "Yeah. Why would that matter though?"

"Because it's where your story begins," he said, looking at me. Summoning the last of my strength, I straightened my back and prepared myself for whatever I was about to hear. I was strong enough to handle this. "Do you know the story of Adam and Eve?"

"Everyone knows it, but I don't see what it has to do with Evey," Caroline said.

"It has everything to do with her." He focused his eyes on me. "You were the first woman God ever created. You are Eve."

I stared at him with a blank expression on my face.

"What are you talking about?" Caroline piped up. "She can't be Eve. Eve lived, like, thousands of years ago."

"God created man and named him Adam, and from Adam, He created Eve. They were to be husband and wife and live together in the Garden of Eden."

As he talked, my mind wandered. Flashes of a garden grew before my eyes. I could see it as plainly as I could see him sitting in front of me. A tree. I walked to it, pushing branches and leaves out of my path so that I could get a better look. It was a small tree with crooked branches curling up toward the sky. I took another step. Its beauty drew me in, beckoning me. An irresistible red apple dangled within my reach. It glistened in the sunlight, making my mouth water. I wanted the apple. I needed it. My fingers longed to touch the smooth fruit. I inched closer and closer before circling my hand around it, plucking it from the tree. A smile spread over my face as I rubbed its pristine skin. Then I drew it to my mouth and sunk my teeth into its rosy flesh.

"He's right," I whispered. All my dreams and nightmares had a purpose. I wasn't supposed to be scared of the things I saw. Instead, those things were meant to remind me of my past, to remind me of who I am. The sudden clarity cut through the dense fog that had been hovering around me my entire life.

Caroline stared at me, bewildered. "You actually believe him?"

"He's right."

"Evey."

"Caroline, he's right. I know I sound like a lunatic, but trust me."

"If you say so," she answered hesitantly.

"Go on with the story."

"You and Adam lived happily in the Garden of Eden until you ate an apple off the one tree God forbade you to eat from. You ate fruit from the Tree of Knowledge. When God discovered what you had done, He was angered at your transgressions, so He cast you out from the garden."

"And as punishment, Adam had to work the land for food and Eve had to experience pain during childbirth. Yes, we all know the story, but it still doesn't make sense," Caroline added.

"It wasn't their only punishment," he said, glancing from Caroline to me. "God put you in the garden, provided you with everything: food, shelter, a companion. Still, you and Adam disobeyed Him. You ate the fruit first, and then you persuaded Adam to eat it. When you did this, God saw that humans could be easily influenced by one another. He saw you had power over the actions of others, and that is why He had you reborn."

"So, Evey is actually Eve reincarnated?"

"Yes," he answered, clearing his throat. "God had Adam and Eve reincarnated so He could have influence over future generations of Man. You see, God gave Man the gift of free will. He wants all of His children to repel sin and follow His teachings, but he also wants us to *choose* such a path for ourselves. He never forces Man into anything." He reached for his glass of water and took a long drink from it. "God realized, through the reincarnation of Adam and Eve, He could use them to guide the rest of humanity to Him. You see, Evey hasn't been reincarnated just once; she's been reincarnated repeatedly over the course of time. She and Adam both have, actually."

"Where do you, my parents, Mickey, and Kit fit into this?"

"We're your secundae. Your protectors," he answered. "Over the years, you and Adam were reincarnated by the *Concilium*. The Concilium is a group of seven men and women who act as the voice of God. They interact directly with Him, and they're the ones who cause you to be reborn."

"That's what my father was talking about when he told us to find the consiliarius?"

"Yes." He paused for a moment to take a deep breath. "You and Adam were always reincarnated into positions of power, reigning over Man as prominent kings and queens throughout history. And you ruled together successfully for many years, changing the way people viewed religion. You helped people change from worshipping pagan gods to following the Christian God."

"What happened to Adam?" As soon as the words left my lips, I realized I already knew the answer. "Aden?"

Conrad nodded. "You and Adam were very happy together. You worked with the Concilium to help bring people to God. That was, until Adam started to change."

"What changed him?" I waited for his answer with bated breath.

"The apple." A new wave of shock shuddered through me. "The apple was just the spark; it was the start of his evil nature. The rest happened because of you."

"I don't understand," I said, shaking my head.

"The apple you ate was from the Tree of Knowledge of Good and Evil. You took the first bite, causing the knowledge of all that is good to come into your body, while Adam took the second bite, consuming all knowledge of that which is evil."

My hand was drawn to my mouth, covering it. Very slowly, I withdrew it from my face. "Then what did I do that made him change even further?"

"You fell in love with someone else."

"You mean I fell in love with you," I replied in disbelief.

"I know it might be hard for you to accept right now, but you did."

"Hard?" I asked, allowing anger to seep into my voice. "It's ridiculous."

"Okay, okay," Caroline said, interrupting us. "Let's all just take a deep breath."

"I need some air." I stood from the table and stormed for the door. I no longer wanted to stare at the man who allowed my family to perish. The wooden beam felt heavy in my hands as I propped it against the wall. A rush of cool air flowed into the room, and just as I was about to open the door all the way, it slammed shut with a deafening crash.

"No going outside alone," Conrad ordered. His hand rested against the door, holding it shut.

"Move aside!"

"That's not happening. I'll gladly go on a walk with you, but I'm not letting you out of my sight."

"So, basically, I'm your prisoner?"

"No, I'm only trying to protect you," he answered. "Can't you see every decision I made tonight was done to keep you safe?"

"I don't want to be safe! I want my family back!"

"I'm sorry."

"You should be!" I shouted. I rushed at him, beating my hands against his chest. "You let them die," I cried. I continued to hit his chest, hoping it would ease the pain I felt.

He caught my wrists, keeping me at arm's length. "Mickey, Kit, and your parents were my family too! I've known them for centuries, and it pained me to leave them behind. I love them as much as you do."

"If you loved my family, then why are you a stranger to me?" I asked. "Why don't I remember my true identity?"

"Your memory was erased in order to protect you. What better way than to hide you in plain sight and let the rest of the world believe you're a normal teenage girl?" His hands released my wrists, sliding down my arms. "There are also some things that are too terrible for you to remember. We wanted to spare you such pain."

"Who makes these decisions?"

"Evey, try to relax for a second," he whispered as he wrapped his arms around me. As soon as our bodies met, my consciousness was transported into the past.

I slammed into a wall, gasping as my back collided against stone. "If gold is what you seek, take it," I shouted, throwing my coin purse at their feet. Three men stood before me, each wielding a small knife. I tried to run, but there was nowhere for me to go.

"Why take your gold when there are more enjoyable things we could take from you, Your Highness?"

Fear fluttered in my chest. There was no way I could fight all of them off. "Please," I begged. "Just let me go."

"You'll be free to leave, once we're done with you," the man sneered. He inched closer to me, holding his knife to my neck. "If you scream, I'll cut your tongue from that pretty mouth of yours."

Just as the man was about to place his lips on top of mine, he was ripped away from me. Now, the three men surrounded Conrad, all brandishing their weapons. Conrad charged at the man on his right. The man barely had time to move before Conrad whipped his sword through the air, slicing the man's head in half at his jaw. The lifeless form collapsed to the ground, blood spurting from the split skull. Undisturbed by the loss of one of his comrades, one of the remaining men lunged forward in an attempt to stab Conrad, but he failed. Instead, Conrad kicked the attacker, dropping him to his knees. Then he took his sword and shoved it down the man's throat, skewering my attacker like a roasted pig.

"If you let me go, I'll never bother you again," the man who tried to kiss me said.

"Why should I show you mercy when you weren't going to grant any to our queen?"

"I—"

The man didn't even have time to finish speaking before Conrad tackled him. The two men struggled against one another, but when Conrad managed to wrench the small knife from the man's hand, I knew the fight was almost over. Conrad plunged the blade into the man's chest six times before finally thrusting it through the side of his neck. As Conrad rose to his feet, his body shook with rage. Blood coated his face and neck. His eyes glowed with hatred. I wanted to go to him, but my body was incapable of moving. I forced my eyelids shut, and when I opened them, Conrad stood before me in the living room of the farmhouse.

"What did you see?"

"Three men were attacking me, but you stopped them. You killed all of them . . . brutally," I whispered.

"They wanted to rape you!" he shouted. "Sorry, but there was no way I was going to allow any of them to touch you."

"Have you died trying to protect me?"

"I believe you already know the answer to that."

"Why would you make that sacrifice for me?"

"Because you mean everything to me," he confessed, moving closer to me. When he reached to touch my face, I backed away. "You're frightened of me?"

"Shouldn't I be? You're a killer."

"I would never hurt you," he replied. "And I've only ever killed for one reason—to save your life. I was one of your personal guards, protecting you was my job. I gladly risked life and limb to keep you from harm."

"Well, I for one am tired. The two of you must be exhausted," Caroline said, moving to stand by my side. "I should probably shoot my mom another text too, otherwise she'll worry."

"Why don't we all go get some sleep? There's still a lot more to tell you, but I think it can wait until tomorrow," Conrad suggested. He retrieved the dishes from the kitchen table and took them to the sink to wash. Caroline and I trudged up the stairs. I heaved my feet over the polished wood, wishing I could block out all the horrific things I'd seen.

"I'm sorry to involve you in all this," I said, hugging her.

"You're my sister. I'd do anything for you. I'm just glad you didn't get hurt."

"I wish I could turn my brain off. I don't think I have any tears left to cry."

"Why don't I stay with you tonight? If I were you, I wouldn't want to be alone."

"You need to rest too."

"What you need is to be around family."

"You're right," I said, smiling slightly. "Thanks for trusting me enough to come tonight."

"Of course." We shut the door to my room behind us and pulled back the covers on the large canopy bed. Caroline set my head in her lap, combing her fingers through my hair. "Tell me about what happened tonight."

I relayed the night's events to her with exact detail. I started with Conrad driving us to Claire's party and ended with the drive to the farmhouse. She didn't interrupt me to ask questions, she simply let me talk. It was therapeutic, and the more I poured my heart out to her, the better I began to feel. Only when I finished did she open her mouth to speak.

"You described your memories of Conrad, and I agree with you, it was terrifying, but do you really believe he'd hurt you?"

"I don't know."

"You're thinking too much. Given what you've been through tonight, it's more than understandable, but from what I've seen of Conrad, I don't believe for a second he'd harm you."

"How can you be so certain?" I asked. "I feel like the world as I knew it was a complete lie."

"I just know," she answered. "The way he looks at you, I can tell he cares about you."

"You didn't see him tonight, Caroline. He was like a killing machine!"

"If I were trying to find someone to protect my family, I'd want a total killing machine watching over them."

"I suppose you're right."

"From what you've told me about the tortured souls at the diner and your house, it sounds like he saved your life more than once."

"He did," I whispered.

"Shouldn't that tell you something?"

"I'd like to think so."

"Let's get some sleep, Evey." Caroline turned off the lamp beside the bed, darkening the room. I nestled under the covers and shut my eyes. I wasn't expecting sleep to come to me so quickly, but as soon as my head hit the pillow, my mind relinquished its reign to exhaustion.

Rest visited me in waves, like the ocean's tide forever waxing and waning. In my dreams, I saw a horde of souls, chasing me through the streets of my neighborhood. I ran, never stopping or slowing down, even as my lungs began to burn. My feet carried me over sidewalks and roads, but with every step I took, the souls were nipping at my heels. I pushed further, barreling down the street with as much force as I could muster, but when the pain in my arm became too unbearable, my body forced me to wake.

A glance to the left informed me that Caroline was still fast asleep. Faint footsteps padded back and forth beyond my bedroom door, causing the wood floor to creak. Conrad was still awake. Quietly, I slid out of bed and shut the door behind me as I entered the hallway. I could see Conrad pacing through his open door. He turned toward me as I crossed the threshold.

"Do you need something?" he asked.

"I couldn't sleep," I replied. I held my arm gingerly to my chest, trying not to touch the burnt skin.

"It seems to be an epidemic tonight because I can't either," he replied with a laugh. "How's your arm?"

"It hurts. I was so distracted earlier I'd forgotten it was burned, but then it started

throbbing enough to wake me up."

"Let me see." Without asking for permission, he extended my arm in a single, gentle movement. The blisters covering it popped, releasing clear liquid all over my skin. "It'll start to look better in a few days. Burns from souls are painful, but they fade faster than real burns, and luckily, they don't scar." He walked over to the closet and grabbed a first aid kit. For the first time, I noticed a small tattoo marking his bare flesh. A beautiful tree adorned the back of his left shoulder, no bigger than the size of my fist.

"You have a tattoo?" The black lines of the trunk spiraled up into a delicate pattern of woven strokes, forming the tree's branches. It was captivating.

"Actually, all secundae do; we call it the *sacramentum secundae*, which translates to oath of the secundae."

"Why is that?" I found myself studying the image, observing all of its intricacies. Bundles of leaves dotted the branches of the tree. As the limbs curled upward, the roots intertwined, developing a maze beneath the tree.

"We're each marked with this tree to serve as a reminder of our duty to the *primums* and the Concilium," he answered. "You see, when you're made into a secundae, you take an oath to protect the primum or consiliarius you've been assigned to. The tree is just a symbol for the oath we take, and we're all bonded together by our service to God."

"I never noticed one on my mother or father, but they must have had one too, right?"

"They did. Because they had to hide their true nature from you for so long, they became very skilled at concealing a great many things."

"This is the tree from the Garden of Eden, isn't it?"

"It is."

"When did you get the mark?"

"When I was made into a secundae. I woke up and it was there. It's been on my shoulder ever since."

"Do the members of the Concilium have one too?"

"Yes, but theirs isn't a tree. Only secundae have a tree."

"Oh," I replied. "What do they have?"

"They have a handprint over their heart." He motioned for me to sit as he opened the first aid kit. "Because the members of the Concilium were chosen by God to act as his voice on Earth, they're marked with His handprint." He spread a thin layer of aloe over my burn before wrapping it with a roll of gauze. "How is that?"

"It feels a lot better, thanks."

"You're welcome." We stared at one another for what felt like ages, his gaze holding my undivided attention. The anger filling his eyes as he protected me from the men in my vision was gone. I thought back to the night Conrad and I had talked in the park. The way he had held me and kissed my forehead was so tender, so full of affection. Could that man and the one from tonight really be the same person? When his hand lifted to caress my cheek, I recoiled from him. "That's right," he said. "I forgot you were afraid of me."

"What am I supposed to think after the things I witnessed tonight?"

"I've no idea. This has never happened before. Any other time you were reborn, you've always wanted to be with me."

"I'm sorry."

"For what? You can't help the fact you think I'm a monster."

"I don't think that."

"Then what do you think?"

I don't know," I whispered.

"You were afraid of Aden because he was cruel and evil. I don't want you to think I'm like him." He crossed the room, putting as much distance between the two of us as possible. He was hurt. The man who was a veritable assassin was wounded by a mere look from me. Lust, love, and fear twirled together within the confines of my chest. Incapable of staying away for another second, I moved to stand behind him. The tips of my fingers slid down the muscles of his back causing him to flinch. "Don't touch me like that if you don't mean it," he said with a sigh.

"And what if I do mean it?"

"Do you understand how badly I ache to hold you in my arms, to kiss you? I've thought of nothing else for the last nine decades," he replied, raising his voice. "You were my wife for five centuries, and it kills me to know you not only regard me as a stranger but as someone to be frightened of!"

"Then show me something worth remembering!" I shouted. "Show me what it felt like to love you."

Without warning, Conrad grabbed my hips, jerking my body into his. Anger gave way to passion as my mouth opened, eagerly returning his kiss. I curled my arms around his neck, drawing him closer as his hands skimmed the length of my body, seeming to touch me everywhere at once. The feel of his lips against mine transported me into a temporary state of euphoria, eliciting a jolt of memories to invade my mind.

Now, I was on the balcony of a large plantation home. My dress fanned around me like a white cloud, draping my body in yards of delicate lace. To my left, a gathering of faces watched me from their seats, smiling broadly. Rows of sycamore trees formed a lush awning of shade that blocked the midday sun while arrangements of peonies and roses cascaded down the balcony railing. Soft thumbs stroked my knuckles, demanding my attention. Conrad stood across from me in an immaculate suit. His kind face filled my heart with joy, and I couldn't fight the desire to touch him.

"I love you," I whispered, caressing his cheek with my palm.

"And you know how much I love you," he replied.

"It's time for the vows," the priest announced. "Do you, Conrad Xavier Bourdet, take Evelyn Alexandra Rhodes to be your lawfully wedded wife, to have and to hold from this day forward, for better or for worse, for richer, for poorer, in sickness and in health, to love and to cherish until the end of time?" I briefly glanced at the priest standing at my right before focusing on Conrad once again.

"I do," Conrad answered, sliding a diamond ring over my finger. Once he finished, he lifted my hands to his mouth for a kiss.

"I didn't tell you to kiss her just yet, son," the priest scolded, unable to temper his amusement. Light sounds of laughter emanated from our guests, echoing my own.

"Please forgive my eagerness, Father Ryan," Conrad apologized with a grin.

"Shall we proceed with this lovely ceremony?" We nodded, our fingers intertwining. A surge of bliss flooded my senses as I looked at my soon-to-be husband. I'd spent my entire life dreaming of the day we would be joined together forever, and it was finally my turn to complete the vows. "And do you, Evelyn Alexandra Rhodes, take Conrad Xavier Bourdet, to be your lawfully wedded husband, to have and to hold from this day forward, for better or for worse, for richer, for poorer, in sickness and in health, to love and to cherish until the end of time?"

"With all my heart, I do," I said, sliding a silver band on Conrad's finger.

"By the power vested in me, I now pronounce you husband and wife. You may finally kiss your bride."

In an instant, Conrad tugged me to him, sliding his arms around my waist as he pressed his lips to mine. He kissed me passionately, much to the raucous approval of our wedding guests. Even as the priest presented us to his congregation, we continued to kiss, never wanting it to end.

Decades later, Conrad and I were still locked in the same embrace. Our lips parted slowly while our gazes remained glued to one another. "I shouldn't have done that." He took a few steps away from me. "You have my sincerest apology."

"It worked." My voice was nothing more than a whisper, but I knew he was hanging onto every word.

"What did you see?"

"We were getting married," I answered. "The ceremony was on the balcony of an old plantation home. It was breathtaking."

"That's when we lived in Savannah. It is one of my favorite cities we've ever lived in."

"What was the year?"

"It was 1858," he answered. "I remember that day like it was yesterday."

"Did you still think of me as your wife on the first day of school?"

"It's almost impossible for me to see you any other way," he answered.

"How do you want me to think of you?"

"However you feel is right in your heart. If you're still frightened of me, then I'll keep my distance and protect you from afar. I want you to feel at ease around me."

In that moment, I wanted him. No, not wanted, needed. I needed him, and the feeling was completely foreign to me. I'd never experienced such a confusing array of emotions in my entire life, and what scared me even more was that I didn't want it to stop. But at seventeen years old, I wasn't emotionally equipped to process everything happening to me. I needed time to think things through, so I asked in a quiet voice, "What do we do now?"

"Act like the kiss never happened?"

"Act like it never happened, it is," I agreed. I sat on his bed, feeling the mattress give as he positioned himself beside me. "Do you really think Aden will kill my mom?" My voice shook as the words left my lips.

"It's hard to say one way or another. Aden is notorious for being unpredictable. If he believes Marie can be useful to him, he'll keep her alive."

I bit my lip hard, trying not to cry. "That's what my dad said too."

"Unfortunately, Guy was right."

"Did they all know about us?"

"What do you mean?"

"Did my parents, Mickey, and Kit all know that we were—well, you know what I'm trying to say."

"That we were lovers?"

"Yeah."

"They knew. They actually helped us hide our relationship from Aden."

"Why did they do that?"

"They could see how empty you were while being married to Aden, and they wanted you to be happy."

"I'm sorry I was so rude to you earlier. You were trying to save me, I know that, but I couldn't sit by and do nothing."

"Honestly, I expected nothing less from you. You've always been headstrong and stubborn. I would've been more surprised if you hadn't tried to help them."

"What am I going to do without them?" I drew in a couple ragged breaths. I didn't have the energy to weep any more tonight.

"You have to keep being strong; it's what they'd want."

"Really?"

"They'd want you to keep going and stay safe."

"I'm trying to."

"You can do it. You have the capacity to do the most incredible things," he said. "And if anyone needs to apologize for this evening, it's me. I should've realized what that old woman was the moment we set foot in the diner. If I'd been on my guard, we would've seen the souls coming."

"It wasn't your fault."

"Yes, it was. Usually, I can see an attack coming from a mile away, and I'm sorry I didn't this time. I shouldn't have been so distracted."

"Why were you so distracted?"

"Why do you think?" The two of us sat shoulder to shoulder on the edge of his bed.

"Oh," I whispered, realization dawning on me. "I should go back to bed and try to get some rest."

"That would be a good idea."

I paused at his door, not wanting to part on such an awkward note. "Conrad?"

"Yeah?"

"Thank you for saving my life."

"Anytime. And . . . Evey?"

"Yes?"

"I know it might not be much consolation, but I promise you'll see your family again. You always do."

"Actually, that thought is a wonderful consolation."

"Good night, my lady."

"My lady," I repeated. "That's what you always used to call me when we first met, when I was your queen."

"You remember that?"

"I do. When you said it just then it clicked in my head and I remembered."

"I'm glad you're getting some of your memories back."

"Me too." I took one last look at him before closing his bedroom door behind me.

8

SECUNDAE

The next morning, I awoke to the sunlight beaming on my face from a nearby window. I rolled over expecting to see Caroline, but her spot was vacant. Pushing myself off the mattress, I made my way to the bathroom. I brushed my wavy hair, clipping half of it back from my face. Dark circles clung to the skin beneath my lower lashes. I felt drained. All I wanted to do was crawl back in bed and block out the rest of the world. But what good would that do me? I had to do what Conrad suggested; I needed to stay strong. Summoning the last of my energy, I rummaged through my bag and found a pair of jeans and camisole to wear.

I could hear the voices of Conrad and Caroline wafting up from the kitchen. Quietly, I descended the stairs, not quite ready to join their conversation.

"Okay, so there's something I kept wondering about after we all went to bed last night," Caroline said.

"What's that?"

"Does everyone that's reincarnated always look the same?"

"We do. As a primum, Evey is reborn as an infant, but secundae aren't. Our bodies are the same ones we had in our previous lives, but instead of being born again, we're healed. It's kind of like being reanimated."

"But wouldn't people notice that? Like you said, Evey and this Aden guy were prominent kings and queens throughout history. Wouldn't they look the same in all the paintings of them?"

"Paintings can be deceiving."

"How so?"

"Well, you remember the painting of Isabella I of Castile in our history book? That is a picture of Evey."

"But it didn't even look anything like her."

"Exactly. Evey was a queen. She paid artists to depict her image differently throughout the years so no one would notice her later on. Aden, of course, did the same."

"That seems like it would be more difficult with photographs and things like that,
though."

"By the time the camera was invented, Evey was put into hiding. She wasn't reborn as a queen anymore. Instead, she was born into normal families with Guy and Marie posing as her parents. The only people who would have pictures of her would be close friends and family."

"Why did I need to be put in hiding?" I asked, entering the kitchen.

"Tired of eavesdropping from the stairs?" Conrad asked.

For a moment, I stared at him incredulously.

He gave a slight shrug. "I heard you come down the steps."

"You don't miss a thing, do you?"

"Not usually," he replied.

I took up a seat at the table as Conrad slid a plate of pancakes toward me.

"Thanks," I said, surprised at how hungry I suddenly was.

"I told you last night that the apple had initiated a change in Aden, but what really set him over the edge was the discovery of our relationship."

"And when did we meet?" I asked, though I had a pretty good idea I already knew the answer.

"We met when you were reborn as Isabella I of Castile."

"Does that mean Aden was Ferdinand II of Aragon?" I asked.

"Yes."

Images of Conrad's face flitted before my eyes like an action flip book, sharpening every feature until he disappeared. I didn't know what I was about to see, but my gut told me it would have everything to do with the warrior sitting across from me.

Night cast a dark shadow over the world around me as my eyes darted in every direction in an attempt to ascertain my surroundings. The wind howled, chilling me to the bone. I knocked on the dilapidated door in front of me. This house was nothing more than a hovel. My own bedroom was almost double its size, and the thought pained me. I lived in the castle, surrounded by wealth and comfort, and yet, there were people right down the road struggling to survive. Immediately, the door opened, permitting my entrance.

"Please come in," the man said. I moved past him, making my way to the fireplace. Before I even had a chance to speak, the young man dropped to his knees. "I know what you have come for and I will return it to you. I was wrong to steal from you, but I took it to help my family," he pleaded. "You may suffer me to any punishment you see fit, but I beg you to show my mother and sister mercy. They're innocent."

I removed my cloak, hanging it next to the fireplace and cast my attention to the man kneeling at my feet. His eyes were the loveliest shade of blue I'd ever seen. In an instant, my heart began to race. "Please don't worry," I said, lowering myself in front of him. The urge to be near this man was too strong to resist. My fingertips traced the lines of his jaw as I drew his handsome face toward mine. The moment we touched, time seemed to stop completely. I knew the monotonous presence time possessed; I understood with perfect clarity how one life could extend into another like an interminable cycle. However, as we stared at one another, it was as if we were the only two souls in existence. One glance into this man's eyes and I knew beyond a shadow of a doubt that he was my salvation. I placed a soft kiss against his forehead. "I'm not going to hurt you." It was the truth. My statement was simple, mere words strung together into a reply, but it somehow felt like the most monumental promise I'd ever made.

"But why?" he asked.

"What reason do I have to hurt you?" The skin of his cheeks warmed my hands as I looked at him.

"I stole from you. That would be reason enough to sentence me to death."

This man had no difficulty realizing who I was and the title I held. I was a queen, a ruler. To him, my position meant I could deliver any one of my subjects into the sinister hands of an executioner, but what he didn't understand was that I too was a prisoner. I lived my life at Adam's disposal, and it was because of this fate I couldn't bring myself to send a man to his death. He might have stolen from me, but he only did so in order to survive, to provide for his family. Even now, he begged for me to spare his mother and sister from harm. He cared more for their well-being than his own. It was this beautiful display of compassion and love that cemented my decision to ask him to become one of my personal guards. I would save this stranger, because one day, I'd need him to save me.

The chill of winter subsided, but my attention refocused on the man I'd first met so many lifetimes ago. "I saw it," I whispered. "No, not saw. I *lived* it. I relived the first time we met."

"And what do you think now?" Conrad asked.

"I think I must have been one of the loneliest people in the world."

"Perhaps your loneliness could see my own because that's exactly how I felt before I met you."

"When I say I lived the past, I mean I had access to all my thoughts and emotions. I was drawn to you, to a complete stranger. I saved you from punishment because I knew there would come a day when I would need you to save me," I said. "Why you?"

"I wish I could answer your question, but I can't. The only explanation I've been able to come up with is that we were meant to be a part of one another's lives."

"It's no wonder Aden was angry at the thought of us together, especially with the way you looked at me. You stared at me like you were in love with me."

"Maybe I was."

"So, you felt that strongly about me from the moment we met? Don't you think that sounds a little irrational?"

"I was born in 1450. Technically speaking, I'm well over five hundred years old. Doesn't that seem more irrational to you?"

"Yes," I conceded. "What happened when Aden discovered I had feelings for you?"

"You've already seen what happened."

I wished I could take back my question as soon as I asked it. Aden executed Conrad right in front of me. Loving me cost him his life. I stood from the table, pacing back and forth. I'd seen grisly images of people being tortured, but if I tried hard enough, I'd always been able to block them from my thoughts. That wasn't the case with Conrad's execution. I've never been able to forget it, and the thought ate away at my soul. Why did my first memory of Conrad have to be so unbearable?

"What's wrong?" Conrad asked. "It wasn't my intention to upset you. You said you'd seen that scenario play out so many times, I assumed you'd figured out why I was being killed."

"I know, and after finding out about our relationship and who Aden was, I knew. But why would my brain force me to recall something so horrible? Why couldn't I remember meeting you or marrying you? Why did I have to see Aden sentencing you to death over and over again?"

"Because your mind wants you to remember the things he's capable of doing. You're the only one who can stop him, and believe me, he needs to be stopped."

"I need a break. I can't handle hearing about anything else."

"You need to know all this. You need to start remembering who you are."

"And what if I don't want to remember who I am?"

"Evey—"

"I'm being serious, Conrad. I've had to watch him cut your head off over and over again, and the only thing worse than that is knowing I'm the reason you suffered such an agonizing fate."

"That wasn't your fault," he said, taking my hand in his. "Aden is responsible, not you."

"How can you even stand to look at me?"

"You saw the first time we met, but you still don't realize what you did for me and my family."

"What do you mean?" I asked.

"Follow me, there's something I want to show you," he replied, increasing his hold on my hand and leading me to his room. Once there, he pulled a long box out from underneath the bed. The width of it was only a couple inches. Immediately, I found myself trying to guess what was inside. He removed an object from the box, and I couldn't help but notice it looked like a picture frame of some kind. Cream cloth covered the mysterious item, and he handled it with extreme care. I watched with curiosity as he placed the object on top of the bed to uncover it. "Do you remember the painting from history class?"

"Yeah," I answered, unsure of where this conversation was going.

"This is the real painting that one was copied from."

I sucked in a deep breath as I noticed my own eyes staring back at me. I moved closer to the portrait, scrutinizing every detail. I sat in a high-back chair, hands folded in my lap. Dark auburn hair fell in soft waves past my chest, and the deep gold brocade of my dress seemed to glow against my fair skin. The pendant hung delicately around my neck while a jeweled crown rested upon my head. I could recognize the similarities between this painting and the one from the book—the dress, chair, crown, and position were all the same.

"So we really do look the same every time?" I asked, reaching out my hand to touch the
gold frame encasing the portrait.

"Yeah, it makes it a lot easier on all of us."

"How did you come to own the painting?"

"You gave it to me as a gift," he said, inching closer to me. "It hung in my room when I lived in the castle. It's gone everywhere I have."

"Oh," I replied. "Where did my necklace come from? If it was important enough for you to hold on to, I figure there must be some sort of sentimental attachment to it."

"I gave you the necklace."

"This was from you?"

"It was our secret actually. I had the painting and you had the necklace."

"Really?"

"You sound surprised," he answered with a smirk. "Is it because I was poor?"

All the blood in my body suddenly rushed to my face. "That's not what I meant."

"If you remembered the first time we met, then you saw my home. We lived in a shack with dirt walls."

"It was rather small."

He laughed at my admission. "Small is a kind way to describe it. We were so lucky to meet you."

"What difference did meeting me make?"

"My mother and sister were very sick when we first met. You brought all of us to live in the castle and then nursed them back to health. You saved their lives; you gave me a job as one of your personal guards. Because of you, I was able to provide food and clothes for my family. There isn't a day that goes by that I'm not thankful I met you." His hand released mine and he moved to trace the portrait's frame. "The necklace was my mother's. Her side of the family had come from money at one point in time, but she gave it to me to give to you."

"Thank you for returning it."

"Anytime," he said, smiling.

"I guess we should go see what Caroline is up to."

He set the painting beside his bed before following me downstairs. When we reached the bottom step, Caroline was sprawled on the floor in front of the television watching a local news channel.

"What's going on?" I asked, sitting next to her.

"They're talking about the diner."

"What are they saying?" Conrad came and stood behind us. A picture of the diner flashed across the screen.

"They're saying it was a gas leak and the entire diner burned down because of it."

"Did they say anything about Mickey and Kit?" I could hear the panic in my own voice as I asked the question. Not a second after I had spoken, a bulletin flashed across the bottom of the screen. Two bodies had been found inside the diner. Horror riddled my body as I realized I would never get to see Mickey and Kit again. Two people who had been in my life for as long as I could remember were stolen away in the blink of an eye. It wasn't right; they didn't deserve this. Without saying a word, Caroline jumped up and bolted for the bathroom. The door slammed shut, but Conrad and I could still hear her getting sick. I covered my own mouth with my hand, feeling I might need to join her.

I glanced at Conrad, hoping he would know what to say or do. "This is my fault. They died trying to protect me."

He moved to kneel in front of me, gently taking my hands in his own. I flinched a bit at his touch, but once his fingers began rubbing my wrists, I didn't want him to let go. "Evey, I want you to listen to me." His fingertips met my chin, adjusting my gaze to meet his. "I've known Mickey and Kit for centuries; they're my family. Trust me when I tell you that they were proud to be your *secundae*. They knew the risks of protecting you, and they still wanted to be by your side. You're the thing that binds all of us together. If you are lost, all hope is lost."

"Is that what I symbolize? Hope?" I stared into his eyes, unable to look away.

"That and so much more." Years of love and affection existed between us. I could see it in the way he looked at me. No matter what I did, he'd always be there for me. Even now, he sat before me, patiently waiting to be remembered. The notion was as much my comfort as it was his condemnation. If he stuck around, would he be doomed to suffer the same fate Mickey, Kit, or even my father endured?

"I'm not quite sure I deserve you."

"That's funny," he said. "I've been saying the same thing about you for years."

He stood and headed in the direction of the kitchen. I listened as he filled a glass with water. Then he stood by the bathroom door, waiting for Caroline to emerge. Once she did, he presented her with the glass.

"Thanks," she replied, taking a drink. They walked back to the living room and seated themselves on the floor beside me. Grabbing the glass from her, I took a drink.

"They're really gone," I whispered.

"I just don't want to believe it," Caroline replied. "I can't believe it." A lone tear trickled down her cheek, mirroring the one that was falling from mine.

"We'll make this right," Conrad said. "I can promise both of you that."

"What do we have to do?" I asked, refocusing myself to the task at hand.

"We have to do as your father said and find the nearest consiliarius and warn them. Then, we have to find the head of the Concilium and tell them what's going on. They have to help us stop Aden," Conrad announced.

"Do you know where to find them?" Caroline asked, wiping her hand across her face.

"I haven't been in touch with anyone but Guy in the last few decades. Most members of the Concilium move around every few years as a safety precaution," he answered. "Guy said it was in the field. Do you know what he was talking about, Evey?"

"I don't. Maybe he got mixed up. I mean, it was right before—" I stopped, leaving the rest of my sentence unfinished.

"No, he knew those words meant something to you. You just have to think about it," Conrad added.

"I don't know. There are so many things running around my head right now. I'm trying to make sense of it all."

"Just try to relax and think about it. I'm sure it will click and you'll remember."

I tugged at a string that hung off the bottom of my jeans. "You have a lot of faith in me."

"When you spend a couple centuries with someone, you know what they are and aren't capable of, and you're definitely capable of figuring this out."

The sound of Caroline's ringtone blared through the room, causing me to jump. "Is that your mom?" I questioned.

"It's the police station," she replied, staring at her phone. "And it's not the extension for my dad's desk either."

"Answer it," Conrad said. "They probably have a few questions about Mickey, Kit, and the diner."

"What should I say?"

"Answer as truthfully as you can and maintain our secrecy. Our very lives may depend on it."

"Hello?" Caroline asked in an uncertain tone. "Oh, hi, Officer Zimmerman. Yes, that's right, I'm with Evey Rhodes." Conrad and I listened closely, desperate to hear what the officer was saying. "You tried calling her phone? Well, she turned it off to try and get some rest last night. She's right beside me if you would like to speak with her."

I accepted the phone, hesitantly placing it against my ear. "Hello?"

"Is this Evey Rhodes?"

"Yes."

"Hello, my name is Officer Zimmerman, and I know this is a terrible time for you, but I was wondering if you could answer a few questions about the break-in at your house last night."

I pulled the phone away from my face, covered the bottom of it with my hand, and stared at Conrad. "He wants to ask me a few questions about my father."

"Same goes to you then. Answer with discretion."

"Okay," I said, speaking into the phone again. "What are your questions?"

"You weren't at your house last night when the break-in happened. Where were you?"

"I was on a date with Conrad Bourdet."

"And where did you go on your date?"

Officer Zimmerman spoke in slow spurts, and it made me realize he was writing down everything I said. I gulped nervously. My answers needed to be perfect in order to not raise any suspicions about what really happened last night. "We went to a party at Claire Newell's house for almost an hour, and then we stopped at the diner and grabbed some food to take with us to Conrad's house. We wanted to watch a movie."

"And what time did Conrad pick you up?"

"At eight."

"And what time did you get to the diner?" Officer Zimmerman asked.

"I guess it was right at 9:30."

"After you picked up your food, where did you go?"

"I heard the diner burned down because of a gas leak. Is that true?" I asked, unable to help myself.

"Unfortunately, yes. The fire chief from Lynchburg came to determine what caused the fire."

"Oh."

"I'm sorry. I know you worked there," he said. "Where did you go after you left the diner?"

"We went back to Conrad's house to watch a movie."

"What time did you leave his house?"

"I didn't, not till today. It was really late when my mom called last night though."

"So, your mother called while you were at Conrad's?"

"Yes," I answered, looking to Conrad for help.

"Keep going," Conrad whispered. "You're doing fine."

"She called around midnight and told me to stay with Conrad."

"I see."

"Haven't you confirmed this with my mother already?" I asked. Perhaps I was teetering on the edge of recklessness, but I needed to know if this man had spoken with my mother. If he had, then there was still hope we may be able to find her.

"I did," Officer Zimmerman replied. "But for my report, I'd like to have a record of where you were last night."

"Am I a suspect or something?"

"Not at all. We're just trying to gather all the information we can. It looks like a cut and dry robbery gone awry, but we want to make sure we aren't missing anything."

"Okay."

"I'm very sorry for your loss, Miss Rhodes. I know these questions seem trivial, but sometimes the smallest details can make all the difference in the world."

"Thank you," I whispered. My eyelids fluttered rapidly as I attempted to blink away the building tears. Caroline took my free hand in hers, squeezing it. "She told me to stay at Conrad's house until she came for me."

"What time did she arrive at Conrad's?"

"I don't remember. I cried for a long time after she called and then I fell asleep."

"When did you get in touch with Miss Brewer?"

"I guess it was around midnight. I'm not completely certain though," I answered. "I asked Conrad to pick her up. I was so upset, I needed to talk to her."

"That fits with the note Caroline left for her parents. Like I said, I know these questions seem trivial, but I appreciate you taking the time to answer them."

"You're welcome."

"Again, I'm very sorry for your loss, and if there is anything you remember, please don't hesitate to give me a call."

"Thanks. I will."

"I'll be in touch if there are any other details we need to go over."

"Okay. Goodbye."

"Goodbye." I handed the phone back to Caroline. "How was that?" I asked Conrad.

"You did great. What did the officer say about Marie?"

"Basically that she provided him with the same story I did, but how could she do that if Aden took her?"

"I'm not sure," Conrad answered. "My only guess is that he's using her to avoid suspicion and keep the cops off his back."

"So, are we going to get Marie?" Caroline asked.

"As much as I want to, it's still too dangerous right now. We don't know exactly where Aden is or what his next move will be. There are too many variables at play for me to risk Evey's safety."

"You know I'd rather get my mom than be safe."

"I know, but allowing Aden to get his hands on you isn't an option. Your mother understands how important you are."

"Fine," I replied in exasperation. I'd just have to think of another way to convince him that we need to rescue her.

"Hey, Conrad," Caroline said, glancing at him. "Can I ask you something?"

"Sure."

"You're one of Evey's protectors, which means you've been trained to fight, correct?"

"Yeah."

"Can you teach me how to fight?"

My head snapped in her direction just to make sure I'd heard her right.

"You want me to teach you to fight?"

"That monster is after Evey, and he's killed people I love. I want him to pay by any means necessary."

"What do you want to learn?" He stood and helped both of us up from the floor.

"I want to know what Mickey, Kit, and Guy knew. I want to help protect Evey like they

did."

"Okay, I can do that. I'm going to get some weapons from the barn out back. We can see what weapon works best for you and I'll teach you how to use it."

She nodded, pulling her long hair into a ponytail. "Good."

"What about me?" They both stared at me as if I were speaking a different language.

"You've been trained how to fight," Conrad answered.

"I have?"

"Yeah, I taught you myself," he said, looking at me. "You'll remember how; the memory of the body seems to be keener than the mind sometimes." Then he turned and left the room.

Caroline and I moved closer to the windows, observing him through the glass panes. "He would do anything you asked him to."

"What are you talking about?"

"I'm talking about the fact he has been in love with you for five hundred years and he's still in love with you right now."

"I know we have this long history together, but I've only been able to remember pieces of it. Everything with him still feels new to me, like I've only known him a few days."

"Really? Because it didn't sound that way when y'all were having a screaming match last

night."

"I'm sorry you heard all that. It's just, I was so scared of him, and then he kissed me and suddenly I saw us getting married in 1858."

"He kissed you?"

"Yes."

"And?"

"And what?"

"And how was it?"

"Caroline!"

"What?" she asked. "Your soul mate for the last five centuries finds you after spending decades apart and he kisses you. And you mean to tell me that you can't come up with half a million adjectives to describe it?"

My gaze followed Conrad as he approached the barn behind the house. "I haven't been kissed like that before . . . It was earth-shattering."

"Sounds amazing," she replied with a smile.

"I didn't know love could feel that way. It was intoxicating, consuming, and frightening all at the same time."

"Why frightening?"

"Because I've never experienced anything so powerful."

Before we could say anything else, Conrad returned armed to the teeth. He presented two different swords, an axe that had a skinny wooden handle about the length of my arm, and what appeared to be a scythe.

"I want you to pick up each weapon and swing it through the air to see how it feels."

Caroline immediately went for the axe, closing both of her hands around the handle. She swung it back and forth a few times, slicing through the air with ease. After she tested the rest of the weapons, she picked up the axe once more. "I really like this one. It feels a lot lighter than I thought it would." I grabbed the smaller sword with a gold cross engraved into the hilt, and Conrad took the larger sword with a curved blade.

"Let's go outside and practice some things," he said, opening the door for us. We walked to the side of the house under the shade of a large elm. "Okay, Caroline, I'm going to swing my sword at you, and I want you to block it with your axe." She looked a little nervous but nodded her head that she understood. He stepped toward her and swung the sword in a graceful arc. As his blade came crashing down, her axe flew upward through the air, meeting his sword with a loud clang. "Good," he said. "That was really good." Caroline returned his smile, clearly pleased with herself. They sparred back and forth for a while, and as they continued to practice, day quickly faded into night. Once she had a good feel for her weapon, Conrad taught her how to counterstrike. His enthusiasm for her skill was apparent with each passing minute. "Are you sure you've never been taught to fight before?"

"Actually, the summer before seventh grade, my parents insisted I fit medieval weaponry in-between tap dance and cotillion."

"All right, smart-ass," Conrad replied with a laugh. "Why don't you take a break and let Evey practice."

"Are you sure about this?" I asked.

"You're going to be fine. Remember, I'm the one who taught you how to fight. You have nothing to worry about."

"I hope you're right," I whispered. As my hand held my sword, beads of sweat accumulated on my palm. Conrad was a formidable opponent, and although I knew he wouldn't hurt me, I was still apprehensive. Maybe it was the look in his eyes. I'd noticed it at the diner when he stabbed his knife through the woman's throat; it was completely predatory. It made me realize I never wanted to be the person on its receiving end, and out of instinct, I tightened my grasp on my sword. However, I didn't have another second to ponder it, because he lunged toward me with his sword outstretched. Even though my mind was reeling with fright, it seemed my body knew what to do. I managed to block his attack, but the force generated from the collision of our blades knocked my weapon from my hands.

"Not bad," Conrad commented, handing my sword to me. "Try again." I readied myself to strike, but as I ran for Conrad, he slid out of my way, smacking the flat side of his sword against my back. "Again, Evey," he ordered.

"I feel ridiculous. What if I can't remember how to fight?"

"You can. Stop being afraid. You've had formal training on how to fight. Let your body recall it."

"If you say so," I muttered.

This time when Conrad attacked, I defended myself, knocking away his blows and countering with a few of my own. He guided his blade in the direction of my head, but when I ducked out of the way, I managed to kick his hands, causing him to drop his sword. However, before I could move, Conrad tackled me. We fell to the ground with him landing on top of me. I tried to throw him off, but he sat across my legs, pinning me in place.

"You aim here," he instructed, taking my blade and holding its tip above his heart. "Or here," he added, moving my sword to the side of his neck. "And whatever you do, don't hesitate."

"Why not?"

"Because a soul or demon never will."

"Understood," I answered, grabbing his shirt and flipping him over my head. I climbed on top of him, holding my sword to his neck.

"Nice counterattack," he said with a grin. When I didn't move, he held up his hands in defeat. "It seems I'm at your mercy, madam." His eyes flickered with mischief, their intense gaze drawing me nearer. I leaned over him, discarding my weapon.

"Would you like me to be at yours?" The question rolled off my lips with ease as I set my forearms on either side of his face.

He grabbed my waist, pulling me closer than I thought possible. "You've no idea how much, my lady," he whispered, brushing his nose against mine. His lips were just an inch away, and every part of my body was screaming for me to kiss him.

"Am I my own person or am I the queen you met so many lifetimes ago?"

"You are that queen, and she is you. You've always been the same person."

"How do you know?"

"Because of the way you're looking at me right now."

"And how is that?" I questioned.

"Like you want to kiss me."

Apprehension overtook my mind, forcing me to increase the distance between us. I climbed off of him and hovered with uncertainty. "Conrad, I—"

"Act like it never happened?" I nodded my agreement, accepting his hand as he helped me to my feet. "Today was a good start, and I'm very impressed with both of you, but for now, we should rest and eat. Tomorrow we can practice some more," Conrad said.

Caroline and I locked arms as we made our way to the house. During our walk, she nudged me with her shoulder, and I had no doubt we'd be having a discussion about the little spectacle she'd just witnessed. As we neared the door, I realized Conrad hadn't kept our pace. Instead, he lingered behind us, his focus darting from one side of the house to the other. He was like a soldier, completing a visual sweep of the perimeter, constantly inspecting for any signs of danger. As I stared at him, I couldn't help but wonder if he ever managed to relax. Was it even possible when he spent every second of the day protecting me?

9

THE HUNT

As soon as we were inside, Caroline went to shower while I cooked dinner. I wasn't one to sit idle when I had a lot on my mind, and let's face it, I had so much drama at the moment, I could spend a year on a shrink's couch and not even scratch the surface of my issues. That's why cooking was such a welcome reprieve. Simple work kept my hands busy enough that I could rest my brain. I could feel Conrad watching me as I chopped vegetables to add to the spaghetti sauce. My fingers gripped the knife as I focused all my attention on the onion I was slicing. An awkward silence hung in the air between us like a dense fog.

"Don't you have a perimeter to check or something?"

He chuckled and took a step closer. "A perimeter?" Heat scalded my cheeks. Not wanting him to see my embarrassment, I tossed the vegetables in the skillet and turned up the burner on the stove, hovering over the spaghetti sauce as if it were the most interesting thing in the world.

"Well, I don't know what to call it."

"The sauce smells good," Conrad said, mercifully changing the subject.

"Thanks," I whispered, giving the sauce another thorough stir. "There is something else I want to ask you." I paused, wondering what he must think of me, this version of me. "I'm sorry, I know I keep having questions, but there's just so much I need explained."

"If you didn't have a lot of questions, you wouldn't be normal."

"Right, because I'm the epitome of normality."

His lips curved in a slight grin. "What did you want to know?"

"I've been watching you the last few days. You always look like you're preparing for battle. Even before the attack at the diner, you acted almost like a soldier. Do you ever wish for a different life? A life where you could worry about paying bills or other trivial things, not running from tortured souls?"

"That's a complicated question," he replied thoughtfully.

"How so?" The only reason he'd been subjected to this life was because of the oath he made on my account. He said he was happy to risk life and limb to protect me, but what if that burden became insufferable? Could he be tired of constantly risking his life in order to save mine?

"I do wish for a different life," he admitted. "But—"

"It smells really good in here!" Caroline announced as she walked into the kitchen. "Wait, did I interrupt something?"

"Not at all." Guilt riddled my body, stinging with the force of a dozen lashes. He wished for a better life, and I was the one thing keeping him from it. He had sacrificed numerous lifetimes in order to protect me. Everyone considered Aden a monster, but did they ever stop to think about what I was? "Conrad told me all I needed to hear."

"Do you need help setting the table?" she asked.

"That would be awesome," I answered. When the three of us were all seated around the table, another awkward silence filled the air. I couldn't stand the thought of eating an entire meal in silence, so I blurted out the first question that came to mind. "What did Aden do to turn the Concilium against him?"

"Aden started to go mad when he discovered our relationship. In the beginning, the Concilium overlooked it, attributing his behavior to jealousy, but what they didn't realize was that he had changed completely. He was never the same man, which became obvious when he started torturing prisoners he held in the dungeons."

"You're talking about the Spanish Inquisition, aren't you? He was reborn as Ferdinand II of Aragon . . . He started the whole thing, didn't he?" I asked, horrified at the reality of what my past decisions had caused.

"Yes," he replied, taking a drink of water. "The Concilium, however, wasn't aware all of this had taken place. So, after the two of you had lived out your lives as Isabella and Ferdinand, you were reborn again. Only this time, he was born as Henry IV of France and you were Gabrielle d'Estrees."

"Who are they?" Caroline asked, helping herself to another serving of spaghetti.

"Henry IV was king of Navarre and France in the late 1500s. He was actually well-loved, because he cared greatly for the welfare of his subjects and he was very tolerant of all religions practiced by his people."

"That actually sounds good. I mean, it's a change from inciting the Spanish Inquisition," I countered.

"Yes, he was a model king at first. I think he was trying to win back your favor, but when he realized you still didn't love him, he transformed into a monster again." I tried to hold Conrad's gaze, but his attention fell to the table. He paused for a minute, as if preparing himself for what he needed to say next. I watched his chest rise and fall with the intake of a deep breath. "None of us ever imagined he would poison you."

"Oh my God! He had her killed?" Caroline's eyes were wide with shock.

"He did." A look of sadness washed over his face, but just as fast as it appeared, it was gone. "Now, history books tell us that Henry was saddened by the loss of his future queen because she died during childbirth. However, that wasn't the whole truth."

"I don't think he killed me just because I wasn't in love with him anymore. Something else pushed him over the edge. What made him do it?" I forced a bite of food down my throat with a stiff swallow.

"In order to answer your question, I have to explain what primum and secundae mean."

"That's what you are, right?" Caroline asked. "A secundae?"

"Yes. Secundae really means secondary, because that's what we are. We're the second set of people to be brought back to life. Evey and Aden are the primums, meaning first or original rebirths. They were reborn first to help influence humanity. Then secundae were created to protect the primums. Evey and Aden each had their own secundae to protect them. Evey's secundae were Guy, Marie, Kit, and Mickey, and I was added later."

The sound of shattering glass startled me. I twisted in my seat, expecting to see a pile of broken dishes on the kitchen floor, but instead, a pair of shaded eyes met my gaze. Caroline and Conrad were nowhere in sight, and I understood with perfect clarity that I was once again reliving the past.

"Am I not your king?" the man shouted at me. "Have I not given you everything you've desired?"

"Adam, what's wrong?"

"I saw him!" he screamed. "Last night, I saw a man who looked just like Conrad leaving your bedroom."

"Is that what you saw?" I asked. "Seems rather ridiculous considering you murdered him."

He seized my arm in a brutal grip, jerking me to my feet. "Don't mock me."

"Why? Because you've killed men for less?" I grimaced at the pain, trying with all my strength to free myself.

"You're mine," he whispered in my ear. "You always have been and always will be."

"Get your hands off me!"

"I can put my hands wherever I want on your body." Shoving me against the wall, his gaze wandered past my face to the open window, and he wondered aloud, "What I don't understand is why the Concilium would bring back Conrad?"

"They didn't. Conrad is dead."

His gaze, now even more furious, returned to my face. "You're lying to me!" he yelled. "I know he's alive."

"You won, Adam! You took the most precious person in the world from me. What other torture would you like me to endure?"

"No torture, my love. I simply want you to bend to my will."

"I'll never bend to your will. Now, get your disgusting hands off me!"

"I'm disgusting?" He pressed my back into the wall as his hands restrained me.

"Stop! You're hurting me!"

"Bend and I won't have to break you," he sneered.

Before I had time to answer, he was yanked off of me. Conrad twisted Adam's arm, causing the bone to snap. Then he slammed Adam against the wall so hard, the room shook. "Touch my wife again and I'll rip your throat out with my bare hands."

"Your wife?"

Conrad's hand tightened around Adam's neck. "I didn't give you permission to speak."

"I'm a king! I can do as I please."

"Not anymore," Conrad replied. "Men will no longer cower in fear before you. It's time for your reign to end." Then he heaved Adam across the room and threw him outside. Once Adam was gone, Conrad locked the door and turned to face me. "Gather your things. We must leave at once."

I ran into Conrad's embrace, holding on to him as if I were afraid he'd disappear at any moment. "I have everything I need right here."

"Did he hurt you?" he asked, combing his fingers through my hair.

"As long as you're alive, he can't hurt me anymore."

When my eyes opened, Conrad was no longer in my arms. Instead, he sat before me, eating the meal I had prepared not thirty minutes earlier. I couldn't help but stare at his hands. Those hands had comforted, protected, and caressed me. And if I asked, how else might they touch me? "I know why he killed me."

"Why?" Caroline tilted her head in confusion.

"He was angry, so angry, the Concilium brought you back as one of my secundae."

"He was," he agreed. "He thought when I died, I wouldn't be a problem anymore and he could have you all to himself again."

"If Evey already had four secundae, why were you made into one?" Caroline interjected.

"The Concilium saw how much I loved her, and they knew I'd do everything within my power to protect her."

"I guess that makes sense. You still haven't told us how Adam became Aden," Caroline

countered.

"Right after Adam killed Evey, the Concilium decided that letting him live was too much of a liability. So they had him assassinated."

"Assassinated?" The question rolled out of my mouth as I stared at him in disbelief. "That doesn't make any sense."

"There was one consiliarius who took pity on Adam. She thought the rest of the Concilium had judged him unfairly. For the most part, all of the Concilium and secundae have favored you over Adam, even before he started to change. But there were a select few who always remained loyal to him."

"The consiliarius brought Adam back to life?"

"Yes."

"And then what happened?"

"Adam was furious the Concilium had killed him, so he in turn murdered the consiliarius who brought him back. He killed her by ripping out her heart and consuming it." He twisted his fork in his hands as he spoke. "By consuming her heart, he absorbed her powers."

"Now the Concilium only has six members?" I asked.

"Yes. After that, Adam pretty much became immortal like the rest of the Concilium. He denounced God, refusing to abide by His or the Concilium's laws. He changed his name to Aden and seeks to undo all the good the two of you have accomplished throughout time."

"Aden can make himself live forever and reincarnate his secundae?" Caroline asked.

"Yes, but the powers he stole won't last forever. He isn't a true consiliarius because he wasn't made into a consiliarius by God, which means his powers are limited."

"And that's why he's after the rest of the members of the Concilium," I added as the

pieces all started to come together into one terrifying whole.

"Exactly," Conrad replied.

I stifled a sarcastic laugh. "So, basically, we're on the run from a homicidal maniac with cannibalistic tendencies?"

Conrad nodded. "Essentially, yes."

"This just keeps getting better and better." I slid my dinner plate away from me, filling the empty spot with my head.

"Evey," Conrad said in a soft voice. "I'm sorry. I know you're overwhelmed, but if we're ever going to stop Aden, we won't be able to do it without you."

I looked up, trying to find strength in his unwavering belief in me. "Are you really saying I'm the key to winning an ancient, biblical, supernatural war that's been carrying on for the last few centuries?"

"Pretty much."

"Fantastic! Must be Thursday!"

"I'm being serious about this."

"I know," I groaned. "It's just that one second I'm thinking about prom dresses, and the next, almost everyone I love has been murdered and I find out I've had not one but two husbands, I've been murdered myself, and I'm the reincarnation of the original woman. So forgive me if I hesitate for a second before jumping on the freaking bandwagon."

"She does have a point," Caroline said.

"I know she does, but I don't think the two of you quite grasp the scale of things. Aden is controlling souls now. He's commanding an army of the devil's minions, and that is something we've never seen him do before."

"What if I don't want to fight?"

"You have to!" he yelled.

"Why? What's the point?" I asked. "If I die, I get reborn

anyway. Why not deny Aden the revenge he wants so much and just leave me dead?"

"Aden is evil, and he has the ability to influence or foster that type of darkness in others. He can transform the kindest people into monsters, but you have the ability to stop him. Your very presence reverses that darkness. Your influence inspires people to be compassionate and good," he said, the urgency in his voice willing me to understand. "You're completely immune to his powers; no one else on this earth can make that claim."

"I never asked to be a part of this!" I shouted, incapable of accepting what Conrad had just confessed.

"Only you can stop him, and if you choose not to act, then you're condemning the world and everyone in it, including Caroline," he said, pointing to my best friend, "to a fate worse than death." The load weighing upon my shoulders multiplied exponentially. All I wanted was to get my mom back. How was I supposed to deliver humanity from the clutches of a madman?

"I know it may feel otherwise, but you aren't alone in this endeavor. I'll always be at your side," Conrad added in a kind voice.

"Even though you wish for a different life?" I whispered, guilt overwhelming my already burdened conscience.

Conrad's eyes stared into mine. "I'm not the one I wish it was different for."

Unable to hold his gaze any longer, I whispered, "I should probably take a shower."

"That's a good idea. I'm sure the two of you are exhausted," Conrad replied. "You go on. I'll clean up the dishes."

As soon as Caroline and I were out of earshot, she bombarded me with questions. "Okay, I have to ask, what the heck happened when we were training?"

"What do you mean?"

"One second, you're holding a sword to his neck, and the next, you're a breath away from making out with him."

"I don't even know. It feels like I'm being pulled to him and it's beyond my control. The more I try to fight it, the more I realize I don't want to."

"Then don't."

"What?"

"Why would you fight it?"

"To feel like I have a choice in the matter."

"You do. What do you want?"

"I don't know," I answered, heading to the bathroom.

"Yes you do. You've been drawn to Conrad like a magnet since he arrived at Tulson. Stop thinking so much," she said. "What do you want?"

"To be with my husband," I blurted out. We stared at each other for a second, thrust into a temporary state of shock. "See what I mean? Is that even me responding, or is it her, the queen?"

"From what I've heard, the two of you are one in the same."

"I'm glad one of us feels so confident about it," I muttered, not sure why I found her wholehearted support of Conrad so frustrating.

"Before you woke up this morning, I asked Conrad how the two of you met. He told me the whole story. He said he stole from you, and instead of condemning him to death, you saved his life. You relived the first time you met him. Would you have acted as the queen did and saved his life? Or would you have condemned Conrad to death?"

I thought of the first time I'd met Conrad. He seemed so fragile kneeling before me, begging for mercy for his mother and sister. "I couldn't have hurt him even if I wanted to."

"And why is that?" she asked.

"Because when I looked into his eyes, my life suddenly seemed bearable again. I was a prisoner to Adam, to my role as a queen, and all that melted away the moment I touched him," I answered. "I saved his life because I knew I would need him to save mine."

"I know you, Evey, and you like him. Whether you want to admit it or not, you do. I'm not saying you have to fall in love with him today, but why don't you allow it to happen naturally? Your heart has chosen this man for the last five hundred years. If I were you, I wouldn't question my own instincts."

"Don't you think he'll be disappointed at having to wait for me to love him?"

"If I had to guess, I'd say he's perfectly happy just being around you."

"Thanks, Caroline."

"No problem," she said with a smile. "You take a shower. I'm headed to bed. After all the training today, I'm spent."

The hot water relaxed my aching muscles as I stood beneath the faucet. As much as I didn't want to admit it, Caroline was right. Just because Conrad was my past didn't mean he couldn't be my future as well. I'd told myself not to fear my nightmares because they were meant to remind me of who I was. Shouldn't I do the same with my good visions too?

I finished my shower and changed for bed, but my body had a mind of its own. Instead of heading to my room, my feet led me to Conrad's. When I got there, the light was on, but he was nowhere in sight. As I turned to leave, one of the curtains floated away from the window frame. I peered outside only to find Conrad sitting on the roof.

"Mind if I join you?"

He stood at the sound of my voice. "Not at all. Allow me," he answered, grabbing my waist and lifting me out of the window.

"Thanks." I circled my arms around his neck, instinctively wanting to pull him closer. When our cheeks slid past one another, images bombarded my brain, highlighting intimate moments between us. Conrad stood beside me at the edge of a great precipice. The setting sun illuminated the sky with radiant shades of red and amber. Waves crashed into the cliffs below. The dark sea created a beautiful juxtaposition where it merged with the sky. I accepted Conrad's outstretched hand, laughing as he spun me in a circle. We held onto one another, dancing to the rhythmic sounds of the ocean. I could've spent an eternity watching the two of us in that moment, but the memory was quickly replaced with another. This time, our surroundings weren't quite so tranquil. Crying people ran on either side of us. Fires covered the land, brightening the darkness. Conrad had a hold of my hand, running for the edge of the woods. The tall trees would be a welcome camouflage, hopefully protecting us from the rampant bloodshed. I sighed with relief as we made it to the forest. Mickey, Kit, and my parents trailed behind us. I yelled, beckoning for them to hurry. I reached back toward them out of desperation, leaning through the trees. Suddenly, I was shoved to the side. Conrad pressed against me, now occupying the space I had just vacated. An arrow ripped through his chest, soaking his shirt with blood. A scream poured from my mouth at the sight. He collapsed at my feet, gripping his wound. Before I could help him, the backdrop faded away.

Back on the roof in present day, but still processing the two memories I had just experienced, I spoke through gritted teeth, "Every time you touch me, I see the past." I kept my eyes shut for fear I might find an arrow protruding from his chest.

"If you don't want me to touch you, I won't," he said, backing away from me.

"That's not what I meant."

"I'm sorry. This time, I don't know how to act when I'm around you."

"You aren't alone in that," I replied, opening my eyes to see him standing a few feet away with a sad and lost look on his handsome face. "So, what were you doing out here?"

"Thinking."

"About what?"

"You." I took the hand he offered, following his lead down a small stretch of sloped roof to a large balcony. It rested on top of one of the house's side porches. "I've spent the majority of the day trying to come to terms with our complex relationship."

"That doesn't sound good."

"I keep remembering things from when I was a queen, and I just want to make sure I have a choice in how I feel."

"You do have a choice."

"Do I? Because whenever I'm around you, it doesn't seem that way." I shifted sideways, positioning myself closer to him. "Every time I'm around you, my will isn't my own."

"My will hasn't been my own since I met you," he whispered.

"I know how I should feel. Believe me, I do. It's just . . ." I whispered, letting my words trail off, too nervous to complete my sentence.

"Just what?"

"As foolish and selfish as it sounds, I want a memory of my own. I want one we've made in this lifetime."

"I can help you with that if you'd like," he said, standing to his feet. I nodded and accepted his outstretched hand. He rested one of his hands against my back while the other held onto mine. "Follow my lead."

To my surprise, Conrad led me through an elegant waltz across the rooftop. We moved together in perfect unison, decreasing the amount of space between us as we glided along. Light from the moon illuminated everything in sight with a beautiful glow. Then he spun me in a circle, dipping me so low that I was almost parallel to the ground. The sudden movement made me giddy and my whole body began to tingle. "I love to dance," I giggled.

His nose brushed against mine playfully. "I do too."

I didn't want to let go, and as soon as I was back on my feet again, I blurted out, "What made you fall in love with me?"

He thought for a moment before answering, "I think it's impossible for anyone to be around you and not love you. You're so kind and always place the well-being of others before your own." He inched closer, pressing our chests together. "And you know how I said my mother and sister were sick when we met you?" I nodded, waiting for him to continue. "They were still sick when we moved into the castle. You sent all the servants out of their room and stayed there for two weeks, nursing them back to health. We were peasants and you treated us with more respect than we'd ever known."

"They did get better, right?"

"Yeah, thanks to you. Cecily, my sister, was very fond of you."

"When did I fall in love with you?"

"Well, as one of your personal guards, I protected you when you traveled and helped you hand out food to people in the streets. As time passed, a close friendship developed between us. Then, about nine months after I met you, Aden went on a hunting trip. He asked me to accompany him in place of a guard who had fallen ill. You didn't want me to go, but because Aden had ordered it, I didn't have a choice," he said. "We set off for a few days to hunt wolves, but the weather wasn't good for our sport. It stormed every day we were gone, making it almost impossible to hunt anything. It wasn't until the last day of our trip that we actually spotted a pack of wolves. After we tracked the pack all day, we were able to surround them, preventing them from escape. Just as Aden was about to strike and kill a wolf, a loud clap of thunder erupted, scaring all the horses. A few of the wolves took off, and Aden dashed after them, trying to catch up. I took off behind him, afraid he was going to get injured. While I was following him, I was knocked off my horse by a low branch. I rolled to the bottom of a small embankment and landed on a pile of rocks."

"Were you hurt?"

"I was knocked unconscious, and the rest of the party couldn't find me, especially since night had fallen. They set off for the castle, assuming the wolves had gotten the better of me. When I woke up at dawn the next morning, I had nothing with me except my sword, bow, and the clothes on my back. It took me the entire day to hike back to the castle. That night, a feast was held to celebrate Aden's kill. When I made it back, I sought out Marie so I could tell her I was all right and find out where you were. She said they thought I was dead. The hunting party found my horse roaming in the forest, but there wasn't any sign of me. Everyone was at the feast, except for you." His bright eyes locked onto mine, claiming my undivided attention.

"Where was I?"

"Marie led me to my room, and as I walked in, I saw you sobbing on my bed. I'll never forget the look on your face when you saw me."

I could still hear his voice ringing in my ears as my mind began to wander. It softened until it disappeared altogether and I found myself in a dimly lit bedroom.

My eyes fell upon his body. Cuts covered his face and hands, saturating his skin with red. He was drenched from head to toe with mud now staining his once white shirt. I sprang from the bed and ran, colliding into him.

"I thought you were dead," I sobbed into his shoulder.

"I'm still here," he said, caressing my hair.

"I don't know what I'd do if you were gone." Nothing he did could stop my tears. After a few moments, he stepped back from me awkwardly, ending our embrace.

"I'm sorry. I shouldn't have been so informal with you. I didn't mean to touch you in that way, my lady," he replied with an uncomfortable bow.

I raised my hand to stroke the side of his face. "You may touch me in any way that pleases you." Encouraged by my caress, he seized my body, pressing it to his with all his strength. His lips were on mine, kissing me passionately. My hands eased his bow off his back. It fell, slamming into the stone floor. Then his lips moved from my mouth to my neck, covering every inch of skin between. I lifted his head to meet mine and kissed him, losing myself in his arms.

"Conrad?" I whispered, breathless.

"Yes, my lady?"

"When you didn't come back, I was scared that not only had I lost you, but there was one thing I would never get to say to you."

"What would that be?"

I took his hands in mine before gazing up at him. "I love you." I could tell by the

expression on his face that I had startled him. "I understand if you don't feel the same way, but I just wanted you to know how I feel about you."

He brought my hands to his mouth, softly kissing each finger. "Then there is something I should tell you," he replied with a grin. "I've been in love with you since the first moment I saw you."

Once again, I was thrust from my past into the present. Conrad watched me, intently surveying the features of my face. "I was ready to lie on that bed till I withered away and died. Until you walked in. I can't describe how happy I was to see you again. How did you do it?"

"What?"

"How were you able to live for years, knowing I wouldn't remember anything about you?"

"I held on to the hope that one day you would remember me and when that happened, you'd be able to live a long, happy life without having to spend each moment looking over your shoulder." The muscles in his arms tightened as he held on to me. No space existed between us, and yet he was still trying to draw me closer.

"Why are you a stranger to me?" I asked. "You're one of my secundae. Why weren't you a part of my life like Mickey, Kit, or my parents were?"

"I was a part of your life for a very long time, but then everything changed. One day, you started remembering the Garden of Eden, Aden, and me," he answered. "The Concilium thought I was the one triggering your memories, so they forbade me to have contact with you." The look of pain written on his face was unmistakable. *I haven't been on a date since 1926.* His words from the other night rang in my ears. "I didn't want to give you up, but I'll do whatever is necessary to keep you away from Aden."

"When you said you hadn't been on a date since 1926, you were talking about when they sent you away from me?"

"Yes," he replied, years of sadness emanating from the depths of his blue eyes.

"Do you want to talk about it?"

"Not really."

"Why not?" I asked.

"I should stop whining about it. I've been luckier than most. I've had the opportunity to spend centuries with you. What are a couple decades compared to that?"

"You don't have to be so resilient all the time."

"Yeah, I do. It's what you need me to be right now."

"And what about what you need?"

His face neared mine with each passing second. "What do you think that is?"

"Something only I can give you."

"If you only knew," he whispered, allowing his lips to linger against my ear.

"They were right though."

"Who?"

"The Concilium. You're the reason I started to remember the past. That first day when we met in class, I grabbed your wrist when you let me borrow your pencil. The flashes started when I touched you. I always had dreams, but they were just glimpses or pieces; nothing made sense until you came along."

"They were right to separate us then."

"Conrad—"

"Aren't we supposed to be dancing?" he asked, spinning me around once more. He guided me through another waltz, turning us about the balcony with an easy grace. Time forged onward, or maybe it stopped completely. Either way, I didn't care. The only thing I wanted to do was to keep dancing, but as soon as I had the thought, Conrad ended our embrace. "We should probably get some rest."

"You're right," I agreed, heading back to his window. When he helped me climb back into his room, I wanted to say something to ease the awkwardness enveloping us, but everything I wanted to say dissipated before I could utter a single word. "Well, good night."

"Evey?"

"Yeah?"

"You don't have to love me. I came to protect you and ensure your safety. I didn't come all this way to force you to be with me," he said. "You have a choice. You'll always have a choice with me."

I stepped toward him and kissed him on the cheek. "I know," I replied with a smile.

M y room and bed felt empty as I lay down to sleep. I could've gone to Caroline's room, but I didn't want to wake her. She was just as worn out as I was. Even though my mind and body yearned for rest, it eluded me. As I slept, I dreamed. Not of kings or masked executioners, but of baskets filled to the brim with ripe blackberries and a field of wildflowers. My father and I lay amongst the flowers, gazing at the clouds floating above us. Bumblebees buzzed in my ear, humming a melodic tune while my father's laughter rang throughout the meadow. I gathered a handful of flowers, methodically tying each one to another to form a long chain. I was almost finished with my necklace when a hand grasped my wrist.

"Evey, it's in the field." My father stood over me. "It's in your field."

"I don't—"

He pulled me to my feet. "Your field."

"You're not making any sense."

"You have to hurry! You're running out of time."

"What field?" I glanced in every direction, desperately trying to piece it all together: my father, a basket of blackberries, and a field of wildflowers. Each thing was a clue meant to point me in the right direction.

I wracked my brain, feeling like the answer was just out of reach, when I realized what my father was trying to show me, what he wanted me to remember. With death just breaths away, he told me where to find the answers. "The field in my painting?" The field he mentioned wasn't an actual place. Rather, it was the field of poppies from my painting.

He smiled. "Take him to the field. He'll keep you safe."

10

PULLED

I jolted awake. We had to get that painting as soon as possible. Ripping off my nightgown, I threw on a pair of jeans and a bra. My shirt was still in my hand as I bolted for Conrad's room. "Conrad!" I screamed. "Conrad, hurry!" As I burst through the door to his room, something shot past my face, sinking into the wall behind me. "What the hell was that?"

"A knife," Conrad answered.

"I thought you were supposed to protect me, not impale me with flying cutlery!"

"If I wanted to harm you, trust me, the knife would be sticking out of you and not the wall."

"How comforting," I replied. "And why exactly are you sleeping with a knife?"

"It's a precaution."

"Are you expecting to be attacked in our sleep?"

He shrugged and sat on the edge of his bed. "It's been known to happen before."

"Anyway, we have more important things to talk about. I know how to find the consiliarius."

"How?"

"It's hidden in a painting at my parents' auction house."

"You're sure?"

"Yes! When my dad said it was in the field, he was referring to my favorite painting at their store. I just had a dream about it."

"Okay."

"Come on, we have to go!" I unfolded my top frantically. "What?" Conrad was staring at me with a smirk on his face. "What is it?" I asked, confused at his lack of urgency.

"I just haven't seen you this undressed in a long time."

"Seriously?"

"What?" he asked, his voice the embodiment of innocence.

"I'm telling you I know how to find a consiliarius, and you're talking about how long it's been since you've seen me undressed?"

"You're the one who ran in here topless."

"I have a bra on! It's not like I'm naked."

"How unfortunate for me."

"You're impossible."

"You're my wife! What do you think I think about when I see you?"

"I don't know!"

"Really?" He stood and gently circled my wrist with his hand, tugging me closer to him. I could feel his lips grazed the curve of my neck as he leaned toward me. "You really have no idea what I'm thinking right now?"

"Enlighten me," I ordered, unable to fight the chemistry that had been surging between us since the moment we met.

"I could do so much more than that."

"What the hell is going on here?" Caroline asked, her surprised voice surprising us even more.

Her eyes focused on Conrad's shirtless form, then mine, before finally settling on the knife still sticking out of the wall. "It's not what you think," I answered.

"I hope not. Because what I'm thinking is pretty weird."

"I can only imagine," Conrad replied, trying his best to suppress a laugh.

"But seriously, is there a reason the two of you are shirtless right now?" she questioned.

"Does one ever really need a reason to be shirtless with a beautiful woman?"

Caroline chuckled at his reply. "Oh, nice save."

"Thank you," Conrad said with a slight bow.

No longer distracted by his bottomless blue eyes and perfectly muscled shoulders, my sense of urgency returned. I tried to explain, "I had a dream about my father. He showed me the field we need to find in order to contact a consiliarius. It's hidden in a painting at my parents' auction house," I blurted out in exasperation.

Quickly grasping the significance of this new information, Caroline replied, "So, we're going to go get the painting? I'll go get dressed."

I nodded, finally pulling my shirt over my head. We both froze at Conrad's next words.

"We aren't going tonight," he answered.

"Why not?" I asked, surprised.

"Aden isn't stupid," Conrad stated, moving to sit on his bed again. "He sent souls to the diner and your house. We'd be fools to assume he isn't still watching the places where he thinks you'll return. He's been looking for you for a long time, and the other night was the closest he's ever gotten."

"Are you saying we need to wait weeks or something? Because I don't think my mother has that much time."

"All I'm saying is when we go, I want to be prepared for any situation that might arise. Why don't we go tomorrow night after we've had some time to come up with a plan?"

"Yeah, you're right. We should be smart about this." I glanced at Caroline, wanting her opinion as well.

"If it's the best way to keep you safe, then you know I agree," she said with a yawn. "I'm heading back to bed. I'll see y'all in the morning."

"I should get some more rest too."

"It would be a good idea," Conrad agreed.

Before leaving, I pulled the knife from the wall and handed it back to Conrad. "You might need this tomorrow night."

"Throw it."

"What?"

"Try and hit the same spot I did."

"You're serious?" I asked.

"Absolutely."

"What the hell," I mumbled. I grabbed the knife by its point and chucked it at the wall. To my amazement, the blade embedded itself in the exact spot Conrad had hit. "You really did train me to be a fighter, didn't you?"

"I trained you to live," he replied. "Just remember that."

The next morning, I was up before Conrad and Caroline. I tossed and turned the rest of the night, my mind too preoccupied with thoughts of rescuing my mother and retrieving my painting without being burned alive by souls. When the sun finally rose, I surrendered to the battle, and after a little deliberation, I decided to wake up Conrad. Hopefully the task wouldn't involve losing any blood. I crept into his room and shook his shoulder. "Hey, it's time to get up," I said, ducking out of sight. Getting stabbed wasn't on my to-do list for the day.

"I'm up," he said, stretching out his arms.

"I was going to make us all breakfast this morning. Is there anything in particular you like to eat?"

"Not really. I'll pretty much eat anything, although there's not much food left in the fridge." He rolled out of bed. "I'll run to the store. It's a couple miles up the road, so it won't take me long."

"Sounds good." He grabbed a blue T-shirt and threw it on as I followed him down the staircase. "I want you to lock the door, and don't open it for anyone but me."

"I won't."

"I'll be back in a few minutes."

Once the door was locked, I went to the kitchen to make a pot of coffee. Caffeine was definitely on my to-do list for the day. While I was waiting for it to brew, Caroline wandered into the kitchen.

"Morning."

"Morning," I said, pulling three coffee mugs out of the cabinet. "Where's Conrad?"

"Oh, he went to the store to get some food. He'll be right back."

"Good! I'm starving."

"Have you talked to your mom and dad?" I poured coffee into two mugs, adding plenty of cream to both. When I handed her the steaming cup, she accepted it with a smile.

"I just talked to my mom. She said everyone is really shaken up about your dad." She grabbed my hand across the table, giving it a tight squeeze. "I told her we'd be heading out of town to be with the rest of your family."

"Thanks for lying to your parents for me," I said in a shaky voice. "Is my dad's body still at the morgue?"

"That's just the thing. My mom said she saw your mom go identify his body this morning and arrange to take it to Indiana." Caroline's mom was a secretary at the police station. If something happened in Estill Springs, she was the first to know about it.

"But how could my mom pick up his body?" I held on to her hand to steady myself.

"I don't know. Aden has your mom; he must be trying to clean up his messes so the Concilium doesn't catch on to what he's doing." A drop of water landed in my coffee, rippling the caramel surface. I wasn't sure when the tears had started, but now they were flooding my eyes. Caroline knelt beside my chair and held my head to her shoulder.

"Sorry I'm such a mess."

"Don't you dare apologize for this," she scolded. "You've been so strong. I don't know how you're doing it, but you're amazing."

"Thanks." She leaned back from me, taking my hands in hers.

"This does tell us one thing though. Your mother is still alive, and we're going to get her back."

"You're right," I agreed, blotting my face with a paper towel Caroline handed me. "And tonight we'll retrieve the painting and contact the consiliarius my dad mentioned."

She went back to her seat on the other side of the table and took a gulp of coffee. "You can also defend yourself, which, after what happened at the diner, is good too."

I nodded my head in agreement. I was surprised by my abilities, especially since I'd never even thrown a punch before, at least, not in this lifetime.

Conrad's knock interrupted my reverie. I peered through the window just to make sure it was him before unlocking the door. He put away the groceries while I started frying strips of bacon for breakfast.

"How do y'all like your eggs?"

"Fried for me," Caroline answered.

"Same here," Conrad replied.

I began cooking the eggs after I flipped the bacon. A few minutes later, we were all sitting around the table, eating our steaming plates of food.

"We know Aden is still in Estill Springs," I said, stuffing my mouth with eggs.

Conrad's brow furrowed. "How do you know that?"

"Caroline's mom is a secretary at the police station, and she said my mother came in to identify my father's body. Apparently, my mother told her that she would be taking him back to Indiana to be buried."

"I'm glad Marie is still alive, but this also means we need to be very careful tonight. I bet Aden's watching the auction house, but unfortunately, it's a risk we'll have to take."

"What's the plan?" Caroline asked, leaning forward in her chair.

"It's best to go at night. That way, we'll at least have a little bit of cover and there won't be as many people out. We'll go in armed and secure the painting as fast as possible."

"That sounds simple enough," she said, looking over at me.

"It is simple, as long as we aren't attacked."

"If we're attacked, we fight back," I countered.

"Yeah, but let's hope it doesn't come to that," he said. "You saw how quickly the diner was overtaken with souls. We'd be foolish to believe Aden doesn't have something more sinister at his disposal."

We spent the rest of the morning evaluating and packing various weapons and equipment. There was so much stuff the living room looked like a bomb had exploded inside of it. We collected knives and polished them until they shone with a deadly gleam. Conrad left out the knives we were going to carry, but stored enough weapons in the trunk of his car to equip a small army. He wanted Caroline to get a little more practice with her axe, so the two of them went outside while I stayed inside to catch up on some rest, as I hadn't slept much last night. I settled on the couch, observing them from a window as they practiced. Caroline was a natural at defending herself. She blocked each blow Conrad dealt with surprising agility. She moved pretty fast, and her speed could no doubt be attributed to her long legs. Though she was only 5'7", the couple inches of height Caroline did have on me made her the faster sprinter. Despite Caroline's speed, Conrad moved gracefully, as if he were dancing a waltz instead of wielding a menacing sword. He'd been a warrior for so long, surely centuries of fighting and running would take their toll.

Lost in thought, I hadn't realized practice was over until Conrad burst through the door. "What are you up to in here?" he asked, brandishing a sword and a grin.

"Just trying to relax. I was about to make us some sandwiches for lunch." He sauntered over to me, leaning his sword against the wall. "You look like you had a decent workout," I stated, noticing the beads of sweat dripping down his face.

"Yeah, Caroline is really skilled. It's kind of surprising actually, but she's fast with her axe. And it's a good thing too, because if we're going to take down Aden, we'll need all the help we can get."

"I don't know why everyone is so surprised I'm such a badass." She was standing in the doorway with her axe slung over her shoulder. "I think it's because I'm a blonde, and I resent that! There's no law saying I can't kick ass and have amazing hair!"

I couldn't help but laugh. "You're too much sometimes," I said, shaking my head at her as I made turkey sandwiches and tossed some grapes in a bowl.

"I think it would be smart to pack some stuff to take with us, like clothes and shoes. That way, if we do get ambushed, we have everything we need. I don't want to lead them back to the safe house if they're tailing us," Conrad said, settling into the chair next to me.

I nodded my head and took a big bite of my sandwich.

"You don't think they've already ransacked the auction house, do you?" Caroline turned toward Conrad, waiting for an answer.

"I don't think so. My guess is Aden still wants to lay low. He wouldn't be stupid enough to tear through everything connected to Evey."

"I wish we knew what his plan is," I added, staring at my plate.

"Have you had any flashes or dreams about Aden?" Conrad asked. He surveyed my face while waiting for my answer. Out of the corner of my eye, I could see Caroline's gaze fixed on me as well.

"Why would I want to remember him?"

"What you see may surprise you. Aden wasn't always evil. There was a time when the two of you were happy together."

His words shocked me. In the back of my mind, I knew Aden had been slowly driven toward hostility, but it seemed impossible I could ever be happy with him. "I don't want to think about it," I answered.

"It would be beneficial for you to try and remember some of the time you spent with him. It might make it less confusing for you when all your memories of him do come rushing back to you."

"I don't want to talk about it," I said, hearing the anger rise in my voice. First, he wanted me to remember our ridiculously complicated past, and now he was encouraging me to embrace the memories of the monster from whom he'd stolen me? Whether I wanted to acknowledge it or not, I belonged to Aden once, and the thought nauseated me. Before either of them could say anything else, I pushed my chair back and ran upstairs to my room. Slamming the door behind me, I paced in circles, trying to block any residual thoughts about my first husband. The door to my room squeaked a little and I knew someone was there. "I don't feel like talking right now."

"I know you don't want to talk about Aden, but he used to be your husband." I could hear the guilt resonating in his voice. "I'm sorry I upset you."

"It's not your fault I was married to a monster."

"Nor is it yours," he replied. "Aden wasn't always that way, but we all have a little darkness in us."

"He kills for pleasure. You don't."

"I still have my fair share of demons, though. I've had half a millennium to rack up a body count." He moved to stand across from me, leaning against the wall. "Do you still believe I'm completely innocent?"

"I don't believe you could ever be like him."

"Well, I had you. You kept me good."

"Aden had me, too, and look what it did to him."

"That's not necessarily true," he countered.

"Isn't it though? I mean, I was the one who gave him the apple."

"You didn't know he was going to change from that, and it wasn't just the apple."

"You're right; we did the rest of it." Regret surged through my veins the moment the words left my mouth.

"I won't pretend like I'm not guilty for that, because I know I am, but I'm not sorry about it. He didn't deserve you then, and he sure as hell doesn't now. I'm not saying I deserve you either, but I won't apologize for the way I felt about you back then."

"Felt?" I asked, staring at the floor. "When you put it that way, it makes it feel like it happened so much longer ago."

"How do you want me to put it?"

"I hardly know myself."

"Can I ask you something?"

"Yeah."

"Why are you afraid of remembering Aden when he was good?"

I let out a deep breath before opening my mouth to speak. "Because there was a time when I loved him, and it scares me to think he could have some kind of control over me. I'm afraid he'll use that power to play off my emotions. I know he's cunning and manipulative. What if he can seduce me back to him somehow?"

"I can understand your reservations," he replied with a nod. "But I also think you don't give yourself enough credit. As I've said before, you're a lot stronger than you think, and you won't succumb to his will. Plus, what you had with him wasn't anything like what we had when we were together."

"What we had was stronger?"

"Yes," he said, taking a step toward me.

I knew he cared about me, but I couldn't help but feel a little disheartened at how he kept referencing our past. We'd been apart for too long to simply pick up where we left off. "What was it like when we were married in Savannah?"

"Your parents owned a large cotton plantation. We farmed the land and lived quiet lives. There was also a house for each of us. Mickey and Kit lived in one, your parents in another, and the third belonged to me until you became my wife. The balcony you saw us getting married on was part of our home."

"We were just peaceful farmers?"

"We were, but it was mostly for show," he replied. "Just because you didn't know your true identity doesn't mean you weren't doing good things."

"What do you mean?"

"Our plantation was one stop on the Underground Railroad. The six of us worked with a network of other homes in the South to help slaves escape to the North. We also gave the people we helped money and supplies so they could start new lives for themselves."

"It's incredible we've lived through all these huge events in history. I almost can't wrap my head around it."

"You've been around since the beginning of time. It'd be impossible to grasp everything you've witnessed."

"All the other times we were married, were we happy then, too?"

"It didn't matter where we lived or what we did, as long as we were together, we were happy."

"I wish it could be like that now."

"It can be, once we stop Aden."

"If he's never commanded an army of souls before, why is he doing it now?"

"I'm not sure, but my gut tells me that we'd prefer not knowing."

"There's one more thing I want to ask you about," I said, biting my lip.

"What's that?"

"When I was Gabrielle d'Estrees and I died, were you there?"

His jaw clenched and he averted his eyes from my gaze. "Yes."

"Well, what happened?"

"That's something I don't talk about."

"Why not?"

"Why not?" he asked, raising his voice. "Because I had to watch you die! I held you in my arms as you started seizing, slowly choking on your own blood. And the whole time, I knew I was the reason why it was happening. I failed you. It's my job to protect you, not get you killed."

"The only reason I'm alive right now is because of you. If you hadn't been at the diner, I'd either be dead or with Aden." I touched his arm gently. "You can't keep blaming yourself for something he did."

"Sure I can," he contradicted. "I've done it for years."

"If you won't allow me to feel responsible for your death, then I won't allow you to do the same with mine."

"How do you plan on stopping me?"

I stepped to him and slid my hands up his arms, rounding his shoulders. "Please, don't blame yourself for his actions for another second," I begged.

"How can I not when he took something so precious from me?"

"Do it for me," I whispered, holding on to him.

"As you wish, my lady."

Unable to stop myself, I ran my fingertips through his hair. "This sensation is so weird. It's like I knew exactly how your skin would feel when pressed against mine."

"That's because you never really forgot."

A loud knock halted our embrace, and we took our time separating from one another. Caroline walked in just as Conrad's hands slid down my back.

"Are y'all playing doctor?" The tone in her voice was nothing short of wicked.

I avoided looking at either of them, but Conrad answered her with all the confidence in the world. "I gave her a clean bill of health."

"So . . ." I said, changing the direction of the conversation. "Did you want to talk to us about something?"

"It's going to get dark outside soon, and I was just wondering when we needed to start getting ready for tonight."

"What time is it?" Conrad asked.

"It's almost six," Caroline answered from the doorway.

"Let's start packing so we're ready to go."

"All right, I'll get my stuff together and get changed," Caroline replied, turning for her room.

Conrad moved to leave, but I stopped him. I held his hand in mine, rubbing my thumb along his knuckles.

"About earlier." I paused trying to collect my thoughts. "What happens to my secundae if I die?"

"We get pulled," he stated in a matter-of-fact tone.

"What does that mean?"

"We don't really die. We get pulled out and then wait for you to be reborn so we can come back."

"Could my dad be reborn again soon? I hoped, since he's a secundae, he would be coming back."

"We can't be reborn until it's time for you to be reborn. You have to live out the rest of your life first."

"Oh," I mumbled, all my hopes to see my father again suddenly deflated. "Do you go to the same place when you die as when you're pulled?"

He nodded. "We go to heaven." He squeezed my hand before leaving for his room.

Heaven? I couldn't stop thinking about the word. It was such a lovely but unimaginable term. A place we all aspired to, and my thoughts turned to my father. When I saw him last, his body was burned and broken beyond repair, but now he was in heaven. Kit and Mickey were there too. Even though they weren't here with me, they were all in a beautiful place together.

But it wasn't time to relax. We had to put a stop to Aden's reign.

I changed into jeans and a long-sleeved black shirt before sliding on my Converse sneakers. I gathered up everything I had and shoved it into my bag. Then, I made my way to Conrad's room and watched as he packed. He threw some clothes and shoes in a bag and slipped his arms into his leather jacket.

"Are you ready to go?"

At the sound of my voice, he crossed the room and switched off the light. "Yeah, we better go downstairs and start getting everything else ready."

He grabbed my bag and carried it in the same hand as his own. When we entered the kitchen, Caroline was sitting at the table, her bag by her feet.

"Now the painting we need . . . you know exactly where it is, right?" Conrad asked, fixing his intense gaze on me.

"Yeah, it's on a back wall by the window," I answered. "I've also got my key to the auction house so we'll be able to go in through the front door. That way, it'll look like no one was there."

"Good, I want this to be a quick trip. The longer we're out there, the more danger you're in." He handed us each a belt with knives and we fitted them onto our waists.

"Don't we need something to cover all this?" Caroline asked. "I mean, if we have to go to a public place, we might look a tad suspicious."

"Hold on." Conrad ran out of the room and we could hear his shoes banging against the stairs. He returned a minute later and handed us each a jacket. I pulled the black hoodie on and zipped up the front, the belt invisible beneath the loose fabric. Caroline covered her blue T-shirt with a navy blue sweatshirt that fit slightly better than mine because she had longer arms. Her brown boots were laced tight; she was ready for a fight. "Good, those work," he said, picking up our bags and carrying them to the door. "I'm going to finish loading up the car."

"You don't have to go through with this if you don't want to," I told Caroline. "All this Concilium, secundae, primum craziness isn't normal. You shouldn't be dragged into it."

"I'm going with you."

"We'll understand if you don't want to go. There's a good chance you could get hurt." "I'm already too involved."

"Caroline—"

"Do you remember when Corey Jones called me a bitch when we were in fourth grade?"

"Yeah, but what does that have to do with anything?"

"Do you remember what you did?"

"Caroline, it doesn't matter!"

"You walked right up to him and kicked him square in the balls," she replied. "Mrs. Tucker saw you do it, too, and she gave you a week of write-offs for it."

"He was a little twit," I said with a laugh. "But I don't want you to get hurt because of me."

She held up her hand, cutting me off. "Would you do this for me?"

"Of course, but—"

"But nothing. You're my sister; I'm staying. That's final."

"Thanks," I replied, returning her hug.

"Come on," she stated, turning back to the kitchen. "Let's make some coffee. I'm sure we'll need the caffeine." Conrad came inside, wiping his hands on a rag. I raised my eyebrows, pointing at the cloth.

"I was just checking the fluid levels on the car." He stepped further into the kitchen. "We'll also need to fill up the gas tank before we stop at the auction house."

I sat at the table while Caroline carried over a fresh pot of coffee and three mugs. "Neither of us have much of an appetite," I said, handing Conrad an empty mug. "We figured caffeine was a good idea though."

"Thanks," he said, taking the mug.

"We should also stop by the bank so we can get some money in case we need it," I added.

"That's a good idea, but there's no need." Conrad rose from the table and went into the living room. He moved the couch from the wall, revealing a safe. He spun its dial to unlock it and pulled out a stack of money.

"Geez. You guys are prepared for anything," Caroline said, staring at the money.

"When you've lived as long as we have, it's kind of inevitable." He separated the money into thirds, dividing it between us. "Here, we'll each take some."

"I thought we weren't planning on splitting up." Caroline's brow furrowed in confusion.

"We aren't, but always expect the unexpected."

Folding the money, I tucked it inside the wallet in my messenger bag. I flinched when Caroline's phone tumbled off the table, smacking against the floor with a loud thud. Our evening plans had me on edge. My brain kept emphasizing all the terrible things that could happen. Death, dismemberment, and destruction—or worse if Aden caught me—were possible outcomes, none of which I wanted to experience. Caroline refilled our empty mugs while I passed around the cream and sugar. We sipped our coffee in silence, too preoccupied with thoughts of tonight to say much. After we drained the entire pot, I washed all the dishes while Caroline dried them, thrilled to have some way to release all my nervous energy.

We waited around until ten before leaving. Conrad locked the door and returned the key to the bottom of the pot holding the dried up tree. Then the three of us climbed into the car and Conrad spun around in the driveway, heading away from the house. We'd be in Estill Springs soon, and the thought made my hands sweat in anticipation.

"I think we should establish some rules before we get there," Conrad said, breaking the silence of the car.

"Such as?" Caroline's voice rang out from the back seat.

"For starters, no one goes anywhere alone. We stick together. If I tell you to do something, you have to do it. If I say run, hide, or leave, you do it. Also, in case we do get separated, we need to have a designated meeting place."

"The movie theater parking lot would be a good place," I said. "It's kind of secluded since it's off the main strip of town."

He nodded, signaling his approval. "Theater it is. Now, do both of you understand the rules?"

"I understand," Caroline stated.

"Evey?"

"I got it." I turned my head to look out the window.

I was so focused on calming my unsteady breaths that I almost didn't hear the quiet conversation that continued between Conrad and Caroline.

"Caroline, I need you to do something else."

"What's that?"

"You have to help me protect her at all times now. She's more important than either of us."

"I know she is, and I'll help you."

My chest tightened at the reality of their words, and I forcefully inserted myself into the conversation. "You both sound crazy. I won't let either of you sacrifice yourselves for me."

"Unfortunately, that isn't your choice," Conrad replied with finality in his voice. He reached for my hand resting on the console, but I withdrew it from his reach and continued staring out the window. He should know I couldn't bear the thought of losing any more people I cared about.

II

THE SILENCE
BEFORE THE STORM

A s the car crept along the deserted street, we could see my parent's auction house on the opposite side of the road. It looked desolate, a single structure immersed in a sea of darkness. Conrad parked the car in front of a neighboring dentist office. My heart was pounding wildly, causing my hands to shake. Caroline wore the same nervous expression that must have been plastered on my face, but Conrad looked completely at ease. He led us to the trunk of the car and handed each of us a weapon. He slid an axe into Caroline's hand and a short sword into mine. He took up the blade he used the previous day and a large iron mallet. The expression on his face was lethal; he was ready for a fight.

"I'm leaving the car unlocked and the keys in the ignition, in case we need to make a quick getaway." Caroline and I nodded to indicate we understood him. "Follow me and be quiet." He stalked off toward the house using the shrubs along the sidewalk for cover. I pulled the building keys from my pocket and tightened my grip on the sword. The air grew heavier with every step we took, as if at any second it would smother the life out of us. We didn't hear a single sound as we approached the house and tiptoed up the wooden steps to the front door. I handed the keys to Conrad and he unlocked it, cautiously stepping inside. He examined every corner of the room before gesturing for us to come in. A deep breath filled my lungs as I crossed the threshold and listened as Caroline did the same behind me.

My eyes surveyed the room, discovering with relief that nothing had been disturbed. Everything looked the same as the last time I had been here. Conrad propped the mallet over his left shoulder and held out his hand for me to grab. He drew me close, and I clutched onto the back of his jacket. The proximity of his body to mine was reassuring, and for a second, I almost felt at ease.

"The painting is through there," I whispered, pointing to the back of the store. He started off in the direction my hand was pointing, but I stopped him. "Wait. Come this way first." Stepping around him, I made my way up the stairs to my parents' office. "Extra inventory is kept up here. I want to get another painting to replace the one we're going to take. That way, nothing seems to be missing or out of place."

"Good idea." He turned to Caroline, jerking his head in my direction. I opened the door to my parents' abandoned office and found spare paintings propped against the wall behind my father's desk. I hesitated, staring at the empty black chair where my father used to sit. My heart seized with pain as I thought back to the last day my father had been alive. I'd sat in that very chair when he told me I could have the painting of the poppies that I loved, though I never would have guessed the way I would be acquiring it. Sensing my apprehension, Conrad reached out and grabbed a painting of a wooded landscape. The scene depicted a forest of evergreens wrapping around the side of a gray, rocky mountain.

"Is this one okay to replace it with?" he asked. I nodded an affirmation. "All right, let's hurry up. I don't want to be here longer than we have to be."

He slid past us and moved toward the stairs. Grabbing Caroline's hand, I took off after him. The floor creaked loudly, causing us to jump. Conrad held a finger up to his lips, prompting us to be quiet. Slowly, we eased our way across the floor to the painting. I could see it ahead of us. The little girl still looked like an angel bathing in a sea of poppies.

"That's it," I said, pointing to it.

Conrad walked over to the picture, lifted it from the wall, and hung the painting of the landscape in its place. The portrait fit perfectly in the space left behind. Then he set his mallet and sword on the floor and retrieved a sharp knife from the belt around his waist. Holding the painting in one hand, he dragged the knife around the outer edge of the canvas, freeing it from the gold frame. I took the empty frame from his hand and darted back up the stairs to hide it among the other paintings in my father's office. I moved as fast as I could and by the time I returned, Conrad had rolled up the painting like a scroll and tied it. A sense of relief filled my body as he handed it to me. We had what we needed, and it was time to go. Conrad bent to pick up his weapons just as the front door flung open and broke off its hinges.

In the blink of an eye, six souls thrust themselves through the doorway, sprinting in our direction. Conrad pushed in front of us, raised his sword, and sliced the heads off the two souls nearest to us. Shrill screams escaped from the others as the heads of the first two tumbled to the ground, disintegrating into a pool of black sludge. As the bodies melted away, three more took their place.

"Get out of here!" Conrad yelled at us. "Now!" He threw the mallet, striking a short old man in the chest. The man heaved backward, crashing into a frail-looking young woman. The woman glared at Caroline and me. She licked her tongue over her rotted teeth and lunged in our direction. I sprang forward, slicing her in half with my sword. Sticky tar exploded from her severed body, desecrating every clean inch of the floor around her. "I said go!" Conrad called as he ran over, pushing us toward the back door. "Caroline, take Evey and get the hell out of here. I'll hold them off for a minute and then follow behind you."

"No!" I shook my head. "You're the one who said we need to stick together!"

Caroline dove ahead of us, embedding the blade of her axe into the face of a deranged elderly woman. As we watched the woman dissolve, a body hurled itself through the window to our left. Caroline gripped my elbow, and we burst through the back door of the house. Souls began running at us from every direction. Conrad slammed the door behind us, wedging it shut with a knife. Then he grabbed another one from his back and brandished the sword in his other hand. Caroline and I trailed him as he sprinted to a small clearing in the yard behind the auction house. Like moths drawn to a flame, a swarm of souls surrounded us. Conrad wasted no time in attacking, destroying three of them within a matter of seconds. I joined his fight, taking out a short soul to my right as Caroline did the same beside me. We had each already killed a few when a towering soul leapt on top of me. His hands squeezed my shoulders, singeing my sleeves.

"Evey!"

My back struck the ground, the impact debilitating my senses. A soft wheeze escaped my lips as I tried desperately to suck in enough air. Scalding hands grasped my sides with an unyielding grip. I bucked against the soul, violently twisting my body until I was able to slip out of his clutch. Freedom was within my grasp, but before I could move another inch, the soul latched onto my foot, dragging me through the grass away from Conrad and Caroline. I tightened my hold on the painting and my sword, kicking against the crazed man with all my strength. In another instant, the man's grip loosened. Surprised, I stared up at him and saw the end of Conrad's sword protruding through his mouth and coated in black.

Conrad jerked me to my feet, shoving me toward Caroline. "Take Evey and leave," he ordered.

I didn't even have a chance to object when Caroline wrapped her arm around mine and yanked me in the direction of the car. As she pulled me away, I glanced over my shoulder in search of Conrad.

Dark oil coated the grass as his sword dropped body after body. I watched Conrad dodge outstretched hands that longed to singe his flesh. My stomach twisted in knots as a large man almost twice his width dove for Conrad's feet, but Conrad was too fast for him. He whipped his sword in a quick ring and sliced the man in half at his shoulders. A river of black blood saturated the grass and a couple of souls slid in the sludge as they moved to take the dead man's place.

"Conrad!" I screamed as I tried to stop Caroline's momentum that was taking me away from him, leaving him alone and in danger.

Hearing me, he glanced over at us in shock. With a fierceness I hadn't heard from him before, he called out, "Caroline, now!"

To my horror, the door broke and ten more bodies poured from the back of the building, heading straight for Caroline and me. Not to be outdone, Conrad threw his sword in the ground like a spear and faced the souls. "I'm her last secundae!" he shouted, sporting a wicked grin. "Come for me if you dare, you mangy bastards!"

His taunt worked. The souls switched course immediately, sprinting toward him as if pulled by an invisible string. Conrad retrieved his sword, meeting them head on. His blade was moving so fast that I could only see the occasional glimmer of silver as it swung through the air.

Caroline tugged at my arm again, urging me to move faster. "Come on! We have to go!"

I dug my heels into the ground, forcing her to stop. "I'm not leaving without him."

"There isn't any time." "Either we go back for him or I offer myself up to the souls right now. I'll let them take me. I'll do whatever it takes to save him." I freed my hand from her grip and stepped away from her. "I mean it!" "Fine," she said in an exasperated tone. "I'll get the car and you get Conrad. When I pull up, be ready to jump in." "We'll be ready." She turned away and sprinted to the car as I started running back to Conrad. Thick tar covered everything in sight. A gash across his chest poured blood, staining his shirt red. One of his hands clutched his sword while the other braced his chest. "Conrad!" His eyes connected with mine and I quickened my pace. It was almost too late by the time I noticed the small body emerging from the bushes. A child approached Conrad from behind, holding a skinny knife. The little boy's eyes were solid black, and his mouth was contorted into a sinister smile. "Look out!"

Conrad barely had time to turn around when the child's knife soared through the air, embedding itself in his thigh. The blow dropped Conrad to his knees, and with a blood-curdling laugh, the little boy pulled the knife from his leg. I watched as the boy drew the crimson blade to his mouth and licked the blood from it.

"Blood of the secundae is always the sweetest," the boy said, cackling. He was about to bring his knife down on Conrad's heart when I leapt in front of him, hacking off the boy's hand. Yellow acid squirted from his wrist and pooled on the ground. He stumbled backward, falling into the dirt. The wail that erupted from his mouth stung my ears. Without hesitating, I swung my sword at the boy, decapitating him. His body imploded on itself, liquefying into a puddle of sizzling yellow slime. However, his head remained intact. Eyes stared up at me from the ground, haunting me with their emotionless gaze. I took the sword and thrust it through each eye. More acid gushed from the hollow sockets and consumed the remaining flesh. Bending down to Conrad, I flung his arm around my neck as the car burst through the bushes of the yard. Caroline threw the passenger door open and pushed the front seat forward. I shoved Conrad in the back seat and climbed in after him, slamming the door shut.

"Go!"

Her foot hit the gas pedal like a ton of bricks, and we spun out of the yard. We were moving with such speed we didn't have time to notice the horde of souls racing across the street to block our only exit.

"Oh my God," Caroline called out. They rushed the car, ramming into its hood. "Hang on!" She threw the car in reverse, turning back toward the side of the house. Just as we were about to crash through the siding, she thrust the shifter into drive. The car tore through the bushes into the yard of the office next door. Through the rear windshield, I could see the souls chasing after us.

Her foot slammed on the gas and we sped away, leaving them in a cloud of dust.

"Drive to Nashville."

"Okay," she replied, shoving the wheel to the right as we skidded around a curve.

Once we were in the clear, my attention shifted back to Conrad. I slid off his jacket, laying it in the front seat. "When we get to Murfreesboro, stop at a drug store. We're going to need a first aid kit."

"How bad is it?"

"I don't know," I answered in a terrified voice. "Conrad, can you hear me?" I shook him lightly, careful not to touch his leg. A groan of pain escaped his lips while blood gushed through the hole in his jeans. Cutting a large slit in his pants, I leaned closer to get a better look at his wound. I fastened his belt into a tourniquet above the gash. Then I ripped my hoodie into strips, tying them around his thigh. When I was finished, I dabbed at the blood covering his chest. Thankfully, the cut wasn't as deep as I had initially expected. "Go as fast as possible," I ordered. The car flew down the interstate, weaving through traffic. "Conrad?" I shook him again to try to elicit a response.

"The demon," he whispered.

"It's gone. Conrad, stay with me. Don't pass out again."

"You saved me." His comment sounded like an accusation more than a revelation.

"I did, and I'd do it again if I had the choice. I can't do this without you," I replied, bending to kiss his forehead. My heart pounded faster every minute we spent driving to Murfreesboro. I just wanted us to get off the road. Holding his face in my hands, I watched to make sure his chest kept rising and falling.

"Evey."

"I'm here." He whispered my name again and passed out. "Caroline!" I cried, panic in my voice.

"We're almost there!" She swerved the car off the interstate at the nearest exit. The bright lights of a Walgreens pharmacy loomed ahead of us. "What do I need to get?" she asked, stripping off her jacket and shirt to reveal a clean top underneath.

Without hesitating to think, I responded, "A first aid kit, a sewing kit, some bottles of water, and a bottle of rubbing alcohol."

"Got it." She turned into the parking lot and left the car running while she ran inside the store. Less than five minutes later, she returned with supplies. "Now where do we go?"

"Take us to the nearest motel. We need somewhere to stay tonight."

We pulled into the parking lot of the King's Inn. I waited in the car with Conrad while Caroline went into the office and got us a room. After driving to the opposite side of the parking lot, we stopped in front of our room. Throwing the motel door open, she flipped on the lights. Then she raced to the passenger side of the car and helped me drag Conrad inside. We pulled back the blankets and heaved him onto the bed closest to the door.

"Go get all the stuff from the pharmacy," I ordered, gently propping Conrad's head on a pillow.

In a surreal daze, I confidently began assessing his wounds. I undid the tourniquet on his leg and opened the first aid kit, my hands taking inventory of the supplies with the grace of a practiced surgeon. I used a pair of scissors to cut the right side of his jeans from his body. Then I slid his left leg out, easing his pants off. Opening the bottle of rubbing alcohol, I grabbed a wad of gauze in my left hand. As I poured the alcohol on his wound, his body writhed in pain.

"Can you fix it?" Caroline stood behind me, watching as I worked.

"Yeah. It's pretty deep, but it doesn't look like his femoral artery was severed. I'll have to sew up the wound, though."

"How do you know what the femoral artery is?"

"I have no idea." I shrugged, applying pressure to his thigh. "Bring in the rest of the stuff from the car."

After holding the gauze to his leg for a few minutes, I threaded a needle from the sewing kit.

"Have you ever done this before?" Caroline's voice was unsteady and her body shook as she stood beside me.

"After my comment about the femoral artery, I'm banking on yes." Placing my hand on his leg, I forced the sides of his wound together. "Hold him down. He can't move while I do this." Caroline laid her body over his abdomen as I straddled his legs. I inserted the needle through his skin, knotting the end of the thread so it wouldn't pull completely through his flesh. His body jerked away from me slightly, but Caroline and I held him in place. I sewed the wound up tight and tied off the thread to keep it from reopening. Then I covered the wound with antibiotic ointment, dressing it with a few layers of gauze and some tape. Removing the remaining shreds of his shirt, I started to clean the gash on his chest. Once I had disinfected the wound, I covered it with a few layers of gauze and taped it all down.

The confidence that infused me during the crisis began to evaporate as I stared at him, still unconscious on the bed. Had I done enough?

"I-I brought in a few of the weapons. They're on the table by the door." Caroline sat in a nearby chair, her facer pale. She asked in a voice much quieter than her usual boisterous tone, "Those creatures we fought tonight, they were same things that attacked you at the diner?"

Realizing this was her first exposure to the nightmare I'd been living, I responded in a gentle tone. "Yeah. Usually, they're controlled by the devil, but now Aden seems to have them at his disposal."

A single tear trickled down the side of her cheek. "I didn't understand what Conrad had meant about the scale of things being bigger than we could imagine, but I do now." With a trembling hand, she wiped her cheek. "I should've gotten you out of there sooner. He's gonna be pissed at me."

"You helped me save his life. I'm sure he'll be grateful for that."

"I hope so," she whispered. "I'm going to wash up and go get us some food." Caroline washed her face as I collected a couple of washcloths and towels from the bathroom.

Dousing the cloths with warm water and soap, I returned to Conrad and scrubbed his flesh until it was clean. The white cloths turned grayish red as I wiped down every inch of his skin. "I'll be back in a few minutes," Caroline announced, a foot from the door.

"I know all of this is a shock to the system. Are you okay?"

"Not really," she answered with a weak smile. "But I will be."

"Caroline?"

"Yeah?"

"Thanks for everything. I couldn't leave him there."

"I know. I wouldn't have either if I were you." Then she left, closing the door behind her. I adjusted the pillows under Conrad's head and covered him with a blanket. As I stroked his hair, he started to stir.

"Conrad, can you hear me?" He answered me with a wheezing moan. Hearing the dryness in his throat, I grabbed a bottle of water from one of the bags and propped his head against the frame of the bed. "Here, take a drink," I coaxed, tilting the bottle to pour a little water down his throat.

"More," he coughed, spiting some back out.

I held the bottle back to his lips, and this time, he drank a third of the bottle before I pulled it away. "Not too fast." My heart clenched with guilt as I stared at him. His flesh had been sliced open because of me, because of who I am. The tips of my fingers continued to comb through his hair, and finally, I sighed with relief as his eyes opened.

His gaze locked on my face. "You were supposed to leave me."

"There was no way I was going to leave you there. That thing would have killed you if I hadn't gone back!"

"That thing is a *dissimulo demon*, and you could've been killed trying to help me."

"A what?"

"Dissimulo demon. It's a higher-level demon. It can disguise itself to look like a normal person. It's the most dangerous because it can trick you into thinking it's an innocent."

"I don't care what it is," I countered. "Do you think I could've just left you there?"

"It doesn't matter because you *should* have left me there." He pushed himself up, adjusting the pillow behind his back. "Damn you, Evey. You're going to get yourself killed."

"And how do you think I'd feel if you died?"

"It doesn't matter."

"It does to me."

"You don't even understand how much more important you are than me."

"You're important to me. If you would die, do you think I could do this without you? Because I can tell you right now, I can't."

"Evey—"

"And you can yell at me all you want, but any time there's a situation like that, you can sure as hell count on the fact that I won't leave you," I replied defiantly.

"I don't understand why you won't listen," he muttered in exasperation.

"Because I feel like I'm waking up. It's as if I've been in a deep slumber for the past seventeen years, and you're the one who brought me back to life. Whether I'm falling in love with you again or simply remembering how I feel about you, I'm not sure. All I know is that for the last five centuries you've been my soul mate, and I'm not about to lose you now that we've found each other." I eased my arms around his neck, holding on to him tight.

"You don't have to worry about losing me because I'll always come back to you."

"Promise?"

"I promise." His hands trailed the length of my back and I sighed at the touch.

"You should probably get some rest," I suggested. "Are you hurting?"

"My leg stings a bit."

"The only medicine we have to help with your pain is Tylenol. Do you want some?"

"No, I'll be fine. The only real pain medicine we had in the Middle Ages was opium, and I never liked to take it," he replied. "I always preferred alcohol when I was injured."

"Well, Caroline and I are under age so we don't have that either."

"I promise I'm fine."

I nodded, still wishing I had something to offer to alleviate his pain. "Caroline went to get us some food. She'll be back in a bit. I'm going to take a shower while we wait."

I showered quickly, scrubbing the blood and filth from my flesh. After I dressed, there was a soft knock at the door. When I looked through the peephole, Caroline was standing outside with a couple bags of groceries.

"Oh my God," she said while staring at Conrad. "You're awake!"

"Yeah, thanks to the two of you."

"Oh, thank goodness. I thought for sure you were going to die in the car." She collapsed on the second bed and kicked her shoes off. "Evey was amazing though. She sewed up your leg and everything."

"I'm sure she was," he replied with a soft smile.

"Are y'all hungry?" I went through the food and took the perishable things to the fridge in the corner of the room.

"I'm starving," Caroline answered. I looked at Conrad and he nodded. I made each of us a ham and cheese sandwich and added a pile of chips to each plate. Handing one to Caroline, I carried Conrad's plate over to him. I waited for him to take a bite of his sandwich before digging into mine. The fear I experienced at the sight of his body covered in blood lay dormant in my bones. I needed to make sure he was okay before I could even attempt to relax. Much to my relief, he finished all of his food before I'd even eaten half my sandwich.

"You want some more?"

"If it's not too much trouble."

After I made him a second sandwich, we ate the rest of our meal in a silence. Even chewing seemed to take an enormous effort. The events of the night had drained all our energy, and I could already feel sleep beckoning. I cleaned up everyone's trash and straightened up the room while Caroline went to the bathroom. When I was done, I crawled into the second bed across from

Conrad. He reached for me and my hand clutched his, our fingers weaving together like ivy. The sound of the shower reminded me of rain, and my eyelids began to droop.

"Evey?"

"Yeah?"

"Thank you for saving my life."

I smiled at him, holding on to his hand with my remaining strength. "Anytime."

12

CONCEALED MESSAGES

We slept in until late in the afternoon the next day. Hearing me stir, Conrad pushed himself up in bed.

"How do you feel?" I asked, taking stock of his color, pleased to see that some of the pink had returned to his cheeks that were so pale the night before.

He examined the bandage covering his chest. "Actually, a lot better."

"Here, let me look at it." Standing in front of him, I pulled back the tape to inspect the gash. His skin was still raw, but it would heal within a matter of days. I applied some more antibiotic ointment and taped the gauze back to his chest. "Let me see your leg." He flinched slightly as I removed the dressing covering his wound. My stitches were holding up well, and I checked his skin closely, searching for any signs it might be infected. There was no obvious inflammation, and I couldn't help but be pleased with myself.

"You did a good job."

"To tell you the truth, I didn't really know what I was doing, but as soon as my hands touched the supplies, it was like I was functioning on autopilot."

"I'm not surprised. You've had to take care of all of us at one time or another."

"I took care of your mother and sister too," I added.

"You did." He brushed a strand of hair behind my ear as he spoke. "So, where are we exactly?"

"Murfreesboro. We're about fifty minutes outside of Estill Springs."

"Oh. We got the painting, right?"

After almost watching Conrad die, I'd forgotten about the painting. My eyes darted around the room in a panic until I finally spotted it on the table, still rolled up like a scroll. I retrieved the painting and opened it, spreading it on the bed between Conrad and me. Behind us, I could hear Caroline yawning.

"Good morning," she said, "What are y'all looking at?"

"The painting."

"Have you found anything yet?" The tone of her voice indicated she was excited and hopeful at the same time.

"Not yet," I replied, leaning close to examine the layers of oil paint. "He said it's in the field."

I could feel them on either side of me, hovering just below my shoulders. Conrad skimmed his hand over the surface, moving in a methodical manner as he tried to detect anything that might seem out of place.

"Nothing," he murmured. "You're sure this is the field he meant?"

"There isn't another one he could be talking about."

"Maybe a magnifying glass would help?"

"Actually, that's a good idea." I glanced at Conrad for his answer.

"It couldn't hurt."

"I can go get one really quick," Caroline suggested. "You know, because Conrad should rest his leg and you're the nurse."

"That's fine," I answered, returning my gaze to the little girl. I couldn't shake the feeling she would help unravel the mystery my father alluded to.

"I'll be back in a few."

"All right."

"I'll pick up some donuts for breakfast while I'm out, too. Either of you want coffee?"

"Please," I replied.

"Conrad?"

"Yeah, that sounds great," he answered.

"All right. Be back soon!"

"Since there isn't much we can do till she gets back, I think I'm going to take a shower," Conrad said, standing up from the bed. His leg was still weak, and it started to buckle as he put weight on it. Jumping up, I wrapped my arm around his waist to steady him.

"Are you okay?"

"Yeah. I'm just a little weaker than I thought."

"Is there something I can help you with?"

"I need to use the bathroom."

"Okay."

He grimaced with each step as we slowly made our way to the bathroom. "I can get it from here," he assured me.

"I'll be just outside if you need me."

I waited patiently by the door to make sure I was close by just in case he needed any help. Every now and then, another surge of anxiety would rip through my gut. If I hadn't gone back for Conrad last night, he'd be dead. The pain and despair I felt watching him die in my dreams was excruciating, and there was no way I was going to allow those nightmares to become our reality again.

The steady stream of the shower was audible from my perch. I was worried about Conrad moving around by himself, especially because he couldn't walk on his own, but then again, he did deserve some semblance of privacy. Just as I contemplated knocking on the door to ask if he needed anything, a loud thud sounded from the bathroom.

"Conrad!" I shouted, rushing inside.

He was sprawled across the bathtub, holding on to the shower curtain with all his strength. But the plastic was slick with water and his hands slid. He landed in the tub with another loud thump before I could even reach for him. "Son of a bitch," he muttered, the shower stream pelting him in the face.

The vast array of emotions I'd been experiencing over the last few days came to a head, and without warning, I burst into a fit of laughter. "I'm so sorry. I know it's not funny, but you look ridiculous." My hand covered my mouth in an attempt to hide my amusement as I knelt beside him and plugged the drain. Switching the showerhead off, I decided to draw him a bath instead.

"I look ridiculous?" He tugged on my arm, jerking me into the tub. Water splashed all around me, soaking my hair and nightgown.

Now, he was the one laughing. "Oh, you did not just do that!" My hands scooped up a handful of water and I flung it at his face. He returned my attack, and we quickly began splashing each other back and forth. "Thank you," I panted, still trying to catch my breath.

"For what?" He collapsed beside me, our childish battle finally at an end.

"Making me laugh." My fingertips traced the curve of his jaw as I stared at him. "It feels like I haven't laughed that hard in years."

"Happy my pain and personal humiliation could make you smile."

At his words, I smiled again. "Why did you come for me?"

"What do you mean?"

"If the Concilium told you to stay away from me, then why did you come back now?"

He paused for a moment before opening his mouth to speak. "I came because you told me to," he answered. "I had a dream about you, and you told me that you needed help, that you needed me. So, the next day I packed everything up and got in touch with your dad. He gave me your address and said he thought it would be a good idea for me to come."

"My dad wanted you in my life?"

He nodded, taking my hand in his. "Your dad said you were happy, but he could tell something was missing from your life. He said when I was gone, you never married, never even tried to date. You were always alone. He figured it was because we'd been separated."

"I missed you, even though I didn't know you. How can you miss someone you've never met?"

"You didn't. You missed someone you couldn't remember."

"Well," I whispered, leaning toward him. "I'm glad I have the chance to remember you now." I licked my lips, wanting nothing more than to experience the kiss we shared at the farmhouse all over again. His eyes studied me intently, watching as I inched closer. Our mouths were just a breath apart when my left hand rose from his chest to cup his face. Red smeared across his cheek, distracting me. "Oh my gosh!" Glancing at my hand, the tips of my fingers dripped with blood. The gash along his chest had reopened, saturating the bandage I'd applied. "You're bleeding again. I'm so sorry!"

"I'm fine, I promise." He pulled off both the dressings and settled back into the tub. "But could you help me get cleaned up a bit?"

"Of course." I stood up, grabbing a handful of towels. Spreading out a couple on the floor to soak up the mess we'd made, I used the rest to dry myself off. Then I turned around while Conrad removed his shorts and set a towel across his lap. When he was done, I sat on the edge of the tub.

"Thank you for this."

"You're welcome," I replied. "Lean back for a minute so I can clean your wound."

He consented and I washed his chest carefully, not wanting to hurt him.

"You've done this before. Do you remember it?"

"No, but will you tell me about it?"

"It was the night I returned from the hunt. I was covered in blood, mud, and who knows what else. I was disgusting." He laughed, and I could tell he was picturing everything that had taken place. "You stripped my clothes off and drew a hot bath for me right by the fireplace."

"Did I tend to your wounds as well?"

"Yeah," he answered. "Marie brought me some food, and you even helped feed me before we went to sleep in my bed. I even remember waking up with you still in my arms. It was the happiest and saddest moment of my life."

"How so?"

"Well, waking up and realizing I was holding you made me so happy, but at the same time, I knew it couldn't last because you were the queen and I was just one of your guards."

"Is that why you wanted to become one of my secundae?"

"It's one of the reasons."

"If you had to do it again, would you make the same choice?"

He grabbed my hand, gently pressing it to his lips. "Yes."

Once I'd finished cleaning up Conrad, I slipped out of the bathroom to change into a pair of jeans and a black tank top. When I returned to help him out of the tub, I averted my eyes while I helped him tug on a clean pair of shorts.

"I think I'm starting to bleed again," he said as we walked the short distance back to the bed.

"Here, I got it." I dried the blood from his chest and covered it with a fresh bandage before turning my attention to his leg. As I disinfected his wound, I could sense his gaze surveying the features of my face with a newfound intensity.

"Do you even realize how lovely you are?" I glanced away, tucking a loose strand of hair behind my ear. "I'm sorry," he continued. "I didn't mean to make you uncomfortable."

"You didn't make me uncomfortable, I promise."

"Then—"

"You have this vivid memory of me and all the lives we've spent together. I just don't want to disappoint you or be less than what you expect."

"I don't think there's any way you could disappoint me. My feelings for you haven't changed in the last five hundred years, and they never will. If there's anything I've learned from living all the different lives with you, it's that you're never what I expect. You're always more."

Moving to sit next to him, I slid close enough to rest my head on his shoulder. When his arm wrapped around my back, I actually sighed with contentment. The embrace felt natural and I couldn't help but wonder how many times we'd done it before. We stayed that way for a while, neither of us feeling the need to talk as we enjoyed one another's presence.

"We should probably look at the painting," I suggested.

"Probably."

While he took another look, I paced back and forth, analyzing every second of the last conversation I had with my father. It was in the field; a way to get in touch with the Concilium was in the field. The only problem was how on earth would I know what to look for? Was our means of communication a phone number, an address, an email? The possibilities were endless. Aden had sent souls and demons after me. None of us could really be sure what he was up to, but there was one thing we were sure of—he was after a consiliarius too. I couldn't fight the nagging feeling that I was missing something. "Come take another look," Conrad suggested, holding out his arm for me to sit beside him again.

I grabbed one end of the canvas and he took the other, helping me hold it. My eyes scanned the painting again, starting at the bottom before gradually moving upward. The soft, green grass spread in tufts around the girl, while her hair fell in golden curls much like a halo. On either side of her, red blossoms opened toward the sky. Nothing seemed out of place. There was no magic key to unlock the door we needed to get through so desperately.

I glanced up as Caroline walked inside.

"Hey," she said, handing me a box of donuts. She dropped her purse on the table and brought our coffee over to us.

"Thanks." I grabbed one with my free hand.

"Did you find anything while I was gone?"

"No, we just started searching again," Conrad answered, taking a swig of coffee.

I opened the box and handed him an almond bear claw. Taking one for myself, I focused on the picture as I ate.

"Here's the magnifying glass." She laid the heavy glass on the bed beside me.

I zoned in on the girl, convinced she would help me solve the puzzle. Her arms were folded underneath her head with a picnic basket lying next to her in the grass. A white and blue scarf was tied around the handle of the brown basket, the ends of it flying in the breeze like a flag. I scrutinized every blond curl of her hair and every eyelet in the lace on her dress, but my search was in vain. The answers I sought eluded me. I shook my head, tearing my gaze away from the girl and dropping the magnifying glass to the carpet in frustration. But I couldn't give up. This was too important. Closing my eyes, I tried to picture the girl in my mind.

"Is something wrong?" Conrad asked.

I shook my head, not daring to speak for fear it might interrupt my train of thought. I envisioned the girl again. Her white lace dress was delicate and pristine in the cradle of poppies. She appeared to be sleeping, her arms crossed into a makeshift pillow beneath her head. Then I realized what I was searching for. At first glance, the way she was holding her hand seemed careless and relaxed, but she was pointing ever so slightly to the basket at her side. My eyelids flung open and I scrambled for the magnifying glass at my feet. I held it up to the canvas. I was right; she was pointing, but just barely. I followed the trail from the tip of her finger and leaned closer to get a better view of what was inside the basket. A bouquet of red poppies rested inside, and next to them sat a glass jar filled with blackberries. I set the magnifying glass right over the lid of the jar. There was a sequence of numbers and letters circling its edge. I could barely make them out, even with the magnifying glass.

"I found it!" Conrad and Caroline stared at me intently. "I found something," I repeated.

"What is it?" Conrad bent low to the painting beside me.

"I think it's an address written on the lid of the jar. See? The girl is pointing at the basket," I said, showing Conrad. "I can't make out the numbers. Here, you try."

"Is there a pen and paper nearby? I'll call it out while one of you write it down." He held the painting close to the glass.

I grabbed a pen and paper from the table beside the bed. "What is it?"

"421 Chicago Avenue."

"Chicago Avenue," I repeated. "As in Chicago the city?"

"What else could it be?" Conrad looked up at me from the painting.

"I guess this means we're going to Chicago," Caroline said.

"It's the only lead we have," he agreed.

"Hey Conrad, I've been wondering, why aren't you in touch with the Concilium, especially since they're the ones who allow you to be reborn?" Caroline asked.

"The Concilium needed to be protected from Aden, so they went into hiding." He paused and then commented, more to himself than to us, "Not that they were ever really available unless *they* needed something. They aren't exactly the most social group of people."

"Oh," she replied. "Then how did Evey's dad have an address?"

"Because Evey is the primum, the Concilium wanted to be sure her secundae had a way of getting in touch with them in case something happened or they needed help."

"How does the Concilium know where to place Evey every time she's reborn, or when to have her reborn?"

"I suppose you could say they receive their instructions from a higher power."

"That's so weird," she muttered.

"I wonder what it's like to talk to God," I added.

"When you remember, you'll have to let us know," Conrad replied.

"I will," I said, glancing back at the girl in the painting. "I guess we should start packing. It's going to be a long drive to Chicago." Rolling up the painting, I set it inside my bag. Even if it was just a clue to get us in touch with a consiliarius, I was still going to keep it. It was a connection to my father, and the more connections I could hold on to, the better. I started to pack up some of the things around the room, but stopped suddenly. "Conrad, do you feel strong enough to travel?"

"I'll be fine. It's just a scratch."

"A scratch?" I asked.

"I've had worse."

"Don't remind me," I whispered.

"Evey and I can take turns driving," Caroline suggested. "That way you can rest."

"I guess we should leave as soon as possible then," he replied.

I3

COMEDERE COR

An hour later, we paid our motel bill and were en route to Chicago. The drive was going to take us about nine hours, and I could only pray the trip would lead us to the consiliarius. In a moment of cynicism, I wondered if we were on a wild goose chase, running all over the country trying to find some great treasure. Caroline offered to drive the first few hours, and I was to drive second. We made Conrad lie across the back seat so he could stretch out his leg.

"Are you comfortable?"

"About as comfortable as you can get in a car this size," he joked.

"How's your leg?"

He lifted his shorts to glance at the tape over his wound. "Surprisingly, still attached to my body."

"You're not as cute as you think you are," I spat.

"Just give it time, my lady," he replied, grinning.

"Smart-ass," I muttered under my breath.

"Now, children, don't make me turn this car around," Caroline mocked.

"As always, you did a wonderful job stitching my leg," Conrad added, reaching for my hand. "I'm in your debt." He pressed my hand to his lips, softly kissing my skin.

"No, you're not," I replied. "I've been in yours for the last five hundred years."

"Not at all. We've always been in yours."

"What do you mean?" I asked.

"When we meet other secundae or members of the Concilium, don't be surprised by how they treat you."

"Why would they treat me differently from everyone else?"

"We all try not to, but it's hard. You have an effect on us, so to speak," he answered. "You make us feel happier, more joyful."

"You make me sound like a drug."

"The best way to describe it is to compare you to light. You never realize how much you need it until you're submerged in darkness."

"I'll keep that in mind," I replied, repositioning myself in the passenger seat. I was their light? I wasn't quite sure what that meant, but it had to be the reason they needed me to counteract Aden's darkness. After an hour of staring at the road, I had to close my eyes for a minute. I hadn't intended to fall asleep, but the last thing I heard was Caroline singing along to the radio and I was out. She was supposed to wake me up at ten, but when I finally woke up, we were at a gas station somewhere in Illinois.

"I needed to use the bathroom, and I was going to see if you wanted anything," Caroline said as she reached through the open door to pull out some cash from her purse.

"It's almost midnight! You let me sleep too long!"

"I wasn't tired at all, so I decided to let you get some rest."

"Where's Conrad?"

"He went inside to get some snacks and use the restroom."

I got out of the car and stretched. My muscles were sore from being cramped up in such a small space for so long. "How far away from Chicago are we?"

"About two hours. It won't be too much longer."

I couldn't believe it. In two hours, I would hopefully be meeting a consiliarius. The thought was as daunting as it was exciting. The Concilium knew me, or at least were familiar with me, but I had no recollection of ever meeting even one of them. I began to wonder what they were like, but instantly regretted it. What if they refused to help us or expected me to face Aden alone? I didn't think I could bear the thought of seeking their advice only to be rejected by them. I clutched my necklace. When Conrad first put it on me, I found myself holding it in my hand because I wasn't used to the weight of the pendant, but now I found the feel of it to be reassuring. It was just another tangible link to my past and everything happening around me.

"I'll drive the rest of the way," I said to Caroline, climbing into the driver's seat.

"Thanks." She took a drink from her steaming cup of coffee. "I was starting to get sore."

"The two of you should take a nap while I drive, and when we get there, I'll wake you up."

"I can drive," Conrad said from the back seat. "If you don't want to, I'll do it."

"You still need to rest, and I don't mind driving at all." I pulled up Google Maps on my cell phone and double-checked the location before turning out of the gas station parking lot. "Do you know each consiliarius?"

"Yes," he answered with a yawn. "Some of them I know better than others, but I've had contact with all of them at some point in time."

"They know who we are, right? And they'll have to help us?"

"Of course they know who you are, and I would think they would be most interested in putting a stop to whatever Aden is up to. He's just as much of a threat to them as he is to you."

"I just hope by working together, we can figure out what he wants."

"Me too," he said.

Switching the radio to the oldies station, I sang along to the

Temptations as I drove down the interstate. I drove a little faster than normal, but it was well after midnight and there wasn't much traffic. According to the directions on my phone, we should be at our destination in forty minutes. My stomach twisted up in knots as I tapped the gas pedal. With every passing second, we grew closer to the consiliarius and to answers. Miles of interstate disappeared into the night sky as we continued on our mission. A few days ago, I thought I was just a regular teenage girl. Now, I knew most of my past was written in the pages of the history books I used to study so intently. Unable to stop myself, I stole a glance at Conrad, still sleeping on the back seat. He had loved, protected, and saved me for centuries. I just wished I could remember more of the years we spent together. I knew it would all come back to me with time, but I didn't want to wait. Allowing my mind to wander, all I could think about was my rooftop dance with Conrad. My thoughts were so distracting, it only seemed like a few minutes elapsed before I parked the car in front of 421 Chicago Avenue.

"Hey! Wake up!"

"What's going on?" Caroline rubbed sleep from her eyes.

"We're here."

"And where exactly is here?" Conrad's voice sounded from behind me.

"I really don't know," I said as I peered up at a building. It was four stories high with modern style architecture. Large windows covered the upper floors, and a formidable door stood in front of us. It was gray, matching the color of the building. "It kind of reminds me of an apartment building or something."

We filed out of the car one by one. Grabbing my messenger bag, I slid the strap over my head, hoping the touch of something familiar would provide me with some sort of reassurance.

"I guess there's only one way to find out if we came to the right place," Conrad said, pressing the buzzer. Nothing in the building seemed to stir. He pressed it again, this time holding it down longer. "That should wake somebody up."

I nodded my head in agreement and checked the time on my phone. It was 2:00 a.m., and it felt like we were the only people in the whole city still awake. The buzzer suddenly sounded and a voice came over the intercom, startling us.

"Who do you think you are that you feel the need to disturb my house at this hour?" The voice was harsh and demanding.

"I'm a brother of the secundae, and I came to this house with the hope I might be welcome." Conrad's voice was direct and unfaltering. It made me glad he was the one doing the talking, because I knew my voice would be shaking as bad as my body was.

"I see," the voice replied. The voice belonged to a man, but I was having a hard time placing the accent. "Is it a matter for the Concilium?"

"Yes, I have the female primum with me."

The voice didn't reply, but instead the buzzer sounded one more time. The door unlocked, and Conrad pressed it open as he glanced back at Caroline and me. He gestured for us to follow him upstairs, and I grabbed Caroline's hand to steady myself. She squeezed my hand, and my heart slowed its pace at her encouragement. As we stepped inside, the door slammed shut behind us, making us jump. We glanced around the empty entryway, noting that the modern decor from the building's exterior continued inside. The floor was made of shiny black tile that reflected our images like a giant mirror. Deep plum paint covered the walls while a large staircase dominated the left side of the room. On the right was a long metal table with a red bowl in the center. A single white orchid bloomed from the bowl. It reminded me of the still-life scenes my art teacher used to set up for our class to draw.

"Let's go upstairs," Conrad ordered.

The three of us climbed the staircase. I was afraid Conrad would have a hard time walking upstairs, but he stepped gracefully, as if he wasn't injured at all. I shook my head at his ridiculous tolerance for pain. At the top of the stairs, we faced an imposing door. As Conrad reached out to knock, it flung open to reveal a tall, slender girl. She looked the same age as Caroline and me, although she was a few inches taller. Her black hair was cut into a trendy bob, and she wore a low-cut black shirt and tight red pants. I barely had enough time to take in her appearance before she called out Conrad's name.

"Conrad!" She flung her arms around his neck, knocking him back a few steps. "It's been decades!" she exclaimed with a tight hug. He gave her a quick pat on the back before she broke away from him.

"It's good to see you too," he replied. "This is Helen Megaera."

"Ah, I see Eve is with you, but who else have you brought?"

"Hi, I'm Caroline. I'm a friend of Evey."

Her brown eyes narrowed as she scrutinized my face. I smiled at her uncomfortably, hoping she would stare at anything but me. "Well, any friend of a primum is a friend of mine," she answered in a voice that was almost too sweet. "Please come in." She stepped back, allowing us to enter. I sucked in a deep breath as we crossed the threshold. The room we entered was as grand as the foyer beneath us. It housed a large sitting area on one side and a library on the other. The entire left wall of the room was covered in bookshelves containing hundreds of books. Helen ushered us to the right. Caroline and I sat down together on a white couch while Conrad seated himself in the chair beside us.

"I assume you're here to see Noah?"

"Yeah, we're sorry to wake all of you up, but it's urgent," Conrad answered.

"It's no problem. I'll go upstairs and get him." I watched her walk to another staircase. A sacramentum was tattooed upon her skin. The same tree marking Conrad's back covered hers as well. Although, as I studied her mark, I noticed it wasn't an exact copy of Conrad's. While the branches on his tree were dense and full of leaves, Helen's appeared to be sparse. Once she was out of earshot, I turned to Conrad and quietly noted my observation.

"Helen is a secundae of a consiliarius. I've known her for years. I used to serve as one of Noah's secundae when I was banned from being yours."

"Oh." It was the only reply I could manage, and the room fell silent.

"Being a consiliarius must have its perks. This place is huge!" Caroline interjected.

"Yeah, it's pretty nice," Conrad agreed with a slight laugh.

I gave her hand a little squeeze; you could always count on Caroline to break an awkward silence. Before either of them could speak again, we heard the sound of feet descending the staircase. To my surprise, it was a young man who appeared to be in his early twenties. He was as tall as Conrad but not quite as muscular. He wore a black button-up shirt and gray slacks. The dark color of his shirt brought out a vividness in his light green eyes.

"It's good to see you again, Conrad," he stated, walking in front of the couch to shake Conrad's hand.

"You too, Noah. It's certainly been a long time."

"That it has," Noah replied, smiling. His hair was bright blond and styled to perfection. "I see we have Miss Eve here with us." He took my hand in his, bowing before me. I returned his gesture with a slight smile. "And you are a friend of Eve?" His gaze fixed on Caroline, taking in her shocked expression.

"Um, yes," she said after she composed herself. "My name is Caroline."

"It's very nice to meet you." He seated himself in a chair opposite the couch. Helen and a short man with dark brown hair and exotically shaped eyes came and stood to the right of the couch. I had no idea where or when he was born, my first guess would be Egypt and a long time ago. "I believe you already know Helen, but this is Milton. He's also one of my secundae." Milton gave Caroline and Conrad a curt nod as he moved to stand in front of me. His eyes were the same caramel color of his skin, and his neck was as thick as his arms, which left me with no doubts about his ability as a fighter.

"I'm happy to see you again," Milton said, kissing my hand.

Somewhat stunned by his gesture, I blurted out the first thing I could think of.

"I'm happy to see you again too," I replied. He smiled at me once more before occupying the chair next to Helen.

"I'm sorry, but you're a consiliarius?" Out of the corner of my eye, I could see Caroline's gaze was fixed on Noah.

"Not what you expected?" he asked her.

"What I expected was a plump, balding man in a brown monk's robe, not an underwear model."

"Well, I'm sorry to disappoint you," he replied with a laugh.

Looking bored with the conversation, Helen jumped in, "Anyway, why have the three of you come here?" Her voice was sharp and to the point.

"Evey was attacked by a group of souls. They killed the Fultons and Guy. Marie was taken by Aden."

I could tell by the expression on Noah's face that this was not what he was expecting to hear. "How did he find her?"

"I don't know. Guy left us with a clue of how to get in touch with a consiliarius. He hid it in a painting at his and Marie's auction house. When we went to retrieve the painting, we were attacked by more souls and a dissimulo. We knew we had to warn you, so we came here as soon as we were able to figure out the clue in the painting."

"I wondered when he would surface again," Noah said, rubbing his chin. "It's quite concerning he's having souls do his bidding—it's not a good sign."

"I think the dissimulo concerns me even more," Conrad added. "Do you think he's trying to wield the *servi satanam*?"

"If he is, we're all in trouble," Noah replied. "But that's only two of the six. If we see all six of the servi, then we know Aden is making deals with the devil."

"What is the servi satanam?" I asked.

"The servi satanam refers to the six types of minions Satan rules over in hell. Five of them are different types of demons and the sixth is tortured souls," Noah answered, turning to face me.

"Do you have any idea what he might be up to?" My voice was so soft that, for a second, I thought he hadn't heard me.

"We know he's after you and members of the Concilium. The powers of the consiliarius he killed must be running out. He's getting desperate again. There's a ritual he could perform to bind the powers of a consiliarius to him, but I don't see how he could know about that. I thought only members of the Concilium knew about it." He directed his attention to Helen. "Helen, would you notify the *Caput* and his secundae about this? I want to make sure everyone knows what's going on."

"Of course." She left with Milton trailing behind her.

"Eve, do you have full possession of all your memories?"

"I prefer to be called Evey, and no. I'm able to remember bits and pieces, but that's about it. What ritual were you talking about?"

"It's called the *Comedere Cor.* It roughly translates to the eating of a heart. Basically, Aden has to cut out the heart of a consiliarius and combine it with the heart of the first sin he committed. Then he has to consume the heart at the Tree of Knowledge of Good and Evil in the Garden of Eden."

"So he needs to eat my heart and the heart of a consiliarius?"

"Not your heart; the heart of the apple." He paused for a moment, before continuing. "Specifically, the seeds of the apple."

"But that's good news, right?" Caroline looked between everyone, waiting for her question to be confirmed. "I mean, those seeds have to be long gone by now."

"Actually, Evey used to carry the seeds around with her," Conrad replied.

"What?" I could hear the panic in my voice as I spoke. "I kept the seeds?"

"Yes."

"But why?"

"You showed me the seeds when I was one of your personal guards in 1476. You explained to me where the seeds came from, and you told me you liked to keep them with you. You said you kept the seeds as a reminder of the penance you owed to God. You had them with you at all times, always hiding them somewhere safe so you could find them again when you were reborn."

"So, Aden thinks I have the seeds or know where to find them, and that's why he's after me?"

"Do you know where the seeds are?"

"I don't," I confessed. "Is there a way for you to give me back my memories?"

"Nothing that would work the way we need it to," Noah answered. "The best thing for you to do would be to just let the memories come back with time."

"The problem is," Conrad started, "I'm not sure how much time we have."

"As long as you're here, you'll be safe. I think it would do us good to see the head of the Concilium. He knows more about the ritual than I do, and he may be able to tell us a way to help Evey's memories come back faster."

"Where is the head of the Concilium?" I asked.

"He's in New York right now, but he moves around every so often."

"We'll be going to New York then?"

"Yeah, but it'll be a day or two. I'm going to arrange for us to take a private plane. It's much safer than driving there, especially since Aden was able to find you before."

"There's one thing I don't understand," Caroline piped up.

"What's that?" Noah fixed his attention on her again.

"If the consiliarius are supposed to be immortal, then how was Aden able to kill one of you?"

"We're immortal in the sense that we don't age or die of sickness; however, we can be murdered."

"Oh."

"No one can be completely immune to everything. If anyone were, it would disrupt the natural order of things," Noah replied, rising from the chair. "All of you must be exhausted. Follow me and I'll show you to your rooms."

"We still have bags in my car," Conrad said.

"I'll send Milton to retrieve your things for you and bring them to your rooms."

"Thank you. I appreciate it," he replied.

We trailed behind Noah as he led us upstairs. "This floor houses the kitchen and dining room, and the one above it is where all the bedrooms are." When we reached the top landing, we veered left down a long hallway. Noah walked forward, coming to a stop at the first door on the right. "Caroline, you can take this room, and Evey and Conrad, yours is the one right beside it. Helen and Milton are in the last two rooms on the left and mine is the last on the right if you should need anything. Is there anything else I can get you?"

"Umm," I began, unsure how to continue my train of thought. Were Conrad and I supposed to sleep in the same bed and change our clothes in front of one another? Sure, we'd been married numerous times, but it wasn't as if I could remember every moment we shared.

"Actually, I think Evey would be more comfortable in her own room," Conrad stated.

Noah's eyes widened for a brief moment before he responded. "Of course. Conrad, you can stay in the first room on the left then."

I sighed a breath of relief. I had no idea how I was supposed to act around Conrad, especially behind closed doors. "Thank you so much for your hospitality," I said.

"It's my pleasure. Good night." He inclined his head to each of us before walking down the hall to his room. I couldn't help but notice his eyes lingering on Caroline longer than Conrad and me.

"I'll see the two of you in the morning," Caroline added, disappearing into her room.

An awkward silence developed between Conrad and me. "How's your leg?"

"It's fine."

"When Milton brings our bags, I'll come to your room and put a new dressing on it."

"Sounds like a plan," he replied, opening the door to his room.

The walls of my room were painted a deep gold, and a giant painting hung on the wall behind the bed. It looked like a Degas. It depicted a ballet studio with young ballerinas lining up to dance. The soft smudging of colors was characteristic of Degas's work. Considering the state of everything in the apartment, I figured it was real. Noah didn't seem like the type to own reproductions. When I ventured through a door on the right, I discovered a large bathroom with generous counters, double sinks, and a deep clawfoot tub. On the other side of the bathroom was a door. As I opened it, I found myself face-to-face with Caroline.

"Hey!"

"It's like we're roommates," she said, looking at everything in her room. Her room was furnished the same as mine, but the walls were painted a royal blue. Instead of ballerinas, a large gold map of the world hung above her bed. It appeared to be museum quality, and the encasing frame was definitely expensive. "Look at this bathroom," she gasped. "This is bigger than my bedroom at home!"

"I know. It's so huge!"

"Gosh, your room is beautiful, too!"

"I can't believe you hit on a consiliarius."

"I'm sorry, but I had this image of a fat old guy locked in my mind. Besides, you weren't expecting him to look like that either!"

"I know! Maybe there's a requirement that all secundae and members of the Concilium have to be ridiculously attractive. I mean, Helen is gorgeous too."

She rolled her eyes. "You say that like you aren't."

"Your opinion doesn't count, you're biased," I countered. "Speaking of Helen, what do you think of her? She was almost salivating at the sight of Conrad, and she was staring daggers at me."

"Well, when you think about it, you've been alive for thousands of years; I'd say it'd be impossible not to step on a few toes along the way."

"You don't think I stole Conrad from her, do you?"

"After everything I've learned in the past forty-eight hours, nothing seems outside the realm of possibility to me."

"Queen, reincarnated biblical character, adulterous home-wrecker, and the list keeps growing!"

"Don't let her get under your skin! She seems like a total bitch anyway."

"Thanks for saying that."

"It's like I always say, we're best friends because we hate all the same people."

"You know, that's got to be the reason," I agreed, laughing.

"Besides, you heard what Conrad said about her. He was one of Noah's secundae, and they worked together. That's all that was."

"I know. I guess I was just a little jealous about the way she hugged him."

"Does that mean you and Conrad are an item?" she asked. "I know you're married or were married, but things seem to be heating up."

"I think so," I answered with a shrug. "I'm pretty sure he still loves me, and he's waiting for me to fall in love with him again. Whatever's happening, it's complicated."

"Ooh, I love complicated!"

"Me too, and the tension between us is getting unbearable!" I cried, collapsing on my bed. "And now I sound like an angsty teen."

"You're not angsty, and I don't blame you for being jealous."

"Thanks. Besides, who dresses like that at two in the morning?"

"Hookers."

"Caroline!"

"What? Am I rude, or am I honest?"

"Honest," I answered. "I'm glad you're here."

"Me too," she agreed, yawning. "Well, I'm off to bed. I'll see you in the morning, roomie."

A soft knock came at my door. Milton handed me my bag, grinning from ear to ear.

"Oh, thank you, Milton."

"As always, it's my pleasure," he replied with a bow. Then he turned and headed to his bedroom.

Across the hall, voices sounded from Conrad's room. I waited until Milton had disappeared before creeping over to the door to listen. The voices belonged to Conrad and Helen. From the sound of hers, I could tell she was upset.

"If the Concilium forbade you from seeing her, then why are you with her right now?"

"Because I couldn't stay away from her, and I don't want to," he spat, raising his voice. "And Noah didn't seem too concerned with the fact that I disobeyed the orders of the Concilium."

"That's because Noah isn't like the rest of the Concilium. He's much more lenient than the others, especially the caput."

"I'm well aware Everest isn't fond of me."

"Isn't fond of?" she questioned. "He told you if you ever disobeyed the Concilium again, he wouldn't allow you to be one of Eve's secundae anymore. Do you know what that means?"

"Of course I do. I'm not an idiot."

"As soon as we go meet Everest, he'll see what you've done. This will be your last life!"

My heart stopped for a second. Had Conrad already set himself on a course to make the ultimate sacrifice for me again?

"I knew the risk I was taking when I went to find Evey."

"You'll never be reborn again!" she screamed. "And you're acting like you couldn't care less."

"The only thing I care about is protecting Evey," he replied. "I'll do whatever it takes to keep her safe, even if it means dying permanently."

"And there you go again, jumping into battle without thinking of the consequences. You never stop to consider the effect your actions have on the rest of us."

"That isn't true," he replied.

"Everest won't forgive you, even if you ignored his orders for a good cause."

Conrad countered, "After all the attacks, does it really matter? Aden would have Evey right now if I hadn't gone back for her."

"The only person who wants to see you dead more than Everest is Aden."

"You're not telling me anything I don't already know."

"Whatever happens, you're screwed! If we win and defeat Aden, Everest will see to it that you're pulled from this life, never to come back again. And Aden . . . We all know how he feels about you. He'll rip your skin off for fun and make her watch while he does it," she replied. "And don't try to put on that reigning hero routine in front of me; I know you hurt your leg pretty bad. You're limping on it."

"I'm not scared of Aden. And my leg is fine. It's just a cut."

"You should be. We all should," she said. "She's his and he wants her back for himself. In his own sick and twisted way, he's still in love with her. He'll stop at nothing to get what he wants. Shouldn't you know that better than anyone?"

"I won't let him have her. She isn't his property!" I could hear him slam something down on a table in the room.

"All I'm saying is it was a good idea to separate the two of you from each other, because you would risk anything to save her, even the safety of the Concilium. And if Aden ever possesses the true powers of a consiliarius, he could play God."

"Evey is at the center of all this. She's the only one who can stop him, and you know it. Besides, why are you so concerned with what happens to me anyway?"

"Because I care about you. She wasn't the only one who lost you," she replied, the tone of her voice softening. "The way I feel about you hasn't changed. You might know that if you would've kept in touch over the years." There was a pause in their conversation, and Helen was the first to break the silence. "I'm sure you're tired so I'll let you get some rest." Dashing back to my room, I left the tiniest crack in the door so I could watch.

"Good night," Conrad said, standing in the doorway of his room.

"Good night." She kissed him on the cheek before leaving.

I ran a hot shower in the hopes it would distract me, but as I stood there, I couldn't keep myself from replaying their conversation over and over in my head. I was right about one thing: I wasn't one of her favorite people. Helen possessed a certain type of disposition. Even though I'd only known her for an hour or two, I could tell she was strong-willed, ruthless, and blunt. However, her voice was so soft when she talked to Conrad, tender even. It wasn't hard to figure out she was in love with him, and I wasn't exactly sure how I felt about that. She held me accountable for Conrad's death and his current situation as well. He came to Estill Springs with the knowledge that doing so would cost him his role as a secundae. The sacrifices he had made for me were so much more than I deserved.

I'd just thrown on a nightgown and burrowed under the covers when there was a knock at the door.

"Evey?" Conrad whispered my name as he opened up the door. "Can I come in?"

"Sure, I just got in bed."

"I thought you wanted to look at my leg again."

"Oh, I'm sorry, I forgot," I muttered, throwing off my blankets. "Why don't you sit down and I'll do that right now."

I pulled at the tape around his dressings delicately, trying not to hurt him. Easing the gauze from the wound on his chest, I dabbed on a little peroxide to clean it. The cut still looked raw, but it was starting to heal. A wave of relief rushed over my body.

"Are you mad at me or something?" I could tell he was studying my face as I applied a fresh layer of ointment and gauze to his cut.

"No, why would you think that?"

"I don't know. You've been really quiet since we got here."

"I guess I'm still feeling a little overwhelmed by everything and everyone. It's a lot to take in."

"That's true." He flinched as I cleaned his leg. "It's a little tender."

"Sorry," I said, gently putting ointment over the stitches and covering them with a clean bandage. "I want to thank you for everything you've done for me. You almost died when we were trying to get the painting. I hate I'm the reason you were injured." My voice quivered as I spoke, and I tried with all my might to regain my composure.

"It's not your fault all this happened. You can't control what Aden does."

"I know, but the sacrifices you've made and the ones you're still making on my account—" I began, pausing so I could catch my breath. "It's too much." A lone tear slid down my cheek.

"There's a lot more to it than that, and it wasn't your fault. Like I said, Aden is crazy. You can't hold yourself responsible for his actions." He reached for me before I could step away from him.

"What's the point in being with someone who you have to give up your own life in order to protect?"

"I'm not sacrificing my life."

"Really? Because Helen's convinced Everest will revoke your role as one of my secundae in a heartbeat." As soon as I said it, I regretted it. I didn't want him to know I'd listened to his conversation with her.

"You heard us?"

"Well, the two of you weren't exactly being quiet."

"What she thinks doesn't matter," he said.

"Really? Because I'm not so sure that's what you believe."

"Why are you saying this?"

"Why didn't you tell me if the Concilium find out you disobeyed their orders, they'll prevent you from being reborn again?"

He backed away from me. In the dark, I could tell he was glaring at me through the shadows in the room. "What happens to me doesn't matter. I'm just a secundae."

"It matters to me!" I raised my voice to match his, returning his glare. "You never being allowed to live again matters to me. And don't even think what Aden did to you was nothing, because it tears me apart to know I'm the reason you were executed."

"Things were different in the fifteenth century. Kings could do as they pleased, even if it meant executing innocent people. Living back then wasn't like it is today."

"He killed you because he knew it would hurt me. You were just a pawn in his game," I spat.

"I was punished for my transgressions against him," he shouted.

"What are you talking about?"

"You were a queen, Evey; you were his wife. In that time, I should never have been with you, let alone loved you."

I shook my head. "No, you did nothing wrong. You didn't deserve to die just because you loved me."

"It wasn't just that I loved you; you loved me too. I made love to you in the bed he gave you as a wedding present, for God's sake. What man wouldn't want to kill his wife's lover?"

"We what?"

"I'm sorry this is getting sprung on you so fast. I can't imagine what it's like to lose your memories," he said, placing his hand on the small of my back and leading me to the bed. "It's been an eventful day. You should get some rest."

"How can I rest knowing this is the last chance I'll have to know you?" I asked miserably.

"I'd rather spend my final lifetime with you than have to keep my distance for forever."

"Conrad—"

"I'll try not to dump so much information on you all at once again. I'm sure there are a lot of things you might not want to remember."

I set my hand on his chest. "I want to remember you."

"Conrad," Noah's voice called from the hall.

"You've got to be kidding," Conrad spat, letting the anger rise in his voice.

"Maybe he'll go away if you don't answer," I suggested.

"Conrad, I know you're in there. I need to talk to you," Noah said.

"Try to get some sleep. I'll see you in the morning."

"Good night," I replied as I watched him leave my room.

14

THE KING'S AMUSEMENT

As I slept, my subconscious revisited memories I both did and didn't want to see. It was as if my body wanted me to know what the Concilium tried to steal away from me, and it fought for my memories of the man I wanted so desperately to remember.

I sat reading at a wooden table in my room. Its spindled legs shone with a coat of fresh polish. A knock at the door seemed to reverberate off the stone walls, drawing my focus away from my book.

"Come in," I said, closing my book and rising from my high-back chair to face the door. A smile spread across my face as Conrad entered my bedroom.

"You wanted to see me, my lady?"

"Yes. I wanted to ask if you would care to accompany me on a walk?"

"It would be my pleasure," he answered with a slight bow.

"You know, you don't have to bow in my presence."

"Yes, I do. You are the queen of Spain, and I'm a simple guard. Actually, I should kneel in your presence, not just bow."

I reached out to take his hand in mine, gently stroking the tops of his knuckles with my fingers. "You're so much more than just a guard to me."

"It's hard to believe you could love someone like me."

"You're right: kind, devoted, tender . . . " I said, caressing his face. "Who could love someone like that?"

"I'm being serious, and yet you insist on teasing me."

"If you don't believe the words that come from my mouth, perhaps the kisses that come from it will convince you instead."

He lessened the distance between us and cradled my face in his hands. His searing blue eyes ignited with an intense passion. The kiss we shared sent a jolt throughout my entire body, stealing my breath away.

"Your kisses seem to be more persuasive than your words," he replied, smiling. "Now, how about that walk?"

He followed me from my room as we made our way out of the castle. We walked side by side to the far end of the grounds. I gathered the train of my dress, bunching it up in my hand so I could walk. The sun was bright above us, casting our shadows over the ground. When we were hidden from sight by the rows of apple trees, he took my hand in his.

"The king met with me the other day," he said, breaking the silence.

"What did he want?" My hand tightened around his as if I expected something to tear him away from me.

"He asked me to join his council. He knows you favor me above all your other guards and says the devotion I show in my duties would be better served if I were to become one of his advisors."

"What was your reply?"

"I told him I would need some time to think about it. I asked him what you thought about his suggestion."

"He never mentioned it to me," I replied nervously.

His arms wrapped around me. "He probably just forgot. It was a few days ago."

"I don't want you to leave me."

"Don't worry, I'm not going to accept his offer. He wants me to sit in on a meeting today, but after that, I'll tell him I'm not interested. Besides, I'd much rather spend my days watching after you."

"I'm sorry I can't give you the things you want," I said, feeling a tear meander down my cheek.

"What do you mean?"

"I'm not free to marry you, give you children, or grow old with you. You have to resort to sneaking away in the shadows to spend time with me."

"I don't care, just being around you is enough for me."

"But it shouldn't be." His calloused hands dabbed at my tears. "I would leave everything to be with you. We could run off together and start a new life."

"He would search for you," he replied. "He loves you more than anything. Trust me, I can see it in his eyes. He wouldn't let you go without a fight."

"I don't belong to him, I belong to you." I threw my arms around his neck and began kissing him all over his face. "Take me away from here," I begged him.

"I want to so badly, but I can't leave Cecily and my mother. They would have no one to take care of them, and the king would throw them out of the castle."

"They could come with us," I stated hopefully. But as soon as I uttered the words, I knew it wouldn't be feasible. His mother had been in bad health for quite some time. I stopped by as often as I could to care for her, but she had never regained all her strength after the fever. She would never be able to survive traveling a long distance.

His lips met mine once more. "I'm sorry."

"Don't be. You love your family, and I love them too. I couldn't ask you to choose me over them, and you wouldn't be the man I loved if you abandoned your family."

"I love you," he whispered.

"I love you too." I rubbed my fingers over his lips, barely touching their smooth surface. My other hand took his and pressed it against the ruby pendant hanging from my neck. He swept me up in his arms, set me underneath the shade of an apple tree, and joined our mouths with such force I couldn't tell where mine ended and his began. The scenery around us melted away as we held one another. Something in my life had always been missing until I met Conrad. He filled the void in my heart, which had eaten at my soul for hundreds of years. He was the one thing in my life I wanted to keep with me forever. A loud sound drew me from his lips. "Did you hear that?" I glanced all around us.

"What is it?"

"I don't know. I thought I heard footsteps."

Conrad tried to hide the concern that washed over his face at my description. "Let's get you back to the castle before they start forming a search party for you."

As we walked back, we were met by one of Adam's guards. Donovan was Adam's lone secundae. He wore a menacing scowl and a grisly scar carved through the flesh of the bottom half of his face. He served Adam with a cruel hand, and Adam rewarded him for it.

"The king's council is meeting soon. He would like you to join him in the hall in half an hour," he said, barking the order at Conrad. "And the king would like you to meet with him in his chambers," he added, focusing his glare on me. "There are a few matters he needs to discuss with you."

I nodded. "Conrad, I thank you for your company on my walk. I shall speak with you later this evening." He bowed his head slightly before leaving with Donovan.

"You don't have to do this," Marie's voice trembled as she layered another gold necklace around my neck.

"You know I do. If I don't, Adam will hurt him, and I can't stand the thought of causing Conrad pain."

"Adam wants you to be humiliated."

"I don't care. Adam can do what he wants with me, but I won't let him hurt the people I love." My lips touched her forehead. My hand brushed the side of her face as I looked into her soft green eyes. "I'll be fine," I said in a soothing voice.

"You're the queen. You are a primum. He can't treat you like this."

"Apparently, he can," I replied. "I hope you know I would do the same for either of you. Both of you have risked so much on my account. I don't know if the debt can be repaid, but I'll try."

"It is our duty to protect you. We can't stand by and allow this to happen," Kit said, brushing my long hair down my back.

"Yes, you can. This is about me, no one else." I stared at my reflection in the mirror as they finished dressing me. "Come and stand in front of me." At my request, both women circled around to stand before me. "Something more than duty or obligation binds the five of us together. You may have been made into secundae to protect me, but we're a family. We all must look out for each other." I kissed their foreheads before turning back to the mirror. "Am I ready?" I asked the question with a magnitude of confidence I certainly did not feel.

"Yes," Kit replied.

I looked in the mirror again. My hair hung in loose waves, flowing beneath the gilded crown circling my head. Long layered necklaces of gold hung over my chest, barely covering my body. The only thing that felt like it belonged on me was the ruby pendant I clasped in my hand. I was naked except for the strips of metal dangling from my neck and the skirt at my waist. My legs showed through the slits in the sheer material that was almost as white as my fair skin. I was dressed as a prostitute, my body serving as proof to expose me for what I am, and according to my husband, I was a whore. I was to enter Adam's council meeting, and he was to make an example of me. Everyone's eyes were to gaze upon the naked body of his queen, while he defiled me with his words. He wanted to demonstrate his power over me. If I didn't go through with it, he would kill the man I loved. He wanted me to understand one thing: I was his property from the moment I came into this world until the moment he decides I can leave it.

Marie and Kit followed me to the hall, draping a cloak over my shoulders in an attempt to prevent my body from being seen. I appreciated their efforts, but it made no difference to me; I would do anything to keep Adam from hurting Conrad. I didn't care if I had to walk naked through the streets of the city, as long as it would keep him safe.

"I'll be fine," I assured the two of them as they removed the cloak from my body. I stood in front of the oak double doors that led into the meeting hall. Their hands each grasped one of the brass handles on the doors, jerking them open. I took a deep breath and crossed the threshold into the hall just as Adam's voice announced my arrival.

"For anyone who dares to think of betraying me or stealing what is rightfully mine, they would do well to remember that I will inflict twice as much pain as they sought to bestow upon me." Adam's voice bellowed around the room, bouncing off the high archways overhead. It was a warning for what was to come. The men of his council were seated at a long mahogany table with Adam at its center. His black hair hung in curls around his face, and his eyes were such a deep brown, the irises almost blended with his pupils. The dark color of his hair and eyes were a stark contrast to his pale skin. He had the same fair complexion I did, but where my cheeks were rosy, his were sallow. Despite his gaunt appearance, it was easy to see that at one point in time he had been quite handsome. Donovan was seated to his left, wearing a sneer that curdled my skin. The scar trailing from the end of his nose all the way past his chin looked painful, even though it had been healed for years. I knew how sharp a knife had to be to make such a cut, and the thought set my teeth on edge. My head rose above their eye level, and my hands clutched the fabric of my skirt as I stepped before them.

"Esteemed members of my council, it has come to my attention some of you have sought after the pleasures of my unfaithful wife's flesh." The hatred in his eyes burned like a roaring flame. I turned my gaze to meet his, refusing to break my stare first. At the very least, I wanted him to know he didn't frighten me. "Bourdet," he growled. "Is what I say not the truth?" My eyes followed Adam's as he focused his sights on Conrad. Conrad was seated in the last chair on the right side of the table. He looked as if he was going to be sick. However, the shock of what Adam said didn't last. Within an instant, Conrad's expression changed. He was infuriated.

"The only truth in your claim is that I love a woman who is no longer in love with you." His gaze locked onto mine. There were so many things I wanted to say in that moment. I tried to force my feelings into the look I returned, but how could I ever atone for what was happening right now? Rage seethed from Adam as his hands turned white from gripping the edges of the table with such force.

"I think it's a sin for us to bicker like this when faced with such beauty," Adam hissed. His voice was subtly smooth, all of the previous vehemence fading away. The tone sent chills down my spine. I could handle his rage, but this air of calm deception sickened me. His attention was on me as he surveyed my naked body beneath the adornments I wore.

"My love, if you would be so kind as to show us what you have to offer." I said nothing, but I held my arms out with my elbows tucked toward my waist. It looked as if I were poised to carry a gift in either hand, bringing my offering to the beast that lay in front of me. The chains around my neck shifted as I moved around the table, revealing bits of my flesh to their lustful eyes. Only one pair of eyes had my permission to gaze at my body, and those were the blue ones across from me.

"It's not hard to guess the nature of the thoughts in everyone's mind right now, but I ask you all to remember one thing: she belongs to me. I am her king; I rule over her body, taking it for myself as I so choose," Adam said.

I walked past each man, glaring at them with iron resilience. They could look at me, have my body as food for their insatiable thoughts, but they wouldn't break my spirit.

"My lips plant themselves on the smooth surface of her skin," Adam said. "She is but a slave to *my* desires."

As I passed Donovan, I shuddered. He licked his lips as he stared at me, breaking into a greedy smile.

"And as for you, Bourdet, your eyes will be cut from your skull so your gaze may no longer fall upon her. Your tongue will be torn from your mouth so that it may no longer know her kiss, and your hands will be removed, preventing you from touching her again."

His words oozed with cruelty and satisfaction. As I stepped in front of Adam, he lunged, seizing my arm. Conrad immediately stood, knocking his chair backward. He was ready for a fight; his hand clutched the sword at his belt. "There is one more thing I want you to take from this," he said, glaring at Conrad. "When you lie in bed at night without your eyes, hands, or tongue, I want you to remember I'm the one sharing her bed. My eyes will guide my hands and mouth over her body as I take what is mine."

I couldn't take it anymore. His joy at all the pain he was causing infuriated me. I could no longer stand by and let him wound us with his speech. All he had were words, and that seemed like nothing in comparison to what I was about to do. I ripped my arm from his grasp.

"I am not some object you can defile whenever you feel like it! You are not my husband. You're a monster, and the sight of you sickens me. Conrad made me happier in one year than you've made me in hundreds. The affection I used to have for you is dead; I do not love you anymore." My voice carried throughout the entire room, stunning everyone. I knew my confession had crossed the line, that our secret was now in jeopardy, but I didn't care. I wasn't some docile wife Adam could control and manipulate; I deserved a life of my own, and I would have it. "And I will do as I damn well please."

I strode away from Adam and made my way to Conrad. Flinging my arms around his neck, I pulled his body into mine. Our lips locked with a desire that seemed to radiate over us, sending shockwaves throughout the room. His hands caressed the bare skin of my back, and I gasped with excitement in response. We were in another place, miles away from this room and the people who wanted to tear us apart.

"That is enough!" Adam's fingernails clawed at my arm, separating me from Conrad.

I tried to lunge for Conrad as Donovan began hauling him to the door, but Adam stopped me. "Conrad!" He scrambled to return to my side, but Donovan and another man pulled him away. "I'm so sorry, please forgive me." He tried to speak, but Donovan hit him on the back of the head, knocking him unconscious.

Adam's hand collided with the side of my face, stunning me so much my knees buckled. "Because of you, his neck will meet the executioner's axe tomorrow night. He will die for his actions," he screamed. "But you will live. I want you to live so that you can wake up every day knowing you are the reason Conrad is dead and that you'll never set your eyes upon his face again!"

"No!" I screamed. "Let him go!"

I woke up screaming, jerking awake so forcefully I almost fell out of bed. Not a second later, multiple bodies burst through the door of my room.

"Evey, are you hurt?" Conrad knelt in front of me, inspecting my hands and face for signs I'd been injured. "Are you okay?"

"No," I cried, sliding into his arms.

"What happened?" Noah asked.

"Evey!" Caroline shouted, running through the bathroom entrance. "What's wrong?"

"I had a horrible dream."

"We rushed in here for a dream?" Helen asked. "We all thought you were being maimed."

"Please don't hide your joy at the thought," I blurted out.

At my words, Helen closed her mouth and rescinded into the background, where she stood behind Noah and Milton.

"Did you dream of Aden?" Conrad's voice was barely above a whisper.

"Yes," I answered.

"It would be my honor to stand guard at your door for the rest of the night," Milton stated. "I can protect you while you sleep."

"Thank you for the offer, Milton, but you need to rest as well. Conrad will stay with me," I said, meeting Conrad's gaze. "Won't you?"

"Of course," he replied. "You can all go back to bed. I'll take it from here."

"Thank you," I said, increasing my hold on him. He stood, cradling me in his arms.

"Conrad, you shouldn't put that much weight on your leg," Helen said. "You'll hurt yourself even more."

"I already told you my leg is fine. You may leave now, Helen." She filed out of the room last, slamming the door shut behind her. "Tell me what happened in your dream."

"Aden made me walk through his council meeting practically naked. He wanted to show me off as a whore because he knew I was in love with you. I wanted him to know how I felt about you, and like a fool, I kissed you in front of him," I mumbled, burying my face in his chest. "When he saw us together, he snapped and then sentenced you to death."

"Evey, look at me." He set me on the bed gently before seating himself next to me.

"I can't."

"Why not?"

"Because my momentary recklessness sealed your fate. You were condemned to die because of one kiss."

"Aden already knew about our relationship before that meeting. One kiss didn't change anything."

"He was going to let you live until I kissed you. He only wanted you to die after he saw us together."

"Aden wouldn't have let me live for very long. It was just a matter of time before he had me killed—kiss or no kiss."

"I still don't understand how you can want to look at me," I replied, lifting my gaze.

"I could stare at you all day long. I've always had more trouble with taking my eyes off you." He pressed our foreheads together, stroking my cheeks with his thumbs, and in an instant, my consciousness was returned to the exact moment my dream ended.

I was alone in the grand hall, unable to move or speak. I heard footsteps in the distance. The sound grew louder as they neared me.

"Your grace," Kit said, lifting my head from the floor. "What happened?" Her eyes surveyed my face, taking in the tearstains streaked across it. Marie was on the other side of me, throwing a cloak over my nakedness.

"They took him. They took him, and they're going to kill him tomorrow night." Looks of horror altered their features. They raised me from the floor and led me back to my bedroom. I listened as they poured hot water into the metal tub. The sound of gushing liquid crashing against bronze was deafening to my ears. Guiding me into the bath, they washed me as I cried. "Would you help me?" I sucked in a ragged breath as tears continued to trickle from my eyes.

"Help you do what?" Marie's voice was soft, almost like a whisper.

"Help Conrad and me escape, help us run away together."

"Tell us what you want us to do," Kit said, taking my hand in hers.

We devised a plan that would allow Conrad to escape that night. As they dressed me, we sent Guy and Mickey to discover where Conrad was being held. Once they ascertained his location, we enlisted the help of a priest who agreed to pose as Conrad, allowing the two of us time to flee. It was a good plan, and I finally felt able to breathe a sigh of relief. They tied the laces at the back of my white dress and pinned back part of my hair, fastening it from my face with gold pins. The soft curls tumbled down my back. I could almost pass for a bride, which was fitting, as I was about to start a new life with the man I loved. My ruby necklace was the only piece of jewelry I wore. I took off my wedding band and threw it into the roaring fire. Kit finished fastening the back of my gown as Marie packed a trunk with some of my clothes and possessions.

"When will he be here?" The anxiety in my voice was overwhelming.

"Soon," Marie answered. "Guy and Mickey took the priest downstairs to see him."

"And the horses are still waiting for us?"

"Yes. They're waiting in the orchard." She closed the lid of my trunk and fastened it shut. "The four of us will meet up with you later. You still need to be protected."

I nodded, unable to form words. My heart was drumming inside my chest; I longed to touch him and see he hadn't been hurt. The guilt over what I had done earlier tore at my insides. I was responsible for bringing pain to so many people. I called Kit and Marie to my side.

"I want to thank you both for everything you've done for me, for everything you have sacrificed for me." Grabbing Marie's right hand and Kit's left, I pressed my lips to their knuckles. "I can never repay you for the kindness you have bestowed upon me, but know I love you with all my heart."

A knock at the door drew my gaze from their faces. The heavy door creaked as it opened, and with a surge of relief, I saw Mickey and Guy enter with Conrad. I ran to Conrad and took him in my arms. Happiness flooded my senses as I realized I was getting to hold him again. The others left quietly, allowing us some time alone.

"I'm so sorry," I cried into his chest. "I was a fool earlier, and I pray you can forgive me."

"You've done nothing for which you should apologize," he replied, stroking my hair.

"My actions have condemned you to death."

"Everyone dies," he said, kissing my cheek.

"Not always. I've arranged for two horses to be left for us in the orchard. They are waiting to take us away from here. We must leave soon, so we have a good start on our journey before they come for you tomorrow night." I took his hand and started for the door, but he held me back.

"No," he said with finality. "We can't run away."

"He'll execute you tomorrow if we don't leave. It's the only way we can be together."

"He would hunt us like animals. He wouldn't rest until he's killed us both. I won't let him hurt you." He bent to kiss me. "I don't care if he kills me, but I could never go through with anything that would cause harm to come to you."

"Don't you think I feel the same way about you? I don't want to live without you."

"But you must. I won't leave with you. I'm sorry, but I won't give him a chance to hurt you." At his words, I backed away from his touch.

"If you die, then I die too."

"No, you can't think like that." He grasped my arms, demanding my attention. "You need to stay alive and defend your people. I know you're aware of the trials he conducts in the dungeons. He uses metal and fire to coerce confessions of guilt from the prisoners. He tortures them, sometimes until they die. It won't be long until he starts torturing people who aren't prisoners, and he'll make the men on his council participate." I shook my head. I couldn't stand to live a life without him. "You have to live; only you can protect everyone. Where he is cruel, you are kind, and your kindness gives hope to those around you."

"How am I supposed to continue living without you?"

"You have to. My mother and Cecily need you to look after them. I can't protect them, but you can." He stood at my side and held me in a tender embrace. "If you love me, you'll do this for me." I stared in his eyes that shone like shimmering oceans, not wanting to believe the words pouring from his lips. "You have to be strong. As the other primum, you are the only one who can stop him."

I clung to his body, hoping I would never have to release him. There was nothing I could say to change his mind, and his determination couldn't be broken. A sudden desire to discover his body ran through me. I walked over to the flames that glittered in the fireplace.

"If you won't run away with me, then there is another request I want to make of you."

"And what is that, my lady?"

"I want you to know me the way any husband knows his wife. I may have been given to Adam, but I choose to be with you. You're the man I love." My hands reached behind me, pulling the laces at the back of my dress. Standing before him, mere inches of empty space separated us. "I want you to take me as your wife," I said, dropping my gown to the floor. This time, there were no gold chains or fabric to camouflage the rest of my body from his view.

"You would have me as your husband?" He took another step toward me, and I could feel the yearning emanating from his body.

"In my heart, you are my husband," I answered. No sooner had the words left my lips and his hands were on me, rubbing parts of my body they had never discovered before. I quivered beneath his touch, desperate to feel him all over me. Easing off his shirt, I tossed it to the ground. My fingertips danced along the smooth surface of his flesh, leading the way for my mouth. A sigh escaped my lips as his discovered the curve of my neck. Dropping my hands to his belt, we stumbled backward in search of the bed. I opened my mouth to his as our lips pressed together with a desire that stole the breath from my lungs. He lifted me onto the bed before removing his pants and boots. As soon as he was free from his clothes, I pulled him on top of me, tasting his mouth as I kissed him. My entire body felt as if it was on fire; every time he touched me, waves of bliss radiated throughout my flesh. I moaned loudly as his lips trailed down my chest to my stomach, his hands rubbing my thighs as he kissed my skin. My fingers gripped the covers as I felt him unite our bodies, curving upward to him as my head fell back in ecstasy. His breath grew ragged as our bodies moved together. Wrapping my arms around his neck, I hugged him to me as our lips met. His hunger for me seemed to intensify as he guided my hips back and forth with his hands. The feel of him was unlike anything I had ever experienced before. We were lost in each other, completely unaware that a world outside of the room still existed. He accelerated our pace, causing me to cry out in response. A rush of pleasure hummed through my body and consumed my every waking thought.

When we had both been drained of our energy, we collapsed to the bed and buried ourselves under the thick blankets. Conrad held me in his arms as my fingertips skimmed along his cheek.

"Thank you," I whispered.

"For what?"

"For giving me this and for loving me in a way I've never known before." He smiled at me, lightly touching his lips to my forehead. "I only wish we had more time." Tears formed in the corners of my eyes and I tried with all my might to push them away.

"Don't cry," he begged as he kissed my face. "Don't feel sad for me. You're everything I could ever want, and I would rather spend my last night with you than live for an eternity never knowing your touch." His hands fastened around my waist, pulling me on top of him. "Before I went on the hunt and you told me how you felt about me, I would have gladly laid down my life for just one kiss from your lips. I never imagined I would know you like this."

When my eyes refocused, Conrad was still staring at me. The memories I had just relived made me blush. Fresh tears stung my eyes as I remembered the last night we spent together before he died.

"You spent your last night alive with me," I breathed.

"I would spend any night with you, especially if I knew it was going to be my last."

"How can you treat this subject so nonchalantly?"

"I wasn't lost to you forever. I'm here with you now."

"Yes, but we didn't know you would be made into one of my secundae back then. I thought I would have to live again and again, never getting to see you or talk to you. The thought of losing you was unbearable."

"I will always find a way back to you."

"Not if the Concilium has a say in the matter."

"Whatever happens, it was worth it," he replied. "You always are."

"What do you mean?"

"The night we spent together before my execution was worth dying for; it was the first time we were ever together like that. Any time I spend with you is worth it to me."

"I think I know what you mean." I smiled slightly, staring up at him through my eyelashes. "What did Noah want to speak with you about?" My fingers pressed along the tape that held the bandage to his chest, resealing its edges.

"Obviously he knows I came to see you even though the Concilium forbade me to, but when we see the head of the Concilium, he is going to take my side on the matter. Noah was the only consiliarius who thought it was wrong to separate us in the first place."

"Why did he think that?"

"He believes we're stronger together and that we're vulnerable when we are apart."

"He seems so different from what I imagined a consiliarius to be like."

"Yeah, he isn't like the rest of the Concilium. I think it's because of his past. He experienced a lot of sorrow before he was made into a consiliarius, and he can relate to the secundae better than he can the Concilium. He remembers what it's like to feel pain, the way we do, living multiple lifetimes." His fingers traced the length of my arms as he spoke. "Actually, Noah was the one who suggested I be made into a secundae."

"Really?" I couldn't help but be surprised at such a revelation; although, after what he'd told me of Noah, I shouldn't be surprised at all. "Why did he do that?"

"I think it's because he never liked Aden. He always thought Aden was too cocky; well, at least that's what he said whenever I was one of his secundae. Either way, I think he could see Aden was power hungry and cruel before anyone else could."

"I guess I should thank him then," I said, leaning back on my hands. "Will you tell me what happened when you were brought back as one of my secundae and we saw each other for the first time?"

A sly grin spread over his face. "I would tell you, but I think this is one time you should definitely allow yourself to remember."

"Why is that?"

"Because telling you what happened wouldn't do it justice." The grin he was wearing was nothing less than sinful, and for a moment, I thought I actually saw him blush.

"I can't wait to remember it then," I whispered. "Did you want to become a secundae before you were made into one?"

"I always hoped I would, but you aren't asked to be one until you die."

"So, you were happy when they asked you to be one?"

"I was relieved. We had been given a second chance to be together, or at least that's how I looked at it," he replied. My cheeks burned beneath the scrutiny of his gaze.

"Me too. I may not be able to remember everything from the past, but there is one thing I do know and that's how I felt about you." He nodded at my words, seeming too lost in thought to speak. "Helen is in love with you, isn't she?"

"Yes," he answered, dropping his gaze.

"I thought so."

"But I don't feel that way about her. You're the only woman I've ever loved."

"I wish I could say I never loved anyone else, but I know there was once a time when I did love Aden," I said, instantly feeling guilty. I stared at the white sheets, absentmindedly tugging at the soft material.

"What's wrong?" He studied my face as he waited for me to answer his question.

"I feel like a bad person because of it."

"It's like I said before, he wasn't always cruel, and you loved him before we met."

"And I fell out of love with him before I met you too?"

"Yes."

"Maybe we were meant to be together all along." He said nothing in reply. Instead, he took my hand in his and planted a soft kiss on it. "Do you think he still loves me?" The words seemed to slip out of my mouth before I could stop them.

He took in a deep breath, balling his hands into fists several times before answering my question. "I believe he still does," he stated with a grim stare.

"But how? I mean, he had me killed."

"Because he was jealous. Love is a much more powerful emotion than hate. I think he's still in love with you and he hates himself."

"Why would he hate himself?" I had to admit that while I didn't want to remember the time I spent with Aden, I was still curious about the man he'd become.

"He hates himself because he drove you away, and he knows you'll never be able to love him the way you once did."

"How do you know?"

"Well . . ." he paused for a moment to collect his thoughts. "I mean, that's how I would be feeling if I were him."

"You don't think he wants to kill me?"

"I think above everything else, he wants to win you back."

I5

REPERCUSSIONS.

I got up the next day to find Conrad still fast asleep on the floor beside my bed. After asking him to stay in case I suffered another nightmare, I offered to let him sleep in the bed. But he insisted on being a perfect gentleman. His main concern was my comfort, and it made me care for him even more. As frightening as it was to admit, I needed him. When he first told me who I was, I struggled with the revelation. Not only that, I fought it. I thought I couldn't be myself and his queen at the same time. However, with each day that passed, I was slowly remembering my true identity, and I'd come to realize the part he had played in making me who I was and who I am.

Carefully stepping over Conrad, I headed to the bathroom to get ready for the day. Caroline joined me from her room as I was curling my hair.

"Hey roomie," I said with a yawn.

"Hey! Did you sleep all right after your dream?"

"Yeah. Conrad stayed with me after everyone left."

"Did he, now?"

"He slept on the floor, so there are no sordid details to bombard you with."

"Ugh! Why does he have to be such a gentleman? I need the two of you to make out already."

"Sometimes I don't even believe the things that come out of your mouth."

"Stop resisting and hop on the Conrad train. You know you want to."

"I'll think about it if you stop sassing me and go take a shower."

"Yes ma'am," she said with a salute. She shut the door to my room and poured all her makeup out on the counter before hopping in the shower. Once she was out, we started getting ready together. "Is that what you're wearing?" I pointed to the outfit she had hanging by the shower.

"Yeah. You think it will look good?"

"How did you even have time to pack something like that?" I asked. "I mean, it'll definitely get some attention."

"Well, when you called me, I kind of freaked out! I didn't know what the heck was going on, and I already had my outfits set out for every day of school next week; so I just grabbed everything and some extra pairs of jeans and shoved it all in my bag."

I laughed at her response. "I can actually picture you running around your room in a fashion-induced panic!"

"What was I supposed to do?"

I shook my head. "Just be you," I answered, applying a layer of lip gloss.

"What are you wearing?" she asked, sliding on her pastel pink miniskirt and low-cut gray shirt.

I went to my room and returned with a pair of denim shorts and a cream sweater. "Conrad packed my bag as a precaution, so there aren't any dresses or skirts like I usually wear."

"I'm still impressed, though! That's a super cute outfit!"

"I'm sure that's why he packed it. You know, priorities."

She rolled her eyes, muttering, "Smart-ass."

"I wonder if Noah likes pink," I teased, tugging on her skirt.

"I guess we'll have to wait and see." She fixed the clasp on my necklace, sliding it to the back of my neck. "I'm so in love with your necklace. I swear it's like it was made for you."

"Thanks." I looked in the mirror, admiring the pendant. Every time I saw myself wearing it, the one thing I noticed more than anything was how the color of the stone matched my hair exactly. "I love it too."

"You ready to go find some breakfast?"

"Absolutely. I'm starving."

When I checked on Conrad, he was still resting, so I decided to let him sleep and walked downstairs with Caroline. We only went one flight down and stopped in the kitchen. A feast was spread out over a large island in the center of the room. We looked at each other with surprise and then over at the food.

"You think it would be all right for us to eat some of this?" Caroline was staring at a plate stacked with pancakes and French toast.

"Help yourself to anything you see before you," Noah answered. His sudden appearance caused both of us to jump, and he moved to stand by Caroline.

"Thank you." Her cheeks flushed just a bit with her reply. She reached for a plate, but before her hands grasped it, Noah picked it up.

"Here, allow me," he said, flashing a bright smile. Taking the plate, he moved closer to the food. "What would you like to eat?"

"Oh, just some pancakes and bacon." He piled the food on her plate and escorted her to the table, setting the plate in front of a chair. Pulling out a seat for her, he beckoned for her to sit down. I watched as she complied and he gently pushed her chair in.

"Evey?" he asked, turning back to me.

"Oh, I can get it," I said, grabbing a plate. "Why don't you fix yourself a plate and then we can both join Caroline." I smiled at him, raising my eyebrows. For a second, his face flushed scarlet, matching the shirt he had on. We loaded our plates with pancakes, eggs, and bacon before joining Caroline at the table.

"I trust you both slept well?" I glanced at Noah as he asked the question and saw he was intently watching Caroline. His eyes followed her hand as she swept a long strand of golden hair behind her ear. I conveniently ate a bite of pancakes, forcing Caroline to answer his question.

"Yes, thank you." She turned her head, meeting his gaze. "Your home is very beautiful."

"Thank you. I'm quite fond of it myself. Although, I find that beauty in objects isn't quite as deserving of notice as it is in people." His green eyes appraised her features, which seemed to be turning a deeper shade of red by the second.

"Noah, I hope you don't mind me asking, but I was wondering if the painting in my bedroom is a real Degas? It's an exquisite piece."

"Yes, it is. I have quite a few works that probably belong in a museum somewhere, but I can't bring myself to part with them. I enjoy art too much not to surround myself with it."

"I know what you mean. Since my parents own an auction house, I've always been exposed to art and various antiquities. I couldn't imagine living in a place where I wasn't surrounded by it."

"Remind me to show you the Rembrandt I have in my room later. It's my favorite piece I own."

"Thank you. I will," I replied.

Caroline, who was never one for small talk, especially about antiquities, abruptly changed the subject. "So, how do you become a consiliarius?" I glanced between Caroline and Noah, waiting for him to answer her question.

"Well, you are chosen. The Concilium was once made of four men and three women, but after Aden removed Thea's heart and consumed it, only six of us remain." For the first time since the three of us sat down, Noah's smile faded. The subtle flash of sadness sliding across his face pulled at my heart. He still felt the ache of Thea's absence. In an instant, my sympathy was transformed into a rush of guilt. I should be held accountable for Thea's death. If I hadn't persuaded Aden to eat the apple or if I hadn't fallen for Conrad, Thea might still be alive today.

"Will there ever be another consiliarius added to take Thea's place?"

"I can't say. There hasn't been any talk to make another consiliarius yet, but that doesn't mean one will never be added."

After noticing the sadness in Noah's face when he mentioned Thea, I couldn't help but recall what Conrad said about him last night. Noah had experienced a lot of pain in his past. I wondered what kind of pain he had endured and if it got any easier to bear with time. "What was your life like before Thea died? I mean the Concilium wasn't always in hiding, were they?" I watched him eat as I waited for an answer to my question.

"No, we weren't in hiding before that. Actually, we all lived in England, relatively close to one another. We were like a family of sorts, especially since we've spent so many years together."

"It must be hard to be separated from them," Caroline replied.

"Does your family know you're here right now?"

"No, they think I'm out of town with Evey and her mom. They don't know what's really going on or Evey's true identity."

"You would lie to your family to protect your friend?"

"Evey is my family, and I would do anything for her. Now that I know who she is, I know Mickey, Kit, and Guy would all want me here with her. Besides, she would do the same for me," she said with absolute confidence.

A broad smile stretched over his face. "Spoken like a true secundae." He took a sip of water, his attention never turning from her. "Where's Conrad this morning?"

Before I could open my mouth to speak, a voice answered his question from somewhere behind me.

"He's in the shower," Helen said, walking up to the table. It seemed like she favored slutty attire because she wore a tight pair of jeans littered with holes and a black bra under a thin white tank top.

"Excuse me?" I questioned, facing her.

The look of triumph she wore made my blood boil. "I heard the water running when I walked past his door just now." She grabbed an apple from the table and threw it up in the air, catching it in her hands.

"Oh that's right, he did say he wanted to take a shower when we woke up this morning," I countered with a triumphant look. From the corner of my eye, I saw Caroline conceal a smile with her hand. For a second, Helen's smug smile faded. However, she was quick to regain her air of superiority before taking up an empty seat at the table. She tossed the apple again and I caught myself staring at it, suddenly wondering where the seeds of *the apple* might be hidden. I could only hope I would remember their hiding place, and the sooner I did so, the safer we all would be. Sensing I was watching her, she set the apple on the table and drew her hands away from it.

"What's the plan for the day?" Caroline's voice was cheery, filling the silence that had elapsed between the four of us.

"Well, we won't be able to go to New York until tomorrow, so the day is pretty much yours," Noah answered. "Is there something in particular you wanted to do?"

"I noticed last night you have a pretty extensive library," I said to Noah. "Would you mind if I looked through some of it?"

"Not at all. You are guests here, and I want nothing more than for you to make yourselves feel at home."

"Thanks," I replied. "That's very kind of you."

"What are all of you talking about?" Conrad asked as he walked into the room. He stood behind my chair, placing his hands on either side of me. He leaned in, almost touching our cheeks together. My eyes flashed to Helen. She was staring in my direction, but I wasn't the one her gaze was fixed on.

"Oh, we were just talking about what we should do today since we can't leave for New York until tomorrow," Caroline answered.

"And what did we decide on?"

"Nothing yet," she replied.

"Here, let me fix you some food." Conrad eased my chair back and trailed me to the center of the room. He pointed to the dishes he wanted while I piled them onto his plate. His hand lightly touched my waist as I worked. A rush of contentment seeped into my bones at the contact.

"You look nice today."

"Thank you," I whispered, trying my best not to blush. I knew Helen's attention was still focused on us. Conrad was aware she cared about him, but I wondered if he realized how much she loved him. Their history together may be a mystery to me, but there was no misinterpreting the way she looked at him. Helen wanted Conrad.

"We could practice some more fighting techniques," Conrad said to Caroline as he took a bite of eggs.

"I'd really like that."

"Caroline is a natural fighter," Conrad added, directing his comment toward Noah.

"Somehow, that doesn't surprise me." At Noah's words, a broad smile lit up Caroline's face.

Conrad finished his food quickly, and I helped him carry everyone's plates to the sink to be washed.

"Are you going to join us?" he asked while scraping the dishes into the trash before handing them to me.

He leaned against the sink as I loaded the plates into the dishwasher. He was dressed in a snug white T-shirt and jeans.

"Actually, I think I'm going to pick a book out of the library and read."

"If you get bored, come find us."

"I will. Thank you for staying with me last night."

"You don't have to thank me for that." His fingers slid along the chain of my necklace, causing my heart to feel like it was about to tear through my chest. "Have you taken it off since I put it on you?"

"No, I don't even notice I'm wearing it most of the time. It feels like I've always worn it."

"That's because you have." He kissed my cheek before heading back to the table. Caroline and Noah were deep in conversation, but they stopped talking as Conrad approached them. "Ready to train, Caroline?" he asked. Then turning to me, he said, "We'll be on the second floor. If you walk past the sitting area by the library, a long hallway will lead to the recreational room." I watched as the three of them headed downstairs and out of sight, leaving me by myself. I wasn't sure when Helen slipped out of the room, but if I had to guess, it would have been when Conrad was touching my neck.

I left the kitchen and descended the steps to the second floor, studying the layout of Noah's building. The library consisted of a wall at least sixty feet long. The black shelves ran from floor to ceiling, and there were no open spaces in sight. My fingers skimmed along the bindings of the books while I read the various titles. The spectrum of his selection was incredible, and I suddenly doubted my ability to choose anything at all. Noah had everything from romance novels to textbooks on mechanical engineering. It struck me again just how long he had lived. He had more than enough time to study anything and everything. I took a second to marvel at the knowledge he must have accumulated over the course of his life, and my thoughts quickly shifted to Conrad. The same must hold true for him as well. On the day I met him, it annoyed me he hadn't taken any notes in class, but now that I thought about it, he wasn't lying about not needing to take them. He'd seen the Spanish Inquisition and who knows what else firsthand. As I continued walking past each shelf, I noticed the books didn't appear to be arranged in any particular order. *Of Mice and Men* was nestled beside a book on how to fold origami. I persisted in my search, reading more than a hundred titles before finally making a selection. Walking over to the white couch, I curled up with a copy of *Pride and Prejudice*. It was one of my favorites, and I couldn't pass up reading it again. I opened it to the first page and soon found myself immersed in the world of Elizabeth Bennett.

"Call me crazy, but I never thought Elizabeth deserved Mr. Darcy."

Helen sat down across from me. She leaned back in the armchair and crossed her legs. Her tall black stilettos seemed as deadly as the expression she was wearing. "Somehow, I'm not surprised by this revelation," I replied in the most polite voice I could muster.

She shrugged her shoulders. "The story is too predictable. Not everyone winds up living a happy ending." Her voice was laced with malice. There was no use in playing nice with her. I knew any attempt I made to be civil would go unnoticed.

"Everyone, or just you?" She pursed her lips together, staring me down. "Is there a specific reason you hate me, or am I just really that unlikeable?" I asked, not hiding the acerbity in my tone.

"You know why I don't like you. There's no use playing games," she spat, her cold eyes boring into mine.

"If I did something to hurt you in the past, I'm sorry."

"It's not just in the past. It's more like one long continuation." I met her stare with one of my own. She could try to intimidate me all she wanted, but I wasn't scared of her. I was the older woman with more experience, even if I couldn't remember all of it.

"Conrad loves me."

"That's the problem."

"If he was in love with you and wanted to be with you, I wouldn't stand in the way of his happiness. I know what it's like to be trapped in a relationship with someone you don't love, and if he didn't love me, I wouldn't hold on to him." I found myself wanting to reach out and make her understand the way I felt about him, but a voice in my head reminded me that she knew all too well.

"You're lying. You'd never allow him to be with me, so it doesn't matter how he feels." The disgust in her voice rolled over me in waves. "And it's not like I could ever compete with you."

"What are you talking about?"

"You are the female primum. You're the original woman. What man wouldn't be in awe of you? Your beauty, your demeanor, it fills the hearts of men with kindness and desire. Even the head of the Concilium respects the power of your presence, and Everest isn't easily impressed."

"I didn't have any say in when or how I was born. The fact that I'm the original woman is something beyond my control."

"Yes, but you can't claim you don't use it to your advantage either."

"Conrad loves me for who I am. You act as if I've cast some spell over him."

"You said you wouldn't stand in the way of his happiness, but what about his safety?"

"What are you getting at exactly?"

"I think you know," she countered, leaning forward. "If you think this fight will end without more pain and death, you're sadly mistaken." A slight smile unfurled from the corners of her mouth.

"Every day Conrad is with you puts him at risk. You know Aden will do everything within his power to kill Conrad and take you for himself. And since Conrad defied a direct order, the Concilium isn't likely to bring him back. The next time he dies is the end."

"I'm not some piece of property Aden can reclaim as he pleases. Conrad is one of my secundae. He knows the risks, and he chooses to stay with me and fight against Aden," I argued. "I'm not ignorant. I know better than anyone what Aden is capable of, but that doesn't mean I shouldn't try to stand against him. He has to be stopped." I heard the words coming out of my mouth, the same words Conrad had said to me every time I started making the points Helen was making now. I still wasn't sure I completely believed them yet, and her next comment shook me.

"I agree, but I think Conrad shouldn't have to stand beside you."

"I'm not forcing him into anything. He wants to."

"He wants to, or does he want to because you want him to?"

I had to think through her comment for a minute before I was able to fully understand it. "He wants to," I said as doubt crept into the crevices of my mind.

"Are you sure?" I stared at her, wishing she would stop talking, wishing she would leave me alone and allow me to return to the world written in the pages of my book. When it became clear I wasn't going to answer her, she continued speaking. "You know you aren't the only person who lost him in Spain."

Raising my head, I returned my focus to her face. "What are you talking about?"

"His mother, sister, and I almost followed him to the grave after he was executed by Aden. Your actions cost Conrad his life, and it deprived us of someone we loved dearly."

"I'm so sorry for that." Shame overwhelmed my conscience. "I shouldn't have paraded my relationship with him in front of Aden; I know Conrad's death was my fault. I tried to get him to run away with me, but he wouldn't."

"He wouldn't because of you." Her voice grew louder as she practically shouted the last word. "You even had the audacity to cry to his mother and Cecily after it happened. You begged for their forgiveness like a fool."

Her voice echoed in my ears, but I was miles away from the apartment in Chicago. I was in Spain hundreds of years earlier.

I bumped into someone, causing them to fall against the stone wall of the corridor. Kit and Marie trailed way behind me now as I ran through the castle. My feet were clumsy, tripping over my skirt as I tore through the hall. Tears soaked my face, blurring my vision. I was driven by the thought that I had to get to them before anyone else did, before anyone else could tell them what had happened. I'd kept them from Conrad's execution on purpose because no mother should ever have to watch their child die. Adam kept it a hushed affair, because his pride prevented him from making the truth of his wife's infidelity a public spectacle. I wanted to die, to dissolve into the floor, to join the rest of the stones that had been encased in a final resting place. The thought of bearing such painful news was overwhelming. I had lost my last hope that I could endure this life. He had been stolen away forever to a place where I wouldn't be allowed to join him. Lurking ahead was the familiar sight of their door. My hand stretched in front of me, jerking it open. Both of them jumped as I ran inside the room and slammed the door shut. Tears flooded my eyes with more force as Conrad's mother approached me.

"Your grace, what is it?" Her hands touched my arms gently, like a child might touch a wounded doe.

I grabbed hold of her hands, pressing my lips to them. "I'm so sorry." Cecily threw herself at me, her arms clutching my waist. Out of habit, I hugged her to my body. How could I tell her what happened? How could I explain to sweet Cecily she would never see her brother again?

His mother, more familiar with the evils of the world, asked with panic in her voice, "Where is Conrad?" I didn't want to say the words. I couldn't make myself say he was dead. "No, it can't be." She shook her head and pulled me forward.

I stood in front of her and she grabbed Cecily, yanking her away from me. I reached out to her, but they were both too far away.

"The king had him executed today." I choked on the words as they spewed from my mouth. "I tried to stop it. I begged for mercy." Cecily crumpled to the floor, her knees smacking against the stone beneath her. Conrad's mother let out a cry of pain that stung my ears. It was the most agonizing sound I'd ever heard. I tried to run for Cecily, but she stood in my way. She was preventing me from going to her daughter.

"This is because of you, isn't it?" Her finger pointed at me, forcing me to freeze. "Everyone knew there was something going on between the two of you. He was blinded by your title, your beauty, and you led him to his death!"

"I loved him more than anyone else in my entire life. I pleaded with him to leave, to save himself, but he wouldn't."

"None of this would have happened if he hadn't met you. I wanted him to marry Helen, but after the first time he set eyes on you, I knew he wouldn't. In an instant, you changed him completely, and he would have never been content with her as long as he wanted you. I never understood why he loved someone he could never have."

Her confession stunned me. "I was given to the king. I didn't have a choice. If I had, I would have chosen your son. I loved him more than I can say."

"Your proclamations of love won't bring him back!" Her voice sounded around the room. "You stole him away from us."

"Please, know that—"

My voice was drowned out by her cries. "You killed him!" Her hand forcefully slapped my face, sending me back into the wall. "You're the reason he is dead." My hand clutched my cheek as I glanced back and forth between her and Cecily. I had done this. I was the cause of their pain, of their despair, and it was more than I could bear.

"Please forgive me," I whispered. I ran from their room as fast as my feet could carry me, not daring to look back. The love they once felt for me was lost forever, along with the man I took from them.

"Did you hear anything I just said?" Helen's voice was harsh. It took me a moment to realize I wasn't in the past anymore. Her stare tore into me, demanding an answer. I wiped my face with my hands. "Do you even feel any remorse over what you've done, over what you continue to do to Conrad?"

"How can you even ask me that?" I averted my gaze. "Of course I feel guilty. I know I'm the reason he was killed, and every day he was gone, I wanted to die myself. I had no idea he was going to be brought back. I thought I would have to live for an eternity knowing it was my fault."

"And what about the sacrifice he's making for you right now?"

"I didn't know he disobeyed the Concilium's orders, that this would be his last life."

"Now you do!" she yelled. "So, do the right thing and release him. Give him a chance to live a life that doesn't have you in it, allow him to find true happiness away from you," she said.

"You want me to give him permission to be with you?"

"I want you to give him permission to leave you, to no longer be one of your secundae."

"I don't think I can." My stomach churned, making me sick. The thought of losing him was something I couldn't handle. I'd just found him again, and I didn't want to let him go.

"Can't you see what your love does to people?" Her voice rang out around the room. "It destroyed Aden and it'll destroy Conrad too."

Her words cut into me like a knife. I could see his mother's face when I closed my eyes. She wore an expression of overwhelming grief mixed with the fresh sting of betrayal. I had betrayed her, Cecily, and Conrad. Helen was right—I didn't deserve him. I had to get away from her; I couldn't let her see me fall apart. I took off for the stairs, taking them two at a time and bursting through the door to my room. Helen didn't follow me or try to stop me, but I didn't really expect her to. I flung myself on the high sleigh bed. My hands found a pillow, clutching it to my chest. As much as I wanted to hold onto him, it would be better for Conrad to be without me. His mother knew what I was capable of. She didn't want me to be with her son in the first place, and she was right to hate me after I had caused his death. If Aden was able to get the true powers of a consiliarius, he would undoubtedly make Conrad suffer. I could imagine and accept a life without Conrad if I knew he was somewhere safe, but I couldn't stand the thought of living forever knowing Conrad endured a fate worse than death because of me. Much to my dismay, the door to my room creaked open. I had just a few seconds to try to compose myself before Conrad walked in. Sitting up, I hung my feet over the side of the bed to make room for him.

"What happened?" He stood in front of me, resting his hands on the top of my legs.

"I'm fine," I mumbled, trying to force a smile.

"You aren't fine. Tell me what happened."

I turned my head upward. "Were you supposed to marry Helen before we met?"

"Is that what she told you?"

"Did I break the two of you up or something?" My voice was so low, I was sure he strained to hear my question. Part of me hoped he hadn't heard it because I wasn't really sure I wanted to hear the answer.

He let out a deep sigh. "Our fathers had worked out an arranged marriage for us. We grew up together, but I never loved her."

"Well, she certainly has feelings for you."

"I know, but I don't feel that way about her."

"When I was talking to Helen, I had another flashback. I remembered visiting your mother and Cecily after you'd been killed." He tried to wrap me up in his arms, but I held my palms against his chest, pushing him back. "Did you know your mother wanted you to marry her? She didn't want you to be with me because she knew I would hurt you."

"What are you talking about? My mother loved you," he replied.

"No, she didn't. She blamed me for your death, and Cecily did too." His body felt warm beneath my hands. It was so hard to keep myself from falling into him, but I had to be strong. I couldn't fail him again. "And she was right, it was my fault."

"It wasn't your fault. I've told you time and time again that you couldn't control Aden or predict what he was going to do."

"If you had married Helen, you never would've gotten killed. You could have grown old and had children and lived a peaceful life."

"I didn't want any of that with her," he said, backing away from me. "I wanted you. When I met you, I knew I never wanted to be with anyone else."

"But being with someone else would keep you safe," I pleaded.

"I'm one of your secundae. It's my job to keep you safe, not the other way around."

"Maybe I don't want you to be one of my secundae," I yelled.

"Is that really what you want?"

"If Aden wins, he'll find some sick, sadistic way to torture you. Do you think I could live with myself if that happened?" I stared at him, waiting for an answer.

"Evey . . ." he said as he grabbed my hands.

"I'm not the woman you married almost four centuries ago, Conrad. People change. I've changed. Stop holding on to the hope I'm still the compassionate queen you fell in love with, because I'm not. She died a long time ago. I'm just a regular girl. I'm not your savior, and I certainly don't deserve to have any more people lay down their lives in order to protect me."

"You are Eve!" he yelled. "You are light. You symbolize hope for those around you. You give us a reason to fight, to defeat the darkness. That's who you are; that's why we must protect you, no matter the cost."

I pulled my hands out of his grasp. "You will no longer be one of my secundae. I release you from my service." My voice was unwavering as I uttered the words with an air of finality.

"You don't know what you're saying. You can't be without any secundae."

"I want you to leave and take Helen with you. The two of you deserve a chance at the life I stole from you."

"Why do I have to keep telling you that I don't want to be with her?" he asked, raising his voice. "This is foolish! You can send me away, leave yourself unprotected, but I won't forget about you and I'll never stop wanting you."

Stepping forward, I placed my fingers over his lips. His eyes met mine with a wounded look that made my heart ache. "But I've stopped wanting you." The words burned like acid as they escaped my lips. It was a lie. I wanted him more than anything else in my entire life, but I couldn't let my selfishness be his downfall again.

"I don't believe you."

"I'm the female primum, and I belong to Aden. If I can't be with him, then I should be alone. He and I are a pair. God made me for him, not you." He opened his mouth to speak, but nothing came out. The blank expression on his face was haunting, chilling me to the bone.

"If what you've said is really what you want me to do, then so be it."

"I think you should leave," I said as I opened the door for him, hurrying him out before I lost my nerve. This whole ruse would fail if he saw how miserable I felt. He stepped into the hall and I turned my head away from his gaze, unable to meet it. When he was gone, I shut the door behind him and ran to the bathroom. Turning on the water in the tub, I waited as it filled before slipping into the water. I was numb, despite the steam rising from the bath. My knees slid into my chest and I cried.

I didn't know how long I sat there, but when the sobbing finally subsided, the water was like ice and my fingertips were wrinkled and soggy. I pushed the handle to the hot water down and waited as it warmed the tub. I wondered briefly if I could stay in here forever and never face anyone ever again, but I knew that dream would never be possible.

As if my very thoughts brought this reprieve to an end, Caroline's head poked through the door leading to her room. "Evey?" Seeing the state I was in, she flung the door open and came to sit beside me. "What happened?"

"I told Conrad I didn't want him," I answered in between sobs, which had come back in full force at her presence.

"Why would you do that?" She looked confused, as if I were speaking another language.

"Helen came to talk to me and she made some good points. I destroyed Aden, and I'll do the same to Conrad."

"Why would you give credit to anything that jealous bitch says? You and Conrad belong together."

"The head of the Concilium told Conrad he only had one life left. They won't allow him to be reborn because he has disobeyed their orders too many times. This is his last life, Caroline," I said. "And I want him to live it. I want him to have a life without fighting, without worrying about protecting me every second of the day."

"But that's what he wants to do."

"Did you know he was engaged to Helen before he met me?" I asked. "I had another flashback, and his mother told me that had all changed when we met. She had known I would hurt him; she hated me for pulling him away from Helen."

"Evey—"

"I told him to move on with his life. I want him to find happiness, even if it happens to be with Helen."

"I think what you don't realize is that you are his happiness." She grabbed a towel off the rack and wrapped it around my shoulders. "Come on, let's get you dried off."

I was nothing more than a helpless child as she brushed my hair and dried it. Loose strands of radiant auburn flew through the air as she passed the hair dryer over them. I stared at my reflection in the mirror, but I didn't resemble myself. I was a ghost. My expression was as empty as Conrad's had been right before he walked out of my room. Blotches of mascara covered my cheeks, and I wiped away the black smudges. I had to seem put together in front of him; he couldn't know how badly I was suffering.

"You want me to walk downstairs with you to dinner?"

Glancing in the mirror, I smoothed out my sweater. After all my efforts, you couldn't even tell I'd spent most of the afternoon crying. "I guess I'll have to go down there sometime."

As we descended the steps for dinner, I was reminded of how grateful I was to have a friend like Caroline. There was no way I'd be able to face Conrad alone, not after everything I said to him. The kitchen was empty, so we continued to the bottom floor where Noah and Milton were already sitting in the living room. Noah's gaze focused intently on Caroline as we made our way to the couch.

"I hope we aren't interrupting anything," Caroline said as she perched herself across from Noah.

"Not at all," he replied. "I was just telling Milton how well you fight, especially since you've had no formal training."

"I wouldn't say I fight all that well," she countered humbly.

"If Noah thinks you're a good fighter, it must be true." Milton's voice was low and quiet. "If you want to spar some with me later, I'd be glad to. I find it helps to fight against a variety of people, since everyone has their own style and way of moving. It's good to expose yourself to a little bit of everything."

"Yeah, I'd like that."

"How long have you been one of Noah's secundae?" I asked.

"Around four hundred years, give or take a few. I used to be one of Thea's secundae, but I was reassigned after she . . . passed." Pain permeated from the depths of his toffee-colored eyes.

"Oh, I'm sorry," I replied. "That must have been hard on you." I felt terrible for bringing it up. Even though it happened a long time ago, it still had to be difficult for him. I may not know much about secundae, but I do know they have a fierce loyalty to the people they protect. Conrad was made into a secundae because he loved me and would die to keep me safe. It was possible for that to have been the case for Milton and Thea.

"Since Thea was a consiliarius, couldn't she just be reborn? I mean, wouldn't the Concilium have the power to bring her back?" Caroline glanced from Noah to Milton as she waited for a reply.

Noah leaned back in his chair. "They couldn't bring her back because Aden cut out her heart and consumed it. Part of our power lies in our hearts. In the Bible, it says love is God's greatest gift. Well, it's with our love for God and our love for mankind that we're able to bring back the primums and secundae."

"I guess I can understand that," she answered.

"Our powers aren't so much physical as they are ethereal."

"And how do you bring people back?"

"I actually can't tell you; the Concilium is entitled to a few secrets."

"Sure," she replied. "After all, what you do is very important."

The room was quiet for a few moments, so I interjected, "Is there anything Caroline or I can do to help with dinner?"

"Oh, no, everything is ready. It just needs to be taken out of the oven in a little while. We have a chef that comes to fix breakfast and dinner for us every day. It's nice because no one in the house is much of a cook. Every now and then, Helen makes an attempt at it, but Milton and I are always sure to eat before we sit down to any dinner she's made," he answered with a grin.

"I'm sure it's not that bad," I said.

"I found an eggshell in a plate of spaghetti one time and haven't tried anything since." He pretended to gag, and we all started laughing. "God only knows what else ended up in that sauce!"

"Are you talking about my cooking?" Helen's voice sounded from somewhere behind me. A look of confusion appeared on Noah's face before quickly vanishing. I turned around to see what he'd been staring at. It was like someone had punched me in the stomach as soon as I set my eyes on them. Helen was standing beside Conrad, her arm wrapped around his. Apparently, he'd taken my request to heart. As I met Helen's gaze, she smiled at me. The urge to jump over the back of the couch and rip out her throat consumed my every thought. But despite my desires, it was imperative for me to maintain my composure.

"Well, your cooking is terrible," Noah said.

"Oh, it's not that bad!" She laughed, squeezing Conrad's arm.

"I think I'm going to check on dinner," I announced. "Excuse me."

"I'll help you," Caroline offered.

I let out a deep breath as soon as we were out of earshot of everyone downstairs. Opening the oven, I checked on the lasagna. The sauce bubbled up, releasing an aroma of cheese and tomatoes into the air. It would be ready in a few minutes. I cut the freshly baked garlic bread, desperate for some kind of distraction.

"Are you all right?"

"Me? Oh, I'm fine." I tried my best to smile. "I was thinking, if I kill her, Noah could still bring her back to life. You think the Concilium would frown upon that?"

"I find it's better to ask for forgiveness than permission."

"That's a great philosophy! All I have to do is take her out, problem solved," I groaned. "As much as I'd like to, I can't kill her."

"You want me to punch her in the face instead?"

I chuckled at her question. "While that would make me happy, it wouldn't be our best plan."

"I could play it off like an accident."

"Like your hand just happened to be flying through the air and accidentally made contact with her face?"

She shrugged. "It's been known to happen."

"I appreciate your offer, but I have to pass on it." Throwing the slices of bread into a bowl, I watched while she checked on the lasagna again. When I was finished, I began searching through the cabinets.

"What are you looking for?"

"The only thing that ever cheers me up."

"Twinkies? Are we having a Twinkie binge-eating party tonight?"

"Oh yeah," I replied, hearing the despair in my voice. "Jackpot!" I pulled a Twinkie out of the box, ripping off its wrapper.

"Feel better?"

"A little," I answered with a full mouth. "If I can't have Conrad, I might as well shoot for something attainable, like diabetes."

"Screw it," she added, removing a golden cake from the box. "Let's both get diabetes."

I couldn't help but laugh. "You're the best. And I think Noah likes you."

As soon as I uttered his name, she started to blush. "He does not."

"Yes, he does! If he stared at you any more, his eyes would be glued to your ass."

"Really?"

"Really! I think you should ask him to watch a movie with you or something after we eat."

"I just might have to do that." The timer for the lasagna went off. After placing all the food on the table, we called everyone to dinner.

"Dinner's ready," I announced. Trudging back up the stairs, I claimed the seat by Caroline. To my dismay, Helen sat across from me with Conrad beside her. I ate in silence, barely hearing the conversations happening around me. I just wanted to eat and get as far away from everything as I could. Against my better judgment, I stole a glance at Conrad. He seemed to have the same idea, because our eyes met for a second and my heart fluttered. However, our stare was short-lived. Helen leaned in to ask him a question, drawing his attention back to her. I finally understood why taking the high road was the path less traveled. But if my sacrifice meant Conrad would have a chance at living a happy life and being safe from Aden, then each ounce of pain I felt would be worth it. I finished eating before everyone else and excused myself from the table. Within seconds, I was in my room with the door locked behind me. Pacing the floor, I studied each furnishing inside the room. The wood of the bed was carved with a floral motif mirroring the frame surrounding Degas's ballerinas. The effect was beautiful, and it felt wrong to be miserable in such a lovely place. But I'd made my bed, and now it was time to lie in it. I needed to be confident in my decision to send Conrad away and accept any consequences. With that resolution ringing in my ears, I decided to grab the book I had started earlier.

As I moved toward the library, I started hearing voices, and without thinking, I followed the noise. The couples were divided between two couches in the small den. Noah and Caroline were snuggled close to one another on a loveseat, and I couldn't help but smile at the sight. However, my expression faded in an instant as I glanced at the second couch. Helen was spread from end to end with her head resting in Conrad's lap. I snuck past the doorway, praying I'd go unnoticed. At the end of the hall was a sliding glass door that opened onto a balcony.

I admired the lights of the city, unable to ignore how isolated I felt. In a matter of days, I'd lost my parents, Mickey, Kit, and now Conrad. Street lamps illuminated the sidewalks below. The faint sounds of car horns and buses could be heard in the distance. I wished desperately I could talk to my mother. She always knew how to soothe every sorrow and ease every pain I'd ever felt. I needed her guidance now more than ever. She would know just what to say to make me feel better, but she was somewhere beyond my reach, and I didn't know if I'd ever see her again.

16

THE HIGH ROAD

Mustering up the last of my energy, I headed inside. I ran past the room where everyone was watching TV and didn't stop until I reached my room. After I shut the door behind me, I slid out of my shorts and sweater and pulled on my gray nightgown. The bed looked warm and inviting, so I nestled myself beneath its sheets with my book. The minutes faded into hours as I immersed myself in the romance between Elizabeth Bennett and Mr. Darcy. From time to time, my mind would wander to a cynical place where I compared the societal expectations these two characters faced, which in my opinion paled in comparison, to what stood between Conrad and me. It was like we were on opposite shores of a swirling river with nothing to bridge the gap between us, making the possibility of a future together nonexistent. I tried to focus on the book, but my thoughts always turned back to him. The clock on my phone informed me it was half an hour until midnight. I was three quarters of the way into my book, but my eyes needed a break. I wondered where Caroline was. I figured she would come and talk to me when she came up for bed, but maybe she was still watching a movie. I decided to go downstairs and find her. At the very least, I could always finish off the Twinkies.

When I reached the bottom floor, Caroline's laugh resonated from the hallway. Sneaking over to the TV room, I stole a glance through the doorway. The two of them were nestled side by side on the couch.

"I still think you were disappointed when you first met me," he teased.

"I was not!"

His laughter filled the room. "Yes, you were."

"Oh, you're right. I wanted the plump middle-aged man with the bald head because that's my type."

"I knew it." He leaned toward her and pressed his lips against her cheek.

"You know my lips are over here, right?" she asked, pointing to her mouth.

I shook my head at her. "Subtle" was not a word in Caroline's vocabulary. Not wanting to intrude any longer, my feet led me back to the kitchen. I rummaged around for a few minutes for a healthy snack but ultimately gave up and grabbed the Twinkies. Sitting on the counter with a glass of milk, I savored my snack in peace. Mom used to keep a box or two of the golden spongy treats just for me. She could always tell if I was having a bad day because there would be Twinkie wrappers strewn all around my room. It was one of my strange quirks. Some people liked mashed potatoes or chocolate cake, but not me. My comfort food was Twinkies. I ate another and finished off my milk before carrying the rest of the box up the stairs with me.

As I stepped onto the landing, I heard voices and immediately recognized Helen and Conrad whispering in the hallway outside his room. It was too late for me to turn back, so I held my ground, hoping they would leave before I reached my door. Right away, I noticed he was shirtless and she had on some kind of slinky night-gown; although according to her taste in fashion, it could've been a dress. It was short, red, and made mostly of lace. I decided that was reason enough to hate it.

Her arms slid around his neck, making me cringe. "I've wanted you like this for so long," she whispered. All I could think was her arms didn't belong there. Mine did.

"I know."

"Do you ever think about how things could've been different between us?"

"If they had, neither of us would be standing here right now."

She raked her fingertips through his hair and his hands were at her waist, holding her body to his. I watched in horror as she stood on the tips of her toes to kiss him. I backed into the wall, praying I would go unnoticed until the kiss was over. I held my breath for fear they would hear me. Their kiss lasted a few minutes before he released her and leaned against the doorframe.

"Good night," she said, smiling at him.

"See you in the morning." He watched as she walked down to her room and disappeared behind the door.

Pushing myself away from the wall, I walked forward. At the sound of my footsteps, he turned. His mouth fell open slightly as I approached him.

"It looks like Helen got what she always wanted," I spat, my voice full of contempt. As soon as the words left my mouth, I scolded myself for being angry with him. The only reason he was trying things with her was because I told him to. I wanted to believe encouraging him to move on with his life would make me feel less guilty about the one I cost him, but it didn't. Seeing him with Helen only made me even more miserable.

"I—"

"She looks happy is all I meant." Clutching the box of Twinkies to my chest, I took a step to my door. "Happy looks good on her," I added. I should have walked into the room and not said another word, but apparently I was a glutton for punishment because my body wouldn't move. We stood on either side of the hall, staring at one another.

"Late night snack?" he questioned, pointing to the box.

"Oh, yeah. I didn't eat much at dinner," I answered. "Are you hungry?"

"Just a little."

"I can make you a sandwich or something if you want." The words poured from my mouth before I had a chance to think about what I was saying.

"I can fix it myself."

I nodded my head as my hand reached for the handle of my door. "I hope you sleep well."

"Same to you."

As soon as I was inside, I dropped to the floor. My mind kept replaying the image of Conrad and Helen kissing. The reality of his hands resting on her waist nauseated me. Why was she leaving his room wearing lingerie? Why didn't he have a shirt on? There was only one thing they could be doing, and I pressed my hand over my mouth to prevent myself from getting sick at the thought. I could count the moments I remembered with him on one hand. She had centuries of love and desire to offer Conrad at her disposal. How could I ever compete with her now? In comparison to what I'd just witnessed, Aden's council meeting seemed like Easter dinner. Anyone who prided themselves on taking the high road in life and encouraged others to take it was an asshole. From now on, I'd be taking the low road every time. A knock at my door forced me to my feet, but the knock wasn't coming from the one behind me. I breathed a sigh of relief when I realized it had to be Caroline knocking.

"Come in," I said, throwing myself onto the bed.

She rushed inside my room, smiling from ear-to-ear. When she noticed the expression on my face, she stopped. "What's wrong?"

I pulled out another Twinkie and tore the wrapper open. "Oh, nothing much. I just watched Conrad and Helen making out in the hallway."

"What?" Her voice was louder than I expected, and it made me flinch. "I mean, doesn't she have any decency?"

"Well, in her defense, she didn't know I was right there, but it gets worse. She was leaving his room in the tiniest dress I've ever seen, and he was just wearing shorts."

"That's it! I'm punching her in the face," she said, storming for the door.

"No, Caroline! It's okay. They're just doing what I wanted. I told him to be with Helen, and I shouldn't be angry with him for doing it."

"Yeah, but isn't there at least a three-day grace period, though? I mean, it was a matter of hours."

"He said he never had feelings for her, but maybe he did. I think it would be hard to be around someone you care about for so long and not have those feelings develop into something more."

Her arms were folded across her chest. She looked ready for a fight. "Don't make excuses for them; they don't deserve it." She moved forward and sat next to me on the bed.

"No, if anyone here is undeserving, it's me. Look at all the pain I've caused over the years. Look at all the sacrifices that others have made on my behalf. I don't want any of that. I should be locked away so I can't hurt anyone else." I sucked in a deep breath. "I'm tired of talking about my depressing life. Tell me about what happened with Noah."

"How did you know?"

"I went downstairs to look for you and heard a snippet of your conversation," I said with a grin. "So, did his aim ever manage to find your lips?" Her faced turned the same color as a fire hydrant and I couldn't help but laugh.

"Actually, he's a little old-fashioned. He only kissed me on the cheek, but I think it's cute."

"I knew he liked you!" Despite everything, I smiled at her. Seeing her so happy gave me hope I might be happy again, too.

"I knew you were going to say that!" She grabbed the Twinkie from my hand and took a bite before returning it to me. "I really like him, too. He's so different from any guys our age. Well, my age," she added with a laugh.

I joined in her laughter. "Don't remind me. I'm basically as old as dirt."

She winked at me. "At least you still look good. I'm going to get ready for bed and then I'll come back in here."

"You don't have to stay with me," I replied, feeling guilty.

"I know, but I want to."

"Thanks." I waited on my bed while she changed. She returned a few minutes later with a comb and some hair ties.

"I'll braid your hair and then you can wear it wavy tomorrow."

"Okay." I felt my body relax as she started to comb through my hair. It was like an instant recipe for sleep. Her fingers worked methodically as she plaited my hair into two braids. My eyes started to droop as she fastened the last elastic band. I crawled to the far side of the bed, and we buried ourselves under the covers. "Caroline?"

"Yeah?"

"Thanks for being such a good friend."

"Ditto," she replied.

I rolled over to face the far wall, but unfortunately my thoughts were plagued with visions of Helen and Conrad. The expression on her face after he kissed her haunted me. It had to be the same one I wore when he returned to the castle after the hunting party had come back without him. It was a look of sheer happiness. However, there was one thing that kept nagging me. Several times, he had insisted he didn't have feelings for her, so why did he jump at the chance to be with her? Maybe the thing he wanted all along was my permission for him to do so. The circular thoughts haunted me, keeping me awake. Caroline was already fast asleep. Turning on my back, I stared at the ceiling. The bathroom door was slightly ajar and a stream of light splayed across the end of the bed, illuminating the room. For the first time, I noticed the ceiling wasn't painted a plain white, as I originally thought. Instead, there was a range of whites and creams. The colors swirled together creating the soft edges of clouds. Deep tones of cream set off the bright gold walls, reminding me of a cathedral. All it needed was a couple cherubs flying through the mist, and the ceiling could pose as heaven. The rolling beauty of the clouds tugged at my memory. A sky just like the one above me surfaced at the forefront of my mind. The scent of grass flooded my senses as I was transported to a rolling hillside.

I sat up on the hill, looking out at the river in front of me. The sun warmed me as I pulled the hem of my dress up to my ankles. The green material was much lighter than my winter dresses, but I was still roasting in the summer heat. Pulling a ribbon from my hair, I let the curls fall around my face, and tied the end of my dress around my waist. Now, my skirt fell to my knees, making it much easier to move around. I removed my shoes and ran my toes through the soft blades of grass. Someone approached from behind me. There was no mistaking the clinking sound of a sword sheathed in a belt. I prayed it would be him, making his way toward me, and as I turned around, I saw my prayers had been answered.

"You really should stop evading your guards, my lady," he said, standing in front of me. "It defeats the purpose of hiring us to protect you." His skin was tan from years of working outside in the hot sun, and his rolled up sleeves revealed muscular arms.

"Despite what you might think, I can take care of myself," I replied, walking to the river. "And who ever said I hired you just to protect me?" Flashing him a smile, I turned back to the river. The cool water called out to me, beckoning me to take a drink. He hesitated for a moment before eventually following my lead. I bent to my knees at the edge of the river and plunged my hands beneath the smooth surface. I cupped them and took a drink of the icy liquid. Conrad knelt beside me and watched as I took another sip. Beads of sweat trickled down his temples. I returned my hands to the water, but this time I brought them to his lips, offering a drink.

"Now it's your turn." His fingers brushed my wrists as he drank the water from my hands.

"Thank you," he replied as he wiped the water from his chin. "You aren't anything like what I expected you to be."

His comment surprised me, and for a moment, the only thing I could do was gaze into his bright blue eyes. "What do you mean?"

"I heard people in the village talk about you. They mentioned your kind disposition and soft heart, but I didn't really believe any of it until I met you."

"And now that you've met me?"

He fell backward into the grass. "You don't disappoint."

"Well, I'm happy to live up to the gossip." His stare followed me as I neared a fallen tree. Layers of yellow moss still clung to its bark, the hot summer air drying out the spongy plant. The massive oak acted as a bridge, reaching to the middle of the river. I jumped onto the trunk and carefully stepped forward. When I glanced over my shoulder, Conrad was sitting up straight. He looked as if he were on high alert. Continuing on my path, I held my arms out to the side for balance. The tree narrowed until the trunk was only a little wider than my feet. I wobbled just a bit, prompting Conrad to run to the base of the tree.

"Please don't hurt yourself," he called out to me. From the way he spoke, I could tell I was making him nervous. I spun around quickly and tried to walk back to him, but as I did so, I lost my balance. Frigid water chilled my body as I sank beneath its surface. The weight of my dress held me down, forcing me to descend toward the bottom of the riverbed. I was only submerged for a few moments before his hands thrust me back into the air. I coughed uncontrollably as he carried me out of the water. We collapsed on the grass, sucking warm air into our lungs. He hovered above me as I rested on the ground. "Are you hurt?" He scanned my body, searching for any signs I might be injured.

"I'm not hurt." My fingers ran along the side of his face and down his neck. He took a strand of my hair in his hand and looped it around his finger. "And I have you to thank for that." His damp shirt clung to his body, and I could just barely feel his skin beneath it as I rested my hands on his chest. Something about the sensation of his body on top of mine felt so familiar, even though I hadn't known him for long. "Who was the girl you were talking to yesterday?" My fingertips trailed up and down the length of his neck and chest, almost acting of their own accord. As he realized I was still touching him, he froze. Withdrawing my hands form his chest, I laid them at my sides.

"You mean Helen?"

"Yes," I answered. "She's quite beautiful."

"I suppose she is. I haven't paid much attention."

"She certainly pays attention to you," I replied. "I can tell from the way she looks at you that she loves you."

"I know she does. She's felt that way since we were young."

"Do you return her affections?"

"No."

My fingers brushed the line of his jaw. "As your queen, do you have to obey my every command? Even if it's something you might not want to do?"

"Yes," he whispered. "What would you have me do, my lady?"

I traced the edges of his lips, savoring the softness of them. "Do you really need me to tell you?"

His blue eyes bore into me as his arms rested by my sides. A mischievous grin covered his face. The space between our mouths lessened by the second, and my body longed to feel his kiss. Another inch and his lips would be pressed against mine.

"I'm sorry to interrupt, your grace." The sound of Marie's voice thrust us from the daze we'd been swept up in. "But the king is requesting your presence at the castle."

"It's quite all right, Marie. I fell in the river and would have drowned if Conrad hadn't have been here."

"Were you hurt?" She dropped to her knees beside us. Conrad was still lying on top of me and made no effort to move.

"I was being foolish," I replied, laughing. "I tried to walk on the fallen tree and lost my balance." Before I knew what was happening, Conrad lifted me in his arms and began carrying me back to the castle.

"I better help her, just in case she feels faint again," he said to Marie.

"Yes, of course," she replied.

My arms tightened around his neck and I laid my head on his shoulder. "Thank you," I whispered.

"I swore an oath to protect you with my life. I was just doing my duty."

"Is that all I am to you? An oath?" His feet stopped dead in their tracks, and he turned his head to look at me. The skin of his neck was soft beneath my hand, and I touched my lips to his cheek.

My body jerked upright, the room around me suddenly coming back into focus. Why did I have to remember being with him like that? It wasn't fair to be constantly reminded of something I couldn't have. The pressure of his arms holding me as he pulled me from the water lingered in my mind. Our bodies had been but a breath apart, and the nearness of his flesh made me want him even more. I was tired of feeling like this; the high road could go screw itself. Five hundred years of wanting someone couldn't be erased overnight. And part of me understood that I'd never stop wanting him. I hopped out of bed and ran to the bathroom, loosening my hair from the tight braids as I moved. Once my hair was free, I tousled the smooth waves with my fingers. After putting on a little makeup, I rummaged around in my bag and found a silky purple nightgown. The dark color of the fabric shone against my pale skin while a band of pink lace covered the top part of the gown, adding to its delicate appearance. The light blush on my cheeks made it seem like I was glowing. It might not have been red lace, but the effect was still pleasing to the eye.

I crossed the hall in two steps. His door was ajar and I slipped inside, shutting it behind me. Conrad stood in front of the window, staring out into the city. The door creaked as it closed, and he spun at the sound. His expression informed me that I was the last person he expected to see.

"I'm sorry. I shouldn't have barged in," I stated, moving to leave. In a second, he was across the room, holding the door shut with his hand. My back pressed against the door as he bent toward me. Mere inches of space separated our mouths.

"I'd like it if you stayed."

"That day at the river, when you were one of my guards, do you remember it?"

"Of course," he answered, waiting for me to continue speaking.

"You risked your life to save me without a second thought, and I just wanted to know why. You weren't one of my secundae then."

"You know why," he whispered, wrapping a strand of my hair around one of his fingers.

He dropped his hand, stepping so close that our bodies were almost flush against one another. It was only a little while ago Helen was the one touching him. With that image plastered in my mind, I said, "It must be hard to be around someone for so long and have to suppress your feelings for them."

"It is." He placed his other hand on the door, right beside my waist. The remaining dregs of hope drained from my body. He cared for Helen more than he let on.

"You should've told me," I replied, my gaze lingering on our feet.

"I thought I'd already made my feelings abundantly clear."

"My mind keeps jumping back and forth between two different lifetimes with you. I feel like I can hardly tell what is real and what is just a memory."

"Isn't it all the same?" he asked.

"I was beginning to think so."

He shook his head. "You don't—"

"I can tell she really loves you," I said, interrupting him. "You can see it in the way she looks at you, but it's a little different from how you look at her."

"And how do I look at her?" Despite the dim lighting in the room, I watched as his brow furrowed slightly.

"I'm not really sure. I haven't quite figured out what your look means just yet."

"Then ask me what it means."

I sighed, clinging to my last shred of hope as I bit my lip. "I'm afraid, because if it's the answer I don't want to hear, it will break my heart."

"And if it's the answer you want?"

"I'll know that I'm the most selfish and horrible person in the world."

His hand at my waist trembled. "Either answer I give causes you pain," he replied, backing away from me. "It hardly seems fair."

"What about our lives has ever been fair? Especially yours." My fingers reached for the scab on his chest.

"Getting to see you again seems fair to me".

"Conrad—"

"I know, I shouldn't say things like that to you."

"How's your leg?" I asked, changing the subject in an attempt to distract myself from how much I wanted to kiss him.

"It's feeling better. I can put all my weight on it when I walk now." Without waiting for permission, I raised the leg of his shorts to assess his wound. Dried blood covered the white gauze taped to his leg.

"Your dressing needs to be changed."

"It's fine. I'll change it later."

"Lie on the bed and I'll do it for you," I ordered with complete authority. Reluctantly, he walked to the king-size bed and sat on top of the dark green comforter. He had a first aid kit perched on a dresser next to the bathroom door. I retrieved it and took off the old bandage with great care, studying his wound. My stitches were still holding; his flesh had started to grow back together. I soaked a cotton ball with peroxide before pressing it to his skin. He winced, the injury still tender.

Suddenly, my eyes darted back and forth as Conrad's bedroom disappeared from sight. Rough logs stacked on top of each other to form the walls of a small cottage. Conrad sat in front of me, propped against a wobbling table. An arrow protruded from his chest, just beneath his shoulder. Blood spilled from the wound, saturating his shirt. His body jerked in pain as I eased the torn linen from his arms.

"Hold still!"

"I'm trying, my lady, but in case you haven't noticed, I've been shot!"

"I know!" I shouted. "Because in case you haven't noticed, I'm the one cleaning your wound!" I broke off the arrow's tip, making him groan. Then I tore a strip of fabric from my skirt, tying it into a makeshift bandage. Every time I touched him, he shuddered uncontrollably. "You could've been killed, you damn fool! The only reason you're injured is because you pushed me out of the way!"

"I had to. You would've died if I hadn't."

"I don't care."

"Evey," he whispered.

"I've got to remove the arrow's shaft," I said, trying to prepare myself for the agony I was about to inflict upon him.

His fingertips lifted my chin upward, raising my line of sight. "Evey," he repeated, "this wound will heal, but the one I'd have from your death wouldn't. I'd never recover, no matter how much time passed."

"Why can't you understand that's how I feel about you?" I asked, focusing on his shredded skin. "I'm still so mad at you, I can't see straight."

"Not words one wants to hear, seeing as how you're about to pull an arrow from my chest." The grin he wore was beyond irritating.

"Cheeky bastard," I muttered, glaring at him. Wrenching the wooden shaft from his flesh, I tried my best to ignore the gasps of pain rattling in the back of his throat. I replaced the arrow with some cloth, deftly staunching the stream of blood.

"Why don't you do me a favor and make this cheeky bastard a husband?"

"You're ridiculous! I can't believe you'd even ask me such a thing right now!"

"And you're beautiful," he replied, pulling me into his lap.

"Distracting me with a marriage proposal won't work. I'm still angry with you."

His lips met my neck, gradually working their way up. "I'm not trying to distract you. I'm trying to make you my wife," he whispered between kisses. "You wouldn't make an injured man beg, would you?"

Unable to suppress my smile, I pressed my mouth to his, kissing him softly. "Yes, I would, so you better start begging."

"Evey Rhodes, will you do me the honor of becoming my wife?"

"No," I teased.

"No?"

"That's what I said."

"Hmm," he replied. "Then, you leave me no choice." He jerked his sling and bandage loose, allowing his wound to reopen.

"What are you doing?" I scrambled to reapply the dressing, but he held me back.

"Bleeding out. If you won't marry me, what's the point in fixing my shoulder?"

I reached for the stained fabric again, trying with all my might to retrieve it. Drops of crimson trickled down his chest, their rate steadily increasing. "Let me retie your bandage!"

"Nope, not the answer I was looking for."

"Conrad!"

"I'm going to ask you again." His hand slid over the curve of my jaw, drawing my face to his. "Will you marry me?"

"Yes," I whispered, "even if you are a damn fool."

As the fog around me cleared, I stared at my hands. All traces of blood and grime had vanished. Conrad was watching me from his bed. "What did you see this time?" he asked.

"How did you know?"

"Your whole body became rigid and your breathing slowed. Then your eyes glazed over. It's what happens every time you remember something."

"I was pulling an arrow from your chest, and you proposed to me while I was doing it," I said. "This incessant war . . . it doesn't even phase you, does it?"

"Not at all. I was born to be a secundae, just as you were born to bring light into this world."

"Where were we?"

"Just outside London. We had a manor on the outskirts of the city."

"Who shot you?"

"I believe it was a stray arrow, probably meant for a soul." Noticing my look of confusion, he continued with his story. "We had to flee from our home because a couple dissimulo demons and a pack of souls attacked the town we lived in."

"Aden almost found me once before?"

"No, the souls didn't know you were there. Their attack was on the village, not you."

"Why would souls attack a village?"

He had his hands folded behind his head as he lay on the bed. "Every so often, Satan releases his minions to wreak a little havoc on Earth. I assume you're familiar with the Black Death?"

"Of course."

"That was caused by souls, too."

"But surely someone would notice demonic creatures attacking and killing thousands of people? I mean, the magnitude of devastation the Black Plague caused couldn't be overlooked."

"Usually people have a tendency to attach a rational explanation to things they can't comprehend."

"I wanted to do the same thing at the diner when that woman disintegrated right in front of me. I couldn't believe what I was seeing."

"Exactly. Most people aren't programmed to believe in the impossible."

"How many times have you been injured while trying to protect me?" I questioned.

"Honestly, too many to count."

I taped a clean piece of gauze on his leg. "I'm sorry."

"Why are you sorry?"

"Because your body has been beaten, stabbed, burned, and bruised. You've had to endure countless injuries, and I'm to blame for it. At what point will you decide you've had enough?"

"There are only two things that would make me leave you, and that's if you asked me to or if it's what I had to do in order to protect you."

My lack of sleep was starting to catch up to me. Before I knew what I was doing, I collapsed on the bed beside him. "Why didn't Helen stay in your room tonight?"

He shrugged his shoulders and gave me an impassive look. "I'm old-fashioned."

"Do you really expect me to believe that?"

"I don't know," he replied, clutching the pendant he'd given me so many lifetimes ago. "Do you expect me to believe you don't want to be with me?"

I should've anticipated he'd see through my attempt to distance myself from him. After all, he knew me better than anyone, including Aden. I wasn't sure how I knew this, but Conrad loved me with a force Aden couldn't even come close to matching. "What makes you think that?" As I sat up straight, his hand slid down my chest, landing in my lap.

"Why else would you be sitting on my bed in the middle of the night?"

"Friends hang out in each other's room in the middle of the night."

"Oh, so we're friends now?" he asked, sounding bored.

"It's not like there's a rule saying we can't be."

"Correct me if I'm wrong, but friends don't usually wear lace nightgowns in front of each other, do they?" His fingers skimmed over the thin material covering my thigh.

"You didn't seem to mind Helen's red dress earlier," I snapped.

"You're the one who told me to be with her."

"So, if I told you to jump off a bridge, does that mean you'd do it?" I knew I was being immature, but the thought of him kissing Helen infuriated me.

"No," he replied, gripping the small of my back. "But if you told me to kiss you right now, I would." Relishing in the feel of his hands, I realized the more we touched, the more I never wanted it to stop.

"Did you ever try being with Helen when the Concilium wanted you to stay away from me?" I moved closer to him as I spoke. My mind and body were contradicting one another. While I had enough sense to steer the conversation away from the topic of kissing, my body was being drawn to his like a magnet.

"She asked me to be with her, but I told her no. At that time, I didn't want anyone but you."

"And now you want Helen?"

"I do care for her," he whispered. "Maybe you were right when you said she and I belong together. I mean, if you and I both die, we don't even go to the same place." The expression on his face seemed oddly calm.

"What do you mean we don't go to the same place?" Fear saturated my voice as I grasped his arm for strength. "I know you go to heaven while you wait for me to be reborn, but where do I go?"

"You and Aden used to go to the gates outside the Garden of Eden."

"But why?"

"Because the Concilium thought it would help both of you remember why you're being reborn. They thought it would remind you and Adam that you're both part of a bigger picture. At least that was the case until they put you in hiding to protect you from him."

His revelation stunned me. "I feel like everyone wants to keep us apart."

"Isn't that what you've been trying to do?"

"I have my reasons."

"Everyone has a million reasons why we shouldn't be together," he said, sliding his arms around me. "We shouldn't add to their list."

I laid my head on his chest. "I just feel like I'm not worthy of you."

"Before I met you, I was failing at taking care of the two most important people in my life. I worked night and day as a blacksmith. Sometimes I'd earn a little money by brawling in different taverns, but most of the time, I lived in a constant state of exhaustion. The only thing I had to look forward to was that one day I'd die and all my pain and suffering would come to an end."

Despair filled my soul, his words slicing into me as if they were knives. "That's no way to live," I whispered cradling his face in my palms.

"No, it isn't, and then I met you. You gave me hope I could change my fate and provide for my family, but more than that, you made me want to live. As soon as I met you, my eyes were opened to how much joy and beauty this world has to offer." He brushed the tears from my cheeks and smiled. "Without you, I have no life."

"Do you love me?"

"I would think that would be obvious," he replied with a grin.

"I want to hear you say it." I placed my hands on his chest and stared into his eyes.

He took a strand of my hair and looped it around his finger. "I love you more than anything in this world," he whispered. "And I always will." His face hovered just above mine as he leaned over me, my breath quickening in response. "Evey, it's been so long."

My hand slid to the back of his neck, and I savored in the way he sighed at my touch. "Then kiss me."

For a moment, we stared at one another. How many times had we done this? How many times had anticipation surged through our veins, intensifying the desire radiating from our bodies? Just as the wait for his touch threatened to become too unbearable, he joined our lips, his hands knotting in my hair as he held me to him. Deepening the kiss, I opened my mouth to taste him. Everything about him seemed familiar, and as if acting out of memory, my body curved upward, pressing into his while he trailed kisses along the length of my neck. The desire I felt for him superseded every other emotion known to man. This is the connection my soul longed for me to remember. His skin warmed my lips as I made a path across his body, grazing his neck and shoulders. Slowly, my nightgown slid over my waist as his fingertips tugged on the delicate material. Then he buried his face in my chest, his tongue gliding over my flesh.

"Do you want me to stop?" he asked, tossing my nightgown to the floor.

"Please don't," I whispered. His rough hands massaged my thighs, making my body tremble, and I gasped with delight as his mouth passed over the curves of my hips. "Conrad?"

"What is it?"

"I never knew what it meant to truly need someone until I met you." Grabbing his arm, I pulled him on top of me once more. "I love you," I confessed, gazing into his eyes.

My fingers ran along the lines of his abdomen, and I relished in the way his skin felt against mine. Our legs intertwined, reinforcing our hold on one another. His breath was hot on my neck as he planted one kiss after the other, taking his time as he made his way to my mouth. Once again, our lips connected, the embrace stealing my breath away. Pleasure flooded my senses, the feeling escalating with each second he continued to touch me. Easing the straps of my bra over my shoulders, he loosened the garment. I straddled his lap and exhaled with contentment as he rubbed my back. We were so swept up in one another, we barely acknowledged the knock at the door.

"Conrad, I couldn't sleep so I thought I'd come back over," Helen said, bursting into his room. As she took in the scene in front of her, Conrad moved to block my half-naked body from her view. "Would either of you care to explain what the hell is going on here?" Her glare could cut through six feet of concrete. Grabbing my nightgown, I slid it over my head in a panic.

"Helen," Conrad said, approaching her. She avoided his gaze and instead focused her hatred on me.

She blamed me for everything that had ever gone wrong for her, and I was tired of her bullshit. "Well, let's examine the facts; Conrad and I were kissing on his bed with the majority of our clothes off. I don't think it's all that hard to figure out," I spat. Her eyes narrowed and I knew she would be out for blood.

"What has she done to you now?" Helen asked.

Conrad stared at her in confusion. "What are you talking about?"

"One second she wants you, the next she doesn't. She's just toying with you," Helen answered, reaching out to take him in her arms.

"You don't understand what you're talking about."

"You don't act like this when you're not around her."

"I'm acting like I always do."

"No, you aren't. We were close once, and there was a time when I knew you better than anyone."

"That was centuries ago. We've both changed since then. We aren't kids anymore."

"She'll ruin you, just like she did Aden."

"She didn't ruin Aden! He was the master of his own demise, and I'm not like him," he replied, glaring at her. "Evey brings out the best in me."

She placed her hands on his chest. "I can do that for you, too. If you give me a chance, I can give you what you want."

"It was wrong of me to lead you on earlier, but I was under the impression Evey didn't want to be with me."

"And now she does?"

"We can't help how we feel about each other," I answered. "I tried to give him up, but I can't. And to be quite honest, I don't want to."

Her eyes turned to me. Ripping her hands from his chest, she charged toward me. "All of this is your fault!" she screamed. "Why couldn't you have just left us alone, all those years ago? Conrad and I were supposed to get married before you came into the picture."

"That was an arranged marriage," Conrad added. "I'm sorry I called it off, but I couldn't go through with marrying someone I wasn't in love with."

"Your mother and Cecily wanted us to be together. Don't we owe it to them to at least try?"

"Helen, I can't love you the way you want me to."

"You don't know that."

"Yes, I do. I've loved Evey since the first time I met her. There will never be a time when I'm not in love with her."

"You don't deserve him," she added, turning her rage to me.

"I can't argue that, but I also finally believe that I make him happy. Isn't that what matters most?"

"I can make him happy too! You've never given me the opportunity to prove it!" she shouted. Her hand soared through the air, aiming for my face, but before it could make contact, I caught her wrist. Her hand stopped midair and I tightened my grasp.

"Don't do that," I seethed, throwing her arm away from me.

Turning back to Conrad, Helen warned in a menacing voice, "You'll get hurt again, and it will be because of her."

"If I get hurt, then so be it. It's my duty to protect her."

"Aden won't stop looking for her. He'll kill you again so he can take her back."

"I'd willingly go with Aden before I'd let him kill Conrad," I said.

"For his sake, I hope so." She stormed out of the room without saying another word and slammed the door behind her. Conrad and

I stood motionless in the wake of her outburst. I opened my mouth to speak but had no idea what to say. There wasn't an appropriate way to express what had just happened.

"I'm sorry," he finally said as he walked to me.

"If anyone should be sorry, it's me."

"No, I shouldn't have led her on like that."

"Why did you go to her as soon as I told you I didn't want to be with you?"

"I was hurt, and I do care for her. I've always known how she felt about me, and I always felt guilty I never returned her feelings," he replied. "I also figured if you saw the two of us together, you'd realize you didn't want me to be with her. I hoped it would make you see you still wanted to be with me."

Flinging my arms around his neck, I hugged my body to his. "As I said before, I never stopped wanting to be with you."

A swell of excitement lit up my skin as his lips grazed the length of my neck. "I'm sorry we were interrupted." His breath tickled my flesh as he spoke. "Just so you know, next time I won't be stopping for anything."

"Is that so?"

"I don't care if someone is standing in the room or an explosion goes off. I'm not stopping."

"After your scheme with the arrow, I'd expect nothing less from you," I teased, planting a tender kiss on his lips. I held on to him as he swept me up and carried me over to the bed. "Evey?"

"Yeah?"

"Meeting you was the best thing that ever happened to me."

"Meeting you saved me." I smiled. "When you came back into my life a few days ago, I came alive. The way you make me feel is unlike anything I've ever known."

"I know what you mean." My heart raced as he covered my neck in kisses. When he finally came up for air, he leaned away from me, obviously lost in thought. "Can I ask you something?"

"What is it?"

"I know what we have is different than what you had with Aden, and I know you love me more, but I just wanted to ask why. It's been such a long time since I've been able to talk to you about the past, and it's something I've always been curious about."

"I remembered the council meeting Aden invited you to where he had you arrested. He was so consumed with hate and rage, it's hard to believe he could possess any kindness at all. I'm so sorry he subjected you to such a horrible fate in order to hurt me."

"I was an adult. I knew falling in love with you was an act of treason and punishable by death, I just didn't care."

"Your blatant disregard for your own well-being is infuriating," I replied. "I wish I could erase that experience for you, like it never happened."

"Being executed is what allowed me to be made into a secundae. And it happened so fast, I don't really remember it," he said, shrugging. "I did manage to piss Aden off right before it happened though. I wish you could've seen his face; it was priceless." He shook his head with laughter.

"What did you do to piss him off?"

"I simply told him that I didn't care if he killed me, because while he was busy planning my execution, I was busy making love to his wife."

I stared at him in disbelief. "You said what?"

"And I told him he was too late in cutting out my eyes and slicing off my hands, because they'd already discovered the entirety of your body."

I stifled a laugh. "I'm sure he didn't like that."

He wore a grin that would've made a lingerie model blush. "Not at all."

My fingertips delicately stroked the line of his jaw, my love for him growing with each second that passed. "I love you for the man you are, Conrad. You're so tender and compassionate." I inched closer to him, needing to feel the warmth of his flesh on mine. "The way you love me is so beautiful and intense. You savor every moment we have together, and when you touch me, I never want it to stop."

"I value every moment with you because there hasn't always been a guarantee that I'll be allowed to have more time with you."

"I want you to know I'll do everything within my power to make sure we have more time together."

"Good, and I believe you were just alluding to how good of a lover I am a minute ago," he teased, looking mischievous.

Heat permeated my flesh, hot enough to scald. He waited patiently for me to answer, and I knew my skin had to be the same color as my hair. "All I can recall is the memory of the night we shared before you were executed, but I have to say, my memory didn't leave me unsatisfied."

"That's because I've never left you unsatisfied." His hand slipped under my nightgown, caressing my back. "And you won't have to rely on your memories much longer."

"I sure hope not," I whispered, the rate of my breathing speeding up as his hand slid down my skin. Whatever hardships we faced were worth it for moments like these. The night we spent together before he died, I had yearned to know his touch. Even though the few hours we had spent in my room were brief, I would've rather had that than spend a lifetime never being with him at all. A love that transcended time itself welled within me and without thinking, I flung my arms around his neck and joined our mouths with so much force, it felt as if we were the only two living beings in existence.

17

SCARS

A single stream of light fell over my eyes, stirring me from the lull of sleep. It danced off the dark wood floor and illuminated the entire room. Conrad was still asleep, so I carefully rolled out of bed to go check on Caroline. Seeing that she was still unconscious, I decided to make my way down to the kitchen. After filling two bowls with milk and cereal, I headed back to Conrad's room.

"Hi," he said, his voice tainted with the dregs of sleep.

"Hi."

"What is that?" His attention fell to the bowls I was carrying.

"Oh, I brought up some breakfast for us." I set the tray holding our cereal on a small table beside his bed.

"Breakfast in bed? How did I get so lucky?"

"It's just cereal."

"It's still very nice," he replied, snatching me on top of him. "Although, I think I'd rather have you for breakfast." My pale skin flushed at his unmistakable implication. Though he had said similar things in the past, I thought about how close we came the night before. For the first time, what he said felt real and possible, and it made me realize that I wanted what he was offering. But the timing was so off, especially because we seemed to be up to our ears in supernatural warfare.

"We better eat before it gets soggy," I replied, smiling as I presented him with a bowl. "What's the head of the Concilium like?"

"He's probably more of what you would expect a consiliarius to be like. Everest is very traditional, and he isn't happy when someone disobeys the orders of the Concilium."

"So, I'm guessing you aren't one of his favorite people?"

"Not by a long shot."

"Helen said he respects me. Is that true?"

"The caput has always been somewhat enamored of you."

"Caput?"

"It means head. It's what we all call him, if you address him in person."

"Oh, but why would he be enamored of me?"

"You were the first woman; you're the ultimate representation of femininity. It's hard for any man to ignore your presence."

"That kind of makes me sound like a witch or something, like I can just cast spells over people."

"It's not like that, but it will come in handy if you ever need the Concilium's support for anything."

"Everest is the one who told you that you'd never be reborn again if you disobeyed his orders?"

"He did."

"I'll convince him to change his mind. They need me to stand against Aden, and I'll only do that if you're by my side. If they want my help, then they can give me something I want in return."

"That will certainly be an interesting conversation."

I slid my hand inside his. "I won't allow this to be your last life."

"Thank you. I'm once more in your debt."

"You saved me from a torturous existence, and don't ask me how, but I know if I hadn't met you when I did, I wouldn't have been able to hold on much longer. Being bound to Aden was destroying me."

"I'm only glad I could be there to help."

"You did so much more than that."

"All I did was stumble into the arms of a beautiful woman," he replied, walking to the bathroom. I piled up our dishes and made the bed while waiting for him to return. "You don't have to clean my room." He was standing in the doorway, wearing nothing but a towel around his waist as he stared at me. The lines that stretched from the bottom of his abs to his pelvic bone appeared to be chiseled into his skin.

I adusted the pillows on his bed. "I don't mind."

"You can talk to me while I take a shower."

"I can do that." I sat on the counter between the double sinks and combed my fingers through my hair, smoothing it over my shoulders. Conrad watched as he waited for the water to heat up. "You're staring."

"When you see something beautiful, do you not feel an inclination to stop and admire it?"

"I suppose so."

Steam billowed from the shower behind him. Without warning, he dropped his towel. It happened so fast, I didn't have time to turn away from his naked body.

"Who's the one staring now?" he asked with a characteristically devilish grin plastered across his face.

"I have no idea what you're talking about."

"Really?"

I shrugged, donning my most innocent look. He laughed before disappearing behind the shower curtain. "So, what are some things we enjoyed doing together?" I asked, curious about the happier and simpler times that we shared.

"Considering the last time we dated was 1926, I'd have to say most of those things have changed."

"Oh yeah," I replied. "Sometimes it feels as though we never stopped being together."

"I wish that were possible." The sound of flowing water was

therapeutic, and I couldn't prevent myself from imagining what was happening behind the curtain. He surprised me when he said, "I did manage to see you a few times, though."

"That must've been hard on you." It had to be painful to know the person you loved couldn't remember who you were. A lesser man would've bailed a long time ago.

"It was, but I knew it wouldn't last forever. Plus, I did get to see you in a poodle skirt."

"What?"

"You worked in a diner in 1954, and I stopped in for lunch one day. I shouldn't have, but I couldn't help it," he said, stepping out of the shower. "I just wanted to hear your voice."

"And did you talk to me?"

"I did." He wrapped the towel around his waist and made his way over to where I was sitting. "You even gave me a kiss on the cheek."

"I kissed you?"

"There was a guy harassing you and being an ass. I took him outside and knocked him out. You gave me a free milkshake and a kiss in return."

"Has there ever been a time when you haven't been my knight in shining armor?"

"As a matter of fact, no." He inched closer to me, his fingers tracing the length of my legs. "You're a very high-maintenance woman."

"I can't help it if people are constantly after me," I protested.

"I wasn't complaining, Evey."

"I should probably go check on Caroline."

"Do you have to?"

"I'm sure she'll be wondering where I am." He backed up, allowing me to jump off the vanity, and I strode through his room back to mine. Caroline stirred from her sleep as I shut the door.

"Hey, were you out all night?" Letting out a deep yawn, she sat up.

"Yeah, I went to talk to Conrad."

"And?"

"And what?"

"And was his bed comfy?"

"Caroline!"

"It's a question! Besides, inquiring minds want to know," she added with a laugh. "Not to mention, every time you two are near each other, it's like watching a steamy soap opera."

"I have no idea what you're talking about," I replied innocently.

"Oh, please. The looks you give one another would embarrass an erotica novelist." I shook my head, but the grin on my face said everything. She scooted over on the bed and I perched beside her. "Did you know Noah was the one who helped Conrad become a secundae?"

"Yeah, Conrad told me," I answered. "Did Noah tell you why?"

"He said the devotion the two of you have for one another doesn't come along very often and shouldn't be wasted because of Aden's jealousy."

I collapsed on one of the pillows lying behind me. "That was nice of him to say."

"I think he felt just like your mom, dad, Mickey, and Kit. They were all rooting for you and Conrad to end up together."

"Yeah, the only reason he tried to be with Helen was because I told him to," I said, staring at the clouds above me. "And he thought if I saw them together, it would make me realize I don't really want him to be with her."

"Lucky for him, he was right."

"It's been hard for him, though, to be in love with me when I didn't even know who he was. I can't imagine what that was like." Glancing over at Caroline, I saw she was staring at the ceiling too. "He was also supposed to marry Helen before he met me. Their fathers had set up an arranged marriage for them."

"Oh," she answered. "That is a long time to be in love with someone who isn't in love with you."

"I have to admit, her hatred of me isn't completely unjustified."

"You can't help who you love."

"I guess you're right."

"Of course I am," she agreed, jumping up from the bed. "Come on, let's get ready. We have a long day ahead of us."

"Don't remind me. We're flying to New York," I groaned, rolling off the mattress. "I don't like to fly."

I showered and dried my hair quickly. Then, once Caroline was in the shower, I started on my makeup. All our clothes and makeup were mixed together in one big mess. Grabbing a tube of her lip-gloss, I leaned toward the mirror and applied a fresh layer to my lips.

"Are you going to sit by Noah on the plane?" I couldn't resist teasing her, especially because she'd done her fair share of teasing me about Conrad.

"Oh please," she replied as she stepped out of the shower. "I'm sure he has to sit with his secundae or in some special chair." She tightened the light blue towel around her body as she came to stand next to me. As I waited for my mascara to dry, I watched her squeeze the water out of her hair; the golden strands hung around her face in tousled waves. I pulled on a pair of black shorts and a maroon sweater before returning to the bathroom. Then I read-justed my necklace, fitting it into the neckline of my shirt. I had just started to drag a comb through my curls when a soft knock sounded at the door. We looked at each other, unsure of which room the sound had come from. A second knock informed us someone was outside Caroline's door.

"Who is it?" I moved next to her, sidestepping into her room as we waited for an answer.

"It's me, Noah."

"Come in!" Caroline scowled at me as I answered for her.

"Evey!"

"What?" I tried to sound as guilt-free as possible, but despite my efforts, I started to snicker.

"I'm wearing a towel!"

"Well, I guess you better keep one hand free to hold it up." She swatted at me, but I managed to duck out of her reach. Running back into the bathroom, I snuck behind the door, making sure I was out of sight. The door creaked as he opened it, and I could see

Caroline standing by the bed from my hiding spot. He stepped inside and closed the door behind him before setting eyes on her.

"Oh," he said, blushing. "I didn't realize you were indisposed."

"It's just a towel," she said with a slight shrug. She was trying to act nonchalant, but her flushed cheeks said otherwise. However, Noah didn't seem to notice because he nervously tugged at the collar of his white button-up shirt.

"Is there anything you need before we leave?" He inched closer to her, his hand barely making contact with the side of her cheek.

"Is that an offer, or a question?" I watched as the ends of his ears turned red.

"Uh—"

"I'm teasing you. I have everything I need, but thanks for asking."

"Good, that's really good. I just wanted to be sure," he said, tucking the bottom of his shirt back into his brown slacks.

"When will we be leaving for New York?"

"About two hours. The plane should be ready to take us by then. The gas tank has to be filled and a final inspection has to be completed before it can fly."

"I guess I better finish getting ready and pack up all my stuff."

"Yeah," he muttered, staring at her. "That would be good." They stood in silence as he continued to watch her.

"Noah?"

"Yes?" His voice was so low that I almost didn't hear him.

"Are you planning to stay while I change?" She placed one hand on her hip as she waited for him to answer.

"Yes," he said with a dazed expression on his face. Realizing what he had said, the color faded from his cheeks. "I mean, what?"

Caroline snickered at his reply, and I had to slap my own hand over my mouth to keep from erupting in laughter. "I do admire your honesty, but seeing as how you haven't asked me on a date yet, I'm going to have to ask you to step outside while I finish getting ready."

"Of course." He tried and failed miserably to regain his composure. Dropping his gaze to the floor, he didn't dare look up at her. She followed him to the door and opened it as he stepped toward the threshold. At the last second, she grabbed his hand, preventing him from leaving her room altogether.

"I'll see you downstairs," she added, kissing him on the cheek.

"I look forward to it."

She shut the door behind him just as I came out of the bathroom.

"What on earth have you done to Noah?" Our eyes met, and before she could answer, we exploded into a fit of giggles.

"I honestly couldn't tell you."

"Whatever it is, he sure doesn't seem to know what to do with himself when he's around you!" I finished combing my hair and packed up my things while Caroline got ready. Gathering all of her clothes, I folded them into her bag while she slid on a light green dress. She threw a brown jacket over it and picked up her bag from the bed. "You ready?"

"I guess," I replied, following her out the door. I had decided to take everything with me because I had no idea if we would be coming back. According to Conrad, it was always better to be over-prepared than under. As we walked down the steps, I noticed everyone waiting for us on the white couches. Milton jumped up to take our bags and set them with a pile of luggage by the stairs. Noah sat on a couch by himself, and Caroline moved to sit next to him. Helen was sulking in one of the armchairs, not caring to acknowledge anyone else's existence while Conrad was on the other couch. He motioned for me to join him, and I shot a quick glance Helen's way before sitting down. She was staring at the floor and took no notice of my presence. I breathed a sigh of relief—I could live with being ignored. When I sat, Conrad grabbed my hand, interlacing our fingers.

"I see everything is in order," Noah stated, watching Conrad and me. "I'm waiting for the pilot to call me about the plane. It shouldn't be too much longer."

"Where will we be going when we get to New York?" I moved my gaze from Conrad to Noah as I spoke.

"We'll be going to see the caput. I've already called to let him know to expect us. He's hosting a fundraiser tomorrow night for one of the charities he heads. We'll be staying in a hotel near his apartment."

"Oh," I replied. "What kind of charities does he head?"

"All sorts. He mostly connects himself to charities for children or medical research of some kind. Since most members of the Concilium don't work, we find other ways to contribute to society."

"That's really nice," Caroline added.

Noah's phone rang, drawing his attention from her. "Thanks Bill, we'll be there in twenty minutes," he said, hanging up the phone. "The plane is ready." He picked up his and Caroline's bags before she could reach them. She smiled at him and followed his lead. Milton and Helen walked behind them in silence while Conrad grabbed our bags.

"I can carry that." I watched as he swung my bag over his shoulder.

"I know," he replied, "but I want to carry it for you."

I kissed him softly on the lips. "Thanks."

"Don't mention it, my lady."

We held hands as we walked down the stairs, trying to catch up with the rest of the group. Once we were outside, we headed to the parking garage across the street and filed into a black SUV. The inside of the car was immaculate, down to the fibers in the carpet. It made me feel like we had stolen a vehicle from the Secret Service or something. I guess it was important for us to travel as inconspicuously as possible. If Aden could find me in Estill Springs of all places, he'd find me here. His reign of death and destruction had to end. It was time he paid for his crimes, and I was the one with the power to make that happen. If I could remember where I put the apple seeds, I'd be able to stop him once and for all. Perhaps if I channeled all my energy, I would be able to remember where they were. Minutes passed while I'd been lost to my thoughts and it wasn't until Conrad squeezed my hand that I even noticed the car had stopped.

"We're here," he said, pulling me from the car.

"Don't remind me," I groaned.

"I can distract you on the plane if you want." Conrad raised his eyebrows at me in a suggestive manner.

I tried to laugh at his joke, but my attention deviated to the sweat covering my palms. Conrad's hand stayed on the small of my back as we headed to the plane, but the knot in my stomach continued to take root and grow. The plane seemed to shrink with each step we took, and I figured it couldn't have more than ten seats on it.

"This isn't a plane," Caroline announced. "It's a freaking minivan."

"It's perfectly safe," Noah said from behind her.

She turned around and shot him a glare. "Just so you know, if I die on this plane, I'll make sure I'm reborn so I can come back and kick your ass."

"For that, I'll bring you back myself," he replied with a wink.

Everyone else filed on without much complaint, but Conrad practically had to push me onto the plane. We shuffled to the last set of seats, him occupying the seat by the window while I sat in the aisle seat. Noah and Caroline sat together just in front of us. Their seats faced one another and a small table stood in between them. My pulse quickened as the door to the plane closed and the engines started. Fastening my seatbelt, I took the hand Conrad offered and squeezed it tight. As I studied his arm, I noticed a long white mark trailing up to his elbow.

"How did you get this scar?"

"Cecily," he said with a laugh. "She wanted to decorate our house to make it more cheerful, so she gathered bundles of wild flowers and hung them everywhere. Naturally, she forced me to help her, and when she was hanging some flowers by the window, the chair she stood on began to buckle. As it turned out, one of the legs was broken, and when I saw her falling toward the glass window, I just reacted."

"So, you caught her?"

"I did. Luckily, I was able to catch her and take the brunt of the fall. But my arm went straight through the glass."

"I bet she was so upset you were hurt."

"Oh, she cried for a whole day. It took me hours to convince her I was going to be fine."

I raised his arm to my lips, kissing his scar. "How can you have the same scars if you've been reborn?"

"We're reborn into our former bodies, so any scars or markings we have before we die stay with us forever. That's also why I'm not reborn as a baby; we're reborn at the same age as we were when we died."

"But then why am I born as a baby?"

"Because you're a primum and the Concilium want you to live just like everyone else. I think they believed it would make it easier for you and Aden to connect with the people around you," he explained.

"Then how do you age?" I questioned. "You do age, don't you?"

"Yes. ," he answered. "All secundae are brought back at the same age they were when they died in their first life. However, we don't start aging until you turn eighteen."

"Why eighteen?"

"Because it's the age you were when you were first created."

"Oh," I whispered. "But why does everyone's age progression revolve around me?"

"You represent life. As a woman, you have the ability to bring life into the world," he replied. "Also, your influence on everything, even the Concilium, has always been more significant than Aden's."

"Everything the Concilium does seems so mysterious."

"They have their reasons for that."

"I guess if they weren't, Aden would possess all of their powers by now."

Conrad nodded his head in agreement. My hold on him increased as the plane started to leave the ground. "It won't take us long to get there." He guided my head to rest on his shoulder. "And at least we have some in-flight entertainment," he replied, pointing to Caroline and Noah. The two of them were leaning over the table, and Noah had a playing card stuck to his forehead.

"Is it the seven of hearts?" As he asked his question, he broke into a grin.

"How did you know?" Caroline peeled the card from his head and stared at him in amazement.

"I told you I can do magic. Sometimes, I even raise the dead," he added in a joking manner.

"I think he really likes her," I whispered to Conrad.

"Me too," he agreed. "In all the years I've known him, I've never seen him act like this before."

"I take it that's a good thing?"

"As far as I know, it is."

Through the window, buildings and trees covered the ground beneath us. They looked like tiny dots from our bird's-eye view. Across from Noah and Caroline, Milton was immersed in a book propped in front of him. He wasn't the most vocal person, but I liked his quiet, strong demeanor. Helen occupied the seat in front of him, but instead of facing him like Noah and Caroline were, she had her seat turned in the opposite direction. Her chair was laid out like a recliner, and I figured she was sleeping. As I watched her, I found myself wondering why she had been made into a secundae. Generally, it seemed you were brought back if you demonstrated an act of pure selflessness or sacrifice. Even if I didn't know her very well, I couldn't imagine Helen was all that altruistic; but then again, she might be. I'd have to make a mental note to ask Conrad about it once we were out of earshot.

The airplane dipped a little and my whole body tensed. Needing a distraction, I turned back to Conrad and asked, "Do you ever miss living in the Middle Ages?"

He nodded, turning from his view out the window. "There are things about it I miss, but for the most part, I like the time we're in now."

"What do you miss about it?"

"I miss how people were closer to one another. Families spent their evenings gathered around the dinner table or the fireplace talking or telling stories. People just seemed to spend more time with one another. I also miss living in the castle with you, Cecily, and my mother."

"Was your room next to mine?"

"No, but it was pretty close."

"Did you ever sneak into my room at night?"

He raised his eyebrows and took my hand in his. "I did one other time besides the night we spent together right before I died," he said, rubbing his fingers along my knuckles.

"What happened?"

"After I came back from the hunt, I had a horrible nightmare every night. I dreamed I was right on Aden's heels as he hunted the wolf through the forest. Once he caught it, I watched as he stabbed the wolf with his spear, killing it. When he stood over its carcass, it turned into you." He studied my hands as he talked. "Every time I had the dream, I couldn't go back to sleep without wanting to make sure you were all right. So, I'd walk to your room and check on you. One night when I opened your door, you were awake."

"And what happened next?"

"You saw me and could tell I was upset. You made me lie down with you, and you rubbed my head while I told you about my dream."

"Why didn't you make it a regular habit of coming into my room at night?"

"I wanted to, but we were always careful about hiding our relationship."

"I hate that we had to hide it."

"Me too. But at least we don't have to anymore."

"No," I whispered, pulling him into a kiss. "We don't."

Out of the corner of my eye, I could see Noah standing beside me.

"I just wanted to let both of you know we'll be landing in a few minutes," he said.

"Okay, good," I answered.

"I arranged for a car to take us to the caput's apartment. After we talk to him, we'll head to where we're staying. I put you and Caroline in the same room. I hope that's fine."

"Sounds good to me," I replied.

"Conrad, you and I will be sharing a room as well. Helen and Milton will each have their own rooms."

"Thanks for arranging everything," Conrad added.

Noah shrugged his shoulders. "It was nothing."

Anticipation festered in my stomach as the plane began its descent back to the ground. I was nervous . . . Not only at the thought of meeting the caput, but also because I could feel myself leaving my former life behind. Estill Springs seemed so far away now. I'd never be able to go back to the life I had there, and while part of me mourned the loss of my simple existence, the other part of me knew it wasn't really mine. Conrad was my life. He was my past, present, and future. Any time I spent without him wasn't living; it was simply existing until I could be reunited with him once more.

As the plane made contact with the earth, I breathed a sigh of relief. The sooner I could get my feet back on solid ground, the better I'd feel. Conrad retrieved our bags, and I fell in line behind Caroline as we exited the plane. Another black SUV was waiting for us as we stepped outside.

"I feel like we're in the witness protection program," Caroline whispered in my ear.

"When you think about it, I kind of am," I replied with a slight laugh.

The outside world morphed into a blur as the car sped away from the landing strip. I wasn't exactly sure where our plane had landed, but the area was deserted. It had to be some kind of private piece of land. No doubt it belonged to the Concilium. They seemed to have power and affluence in spades. I felt the warmth of Conrad's hand move on top of mine. My nails were embedded in the black leather seat. I hadn't even realized what I was doing. Perhaps I was even more nervous than I thought. At the gesture, my grip loosened. I knew he was staring at me, and I couldn't resist the urge to meet his gaze. I always tried to think of the best way to describe the color of his eyes. They were like shimmering sapphires or bright oceans of blue, but even those comparisons failed to capture their true essence.

Scenes of the countryside flew past the windows, transforming into an urban environment. I had never been to New York before, at least not in this lifetime, and I found I couldn't look at everything fast enough. Buildings that seemed to be made entirely of glass jutted up into the sky, and the city vibrated with life. I'd never seen buildings so tall; they appeared to merge into the clouds floating above us. We rode deep into the city before stopping in front of a smaller building. It was miniscule compared to the skyscrapers towering around it, but something in my gut told me the inside would be grander than any other building near it.

After we left the car parked in front of the building, a plump doorman ushered us inside the lobby. I was right about the building being impressive. Large crystal chandeliers dangled from high ceilings, and an oversized desk held two large arrangements of roses. The lobby was exquisite. The dark gray floor shimmered with swirls of gold. People walked around the lobby, continuing with their busy schedules as we followed Noah to the metallic gold elevators ahead of us. The six of us piled inside, and Noah scanned a security card he had retrieved from the front desk clerk before punching a button, illuminating the number ten. A quick scan informed me we were headed for the top floor, the penthouse, and the ride was over in a matter of seconds. As the doors opened, a short hallway ending with a red door loomed in front of us. The color was a deep red, almost the color of dark wine. It appeared to be a normal door at first, but upon further examination, I could tell it'd been made of some kind of reinforced steel. The caput didn't take security lightly. I huddled close to Conrad and Caroline, unsure of what to expect next. Noah, however, knew exactly what to do as he announced our presence with three swift knocks.

18

CAPUT

A small crack appeared in the door and a single eye peered at us through the opening.

"Yes?" The voice behind the door was deep.

"It's Noah. We're here to see Everest."

"In that case, please come in." Four locks clicked in succession before the door opened, admitting us into an expansive room. In an instant, I could tell this apartment had to take up the entire floor. The man at the door was a little shorter than Conrad and Noah, but what he lacked in height, he made up for in width. He had a stocky yet muscular build, and his hair was bright, like a patch of flames covering his head. A thick beard concealed his chin and matched the color of his hair. He led us into the center of a large room where the furthest wall was comprised of nothing but glass. Window after window lined the wall, allowing us to see out into the city. To our right sat a grand piano, and to the left was a collection of black leather couches. The man motioned for us to sit.

"It's good to see you again, Terrick," Noah said, extending his hand to the man.

"Same to you," he answered in his deep voice. "Conrad, Milton," he said as he shook each of their hands. He gave a curt nod in Helen's direction.

"I believe you already know Evey," Noah said, waving a hand at me.

"Of course," he said. Just as Milton had done, he kissed my hand and bent into a low bow. I smiled at him as he straightened his back. "I'm always so glad to see you."

"I'm glad to see you too," I replied.

"And this is Caroline. She is a close friend of Evey's." Terrick bent his head toward Caroline.

"Nice to meet you," she said.

As she was talking, another man walked up and stood next to Terrick. He was an exact replica of him except for his hair. Where Terrick's was a flamboyant red, this man's hair was dark. It was such a dark color of red, it almost appeared violet when the light shone on it. He had the same honey-colored eyes as Terrick and the same stocky build. Each man had a thick tribal-looking tattoo on his left arm. I could just make out the black ink from under the sleeve of their shirts, and I wondered how many years ago the ink was first set into their skin.

"This is my brother, Warrin." Warrin inclined his head to the others but greeted me in the same fashion his brother had.

"Will you be staying with us for very long?" Warrin asked.

"That's yet to be decided," I answered.

"I wish you could stay," he replied.

"Thank you," I said, smiling at him.

"Everest will be out to talk to you shortly," Terrick stated.

"Thank you," Noah replied.

I glanced around the room to try to get a better feel for my surroundings. The dark wood of the floor shone with a fresh coat of polish. Large black and white landscape photographs hung on a wall to my left. I felt myself drawn to one of what had to be a small orchard. Rows of trees cast angular shadows onto the dark gray of the earth. The entrance of a middle-aged man in a charcoal-colored suit diverted my attention away from the image. The light blue shirt under his jacket was buttoned all the way up his neck. He had a slight build and short gray hair, which matched his suit. His eyes, like everything else, were dark gray and his face, which was devoid of any emotion, gave the appearance that he was not someone with whom you could easily converse. He came to stand in front of us with the twins on either side of him. As I studied the three of them standing together, I could only think that they were a force to be reckoned with.

"Thank you for agreeing to see us on such short notice," Noah said, standing to shake his hand.

"Of course," Everest replied. "Helen, Milton, it's good to see you again," he said with a nod. "Bourdet." The way he said Conrad's name made it clear that he was not pleased to see him. Conrad's body tensed as he and Everest made eye contact. He hadn't been kidding when he said he wasn't one of the caput's favorite people. They stared each other down for a minute before the caput's attention focused on me. "And it's always a pleasure to see you, Eve," he said, pulling me into a tight embrace and kissing me on each cheek. I fidgeted in his arms.

"It's very nice to meet you," I said. "This is my good friend, Caroline."

"It's our honor to host you," he said, turning to her. "Now, I know your message was brief, but you said Aden has resurfaced. Tell me what happened." His attention shifted back to Noah.

"Evey was attacked by a group of souls a few days ago. She was with Conrad, Mickey, and Kit. The Fultons didn't make it, but Conrad was able to save Evey," Noah said.

"What about Guy and Marie?" Everest stared at him intently. His gaze wasn't cold, but it lingered on the side of being austere.

"Guy was murdered, and Marie was taken by Aden."

"Oh," the caput said, rubbing his chin. "That isn't good."

"What concerns me more is that when we went to Guy and Marie's auction house to secure the location of the closest consiliarius, we were attacked again by more souls and a single dissimulo," Conrad added.

"The servi," Everest muttered to himself.

"That's what I thought too," Noah replied. "I know there hasn't been an appearance of all six, but it still isn't a good sign. If Aden is making deals with Lucifer, it's a thousand times worse than we thought."

"I'll make sure the other secundae know to keep their eyes open for any signs of the servi," Everest answered. "We all need to be very cautious right now, especially until we can discern more of Aden's plans."

"Do we have any reason to believe Marie may still be alive?" Everyone turned to Terrick as he spoke. "Or do we think Aden killed her?"

"I would think the first option," Everest said. "She's much more valuable alive than dead because she could lead him right to Eve."

A knot formed in my throat. The loss and guilt I struggled with in the immediate aftermath of the attacks they were talking about so casually resurfaced, and I felt as though I couldn't breathe.

"Stop," I demanded, stunning everyone, including myself. I jumped up from the couch and looked around the room. "Stop talking about my parents and Mickey and Kit as if they weren't real people, because they were! They were my family, and now they're somewhere beyond my reach. And it doesn't matter how hard I try to bring them back, because there's nothing I can do about it!" Anger coursed through my body like an electric current. I knew they weren't trying to upset me, but my emotions were running high at the moment, and I wouldn't apologize for it. Conrad was on his feet beside me. I hadn't noticed when he stood, but I turned to him, burying my face in his chest. His arms wrapped around me, blocking me from everyone's view. The feel of his body against mine was reassuring and calming.

"Are you okay?" He raised my chin with his fingers.

"Not really," I whispered.

"You're strong enough to handle this."

"I know."

"Eve," Everest said.

"Just give her a minute." Conrad's voice was harsh. I had never heard him speak with absolute anger, but his dislike of the caput was apparent. Everest said nothing in reply, but the scowl he wore was downright livid.

Admiring his strength of character helped me find my own. "I'm fine," I said, backing away from Conrad. Moving forward was the only way I knew to honor their sacrifice. I turned back to the group and explained, "My dad hid Noah's address in a painting at his auction house. He wanted us to get in touch with a consiliarius and warn them that Aden was hunting us down. When we went to retrieve the painting, we were attacked again." I shuddered as I remembered the demonic child licking blood from his long knife.

"I think Aden believes she has the seeds," Noah said to Everest. "If he gets ahold of them——"

"I had the same thought just now," Everest replied. "It could mean the end for all of us." Turning to me with a grim look on his face, he asked, "Do you know where the seeds to the original apple are?"

"No," I replied in a low voice. "I don't have all my memories yet."

"Do you think you were followed here?" Warrin's voice rang out.

"No," Conrad answered. "The last time we saw any souls was back in Tennessee. We didn't see any in Chicago or here."

Never one to be intimidated by a situation, even one as strange and serious as this one, Caroline interjected, "What should we do now?"

We all looked to Everest, who sighed before responding. "Well, it's unfortunate timing that my fundraising party is tomorrow night, but I think all of you should come. It would be the safest place for you in the city, and with all of the secundae we have in the room right now, every entrance to the apartment could be covered," Everest said. "Not to mention, you have to have a security card to even reach this floor. The elevator doors won't open without it."

"I agree," Noah replied.

"Good," Everest said. "I'm going to get in touch with the rest of the Concilium and call them to New York for a meeting. We need to decide our plan of action against Aden collectively —that way, we're all prepared." I watched as he rose from his seat and buttoned the front of his suit jacket. "Helen, Milton, Caroline, the three of you must be hungry after your trip. Terrick and Warrin will show you to the kitchen so you can get something to eat. Noah, Eve, Conrad, if you would follow me to my office, I wish to speak with the three of you."

Everest took off, striding toward a long hallway on the other side of the room with Noah right behind him.

"Why do I get the feeling we're being called to the principal's office?" I asked Conrad.

"Because we are," he replied with a laugh. "Don't worry though, he adores you. He won't be mad at you. I, on the other hand, won't be so lucky."

"I suppose it's time for me to use the appeal of being the original woman to your advantage," I whispered.

"I would certainly appreciate it if you did."

Conrad and I jogged to catch up with the two men in front of us. We were led through a dark hallway containing three doors. The metallic gray paint on the wall seemed to glisten when illuminated by light. Everest beckoned us inside a small room with the same walls. It was obviously Everest's color of choice. There was an expensive-looking desk on the far side of the room. Four matching leather armchairs sat in front of it. The sensation of power and intimidation was very reminiscent of going to the principal's office, indeed.

"Please, have a seat," he said as he moved behind the desk and sat in a high-back leather chair. His image was reflected in the polished wood of his desk. He looked like a monochromatic picture, with the contrast of his gray hair and suit against the black chair. The three of us sat, and I waited anxiously for him to start yelling at us. Instead, he had a stern but even tone when he said, "Bourdet, I know you care about Eve very much, but when the Concilium asked you to stay away from her, we did it with good reason."

"I know, and believe me when I say I want her to be safe more than any of you, but at the same time, I can't live without her," Conrad said in his defense.

"While that is a touching sentiment, it isn't within your authority to decide when you get to see her. I informed you that if you ever disobeyed my orders, you'd forfeit your life as a secundae."

"I'm aware."

"I was never in favor of having you join us, but Noah insisted on it. You're doing him a dishonor by not following the Concilium's orders."

"This is my doing," Noah replied. "I asked him to go and watch over her. The two of them are stronger when they're together. It's part of the reason we had to bring back Conrad in the first place."

"If that's the case, then we may have to hold a trial and test your loyalty to the brothers and sisters of the Concilium. Maybe a trial will reveal that you're no longer worthy of the powers you possess." Noah flinched at his words and Conrad appeared stunned. I wasn't sure what a trial held by the Concilium would entail, but something in my gut told me it wouldn't be a pleasant experience.

"Noah didn't send me there. None of the blame should fall on him. I went of my own accord. I didn't want to stay away from her any longer," Conrad pleaded.

"Don't think we're unaware of all the times you watched her from afar."

"I didn't think it would harm anything if I saw her from a distance and she didn't even know who I was."

"It did," Everest countered, raising his voice. "Your very presence put her in danger!"

"You know what she means to me!" Conrad's pitch rose as well, and his hands tensely gripped the arms of the chair.

"She's important to all of us! You aren't the only one who loves her; we all do."

"Then why was I the only one you sent after him?" Conrad asked. "I handed you his head on a silver platter, and you still doubt my loyalty."

"Your loyalty to us is something which must stand the test of time!" Everest shouted.

"And five hundred years of protecting Evey doesn't meet that standard?" Both men jumped from their seats and glared at one another. The tension in the room was so thick it was almost visible. I wanted to speak, to defend Conrad, but I didn't know what to say in the face of two forces dedicated to me with such different points of view.

"She's the only one who can save us from Aden. She is more important, and more valuable, than all of us put together."

"You think I don't know that?" Conrad's fists clenched as he spoke. "I've given my life to protect her time and time again. I understand with perfect clarity just how important she is."

"And yet you're incapable of keeping your distance."

"You say that like you think I want Aden to get her again."

"Well, you claim you don't want it to happen, yet your actions would suggest otherwise."

"Of course I don't want Aden to find her! You weren't there when he killed her in France!" Conrad shouted. "You didn't see what I had to see." His entire body shook as he scowled at Everest. I knew from what Conrad had told me that I was poisoned by Aden, but other than that, he hadn't been forthcoming with information. Any time I broached the subject, his entire demeanor drastically changed. I knew that if Conrad wanted to tell me what happened, he would do so in time.

"I didn't have to see it! Ever since that happened, we've been trying to keep her from getting killed again, but it looks like I can't say the same for you," Everest said with a scowl.

Why was Everest so convinced that Conrad was putting me in danger when everything he had done showed that he was protecting me, and arguably, better than all of my other secundae and the Concilium? None of this made sense, and I couldn't allow Everest to continue lashing out at the one person I trusted to keep me alive.

"That's enough!" In unison, they turned from each other to stare at me. "Conrad saved me. If he hadn't been at the diner, Aden would have me right now. I know the Concilium was trying to keep me safe, but my loyalty lies with the man standing next to me. If you want my help, then I expect to have my husband protecting me."

"He disobeyed our orders," Everest whispered, clearly torn by his need to be respected at all costs and his love for me. "He must be held accountable for his actions."

"I can't defeat Aden without Conrad. He is to remain as one of my secundae indefinitely or I'll walk out this door and never come back."

"I already made a decision regarding Conrad's fate as a secundae. I can't alter my verdict."

"I respect your position, Everest, and the choices you're forced to make, but seeing as how I'm the oldest person in this room, don't you think I should have a say in how my life is run?"

"I—"

"Do you know what it feels like to be owned by another person?" I waited for Everest to reply, but he never opened his mouth to speak. "Since the first breath I took into my lungs in the Garden of Eden, Aden has believed he owns me. I was his and had no say in the matter." I stood from my chair and took Conrad's hand in mine. "But I choose to be with Conrad, and that will never change. You may be able to take away my memories and order him to stay away from me, but after everything he and I have been through together, why would you be so cruel as to keep us apart from one another?"

"It was never our intent to hurt you."

"I know," I answered.

"I've never been able to say no to you," Everest said, sitting back in his chair. "Either way, it appears any attempts we make to keep the two of you apart are useless." His eyes met mine and he smiled at me. "Go get something to eat. I'm going to call the rest of the members of the Concilium." The way he said "rest" was drenched in heaviness. The Concilium was one member short, thanks to Aden.

Conrad and Noah were at the door as soon as he gave us permission to leave. I rounded Everest's desk and hugged him. "Thank you so much," I said. "You don't know what this means to me."

"I have a good feeling I do," he replied.

I closed the door to his office behind me and we made our way to the kitchen.

"Well," Noah said, "that went better than I expected."

"Is he always like that?" I asked, remembering his fierce reaction to being disobeyed. It was obvious he was used to getting his way, and I wondered how having that much power for so long could affect a person.

"I don't think he knows how to be any other way," Noah answered.

We met up with the others in the kitchen. I hadn't realized how hungry I was until I smelled the fragrant food that covered the countertops. As soon as we walked in, Caroline shoved plates at us full of chicken and shrimp stir-fry piled on top of steamed rice. The atmosphere was almost cozy except for Helen staring at me as I ate. She was standing between the twins and had her arms folded across her chest. Every now and again she would look at one of them as she spoke, but for the most part, her attention was focused on me. I knew it'd been unfair to push Conrad at her only to take him back, but I needed to lose him in order to realize that we deserved to be together. I'd bear the consequences of my actions, even if it meant enduring her overt disdain for me.

I came out of my reverie as Terrick said, "Conrad, I've heard you're the best fighter out of all the secundae."

"I don't know about that," Conrad replied, turning to face the man with flaming red hair.

"You're one of the best I've ever seen," Milton piped up.

"He really is," Helen said. "He used to win all kinds of tournaments back in Spain."

"Why don't we have a friendly match? That way, we can find out just how good you are," Terrick suggested with a grin.

"If you insist," Conrad answered.

"It's a shame fighting isn't how it used to be. In my time, when two men were engaged in a duel, only one man was left alive. Not to mention, the triumphant man was always rewarded with a woman," Terrick said, staring at me with a wicked smile.

"Lucky for you, we aren't in your time anymore. I daresay

Everest wouldn't be happy if you lost your head." The words spilled from my mouth before I even realized I was saying them. Caroline and Noah laughed hysterically as Conrad took my hand in his. He was grinning from ear to ear.

"Have I ever told you how much I love you?"

"Not today," I whispered back to him.

We left the kitchen and followed Terrick to a large room on the other side of the apartment. The room was three times the size of Everest's office. Black rubber mats covered every inch of its surface, and one wall was littered with weapons. The contrast of gray metal upon the white paint was striking, although more shocking was the quantity of weapons on display. Swords, maces, hammers, axes, and crossbows took up every inch of open space. A couple of benches were placed opposite the armaments. Caroline and I sat on one of the benches and watched the others approach the far wall. Noah stood by as Conrad removed a sharp sword from a pair of metal hooks. Terrick chose a sword of his own, and the two men made their way to the center of the room. Helen inspected a couple daggers as she talked to Warrin. Their heads were bent together, and they were pointing at Conrad. The two secundae circled one another, brandishing their swords. While Conrad was the taller of the two men, Terrick was broader.

"Do you think Conrad will beat him?" Caroline asked, shifting her attention from the unfolding scene to me. Before I could open my mouth to speak, Milton answered her question.

"Conrad will most definitely be the victor." He sat on the bench to my right as he spoke. "I've never seen anyone fight like he does. I think it's part of the reason Everest finally agreed with the rest of the Concilium to make him a secundae."

"Why else do you think Conrad was made into a secundae?"

"I think it's hard for most men to resist doing something that would bring you joy."

"That's what everyone keeps telling me," I replied, turning from Conrad and Terrick.

I adjusted my focus from Milton in time to see Terrick's blade fly forward as Conrad lunged to meet him. Their swords clashed, the sound of striking metal echoing around the room. Each time Terrick attempted an attack, Conrad stopped him. He moved twice as fast as Terrick, and his feet stepped lightly as he danced around his opponent. Even though they weren't fighting to the death, the sight of a sword cutting through the air toward Conrad still made me nervous. My thoughts wandered to the night he was stabbed by the dissimulo demon. Dread filled my heart. A world without him was unimaginable. There was once a time when he was lost to me forever, and I didn't want to live through that again. I couldn't comprehend how Milton must be feeling. It was obvious he had been in love with Thea; now, he was destined to live forever without her. "Can I ask you a personal question, Milton?"

"Of course," he replied.

"You were in love with Thea, weren't you?"

His hands twitched, and he rubbed them together to stop the shaking.

"Yes. I was very much in love with her."

"She didn't share your love, did she?"

"No, she didn't." He sighed. "I'd been one of her secundae for nine hundred years before she died. I loved her for all those years, and she cared for me, but not the same way I did for her."

I leaned forward and took his hand in mine. "I'm sorry," I said, squeezing his hand.

"You can't force someone to fall in love with you, especially when that person is in love with someone else. Either way, I was still the person she trusted most. Being trusted by her was a great honor, especially since she was the caput."

"Thea used to be the caput?"

"Yes. She was the first consiliarius. She brought back the first secundae and wrote the Book of Adam and Eve."

"There was a book about me and Aden?"

"Yes, but for obvious reasons, it wasn't included with the rest of the Bible."

"What's the book about?" Caroline asked.

"She never told me exactly what it contained, but she did say it was the key to your and Aden's history, as well as the history of the Concilium."

"The Concilium is so secretive," I said, more to myself than anyone else. My attention shifted back to Conrad and Terrick at the sound of a loud grunt.

"After what happened to Thea, can you blame them?"

"I guess I can't," I whispered. "How many people actually know about the Concilium?"

"Only those directly involved in its matters. The primums, secundae, and members of the Concilium know, but other than that, no one except Caroline."

"Is my body going to turn up in a river somewhere, like in a mob movie or something?" Caroline asked.

"No," Milton answered, laughing. "But I would advise you to practice the utmost discretion with the information you are now privy to."

"Of course. Evey is like my sister; I'd never do anything to put her in danger."

"Good."

"So, Everest was named caput only after Thea died?"

"Yes," he answered. "He is a great caput, just like Thea before him."

"Then why did you choose to be one of Noah's secundae instead of Everest's?" Caroline glanced in Noah's direction as she waited for Milton to answer her.

"Noah is different. He's more understanding than the rest of the Concilium. I also liked how he openly stood up to Aden before we were aware of his true nature."

A terrifying grumble forced the three of us to glance back at Conrad and Terrick. Terrick was slashing left and right. He was trying to corner Conrad against the wall, but Conrad slid past him, kicking him in the back. Terrick stumbled forward, trying to brace himself. Once he regained his balance, he swung his sword at Conrad's head. Conrad ducked underneath it and jabbed the hilt of his weapon into his opponent's exposed stomach. Doubling over, Terrick dropped his weapon to the floor. Conrad lashed his foot out and knocked Terrick's feet from under him. Conrad stood triumphantly as the victor, Terrick staring up at him in surprise.

"I yield," he said, gaping at the blade held to his throat. "I have to admit, you're the best I've ever fought." Terrick accepted Conrad's hand and was hauled to his feet. Following the conclusion of their match, Conrad returned his weapon to the wall and came to stand in front of me.

"I'm going to go talk to Noah," Caroline announced. She rose from her seat and crossed the room to stand beside Noah, who began smiling at her approach.

Conrad took her spot beside me and set his hand at my back. "You seemed nervous when I was sparring."

"I'm always nervous when you're fighting. My mind keeps recalling the demon stabbing you outside the auction house or the time I pulled an arrow from your chest. I never want to watch you get hurt again."

"I know. When we stop Aden, you won't have to." He leaned in to kiss my cheek and, at the last second, I turned, meeting his lips with mine. His hands grasped my shirt in response.

"If only all these people weren't in here right now," he whispered.

"You might find yourself in trouble," I said, surprised by my own brazenness. But embracing my feelings for him somehow filled me with a confidence in myself and in us that I never could've imagined.

"Is that so?"

"Wouldn't you like to know?"

Caroline's laughter resonated from the other side of the room. Noah was talking, and his hands were moving about wildly. He must have been telling a captivating story, because she never turned to watch the commotion Milton and Warrin were starting. They'd challenged each other to a friendly duel, but neither man resembled anything close to friends. Both of their faces were set in a snarl as they appraised one another. Tension mounted between them as they prepared to fight. Without warning, Warrin ran toward Milton, his axe raised, and Milton jumped to meet his attack.

"They look like they're about to kill each other."

"That's just the twins. They never turn down a good fight."

"I'm guessing that's how they became Everest's secundae?"

"That's part of it."

As we watched the two men fight, neither seemed superior. Warrin would try his best to land a blow, but Milton thwarted him at every opportunity. If Milton tried to advance, Warrin blocked him. They battled back and forth, covering every inch of the rubber floor. Sweat poured from their faces as the bout continued. I was amazed at their athleticism but wondered how long they could endure this pace. After a few more minutes in which both men landed a couple of punches, the two finally reached the point of exhaustion and called an end to their sport. Unlike Conrad and Terrick's fight, there was no victor. Warrin and Milton were at a draw.

When the fighting was over, we left Everest's apartment and drove downtown. Nighttime had begun its reign, all traces of sunlight vanishing from sight, and the moment we pulled up to the Hudson Hotel, I could tell it was an upscale place. Caroline was right about one thing: being a consiliarius certainly did have its perks. As we walked toward the main desk, I couldn't take my eyes off the ceiling. Thick vines of ivy concealed the dark sky hovering just above the glass roof. The warm, earthy tones of the floor and desk, combined with the ivy, created the perfect blend of nature and architecture. We waited while Noah retrieved our keys from the clerk at the desk before heading upstairs to our rooms.

The room Caroline and I shared was on the seventh floor, right across the hall from Conrad and Noah's accommodations. It had a large king-size bed centered on the far wall with a fluffy white bedspread draped across it. A vase beside the bed held a beautiful arrangement of orchids. Conrad set my bag alongside the bed, and Noah followed behind him with Caroline's.

"Nice room," Conrad said, looking around. "Does ours have a king-size bed too?" He looked toward Noah as he spoke.

"No, it has two beds."

"Oh . . . for a second there I thought you put us in the same room because you wanted to cuddle with me."

"You should be so lucky," Noah retorted.

Caroline and I tried our best to conceal our amusement at their bickering but failed miserably. "The two of you sound like an old married couple," she said after a long pause.

"It's the price we must pay for living around each other for so long," Noah countered.

"Well, Evey and I are exhausted and I'm sure the two of you must be too. We're going to unpack and turn in." Caroline ushered Noah toward the door with haste. "Thank you so much for carrying our things up."

"It was my pleasure," Noah answered with a slight bow, his attention never leaving her face. Conrad raised his eyebrows at me. I shrugged, just as baffled by the quick dismissal as he was. Reluctantly, Conrad exited our room, closing the door behind him.

"What was that about?" I asked, rounding on her.

I watched her remove her shoes and pull a pair of black shorts from her bag. "I don't know. I guess I just got a little nervous with the four of us all hanging out in here. It felt kinda like a double date or something."

"Seriously?"

"Okay, I panicked. What if Noah doesn't like me as much as we think? Maybe he's just being polite."

"Yeah, right," I replied sarcastically. "And maybe Helen and I are going to become best friends."

"I'm being serious."

"I am too! Noah is crazy about you. Did you see how he walked out of here like a lost puppy?"

"I guess so." She dressed in her shorts and a tank top before sliding under the covers.

"He likes you. Conrad told me he's never seen Noah show feelings for another woman, and he was one of Noah's secundae for years."

"You can really tell he cares about me?" Her voice was so soft I had to read her lips to make sure she was talking.

"Yes. Every time you're in the same room as him, he can't take his eyes off you."

"I really like him too."

I took off my shorts and sweater, replacing them with a blue nightgown and gray sweater. "I know you do. Why don't you invite him to eat and watch a movie with you? I know that's what both of you want."

"Yeah," she mumbled. "Where are you going?"

"To send you a tall, blond surprise." I could see her grinning as I closed the door behind me. In two steps, I was across the hall, knocking on Conrad and Noah's door. "I thought we would do a swap," I said to Noah. "I want to talk to Conrad, and Caroline wants to talk to you."

"Really?" The tone of surprise was evident in his voice.

"She's waiting for you as we speak." Stepping back, I watched as he ran to our door, not even bothering to knock before walking inside to meet her. When I entered their room, Conrad was lying on one of the beds.

"What's going on?"

"Caroline wants to talk to Noah, and I want to see you," I said innocently. I stepped to his bed and crawled on top of it. The white comforter was soft to the touch.

"I was just about to order some room service," he said.

"Will you get me some too?"

"Of course." I curled up beside him as he picked up the phone. He ordered each of us a hamburger and fries with a sundae for dessert. I turned up the volume on the television and snuggled closer to him. "The food will be up in a little bit. You want to watch a movie?"

"Whatever you were watching is fine."

"Well, I just turned on a documentary, so if you want to change it, I understand. Will you stay in here with me tonight?"

"It hadn't occurred to me to stay anywhere else," I answered. "And I don't think Noah will be back tonight. I'm sure he'll be trying to charm his way into Caroline's good graces until dawn."

"I wouldn't put it past him."

We watched a documentary on Leonardo Da Vinci, who Conrad considered to be one of the most intelligent people he'd ever met. It was incredible to think that we belonged in a documentary right alongside Da Vinci, especially because we had the opportunity to acquaint ourselves with these illustrious names from the past. Moving so my back was resting against the headboard, I combed my fingers through Conrad's hair as he rested his head in my lap. About thirty minutes later, a knock sounded at the door. Conrad sprang off the bed and accepted a tray of food from the bellhop while I grabbed a towel from the bathroom, spreading it across the bed so Conrad could set the food down.

"Here," he said, handing me a bottle of water.

I took a drink from it before I started to eat. "It's almost like having a picnic."

"Evey?"

"Yeah?" I ate a couple of fries before meeting his gaze.

"Do you want to go on a date with me tomorrow?" His burger was still in his hands, but his focus was on me. "Our first date didn't go as planned, and I was wondering if you'd be willing to try again."

"I'd like that."

"Good, because there's a terrace on the fifteenth floor and I thought we could have a real picnic up there."

"That sounds nice," I answered, picking up my burger and taking a bite. As I chewed my food, my mind began to wander, and the moment I swallowed, I blurted out, "There's something I've been meaning to ask you about."

"Okay, shoot," he said in between bites.

"When I have flashes of when you first became one of my guards, one thing I notice is how I always made advances toward you. Didn't you realize I was flirting with you?"

"I knew there was a possibility you could have feelings for me, but I always told myself I was crazy. It just didn't seem possible the queen I was supposed to protect could want me in that way."

"I practically ordered you to kiss me. Did you need me to be any more obvious?"

"It was different back then. Everyone but you lived and died by the rules of society."

"And how did I live?"

"You lived to help others and be happy."

"I should've lived to make you happy."

"You did and still do," he replied, placing his hand on my leg. We continued the rest of our meal in silence as I thought about what he said. I should try harder to make him happy, especially after everything he had to endure to be with me. "Whatever you're thinking, just stop." He took my chin in his hand, his thumb grazing my bottom lip. "For the first time in centuries, we have a chance to be together. Don't spend it dwelling on a past we can't change," he said, pressing a kiss to the tip of my nose. "Now, why don't we dig into this dessert?"

I couldn't help but grin as he set the towering sundae in front of us. The mounds of vanilla ice cream were drenched in chocolate syrup and chocolate chips with a dollop of whip cream on top. The only pop of color was the glistening cherry, the pinnacle of the dessert. We each took a spoon, glad to dig into the mountain of sugar in front of us. I took a bite, savoring the decadence of it. "This is so delicious," I mumbled with a full mouth. We kept working on the sundae, but it didn't even look like we'd made a dent in it. Scooping up a spoonful of ice cream and chocolate, I watched as Conrad took a bite from his side of the sundae and laughed. "You have a little chocolate on your cheek." I leaned over the sundae to wipe the chocolate from his face. As he waited for me to clean his cheek, I took my spoonful of ice cream and spread it over his face. For a second, he was completely stunned.

"Oh, you're gonna get it!" He loaded up his spoon and lunged for me. Jumping off the bed, I ran toward the door screaming.

"You wouldn't do such a thing to your queen, would you?" I asked, dodging his grasp.

"You've no idea about the kinds of things I'd do to you, my lady," he answered with a bow.

I darted past him, squealing as he made another attempt to lunge at me. "I thought you were raised to be a perfect gentleman!"

"Oh, I was," he countered, smiling devilishly. "But that doesn't mean I have to be one right now." I hopped on the bed again, thinking I'd escaped him. However, when I turned around, I was met with a face full of ice cream. He ran toward the bed and grabbed the bowl. "I hope you wanted to wear this tonight," he taunted.

"No, please don't."

"I think it's only fitting," he said. "Especially since you started it."

"No!" I struggled against him, laughing as I tried to keep the dessert as far away from me as I could. But it was no use. Within the span of a few seconds, Conrad overpowered me and smeared a handful of chocolate over my face and chest. Every inch of my skin above my waist was drenched in vanilla ice cream and chocolate syrup. Deciding to just go with the moment, I stepped to him, licking some chocolate from his neck. "I don't know if I've ever told you this, but you taste delicious," I replied, giggling. My legs wrapped around his waist as he lifted me from the floor. I kissed every inch of his face I could set my mouth on while his lips made contact with my shoulder. Warm arms supported my weight, forcing our bodies as close together as possible. To our surprise, the door to the room flung open, leaving us exposed to the world outside.

"I'm not even going to ask," Noah said.

"He started it," I stated in the most innocent voice I could manage.

"Do the two of you do anything else?" I could tell he was exasperated with us—not to mention, the room looked like a tornado had torn through it.

"Would you rather us answer that question, or would you rather find out what Caroline looks like covered in chocolate syrup?"

He thought about what I said for a second. "Bye," he called out, running back to the other side of the hall. The door to the room slammed shut behind him and the two of us were alone again. Conrad erupted in laughter as he carried me to the bathroom.

"I guess we should get cleaned up." Conrad set me on the counter next to the sink and started cleaning up the room. He piled the empty dishes back on the tray, folded up the stained bedspread, and set it in a corner of the room. He turned his back as I removed my clothes and stepped inside the shower.

A swell of confidence rushed through me. I wasn't just Evey Rhodes, diner waitress and high school student. I was Queen Isabella, Eve, and countless other powerful women throughout the course of time. "I don't care if you see me," I announced.

"You don't? And why is that?"

"Because we were married for, like, four hundred years. If that's not commitment, then I don't know what is."

I finished showering, and as I stepped out, he wrapped a towel around me. "I used to be one of your knights. Commitment comes with the territory." He took his shirt off and threw it on the floor. "I put some clothes on the counter for you." I watched him in the mirror as he removed the rest of his clothes and disappeared behind the shower door. I dressed in the white T-shirt and red boxers he had set out for me. Combing through my hair, I watched him dry off before throwing on a pair of shorts. "You look good in my clothes."

I grinned. "And you look good without them."

Now that we were as clean as the room, we headed back to his bed. Conrad grabbed the bedspread off Noah's bed and tugged it over us. "I know I told you that the next time we get caught up in the moment I wouldn't stop, no matter who was in the room, but I've changed my mind," he confessed.

"Really?"

"Yeah, we finally have the opportunity for a fresh start, and I want us to take full advantage of it."

"I'd like that." I never felt more safe or loved than when I was in Conrad's arms. His hand slid underneath my shirt, resting against my stomach, and it wasn't long until my eyes sealed shut.

We slept late the following day, never stirring throughout the night. By the time we finally rolled out of bed, it was already one in the afternoon.

"Where are you going?" Conrad sat up as he watched me open the door.

"I have a date to get ready for," I answered with a smile. Shutting the door behind me, I opened the one leading to my and Caroline's room. With the curtains drawn, it was dark when I walked inside. I could just make out Caroline and Noah cuddled together in the large bed. Caroline roused from her sleep at the sound of the closing door.

"Morning." She stretched out her arms and yawned.

"More like afternoon. It looks like you got a good night's sleep," I said with a grin.

"Absolutely." She smiled, her gaze dropping to Noah. "What are you wearing?"

"Some of Conrad's clothes. We had an ice cream fight."

"I heard about that."

Noah sat up with a start, glancing between Caroline and me. "Noah, you have a little bit of chocolate on your chin."

He rubbed his chin vigorously before realizing my joke. "I see you got all the ice cream out of your hair," he replied.

Caroline jumped up from the bed, retrieving a brush from the bathroom. She combed it through her long hair, Noah watching her every move. "What are you and Conrad doing today, Evey?"

"We're going to have a picnic on the terrace." I grabbed my bag from the floor and pulled out a pair of jean shorts and a floral camisole.

"That sounds nice."

"There's a great diner down on Fifty-Seventh Street. Would you let me take you to get something to eat?" Noah stood and smoothed out his gray T-shirt.

"I'd love to," Caroline replied, smiling. "Just give me a few minutes to change."

"Of course." Noah walked over to her and took her hand in his. "Knock on my door when you're ready," he said, kissing her hand.

"I will." We both watched as he exited the room.

"So, did anything happen between the two of you?"

Caroline laughed at me as she changed into a red dress and a pair of brown cowboy boots. "Unfortunately, Noah was an absolute gentleman, as always. I'm not saying I'm always the perfect lady, but

I wouldn't mind if he made a move, or two, or three." I couldn't help but laugh at her. If she ever made a move on Noah, he wouldn't know what hit him. "We just ate dinner together and then fell asleep while watching a movie."

"You should have seen him last night when I told him you wanted to talk to him. He looked like he'd just won the lottery," I said as I pulled on my clothes.

"Really?"

"Oh yeah. I'm guessing he thought you were mad at him after you kicked him out of the room yesterday. He was across the hall in one step." We finished our makeup and hair in no time, and Caroline rushed out the door to meet Noah. I could hear the two of them talking as they walked down the hall. After one last glance in the mirror, I left the room as well and noticed a note taped to the door of Conrad and Noah's room. *Meet me on the terrace, fifteenth floor. Love, C.* I snatched up the note, sprinting to the elevator as fast as my feet could carry me.

It turned out the entire fifteenth floor was a lush display of greenery. Delicately trimmed shrubs decorated every nook and cranny of the veranda. I spotted Conrad sitting on a blanket next to a hammock. Tree limbs hung over our heads, forming a living roof above us while a silver tray lined with food lay in front of him.

"Hi." He moved over, giving me enough room to sit beside him. "I wasn't sure what you'd want to eat, so I ordered a little bit of everything."

"Thank you." He leaned in to kiss me on the cheek and handed me a glass of water. I took a long drink before plucking a strawberry from the bowl in front of me. The terrace was deserted except for the two of us. "It's so pretty up here."

"Yeah. I like it. It reminds me of the orchard on the grounds of the castle. We always used to sneak off there so we could be alone together."

"I was thinking that it reminded me of our wedding in Savannah. The trees surrounding the house made a canopy very similar to this one over the balcony."

"You're right. I loved that house."

"What happened to it?" I asked.

"I still own it," he replied, picking up a warm croissant. "But for now it functions as a museum. People can come and tour the home and the grounds."

"I bet it's still beautiful to see."

"It is. I've had it immaculately kept since we left. I wanted it to remain as beautiful as you remember."

"What for?"

"So that when all this fighting and running from Aden is over, we can live there."

"Our fresh start?" I leaned on my elbows, watching him devour the flaky pastry.

"Exactly."

"How are you always so wonderful?"

"One of my many charms." He retrieved another strawberry from the bowl and held it to my lips for me to taste. The tart flavor dissolved on my tongue as I finished the decadent fruit.

"Would you tell me about some of our other lives together?"

"What would you like to know?"

"Anything. Everything."

"The place we lived after you were first put into hiding, after everything that happened in France, was Piedmont, Italy. You, your parents, Kit, Mickey, and I all lived on a small vineyard together. Our home was near the Alps and it was very isolated. We kept to ourselves, mostly. I think all of us were so scared of losing you again that we were a little overzealous in protecting you." He stretched out next to me, propping his head in his hand as he spoke.

"That's understandable."

"We relaxed a little as more time passed, but those first few years were tough, especially since, by that time, Aden had killed Thea too."

"Were we married in Piedmont?"

"The day you turned eighteen, we had a small ceremony."

"You didn't waste any time, did you?" I asked, leaning toward him.

"Eighteen years seemed like an eternity after I'd lost you."

"I'm sure it did." My fingers found his face, drawing him closer until his lips were on top of mine. The kiss was so tender, so filled with love, that a rush of warmth radiated over my entire body.

In a flash, Conrad jumped up from the blanket and gathered me in his arms. "Let's see how strong that hammock is." Our bodies pressed together, swaying slightly as we stared up at the leaves. His hands rested against my waist, and he smelled like pine.

"You smell nice," I whispered.

"You do, too—like a fresh bouquet of flowers," he breathed in my ear.

We swayed together for a long time, enjoying the comfort of one another's presence. No talking or running. Instead, we rested in a peaceful silence, never wanting it to end. Eventually, my eyelids drooped as the hammock continued to swing back and forth. The movement was like a rhythmic lullaby, willing me to see glimpses of my past.

I was holding a white shirt in my lap while my right hand grasped a sewing needle. I pulled the thin needle through the material, fastening a button to it. I'd stolen the shirt out of Conrad's room earlier that day, and I wanted to mend it for him as a surprise. It was a small token of my gratitude for what he'd done for me, but I knew he would still appreciate it. My lips spread into a smile as I thought of how happy it made me just to be near him. A few days ago, he'd saved my life. He pulled me from the water where I could have drowned. I'd wanted to walk into the river before. I considered stepping into its icy waters and allowing myself to be consumed by them. For years, I'd longed for some sort of end to my suffering, but the day I met Conrad, I was filled with the desire to live.

A heavy knock sounded on the door to my room, and I rose from my chair to answer it. Before I could open it, Conrad burst through and slammed it shut behind him.

"Who are you?" His voice quavered with anger as he spoke.

"What are you talking about? You know who I am."

"Tell me who you are, right now!" he shouted. His tone startled me, and I clutched onto his shirt, hoping it would give me the strength I needed to answer him. "Tell me!"

"I am Isabella, and you need not address your queen in such an indignant manner," I declared.

"You're lying."

My body began to shake as he moved closer to me. I wanted to tell him the truth; I wanted to hear his lips utter my true name, but I couldn't. Adam would never allow me to tell him our secret. "So, after everything I've done for you, you accuse me of being a liar?" I asked.

"I—I just want the truth," he replied, his fury now diminished.

"And I've given it to you."

"Have you?" He turned from me and walked over to the window on the other side of the room. "I overheard Guy and Marie talking about you the other night. They didn't know I was listening to them. They mentioned something about primums. What does that mean?"

"It's nothing."

"Nothing?" he snorted. "You must think very little of me if you think I would accept such a flippant answer."

"You know I think nothing of the sort," I replied.

"Then prove it. Tell me what I want to know."

"I can't."

"You said before that you thought I could save you from centuries of emptiness. How can you mean centuries?"

"I didn't know what I was saying that night."

"Then consider this my last night as one of your guards," he answered. He retreated to the door and grabbed the handle. "How am I supposed to protect you if I don't even know who I'm defending?"

Panic rose in my chest, making it hard to breathe. I didn't want to lose him; I couldn't lose him. "Please stop," I begged. He acquiesced, spinning around to face me. "I'll tell you everything you want to know, just don't leave."

"Who are you?"

I took his hands in mine, holding them to my chest for fear he might try to leave again. With a shaky breath, I began to tell him a story I had never told another soul. "I'm not Isabella. I was given that name when I was born, but I have been born many, many times. Ferdinand is really Adam, and I'm Eve. Primum means original. Guy and Marie refer to me as a primum because I was the first woman God ever created and the first one to be reincarnated." Several minutes later, we sat in silence, Conrad absorbing the unbelievable truth I'd just told him. I sat rigidly, every muscle tense as I waited for his reaction. Who would accept such a preposterous tale?

"You could've told me," he whispered.

"I wanted to, so badly. I wanted you to know the real me."

"How is it Guy and Marie know who you are?"

"They're my secundae. They were reborn in order to serve as my protectors. They help protect me and conceal the truth of my identity. Kit and Mickey are secundae too. The four of them have protected me for centuries."

"I want to become one of your secundae. I'm already one of your guards, and you know I'd gladly risk my life to protect you."

"I tell you I'm Eve reincarnated, and you don't hesitate in believing me? Why is that?"

He squeezed my hands. "I know you're telling the truth. I don't know how, but I can feel it."

"And without a second thought, you want to be one of my secundae? Why?"

"If you're destined to be reborn over and over again, then I want to be there with you," he replied. "I'll always protect you." I didn't reply but instead flung my arms around his neck, pulling our bodies together. My grasp on him was firm, but our embrace ended and he backed away from me. "I apologize for yelling at you. I realize now it wasn't my place to say such things."

"Conrad," I said, keeping his hands in mine. "There is nothing you need to apologize for, and I want you to know you can always be honest and speak your mind with me. Don't think of me only as your queen. I want you to think of me as a friend as well."

My gaze met his, but the soft sound of voices began to surround us. I knew if I focused my attention on the noise for even a second, the scene around me would be gone. I enjoyed these views into our lives. They allowed me to watch Conrad and me as we fell in love with each other; they helped me regain my memories of him. The voices sounded again, becoming increasingly loud with each passing moment. I let out a deep breath and roused from the haze of the past. When I opened my eyes, Conrad and I were still in the hammock, and Caroline and Noah stood near us.

"What time is it?"

"It's almost six," Noah answered. "We should head downstairs to get ready for the fundraiser. It'll be starting soon."

"I almost forgot about that," I said, sitting up. The timing was fortuitous as hotel staff emerged from the foliage and began clearing away our picnic and setting out small candles throughout the terrace. I could only imagine how much more beautiful it would be at night. Caroline and Noah stood as close as possible to one another on the elevator ride back down to our floor. Conrad and I exchanged a quick smirk as we observed the two of them. The boys escorted us back to our room, but both seemed reluctant to part from us, even though we had spent the majority of the last twelve hours with them.

As we opened the door, I noticed two clothing boxes on the dresser by the bed. "What are those?" I asked.

Noah, who was still lingering in the hallway, replied, "Oh, I took the liberty of doing a little shopping for all of us. The fundraiser is a black-tie event, and I knew none of us had packed anything appropriate."

"Holy shit," Caroline walked over to the box, her fingers dancing along its top.

"What is it?" I asked.

"You got us Armani?" She looked at Noah incredulously.

"Is that acceptable?" he asked, looking nervous.

"It's freaking Armani. It is far more than acceptable!" she cried with glee.

"Well, I hope you like what I picked out. I think I was able to choose something that fits both your tastes." We approached the boxes, eager to see what was inside, but before we could peek, he continued, "We have two hours before we need to leave for Everest's apartment. Meet us downstairs in the lobby at ten till eight and we'll all leave together."

"Thank you so much," I said, excited at the thought of getting to dress up in an expensive gown. Maybe it was juvenile, but the prospect of dressing like the queen I used to be made me feel even more confident in the woman I was now.

"Yes, thank you!" Caroline squealed.

Noah nodded at us before turning in the direction of his room. Conrad kissed me on the cheek and shut the door behind him, following Noah's lead.

"Open them together on three?" I stood in front of my box as Caroline did the same with hers.

"One, two, and three!" she yelled, tearing off the lid of her box. I tore the lid off mine, throwing sheets of tissue paper into the air. I let out a gasp as I lifted an emerald green dress from the box. The dress was made of chiffon, and the material flowed to the floor in waves of green. I held it up to my chest, admiring it in the mirror in front of me. It was so beautiful, it rendered me speechless. The bodice was cut into a sweetheart neckline. I shifted my attention to Caroline. She was holding a purple dress made of satin. The dress had delicate straps that ran into a plunging neckline.

"Oh, Caroline!" I said, touching the fabric of her dress. "That'll look beautiful on you."

"The color on yours," she said, pointing at my dress. "That contrast with your hair is amazing!"

"Okay, I'm super pumped about getting all dressed up tonight!"

"Me too," she said. "Oh my goodness! He got us shoes, and they're Armani too. I think I love that man!"

I laughed as she caressed the black heels sitting in her box. "You really are too much sometimes." I peeked inside my own box, finding a pair of gold heels. "Noah does have exceptional taste, though. I give him points for that."

She beamed at me and went to the closet to grab two hangers. She hung both of our dresses up before grabbing my hand and pulling me into the bathroom. "We're going to knock those boys' socks off when they see us!"

"I can't wait!"

I curled Caroline's golden hair and pinned it to the back of her head in a loose chignon before starting on her makeup. Later, her fingers worked deftly through my auburn locks, twisting each strand into place. When she was finished, it reminded me of the retro hair-style worn by Lauren Bacall in the old movies my mother used to watch. By the time we finished with our hair and makeup, we had ten minutes to change and meet the rest of the group downstairs in the lobby. Sliding into my green dress, I waited as Caroline zipped it for me. The gown's bodice fit well and the material gathered across the top, accentuating my curves. The dress fit tight through my thighs before gradually fanning out into a small train. I fastened my heels and stepped in front of the mirror to gauge my appearance. My necklace offset the emerald hue of my gown, complementing it perfectly. I was surprised at the reflection gazing back at me.

"You look gorgeous!"

"Thanks," I said, turning to Caroline. She was pulling her dress up, and I moved to fasten it for her.

"Well?"

"Wow, you look beautiful!" I cried, pushing her toward the mirror.

The dress cut into a deep V in the front, and the purple satin fit her body like a glove. She was a few inches taller than me in our heels and looked like a runway model. "Not too shabby," she said, turning to look at the back of her dress.

"We better get downstairs. We wouldn't want to be late."

We left the room, heading for the elevators at the end of the hallway. Nervous energy filled my bones at the thought of seeing Conrad so dressed up. I could only hope he would like my dress. We proceeded through the lobby, searching for the rest of the group. Conrad and Noah, both in expensive-looking suits that fit them impeccably, were deep in conversation with their backs to us. Milton stood to the side next to Helen who was wearing a short red dress made entirely of lace. It was practically see-through in some parts, but she was still stunning. As I studied her, a wave of self-conscious-ness came over me.

"She does look good," Caroline whispered, noticing my hesitancy. "But you look beautiful and classy, and there's a big difference."

I squeezed her hand and continued on my path to Conrad. It seemed as if the men could sense our presence, because they both turned to face us. A wide grin spread over Conrad's face as he stared at me. His suit was black, contrasting with the crisp white of his shirt. Thin lines of silver crisscrossed over the material of the tie.

"Hi," I said with a smile.

"Hi," he said, staring at me. "You look—" He set his hands on my waist and continued to look me up and down.

"I look what?"

"We've been together five hundred years, and you still take my breath away." His lips pressed against mine softly. "You're the most beautiful thing I've ever seen in all my lives."

I stared back at him. "I know exactly what you mean." His finger traced the chain of my necklace, continuing all the way down my chest to the top of my gown. My heart jumped at the sensation of his skin on mine.

"Well, aren't you going to say anything?" Caroline was standing in front of Noah, a hand on each hip. The overt irritation lacing her voice drew my attention from Conrad. I glanced at Noah, wondering how he could remain silent when Caroline looked so beautiful. But he just stood there, staring at her. After a painfully long time, he took a step toward her, shaking his head no. Caroline, never one to need a defender, said huffily, "So you aren't going to talk to me now?"

The tone of her voice seemed to penetrate his trance. "Of course I'm going to talk to you, but to be quite honest, I think I'm just going to keep staring at you for a few more minutes."

"Oh," Caroline replied, blushing. "In that case, look all you want." He took her hand in his, bowing slightly to kiss it. Then she accepted his offered arm, allowing Noah to escort her from the lobby. Helen and Milton stalked after them, leaving us alone in the room.

"My lady," Conrad said, holding his arm out to me.

I took the arm he offered. "Thank you, my knight."

"When did you remember that's what you used to call me?"

"I don't know; it just came out. Why? Do you not like me calling you that?"

"I don't mind at all. Although, I do have to say my name is my favorite thing to hear you call out," he whispered, unable to fight the grin spreading across his face.

"Well," I breathed in his ear, "I'll be sure to remember that for future reference."

19

THE HIDING PLACE

Terrick was at the red door to the caput's apartment when we walked inside. Warrin stood at his side, and they wore matching midnight-blue suits. Terrick resembled an ocean set ablaze. His bright hair contradicted the serenity of the suit. Warrin, on the other hand, looked like the sea during a stormy night. His hair appeared to be even darker when paired with the deep color of his jacket. I clung to Conrad, not wanting to be separated from him amidst the sea of people. Glistening jewels hung from the necks of women, and black suits dotted the room at every turn. I watched as Helen and Milton disappeared into the swarm of guests. Finally, I breathed a sigh of relief upon seeing Caroline and Noah approaching Everest in the center of the room. Everest bowed to Caroline and pressed his lips to her hand. He must have complimented her in some way, because her skin flushed and she glanced away from him.

"Bourdet," he said, extending his hand to Conrad to shake. "And Eve—I mean Evey. I must say, you look more divine than should be possible." He showed me the same courtesy he had to Caroline and kissed my hand.

"Thank you. That's very kind of you to say."

"Kindness has nothing to do with it; it's merely a fact." I glanced sideways at Conrad and noticed he was staring off to the side. Everest's comment must've made him a tad uncomfortable as well. "Well, I see some potential donors over there I need to talk to. If you would excuse me for a few minutes," Everest added, strutting to the other side of the room.

I watched as Noah handed Caroline a glass of champagne. His hand was on her back, barely leaving any space between them. He really did care for her.

"Come dance with me," Conrad requested, holding out his hand. I placed my palm on top of his, allowing him to pull me out to the dance floor. The other couples seemed to be doing some kind of formal waltz, but apparently, that didn't involve enough touching, because Conrad wrapped his arms around my waist and pressed our bodies together. All the noise and people faded away as we started to sway.

"So, what kinds of adventures will we have when all this stuff with Aden is over?"

"I could take you on a trip to see all the places we've lived throughout the years." His lips met with the skin on the side of my neck.

"Really?" I asked, hopeful at the thought of getting to travel the world, just like Caroline and I always dreamed of doing.

"Yeah, and we could end the trip at our house in Savannah."

I thought about that offer and all the memories that hadn't come back to me. "I don't think it's fair that you remember what it's like to be married and I don't."

"Are you asking me to marry you?" I could tell by the way he posed the question that he was teasing me. My cheeks burned beneath his scrutiny as if I were being held over an open flame. "Because of course I would say yes, but we have a sort of tradition concerning engagements."

"What kind of tradition?"

He gave me a swift peck on the lips. "I always ask you."

"And why is that?"

"Because I'm old-fashioned," he replied with a wink as he grabbed two champagne glasses from a nearby tray. The drink fizzed all the way down my throat, making me feel like I was bubbling from the inside out. Once we drained our glasses, Conrad discarded them for us and led me through another dance. A string quartet played song after song, the sounds of the violin humming beautifully in my ears. Conrad moved us across the floor at a steady pace as we twirled in a pattern of small circles. While we danced, every eye in the entire room seemed to shift in our direction.

"Everyone is watching us," I whispered, glancing at all the guests lining the dance floor. Their attention drifted to and fro, keeping in time with our steps.

Instinctively, his arms tightened around me, eliminating any space remaining between us. "Really?" he asked, brushing his nose against mine. "I wouldn't know, because I haven't been able to stop staring at you." Before I could even attempt to reply, his lips enveloped my own with so much passion it was as if he were attempting to consume my very soul. Happiness filtered through my bones, warming me from the inside out.

After we danced to half a dozen more songs, he led me off the dance floor and over to a buffet filled with food. The leather couches we'd been sitting on the previous day had been replaced with tables and chairs. The tables were round and made of glass, with six chairs around each one. Conrad and I fixed two plates with food before sitting at an empty table. As we started to eat, a waiter came by and placed two more glasses of champagne in front of us. Apparently, it wasn't necessary to check anyone's ID at this party. However, even if they did, it's not like they would tell true ages. The youngest looking people in the room were at least a couple hundred years old, and I had no clue what my true age was. I ate my food, watching the couples littering the dance floor in our absence. When we were out there, all the other couples had quietly left, allowing us full use of the space. Everything about this place was enchanting, from the tables and chairs strewn about to the arrangements of white peonies cascading from crystal vases. I was so enraptured with the ambiance of the party, I didn't notice Conrad stand up from his chair.

"I'll be right back," Conrad whispered in my ear. Grabbing ahold of his tie, I jerked it down untill his face met mine.

"Just make sure you hurry back to me," I said with a kiss.

"Don't worry, I will." I released him and watched as he maneuvered through the crowd of guests. Noah and Caroline were in the center of the dance floor, turning about the room. Noah, it appeared, was a trained dancer, because he swirled Caroline in circles before dipping her so low she was almost on the ground. She liked him as much as he liked her; that much was obvious. They were well on their way to being as inseparable as Conrad and I.

"Would you like a dessert plate?"

To my left, a waiter in a crimson jacket held a tray lined with various desserts. "What kinds of desserts do you have this evening?"

"There's chocolate cake, French apple pie, tiramisu, and strawberry lemon cake."

"I'll have some apple pie," I repled. He set a slice of pie in front of me and pointed to Conrad's seat. "Oh, he'll want the chocolate cake," I said with complete certainty. I stared at the cake at Conrad's place as I realized I really was starting to remember things. How else would I know Conrad would want the chocolate cake? A surge of joy flooded me, and I took a bite of apple pie. The filling tasted sweet and juicy against my tongue. As I lowered my fork for another bite, I saw images of the red apple hanging from a branch, begging to be plucked. My fork slipped from my fingers, clanging against the plate. The picture of the apple was burned into my mind. Its peel, which was a glowing red, only seemed to strengthen in color. I had another flash; this time, I was holding three brown seeds in my hand, and I was running through the castle. I knew, without a shadow of a doubt, those were the seeds I needed to find, the seeds Aden was looking for. Another memory thrust itself before my eyes. Now I was sitting at a small wooden table, a cup of piping tea in front of me. On the opposite side of the table sat Conrad's mother. Her dark hair was pulled back into a tight bun, and a brown shawl covered her arms.

"It's very nice of you to still come and visit me," she said, pouring more tea into her cup.

"It's my pleasure to do so, and I'm glad to see you're doing well."

"Cecily and I were fortunate enough to have our health returned to us. I believe we have you to thank for that." The one feature she shared with her children was her beautiful blue eyes—a color that couldn't be matched by any jewel I'd ever seen. However, where Conrad's shone with light and kindness, I always had the strange feeling hers were boring into me, trying to discover my secrets.

"I did what anyone else would have. I just hope the three of you will continue to be happy here."

"In the months we've been here, we've been very happy. Especially Conrad, he loves it here. I think he was always meant to be more than just a blacksmith's son." She took a drink from her cup and watched as I did the same. "You're very fond of him, aren't you?"

"Yes," I replied, setting my tea back on the table. "I am."

"He loves you. That's why he gave you that necklace." Her finger pointed to my neck. My hand clutched the pendant, touching the pearl that hung from it.

"I know, and I treasure it more than any other possession I own."

"Do you feel the same way for him?"

"I think that would be quite obvious."

"I know you do, but as his mother, surely you can understand my need to hear it from you."

"I love your son more than anyone else in this world."

"To love another man is to commit treason against the king." Her blue eyes were staring into mine with a subdued intensity.

"Then it would seem I am a traitor."

Her mouth unfolded into a slight smile. "There is something Conrad never told you about that necklace." She held out her hand, waiting for me to place my adornment in it. Taking off the necklace, I delicately set it in her palm. She turned the pendant over and pressed a tiny lever down, opening a small compartment behind the ruby on the back of the pendant. "It has a secret hiding place." She handed the necklace back to me, and I stared down at it. "When my mother wore the necklace, she kept small tokens from her lover in there. Her parents arranged for her to marry a rich man, but she was already in love with my father. She used the necklace to hide the things from her parents."

"She ran away with your father, didn't she?"

"She did. She gave up a comfortable lifestyle and money for love." She reached over the table and took my hand in hers. "And I have a feeling you would do the same."

The sound of smashing glass drew me back to the present time. To my right, a waiter was picking up shards of broken glass. My hand grasped the necklace. It had a hiding place, a small niche large enough for three apple seeds to fit inside. Were they there? Quickly, I unclasped it, but before I could examine it any closer, someone bumped into me. Glancing up, I saw the same waiter who had the dessert tray earlier; he was trying to get out of the way of a couple dancing around him.

"I'm sorry, please excuse me."

"It's not a problem." He set fresh glasses of champagne in front of me and hurried away to serve other guests. My attention followed him as he weaved in and out of the crowd, handing off glasses filled with golden liquid. A sudden jolt of shock coursed through my body. On the other side of the room, I saw my mother. Donovan held her captive with his arm wrapped firmly around her neck. An uneasy mixture of dread and hope churned in the pit of my stomach. I shot up from my chair and tried to make my way to her, but I was slowed down by the masses of people in between us. I hurried forward, maintaining my focus on her even as the weaving crowd blocked my view. As I sped past Caroline and Noah, who were still on the dance floor, Caroline called out for me. But I didn't slow down until I reached the window where my mother had been standing. She was nowhere to be found. Scanning the entire room, I was desperate to find some trace of her. My pulse beat like a drum in my ears as my eyes darted futilely around the room in search of her. What if that was it? What if that was the last time I would ever see her?

"Evey, what's wrong?" Caroline and Noah interrupted my panicked search.

"I saw my mom." I didn't have time for explanations. I had to find her.

"You saw Marie?"

"Yes, she was right here, and Donovan was beside her," I said, answering Noah in an annoyed tone.

My attention switched from face to face, hoping one of them belonged to her. Suddenly, I caught a glimpse of her as she was being yanked to the door. Without a second thought, I took off after her, running as fast as I could. Noah and Caroline followed behind me, shouting for me to stop. But I couldn't heed their calls. That was my mother and this was a matter of life or death. Flinging the door open with all my strength, I rushed toward the elevator. The numbers were counting down and then they stopped. Donovan was getting off the elevator with my mother, and all I could do was wait helplessly for it to return. After what felt like an eternity, the doors finally opened. Noah, Caroline, and I hurried inside, and I slammed my fingers against the ground floor button. Right as the doors were about to close, a hand shot through, opening them back up. Conrad stood opposite us with Helen and Milton flanking him.

"What's going on?"

"Donovan has my mother. They were at the party, and then they vanished. We have to go find her."

"Evey," he said, taking my hands in his.

I knew he was going to stop me from going after her, but I didn't care about danger. I had to save her, no matter the cost. "Conrad, I have to go! We can't let Aden kill her too." The tears were already filling up my eyes as I stood before him, hoping for his support. Fear challenged my resolve, because I knew I had to go, even if he didn't agree.

"There are six of us," Helen said. "We can take Donovan."

The mere seconds he thought about it seemed to extend forever, but even in my panic, I knew we would be stronger with him there.

"No," Conrad replied with complete authority. "It's a trap, and I won't risk Evey's safety."

"But—" I pleaded.

"No!" he shouted. "Noah, back me up on this."

"He's right."

"As long as they have Marie, Aden can use her to come after Evey," Helen added.

I took Conrad's hand, willing him to understand my need to save my mother. "What would you do if it was your mother?"

A muscle in his jaw twitched and after a few quick moments, he relented. "If things start to go bad, we turn back," Conrad ordered. "And we protect Evey at any cost."

They all nodded their heads in agreement. With everyone in the elevator at last, I exhaled in relief as the metal doors closed. A couple feet from me, Milton knelt and pulled two short swords from underneath the back of his suit jacket. He handed one to Conrad and kept the other for himself. Helen removed a small knife from her purse, and Noah lifted the leg of his pants to reveal a narrow dagger.

"Geez, you people are prepared for anything," Caroline said. Her hands grasped a wad of purple material. She'd been holding up the bottom half of her skirt so she could keep up with me.

"That's because we have to be," Helen replied.

"Can I see that?" Caroline pointed to the knife in Noah's hand.

Cautiously, Noah handed off his weapon. Caroline took the knife and cut the bottom part of her dress off, letting the material hang at the middle of her thighs. Noah stared at her in disbelief. "I've lived thousands of years and women never cease to amaze me."

Caroline tossed the spare material over her shoulder and grinned. "I know things you've never dreamed of."

Conrad held on to me as I waited anxiously for the elevator to land at the bottom floor. When the doors finally opened, we burst through them, charging through the lobby. A cold wind swept through my hair as we stepped outside. Glancing left and right, I tried to figure out which way Donovan had taken my mother.

"I don't see them," I said to Conrad. "Do you?"

"Up that way!" Caroline called out. She pointed up the street, and I squinted through the darkness, hoping to see my mother. I could just make out the two figures moving up the sidewalk. They moved at a sluggish pace, and without a second thought, I sprinted after them. Conrad held on to my hand as he ran by my side. Two blocks from the apartment building, Donovan and my mother cut left down an alley. Conrad cautiously led the group into the dark, narrow space with his sword drawn in front of him. I knew his senses were in overdrive, and I trusted his instincts implicitly. A glance to my right informed me that Noah had one hand on Caroline, guarding her with his body, and the other hand held his dagger. Milton and Helen looked intimidating as they brandished their weapons behind us. Ahead of us, Donovan and my mother disappeared into a dilapidated building. Crumbling bricks formed its exterior, and the door remained attached to its frame by a single hinge. Conrad shoved me further behind him, and my hands gripped his waist. My heart pounded inside my chest, it's rhythm as steady as a jackhammer. Cobwebs and dust hung in the air like curtains. We stalked through the doorway into a large room strewn with scraps of wood and metal. It looked like a renovation had been scrapped part way through the project. The emergency lights were on but gave off a weak light since the bulbs were covered with an inch of grime. Peering through the dim and dirty air, I saw Donovan holding my mother only thirty feet in front of us. Remembering the jousts I had witnessed earlier, I momentarily rejoiced. Donovan didn't stand a chance against the muscle that was on my side. However, my optimism was short-lived. I watched with horror as a horde of souls emerged from the darkness, fanning out behind him. They charged toward us, their screeches penetrating the silence. I flung my hands over my ears, praying to God that He would put an end to it.

20

BETRAYAL

onrad shoved Caroline and me together before running to meet the souls. Noah, Helen, and Milton were right on his heels. They brought their weapons down, spilling black liquid as they made their way through the crowd. I clung to Caroline as the entire room erupted into a river of darkness, unable to see anything but her. I searched all around me in a state of panic for glimpses of Conrad and my mother. Conrad knew Donovan's intent was to lure us from the safety of the caput's apartment, and I should've heeded his warning. Out of nowhere, a soul came up behind Caroline, grabbing her shoulder. Her flesh sizzled at the touch, and as the hand burned her, a scream escaped her lips. I jerked her away from the diseased creature. Immediately, huge welts appeared over her entire back, and she crumpled in pain. It was still moving toward us, and fast. Pulling her backward, I tried to cover her with my body, resolute to the fact that it would reach me in seconds, but I was prepared for the pain if it would save her. Just as the gruesome hand was nearing me, a glint of metal separated it from its owner. We covered our ears, desperate to stifle the soul's screaming. Noah's knife sailed through the air, slicing at the soul's throat. Its head tumbled off its neck before colliding with the concrete floor. He reached for Caroline, helping her to her feet.

I stood, trying to fight the urge to shrink back to the floor. The three secundae were in the midst of battle with the souls. Milton was taking on three at a time, while Helen and Conrad were fighting back to back. Helen's movements were fast and precise. She threw her dagger into the eye of a soul and retrieved it before the soul disintegrated into a pool of black slime. The speed, agility, and accuracy she was demonstrating answered my unasked question about why she was made into a secundae. As fast as they took souls down, more seemed to emerge from the framework of the building. In my fear, I had almost forgotten the bait that had drawn us into this trap. Where was my mother? I peered through the darkness, my desperation to find her increasing with each passing moment.

In the midst of the decaying rot of the souls, I saw the gnarled scar covering the bottom half of Donovan's face. I met his eyes and he stared at me, full of malicious intent. He had my mother by the neck with a sharp knife under her chin. She flinched at the pain it inflicted.

"Mom!" I lunged toward her. She tried to say something, but Donovan's grasp prevented it. She struggled against him, trying to break away. Her head flung backward, colliding with his face. Blood gushed from his nose, and he grabbed her arm, turning her to face him. His knife slashed her throat before I could reach them. Scarlet coated her skin as she fell to her knees. My heart seized. "No!" I was in a daze, every instinct pulling me forward to her, but I couldn't move. Caroline's hands latched on to both of my arms, holding me back as my entire body leaned forward. My mom lay dying on the floor, and I couldn't go to her.

"No, Evey. Donovan wants you to come to him. It makes his job easier, and then he'll take you to Aden."

"She's dying!" I cried.

"And she wouldn't want you to risk your life. She wouldn't want Aden to get you."

"Let me go," I spat, struggling against her.

"Don't let her death be for nothing. You still have to be protected!" She yanked me back from the center of the room, but my focus was still on Donovan.

He grinned as he wiped the blood from his blade. Then he pointed it at me. "You're next," he mouthed. My body shuddered uncontrollably. He was already moving in our direction. Caroline, still holding my hand, dragged me to where Noah was standing. Glancing back at Donovan, I saw he had disappeared in the swarming mass of souls.

"Noah, you and Evey have to get out of here! I can help the others distract them so you have time"

"I'm not leaving you here," he said to Caroline.

"You have to! If Aden gets you, you'll be as good as dead," she yelled, trying to push him to the door. "He'll cut your heart out."

"I'm not leaving you here!"

Neither of them was going to back down. Suddenly, Caroline threw her arms around his neck and kissed him. The knife fell from his hand, his arms wrapping around her waist. I just stood there, watching the two of them kiss.

"I'm sorry," she said when she pulled away from him.

"Why would you be sorry for that?"

"I'm not. I'm sorry for this." As she spoke, she lifted up a scrap of wood and hit him on the head. His face twisted with confusion as he collapsed.

"Caroline! What the—?"

"Evey, you have to help me hide him!"

"What are you talking about?"

"I knew he'd never leave, and I can't bear the thought of Aden getting him. Please, help me hide him!"

"Caroline—"

"Please!" Tears dripped down her cheeks as she grabbed his arms and started dragging him toward a small door. "I can't lose him, Evey."

I grabbed his legs and followed her lead. "We better hurry then." We pulled him over to a small closet faster than I thought possible. Inside was a broom and a couple buckets. We shoved Noah inside and covered him with a tarp. You couldn't even tell there was a body lying beneath. We shut the door and headed back into the room. Masses of souls swirled into a black sea. Conrad, Helen, and Milton stood in the center of the room. Each had a weapon poised at the ready.

"Enough!" A voice from above us called out, ending the fighting. As if controlled by an unseen hand, the souls slithered back to the shadows from which they came. A wave of utter fear washed over me. I knew who that voice belonged to. Aden loomed above us on a small landing that jutted into the room. Before I even knew what I was doing, I ran to Conrad, wrapping my arms around his waist.

"I'm so sorry. I should've listened to you. You knew this was a trap."

"It's not your fault," he replied, kissing my forehead.

When my gaze turned upward, Aden was watching us. His dark eyes narrowed to nothing more than slits. I moved in front of Conrad, trying to block him from Aden's view. He descended the steps as if he had all the time in the world and made his way toward us.

"Hello, my love," he said. "It's certainly been a long time."

"No one here needs to get hurt. I'll go with you and not put up a fight, if you promise everyone else here walks away," I said, still standing in front of Conrad.

"One thing I'll always admire about you is your heart." His words were offset by a sinister smile. "You never cease to put the welfare of others before yourself."

"Aden, I'm begging you. No one has to get hurt." I took a step toward him. "I'll go with you, if you'll agree to that."

"No, you won't," Conrad said, grabbing my hand.

"Let her speak for herself, Bourdet," Aden replied. "Maybe she wants to come with me."

"That'll happen over my dead body," Conrad growled.

Aden pulled out a long sword. "It would be my absolute pleasure to assist you with that."

I stared at the two men. Conrad had his weapon out in front of him. He was ready to strike at any moment.

"No!" Everyone turned to stare at Helen. "You promised that if I told you where to find her, you wouldn't hurt Conrad!"

"You did what?" Conrad shouted, anger rising in his voice.

"I knew it would only be a matter of time before he found her, I just knew it," she sobbed. "I've seen you get hurt too many times because of her." She took a few steps toward Conrad and held out her arms to him. "Please, Conrad, just let him have her and leave with me. We can walk away from all this and start a normal life together."

"No. I'm not going to leave Evey, and I never will." He clutched his sword with one hand and squeezed mine with his other. "You've betrayed the Concilium and all secundae by aligning yourself with him."

"I'm trying to keep you safe! It's what your mother and Cecily would've wanted."

"You don't know anything about them!" he yelled.

"I know what they went through after you died, because I was there! I stayed with them for weeks. I held Cecily at night as she cried for you. And you know what happened to me when you were gone; you know what I did." She enunciated her last statement as she stared at Conrad.

"And yet you teamed up with the man who had me killed."

"It was the only way to protect you. It was the only way to be sure I'd see you again," she pleaded.

"It doesn't matter either way, because I'm still going to kill him," Aden stated, brandishing his sword.

"What?" Helen turned to him in surprise.

"Oh, come on," he said, brushing a dark curl from his forehead. "You didn't actually think I would let him go just like that, did you?"

"I—"

He took a few more steps in our direction before stopping. He was a couple of inches shorter than Conrad but seemed just as strong. I wanted all of this to end. I didn't want to inflict pain on anyone else. "Please, it doesn't have to end this way," I begged.

316

"When a man sleeps with my wife in the bed I gave her as a wedding present, I'm afraid it does." Everything about him appeared to be masked in shadows, from his dark eyes and hair to his black clothes. His mouth contorted into a snarl. "Donovan, ready your sword," he ordered with a smile. "This all ends tonight."

21

THE SACRIFICE

"No!" I shouted, standing in front of Conrad.

"Evey, step aside so I can kill him," Conrad replied. He moved in front of me, advancing toward Aden with a dangerous glint in his eye.

"Do something, Evey!" Helen grasped my shoulders, shaking me roughly.

My hands shoved her away from me. "I'm trying!" I had to buy us time, even though I knew his pride wouldn't allow it. I pleaded, "Aden, please just let me go with you and leave Conrad out of this."

"As much as I would like to see you happy, I'm afraid that's something I just cannot do." I glanced around the room. Aden stood on one side with Donovan, while Conrad, Helen, and I stood on the opposite side. Milton had moved to stand on Conrad's left. Caroline was lurking away from the group, leaning against the door of the closet where we had hidden Noah.

Catching her eye, I gave her one of our patented looks. *Stay there.* She nodded to let me know she understood what I was telling her.

When I shifted my attention back to the situation unfolding in front of me, I noticed Aden was staring at me.

"Wait," he said. "Where is Noah?"

A glimmer of panic fluttered in my chest, and as fast as it arose, the feeling disappeared. "He ran off," I answered confidently.

"So, he's too much of a coward to face me like a man?"

"No, he's denying you the chance to steal his powers. He left to get Everest and escape somewhere you'll never find them."

"He never was one for violence," Aden replied with a smile. "Donovan, kill the others and take Eve. Leave Bourdet for me."

As soon as the command poured from his mouth, Aden dropped to his knees and slammed his hand against the ground. At the movement, the souls that had retreated into the gloom sprang forward like rabid dogs on a leash. Somehow, Aden seemed to control the sinister creatures, because the moment he signaled their advance, they swarmed upon us again with a vengeance. The secundae rushed to meet them with Helen in the lead. She took a particularly nasty looking soul down with her knife. I turned my head in time to see Donovan descend upon Milton. The two men engaged in a rapid battle of flying swords. Their fight was mesmerizing, but I drew my attention away in search of Conrad. He had sprinted to meet Aden, and as I looked, their swords clashed in midair. I watched in horror as the love of my life battled the man set on ruining it. In my heart, I knew that I wasn't meant to be a passive onlooker. Quickly, I assessed my situation. I didn't have a weapon, and I had to be careful not to distract Conrad with my actions. I couldn't think of anything I could do that wouldn't put him in more danger. My knees buckled as I sank to the floor, letting the tears fall as I watched Conrad and Aden fight to the death. Conrad had to win. The alternative was incomprehensible. This helpless, weak feeling was unbearable. I hated that my heart was beating so fast it felt like it would burst through my chest and leave a gaping hole in my ribcage. Holding my hand to my heart, my pendant pressed against my skin. The seeds. My eyes scanned the room with haste. Milton had left an injured Donovan bleeding on the floor to help Helen hold the remaining souls at bay. Seeing that everyone was distracted, I rushed to Caroline and jerked her behind a pile of scrap wood. Thankfully, the pile of broken lumber was large enough to block us from the rest of the group. I undid the clasp on my necklace and flipped the pendant over in my hand. I had to stare for a minute before I saw the tiny fastener and opened it, revealing a hollow cavity beneath. I turned over the necklace with caution. My assumption about where the seeds were hidden had been right. Three brown apple seeds tumbled out of the necklace and into my palm.

"Evey, how did you know where they were?"

"I had another flashback. Conrad's mother told me about the hiding place."

"Where are we going to hide them?"

"We aren't going to hide them," I answered. "You are."

"No, I can't do that," she protested. "We should find somewhere to put them."

"They have to stay with you, Caroline. You'll be able to protect them, I know it." I opened up her hand and dropped the seeds in her palm. Her hand closed securely around them. As I put my necklace back on, I stole a quick glance to the middle of the room. "Caroline, I want you to hide and wait till everything is over before coming out. If things don't go our way, I want to make sure you and Noah will be safe. The two of you can protect the seeds and each other."

"I won't leave you."

"You have to. Noah will take care of you; he really cares about you. He won't let anything bad happen to you."

"But Evey—"

"Caroline, I know how tough you are and that you want to fight, but right now, your mission is to protect these seeds at all costs." I took her hands in mine and squeezed them. "If Aden is killed, I will come and find you, but if he isn't . . ." I said, taking a deep breath. "If he isn't, then you have to hide until it's safe for you and Noah to come out."

"I don't know if I can do that." A single tear trailed down her cheek, running into the corner of her mouth.

"You can. You're so much stronger than I am. I know you can do it."

"But you're my family."

I stared into her green eyes swimming with tears. "I know." I pulled her into a tight hug. "You're the only family I have left. That's why you have to do this for me."

"Okay," she whispered. "You can count on me."

"I know I can." I held onto her for another second before slipping out from behind the stack of wood.

Helen was still making good work of the souls, but Donovan and Milton had resumed their duel. Now, both men had sustained various injuries. Donovan had a large gash across his abdomen and blood was dripping from Milton's right leg. Conrad and Aden were moving about with incredible speed as they continued to fight one another. I had never seen a look of absolute hatred like the one Aden wore as he fought Conrad. The waves of animosity rolling off him were almost visible in the air between them. When he swung his sword at Conrad's head, Conrad ducked just in time and thrust the tip of his blade into Aden's side. The gleaming silver was stained with Aden's blood as Conrad jerked it from his flesh. A small amount of hope blossomed in my heart, but it was cut off by an agonized scream that pulled my attention away from the battle between Conrad and Aden. A soul gripped Helen's knees and refused to let go. He dragged her behind him, leaving a smeared pathway through the black muck and blood coating the floor. I ran over to where Noah had dropped his knife what seemed like eons ago and set off to help Helen. My feet were unsteady on the slick floor, and I almost collided with the soul as I reached them. Another knife rested near his feet. I picked it up quickly and severed both hands from her legs before he could drag her any further. Then I thrust both knives into his stomach and jerked my hands in opposite directions through the soul's putrid flesh. His insides surged through the gaping hole like a black waterfall. To my left, I could see another soul charging for us, and I threw the dagger into its chest. Bending toward Helen, I held my hand out to her.

"Thanks," she said as I yanked her to her feet.

"You're welcome," I replied, trying to catch my breath. Five more souls appeared out of nowhere, rushing toward us. I handed her the one knife in my hand and ran to get the knife I had thrown. We regrouped, standing back to back, facing the wretched souls as they charged forward. "We can take the last of them together," I shouted to her.

I thought she said something, but her voice was cut off by the shriek of another soul. I ran to meet the ones that were sprinting in my direction. Dodging their outstretched hands, I plunged the dagger through the ribs of a young girl. She looked to be the same age as me, and I cringed as I jerked the blade from her body. However, I didn't dwell on the thought for long, because a tall, skinny figure hurtled over the melting girl, almost smashing into me. It was a boy. He couldn't be older than fifteen, and his gaze locked onto mine as I faced him.

"Eve, daughter of God." His face was covered in burns, proof that he had suffered in hell.

"How do you know my name?"

"He wants to see you burn," he said. His teeth were black, and his white hair was matted with grime and debris. "He wants to claim your soul."

"Who does?" The words were out of my mouth before I could stop myself.

"The one who tempts us all," he cackled, sliding a gray tongue over his lips. Despite my curiosity at this unexpected source of information, I wasted no time in stabbing the knife deep into the boy's neck. In spite of the seriousness of the wound, he lurched forward in an attempt to plant his mouth upon my own. My grasp on the handle of the knife tightened and I rammed it into the side of the boy's skull. As I withdrew the blade, he disintegrated into a pile of sludge. Before I could think any further about what he had said, my body instinctively turned back to Helen to see where she was. She cleaned her knife with the bottom of her dress. We surveyed the room, searching for any remaining souls. However, I didn't have time to be relieved at not seeing any, because just then a gasp of pain rang out through the room. I looked for Conrad and saw that he was still fighting Aden, relatively uninjured. That meant the noise had to come from Milton or Donovan. When I spun around, Milton was kneeling on the ground in front of Donovan. His sword was on the floor, too far away for him to reach. Donovan stabbed him through the shoulder, causing Milton to double over. Helen ran to help, but Donovan smacked her with the back of his hand, hitting her with such force that she flew through the air like a rag doll and landed in a heap a few feet behind him. I grasped the hilt of the dagger in my hand and prepared myself to attack Donovan. But it was no use. Before I could reach him, he kicked Milton over and cut off his head. My stomach turned as I watched his kind face roll away from the rest of his body. This wasn't supposed to happen. I only wanted to rescue my mother. Now she was gone and Milton was too. Conrad and Aden were at each other's throats, and so far, it was an equal battle; either could win. Overwhelmed, the knife slipped from my fingers, and I collapsed to the floor. I had failed Conrad again. I put all of us in this position, and the responsibility for any deaths rested on my shoulders. My entire world was crumbling around me, and in my heart, I knew there was nothing I could do to stop it.

Aden's shirt was wet with blood from the wound on his side. He and Conrad were both starting to show signs of fatigue, and I wondered how long they could continue fighting. Resolve thrust me from the floor. Not a day ago, I'd made a vow to work harder to make Conrad happy. He always said us being together was his greatest happiness, and I wasn't about to fail him now. I charged for my soul mate, sprinting as fast as I could. In a few more feet, I'd reach him, but without warning, a pair of arms tightened around my waist, heaving me into the air. I tried to fight against Donovan, but he was too strong. The scream left my throat before I had time to think about it. Hearing it, Conrad spun around, searching for me. My teeth sunk into Donovan's arm with as much force as I could muster. Drops of blood dotted his skin where I'd bitten him, and he released me. My body smacked against the concrete floor. Conrad was already moving in my direction when he suddenly came to a stop inches away from me. Confused, I scanned his body until I saw a silver tip sticking through his chest, right beside where his heart rested. My own seemed to rip in two as I watched the metal disappear from his body, causing blood to soak through his shirt.

"Conrad!" I caught him just before he crashed to the floor. "No, no, no," I cried, hot tears surging from my eyes. My hand pressed against his wound in an attempt to staunch the blood flow. "You're going to be okay."

The piercing blue of his eyes softened with each passing second. "You can't fix this."

"I pulled an arrow from your chest and sewed up the wound on your leg. I can fix this," I replied, clutching his body to mine. "You're going to be fine. I'll fix your wound, and we'll go home, and no one will take you away from me again."

"Evey," he whispered.

"I can't live the rest of this life without you."

As I bent to kiss his lips, strong hands jerked me away. I struggled to find my footing as Aden increased his hold on me. "It's time to leave."

"Let go of me!"

"I'm afraid that is a request I can't grant you."

Donovan stood behind Aden, brandishing his blood-stained weapon. "I want to say goodbye to Conrad. You owe me that much."

"I owe you?" Aden asked, laughing.

"Please."

"No."

Before he could pull me further from Conrad, I plunged my knee into Aden's stomach as hard as I could. He doubled over for a moment and released me. Grabbing a shard of glass, I pressed the sharp end to my neck. "You will let me say goodbye to my husband, or I swear to God, I'll slit my throat right in front of you."

"Eve," Aden said, moving toward me.

"Do not test me!" I shouted, pushing the glass hard enough to draw blood. "If you deny me what I desire most, then I shall do the same to you."

"Evey, don't do it," Conrad pleaded, coughing up blood. "Don't hurt yourself on my account."

"I have to."

"No, you don't. Just come sit with me instead." I glanced at Aden, the glass never moving from my flesh. His hands twitched as he motioned for me to sit, and I knelt beside Conrad.

He took my hand in his, interlacing our fingers. "I remember the first time I ever saw you," he said. "The flames of the fire danced off the strands of your long hair and made it shine. You were more beautiful than I ever thought possible, and there you stood in front of me, glowing like an angel." He removed his hand from mine and wrapped a strand of my hair around one of his fingers. "In an instant, I knew I would never be able to love anyone else."

"Shh," I whispered, lightly touching his lips. "You need to save your strength so we can get you out of here."

"You're everything I ever dreamed of."

"Conrad, you have to hold on, because you aren't dying today. I won't let you."

"I know you don't want me to, but you can't stop this."

"I have to stop it," I sobbed. "You're supposed to propose to me, and we're supposed to get married and live out the rest of our lives together."

"I wish we could." He coughed, leaving tiny specks of red on his mouth. I wiped blood from his lips, careful to be as gentle as possible. "We tried once before, and he stopped us then too."

"What do you mean?"

"When you were Gabrielle d'Estrees and Aden poisoned you. You know how I said history cites you as having died in childbirth?"

"I don't understand."

"You were with child," he replied. "You were about to give birth to our son." He reached forward to set his hand against my stomach.

"We were going to have a baby?"

"It would have been our first child."

A rush of air propelled from my lips. Aden murdered my child. He'd stolen too many people away from me, and I wouldn't let him have a chance to prevent me from telling Conrad how I felt about him. "Thank you," I whispered as I ran my fingertips along the side of his face.

"For what?" He removed the chunk of glass from my grasp as he posed his question.

"For being everything I wanted and everything I longed for. You saved me from the lonely existence I'd been living for hundreds of years. I never knew how beautiful love could be until I met you, and I love you more than anyone else in this world."

Blood continued to pour from his wound no matter how much pressure I put on it. His white shirt was saturated with red.

"I would die thousands of times if it meant I could hold you in my arms just for a minute."

"You have me in your arms."

"Yes," he agreed. "I do." His breathing slowed, and his chest barely moved as he drew in a shallow breath. "I love you, my lady."

"And I love you, my husband." Holding his head in my arms, I leaned in and pressed my mouth to his. I kissed him like never before, wanting to savor the feeling of his lips against mine one last time. When I lifted my face from his, I felt his body release its final breath beneath me, and his eyes went still—they were glistening sapphires no more. "Conrad!" I screamed out, shaking his limp body. "Please don't leave me." Grief overwhelmed me, and I fell onto his chest as fresh tears gushed from my eyes. He was gone, taken away to a place where I couldn't follow.

The touch of a hand at my back startled me, and I jumped at the feel of it.

"Eve."

"Get away from me!" I screamed as Aden's hand reached out to touch me again.

"I'm not going to hurt you," he coaxed. He knelt beside me on the cold floor.

"Hurt me?" The anger in my voice exploded as I flung myself at him. "Can't you see you've practically destroyed me?" His hands caught my arms as I struggled to strike him. "You killed everyone

I've ever loved." I stared into his dark eyes, wondering if he even possessed a soul anymore.

"They wouldn't let you come back to me, and I need you."

"Why can't you just leave me alone?"

"I don't know. I've tried, but I can't," he answered. He loosened the grasp he had on me and started to massage my wrists with his thumbs.

"Don't touch me like that!" I yelled so loud, my voice reverberated from every surface of the abandoned room. "I don't want you to ever touch me again!"

"Eve—"

"You killed him, and I will never forgive you for that. Don't you understand what I'm saying to you, Aden? I hate you!"

"You think what you did with him never hurt me?" He raised his voice to match the level of mine. "You think I felt nothing when he told me about how he slept with you in our bed? I felt like someone was yanking a knife through my stomach, spilling my insides onto the ground."

I jerked my arms away from him and started beating against his chest. I wanted to inflict on him all the pain I felt. He needed to suffer as I was suffering, knowing it would never cease.

"I hate you!" I screamed as I continued to pound his body. I punched his wound as hard as I could. He contorted with pain as he clutched his side. "Why won't you just die and leave me be?" He stopped moving and turned to look at me. His expression transformed into one of sadness as his brown eyes filled with tears .
"Don't you dare look at me like that," I demanded. "You don't know what it means to feel sorrow. You only know how to inflict it on the people around you."

"You're right," he agreed, moving closer to me. My attention never left his face as I pushed myself up from the ground. He stood in front of me and threw his arms around me. My body was thrust against his as he embraced me. I fought back, but I couldn't overpower him. The only thing I could do to free myself was to go for his wound again. I thrust my thumb into the hole in his side, twisting as hard as I could. He gasped and I withdrew my hand, slamming my fists into his body.

"You killed him," I said, breaking into sobs. "You killed him." My knees buckled, and he caught me in his arms, sweeping me off my feet. Tears poured from my eyes as I buried my face in his shirt. I wanted to cry until I felt nothing at all, until I became an empty shell. The life I hoped for was lost. All hope was lost. I'd never again see my handsome knight with glistening blue eyes. I'd never again feel his hands against my skin, and I would never again hear his lips utter the words, "my lady." I was to be Aden's for eternity.

I was his prisoner.

22

AWAKENING

I awoke in a panic, and it took me a second to notice the strong arms wrapped around me. "Thank God, it was just a dream," I mumbled. It was just a silly dream. Closing my eyes, I pressed my body against his.

"I'm cold," I whispered through the haze of sleep. Instantly, the pair of arms tightened, and the warmth of his body spread over mine. I felt the soft touch of his lips on the back of my shoulder. After the dream I had, he was about to get awakened in a way he would like very much. Taking his hands in mine, I guided them along the silky material hanging over the curves of my body. When his fingertips reached the bottom, they tucked under the satin and met with the skin on my thighs. I rolled over to face him, but my body froze as I was met with a pair of dark brown eyes. My voice died in my throat. It hadn't been a dream. This was real. Conrad was gone from my life, and someone else sought to take his place.

"Good morning, my love," Aden said, breaking into a wide smile.

· · ·

End Book One of The Concilium Series

Keep reading for a preview of . . .

A

FALLEN

SON

THE *CONCILIUM* SERIES

A. P. WATSON

Book Two of The Concilium Series

I

LOST

Throwing off the covers, I scooted away from Aden until my hands found the edge of the mattress. There was nowhere else to go, but I yearned for escape. As I pulled myself further away from him, I fell to the ground, my arm thrashing against a small table. Fear overwhelmed my senses, coursing through my veins like a volt of electricity. How could I be here? Why were the eyes boring into mine darker than the deepest abyss? Aden rounded the bed and made his way toward me, his expression unreadable. Panic consumed my every waking thought and my body trembled uncontrollably in response.

The last time I rejected this man, he sent me to an early grave. Now, he stood before me claiming he needed me back, but to do so he had stolen away the ones I loved the most. My instincts told me not believe his lies, that he was no doubt hungry for more carnage. I knew the depths of love and this twisted version wasn't even close to the word.

As he advanced toward me, I scrambled across the cold, wooden floor. I was nothing more than a caged animal. When Aden bent before me, I fought the urge to scream. My eyes clasped shut. The thought of staring into his dark gaze sickened me. The moment he grabbed my wrist, a shudder slithered down my spine. His touch was like ice, stinging my skin with the pressure of his fingers.

"If you're going to kill me, just get it over with," I spat defiantly. Fighting against my instincts, I opened my eyes and watched as his hand rescinded.

"I'm not going to hurt you," he whispered. Pain harshened the lines of his face. "You're bleeding." His fingertip pointed at my arm that had bashed against the table. A small drop of blood trickled over the inside of my wrist. Taking my hand in his, he delicately kissed the spot where I'd been cut, cleaning the blood away with the bottom of his shirt. Then he picked me up in his arms and set me on the bed, handling me like I was a crystal vase, as if the slightest disturbance would cause me to burst into a million tiny shards of glass. As Aden sat at the end of the bed, all I could do was stare at him in bewilderment. "There's no need for you to be afraid of me," he reassured me softly.

His gentle answer fueled my anger. "Isn't there?" I questioned, not even attempting to suppress the malice in my tone. "You murdered everyone I care for." I knew my eyes were filled with all the venom I felt in my heart. I didn't care if my salvation lay in his love for me. The life he offered wasn't worth the price.

"I did what I had to in order to have you in my life again."

Confusion began to replace my anger. I was so sure he wanted me to suffer. The only reason he'd been so eager to find me was to hurt me again. Why was he being so gentle, tender even? "I don't understand, I thought you hated me."

"I've tried to hate you so many times and no matter what I do, I'm incapable of harboring even a minute shred of ill will toward you."

"So, you aren't going to kill me?" I understood the influence I had over people, how they were innately drawn to me, but his sincerity and the forgiveness he was claiming seemed unfathomable considering I'd experienced the depths of his cruelty first-hand.

"In this moment, all I want is to hold you and know that you're mine, just like we were always meant to be since the beginning of time."

ACKNOWLEDGMENTS

As always, I want to thank my parents and my sister, Steph, for their unwavering support and love. None of my books would be possible without the three of you!

I also want to give a huge shoutout to Beth who helped me refine this story, and my new editor, Tamara who helped me make it even better! Thank you so much!

Susan, you took the time to edit my first manuscript and all your advice and input has been invaluable.

Tiffany, you are my best friend, my rock. You have read every word I've ever written, even the awful ones, and I'm so blessed to have you as my loudest cheerleader. Without you, this story would not exist.

And how can I not mention Lindsey? You are as attached to these characters as I am. You took the time to read and really connect with this story. Thank you for encouraging me and giving me a swift kick in the butt I sometimes need to stay on track.

I also want to give a shoutout to my betas, you guys are amazing!

And last, but not least, I want to thank you to Will, who helped me develop this story when I didn't believe in myself.

OTHER BOOKS BY

A.P. WATSON

Contemporary Romance:

I Know Better (By Your Side Series: Book One)

You Deserve Better (By Your Side Series: Book Two)

Not Without You (By Your Side Series: Book Three)

Burning Violet

ABOUT A.P. WATSON

A.P. Watson grew up in the small town of Estill Springs, Tennessee. Living in a rural area allowed her imagination to run wild, and she began making up stories in her head at a young age. Being an avid reader furthered her love for storytelling. Her favorite books to read have almost always been heavily doused in romance, but she continues to enjoy a variety of authors—from Jane Austen and Charlaine Harris to Ayn Rand and Edgar Allan Poe. Finding herself immersed in unfamiliar worlds only inspired her to put pen to paper, and eventually, her love for reading transformed her into a writer.

While her reading preferences have no limits, she tends to write stories in the realms of contemporary and paranormal romance. Her stories are the culmination of her passions, combining her love for art, history, dance, and medicine. As she grows as a writer, A.P. would like to branch out into other genres while maintaining a central romantic theme.

When she isn't reading or writing, A.P. spends the majority of her time dancing. She has been an avid pole dancer for several years and has performed in major cities all over the South. She is constantly enraptured by the athleticism, grace, and beauty of the sport and always looks forward to choreographing her next routine. A.P. has a Bachelor of Science in Nursing from East Tennessee State University, and in 2019, she obtained a Master of Science in Nursing with a Family Nurse Practitioner concentration from the same university. She has worked as a critical care nurse for over eight years and loves to incorporate her medical knowledge and experience into her writing. Her goal as an FNP is to combine her love for aesthetics and skincare by becoming certified to administer Botox and dermal fillers. She currently resides in Johnson City, Tennessee, with her adorable rescue pup, Elle.

FOLLOW ME:

www.apwatsonauthor.com

Facebook: A.P. Watson Author

For giveaways, sneak peeks of cover reveals and new book material, join my Facebook reader group: Elementary My Dear Watsons

Instagram: @apwatsonauthor

www.ingramcontent.com/pod-product-compliance
Lightning Source LLC
Chambersburg PA
CBHW050918250626
47155CB00001B/289